Praise for Nigel Balchin

"A writer of genius" – John Betjeman

"The missing writer of the Forties" – Clive James, *The New Review*, 1974

"Balchin writes about timeless things, the places in the heart" – Ruth Rendell, *Sunday Telegraph*, 1990

"…among the great masters of English fiction…" – Julian Fellowes, Foreword to *Separate Lies*, 2004

"Probably no other novelist of Mr. Balchin's value is so eminently and enjoyably *readable*" – Elizabeth Bowen, *Tatler*, 1949

"…his characters have only to open their mouths to reveal a personality" – L. P. Hartley, *Sketch*, 1945

"Mr. Balchin is a writer of real skill… He has established a firm monopoly on his peculiar but admirable territory" – Philip Toynbee, *New Statesman*, 1943

"To some good judges, Balchin, rather than C. P. Snow, was the novelist of men at work" – *The Guardian*, 1970

"I'd place him up there with Graham Greene…" – Philippa Gregory, BBC Radio 4, 2005

SIMPLE LIFE

NIGEL BALCHIN

First published by Hamish Hamilton, London, 1935

© Nigel Balchin 1935

Editorial content © Derek Collett 2022

This edition published in 2022 by Penhaligon Press.

ISBN 978 1 914076 21 3 (paperback)

ISBN 978 1 914076 22 0 (ebook)

Contents

Acknowledgements

I would like to express my gratitude to Nigel Balchin's son, Charles, for kindly granting me permission to republish this novel on behalf of the estate of his late father and to Nigel Balchin's daughter, Freja, who lent me her copy of *Simple Life*, the text of which I have used as the basis for this new edition.

I am also exceedingly grateful to Andrew Chapman of Penhaligon Press, not only for typesetting the book, preparing it for printing and designing the cover but also for his shrewd advice concerning the overall concept of the Nigel Balchin Collection.

Derek Collett

Inside *Simple Life*:
The Story Behind the Story

It is respectfully suggested that, so as not to spoil your enjoyment of *Simple Life*, you should read it *before* reading this introduction.

Sources

The opening chapters of *Simple Life* constitute an exuberant satire of the world of work, and of the advertising profession in particular. When Nigel Balchin began writing the book, he had been living and working in London for about four years. Between August 1930 and February 1935 he was employed by the National Institute of Industrial Psychology, which had offices in Aldwych in central London, very close to those of the fictional advertising agency J. Ritson and Partners in *Simple Life*, which are described as being 'just off the Strand'. For roughly the last eighteen months of his time with the NIIP, Balchin lived just a short walk away from Maida Vale Underground station, and it is reasonable to assume that he travelled to work by Tube at least some of the time. He was therefore intimately acquainted with both the experience of commuting in London and the treadmill-like quality of working life that Rufus Wade complains about at the beginning of *Simple Life*.

When he reviewed *Simple Life* for *John o'London's Weekly*, John Brophy seemed confident that he could identify the source of the advertising agency that Balchin delights in sending up in Chapter II: 'Rufus is a copywriter in one of those big agencies (I could name its original) where advertising is treated with a solemn reverence usually reserved for religion.' Brophy must have been referring to J. Walter Thompson, as that was the only advertising agency that Balchin had any significant experience of when he was writing *Simple Life*. JWT had been awarded the Rowntree's account in 1931, and Balchin worked in close cooperation with the agency's staff as he carried out the market research that led to the launch of the Black Magic chocolate assortment by Rowntree's at the beginning of 1933.

In the mid-1930s, JWT was the second largest advertising agency in the country, with annual billings of £1.3 million (about £90 million today) and a staff in excess of 300. Its offices were located within the gargantuan Bush House (the model for Balchin's Gargantua House), which occupied most of the segment of land between Aldwych and the Strand. Some of JWT's offices had glass walls, and there was a swimming pool in the basement. Intended originally as an international trade centre, and described as being the 'most expensive building in the world' when construction was in progress, other amenities offered by Bush House in the 1930s included a cinema, theatre, restaurant, badminton court and shops.

The second pivotal moment in *Simple Life*—the first occurs when the hero, in quick succession, casts off both his job and his fiancée—occurs at the end of Chapter IV when Rufus bids farewell to his removal men companions, who have transported him from London to Wiltshire, and begins walking on Salisbury

Plain. From this point until the end of the novel, Balchin is very much on home ground geographically speaking. He was born in Potterne, on the edge of Salisbury Plain, moved later in childhood to the similarly located West Lavington and, as he said himself, was 'continuously associated with that part of Wiltshire which lies between the rim of Salisbury Plain and Devizes' for all but a few years 'from birth until I finally left my parents' home for good when I came down from Cambridge'. Balchin's love of that part of Wiltshire that he knew well as a boy emanates strongly from the later chapters of *Simple Life*. He draws a vivid portrait of a swathe of the English countryside that 'depends for its beauty on line rather than on decoration' and he confessed that, as a child, he considered 'those bare windswept chalk downs' to be 'one of the most beautiful places in the world'.

Some of the locations, events and people described in *Simple Life* were probably inspired by memories of Balchin's childhood. The village of Leaford St. Michael, the first substantial habitation that Rufus encounters after his initial walk on the downs, may well have been based on Potterne, West Lavington or both. (As Balchin admitted, many Wiltshire villages consist primarily of a single main street that 'straggles on for a long way'.) And when Rufus collapses the next day, lost and exhausted, on the threshold of Three Trees Farm, one is reminded of this anecdote from the author's youth:

> I know of one man who had lived all his life of 50 years in the same cottage on one of the hill farms. One day there was a fog and he went out to do something which would not have taken him more than 50 yards from his own garden gate. He was found two days later when the fog lifted, five miles away, having wandered in circles, searching for his cottage, until he fell exhausted.

Analysis

The writer and critic D. J. Taylor has observed that one 'recognizable genre' that can be discerned among fiction published in the 1930s is the 'war is coming' novel. Under that heading one can file books such as George Orwell's *Coming up for Air* (1939) and *Of Love and Hunger* by Julian Maclaren-Ross which, although not published until 1947, is set in the 1930s. In Chapter III of *Simple Life*, Rufus eavesdrops on two men in a pub who are arguing about the likely nature of a forthcoming conflict: 'Armies and navies [...] is finished. The nex' war will be in the air.' It may seem a stretch, on the basis of this single piece of evidence, to bundle *Simple Life* in with the works of Orwell and Maclaren-Ross as another 'war is coming' novel. However, like George Bowling in *Coming up for Air*, who returns to his Thames Valley birthplace of Lower Binfield, Rufus, by leaving London and moving to Wiltshire, effectively removes himself from the likely theatre of action of a war that was only just over four years away when *Simple Life* was published. Written at a time when Nazi Germany was vigorously rearming, the threat of war hangs over *Simple Life* like an ugly black cloud.

Another thread of *Simple Life* concerns the ménage à trois that develops at Three Trees from Chapter VII onwards, as Rufus and Mendel butt heads in their quest to win the affections of Ruth. This was to become a very popular theme of Balchin's, one that he would return to time and time again as his writing career progressed. Although subtler, more polished and more fully developed examples of the love triangle are to be found in later novels such as *Darkness Falls from the Air* (1942) and *A Way Through the Wood* (1951), the one in *Simple Life* is of interest by virtue of being the first to be found in any of Balchin's published fiction. There is also a link between *Simple Life* and 1962's *Seen Dimly Before Dawn*, which was republished last year as the first entry in the Nigel Balchin Collection. As Balchin's granddaughter

Justine Hopkins has astutely pointed out, the two books are related because they 'revolve around the attempts of a naïve and bewildered [male] protagonist to understand women who are erratic, incomprehensible and ultimately unreliable'.

The other notable theme of *Simple Life* is that suggested by its title and much of the second half of the novel is taken up with the exploration of psychological and philosophical issues. It is not known how Balchin first became interested in the theory and practice of simple living but a few plausible suggestions on that score are put forward in the essay that follows this introduction. What is clear though is that, for the entirety of the period during which Rufus resides at Three Trees, *Simple Life* concerns itself with, as the book reviewer in *The Times Literary Supplement* observed, 'the exposition of a philosophy'. The dilemma that Balchin poses for the reader can be expressed like this: is it better to live a sedentary urban existence with a steady, well-paid job and all the other conventional trappings of bourgeois society or is the simple, more physical rural life enjoyed by Mendel and Ruth a more palatable alternative?

The inhabitants of Three Trees do more or less what they want. They work for pleasure, not to earn a living; they do not observe regular meal times; they go to bed at night and rise the following morning whenever they choose to do so; they have abundant time at their disposal to indulge in leisure activities such as walking, tobogganing, wood-working, reading and playing chess; and their lives are not ruled by the clock because there are no clocks at the farm, Mendel never wears a watch and Rufus removes his on arrival and only reattaches it to his wrist when he prepares to return to London. (Interestingly, we are never told what Mendel and Ruth do for money. They spend it when they take Rufus to the pub, when Ruth goes shopping in Leaford and when she purchases milk or eggs from neighbouring farms. Prior to his relocation to Wiltshire, Mendel was 'making a lot of money' as a barrister, which prompts the reader to assume that the form of simple living practised by Ruth and Mendel is being made a lot easier than it might otherwise have been by the couple's ability to draw on Mendel's substantial savings.)

It is unsurprising that Balchin, being a man who apparently spent about seventy-two hours a week engaged in work activities in the mid-1930s, ultimately comes out in favour of the daily grind as opposed to the simple life. As he explained in a letter to his publisher when *Simple Life* was in press, 'a life where time means nothing, there is no work, no conventions, and superficially no difficulties, is, in fact, completely bogus and impossible'. Or, put another way: 'you can't just detach from life the things you like and keep the rest'.

When Balchin was writing *Simple Life* he was inexperienced as a novelist and his mature style had yet to form. The book therefore possesses some faults, the most prominent being that it is too long. It is hard to believe that the author who wrote *The Small Back Room* in 1943, and who removed a chapter from that book because it 'added nothing to the story' and 'merely held up the action', would not have deleted Chapter XI from the manuscript of his second novel for the same reasons. But *Simple Life* makes for enjoyable reading, the evocation of the Wiltshire countryside is very well done and the book is packed with thought and incident. In 1935, reviewers derived great pleasure from arguing about which section of *Simple Life* was the most successful. Now, for the first time in over eighty-five years, you have the chance to decide for yourself.

Press reaction

Critical reaction to *Simple Life* was mostly very favourable.

The Times Literary Supplement felt that *Simple Life* possessed the 'virtue of originality' and that the latter, philosophical section of the book was 'difficult, puzzling, but finally satisfying'. Writing in *The Observer*, L. P. Hartley said that Balchin had 'fastened upon an interesting theme' and Brophy in *John o'London's Weekly* observed that *Simple Life* was 'unusual and packed with thought' and that, considered as 'a double-barrelled satire', it succeeded in hitting 'both its targets fair and square'. In the *Daily Telegraph*, thriller writer Francis Iles was also impressed by *Simple Life*, which he said was 'a great pleasure to read'. The fiction critic of the *Sunday Times* expressed the view that 'The first part of the book is funny and exhilarating' and went on to say that 'The advertising office is particularly well done.'

Cyril Connolly in the *New Statesman*, one of the leading book critics of the time, was perhaps *Simple Life*'s most enthusiastic adherent. He described the second half of the novel as 'fascinating' and observed that, taken as a whole, it constituted 'a graphic and interesting book'. Clive James, writing about *Simple Life* almost forty years after it was first published, was also impressed by it, stating that 'With the front shorn off and the rest trimmed of some of its commentary, *Simple Life* could still be an interesting novel.'

Most of the negative comments about *Simple Life* emanated from the left-leaning periodical *Time and Tide*. Their book critic felt that the novel was far too long and he complained about the wearily familiar nature of one of the book's principal settings: 'Mr. Nigel Balchin's Simple Life begins, like so many other modern novels, in an advertising agency.' However, he did concede that 'dozens of less readable novels [are] published every week'.

UK publication history

First published in hardback on 29 April 1935 by Hamish Hamilton. First paperback and ebook editions published in 2022 by Penhaligon Press.

Interesting fact

Simple Life was the second (and last) Balchin novel to be published by Hamish Hamilton. All of Balchin's subsequent fiction was published in the UK by William Collins.

Simple Living: A Very Brief History

The practice of simple living can hardly be said to be a modern one. In a Wikipedia article devoted to the subject, names of possible simple lifers down the ages include the likes of Jesus, Muhammad, Confucius, Buddha and the Greek philosopher Diogenes, who is believed to have sometimes slept inside a large ceramic wine jar.

What is simple living? Definitions vary widely but some common features can be outlined. Essentially, simple living means escaping from the technological complexity of modern life and pursuing a simpler, more physical form of existence. Often it means moving out of towns and cities and settling in isolated, relatively uninhabited parts of the countryside. It can mean downsizing and reducing one's possessions. Some simple lifers—and here one must exclude Mendel, Ruth and Rufus in *Simple Life*—attempt to achieve self-sufficiency by growing their own crops and by rearing animals for the pot. As Mendel says: 'If I were the true simple lifer I should grow my own corn—make my own bread, and so on.' Those who adhere rigidly to the tenets of simple living will tend to make the things that they need instead of automatically buying them (Mendel does qualify as a simple lifer in that respect).

Emphasis may be placed on learning and the acquisition of new skills and leisure time is often spent participating in artistic pursuits such as painting and writing. Leaving aside religious communities such as monasteries, consideration of which is outside the scope of this essay, there is frequently a religious or spiritual basis underpinning the quest for a simple life but, again, that does not apply at Three Trees. (Intriguingly, there was originally a mystical element to *Simple Life* involving Mendel but Balchin removed what he described as a 'strange Gods business' from the end of the book so as not to confuse the reader.)

Moving from antiquity towards the modern age, some key milestones in the development of simple living may be identified. In the 1750s, Genevan philosopher Jean-Jacques Rousseau wrote two books praising the simple life. The American naturalist and writer Henry David Thoreau published *Walden; or Life in the Woods* in 1854. In this classic pro-simple life text, Thoreau described his experience of living simply for two years in rural Massachusetts in a log cabin that he had built himself. Still in the nineteenth century, but on this side of the Atlantic, the artist and designer William Morris was an advocate of simple living and the poet and philosopher Edward Carpenter popularized the phrase 'simple life' in an essay published in 1887. In the Middle East, the first kibbutz opened in Israel in 1910 and kibbutzim, designed originally as utopian communities, flourished over the course of the next thirty years.

And so to the 1930s. For a work by a relatively unknown author, *Simple Life* was reviewed quite widely when it first appeared in 1935. None of the reviewers indicated that there was anything new or out of the ordinary in Rufus's desire to exchange his complicated urban life in London for a simpler rural one in Wiltshire. In other words, in the mid-1930s, it was widely accepted that some people in Britain either practised simple living or aspired to do so.

Two of *Simple Life*'s reviewers suggested that the principal theme of the book may have originated in the actions of two well-known novelists. Cyril Connolly in the *New Statesman* was of the opinion that, when Rufus starts tramping on Salisbury Plain, he 'goes Lawrence'. In 1924, D. H. Lawrence had bought a ranch in Taos, New Mexico in the hope of establishing a utopian community there. He invited many of his English friends to seize the opportunity to begin what he described as a 'new life on earth'. But only one person joined Lawrence and his wife and the project soon fizzled out.

In his review of *Simple Life* in *John o'London's Weekly*, John Brophy said that Rufus seemed to be searching for 'a kind of DH Lawrence–JC Powys simplicity'. Welsh writer John Cowper Powys had departed New York City in 1930 and moved to an isolated cottage in upstate New York. There, he communed with nature, flirted with mysticism and wrote a number of books, in one of which, 1933's *A Philosophy of Solitude*, he came out in favour of the simple life.

Balchin may also have been aware of the Adelphi Centre. This was a commune that opened near Colchester in Essex in 1934 and survived until 1937. It was owned and run by two English writers: Max Plowman and his friend John Middleton Murry, founder and editor of the literary periodical *Adelphi* and an admirer of Lawrence. In fact, Murry had been offered a place at Lawrence's community in Taos but turned it down.

And what of Balchin's own interest in simple living? After he became a successful novelist during World War Two he lived far too regally to be awarded the appellation 'simple lifer'. He did, however, own a series of properties in the English countryside. At most of these he attempted to grow fruit trees and at a house near Rye in Sussex in the 1960s he and his wife kept some livestock. But as for his written interest in the simple life, he seems to have said everything he wanted to say on the subject in his novel of the same name.

In the twenty-first century, interest in simple living persists and that interest has been spurred over the last few years by the impact of COVID-19. In the early days of the pandemic, as most people found themselves spending far more time in their own houses than usual, there was a surge of enthusiasm for some of the home husbandry practices that represent core skills for the simple lifer. To give just a single example, the spring of 2020 saw, according to one source, an increase of 250% in sales of seeds and compost in the UK as a significant tranche of the population decided to have a go at growing fruit and vegetables.

One thing seems certain: as we become more and more reliant on technology, and our lives become increasingly dominated by computers, the desire for a simple (or simpler) life is unlikely to go away any time soon.

Postscript

Within a month of writing this essay I was made aware of two new releases in the popular media—a major television series and an acclaimed documentary film—devoted to the practice of simple living, further evidence that the pursuit of a simple life is a contemporary phenomenon and not just a 1930s concept.

Firstly, on 22 March 2022, Channel 4 in the UK began a six-part series entitled *The Simpler Life* in which a group of people were abstracted from the modern world, relocated to an isolated farm in Devon and asked to live in accordance with the principles of the Amish religious community. Secondly, *The Hermit of Treig* was released into UK cinemas three days later. The film tells the story of Ken Smith, who has practised self-sufficiency while living as a hermit—an extreme form of simple living—for forty years in a remote part of the Scottish Highlands. *The Hermit of Treig* won the audience award at this year's Glasgow Film Festival.

SIMPLE LIFE

*To the Society of Wiltshiremen in London this story of
a Londoner in Wiltshire is respectfully dedicated.*

I have desired to go
Where springs not fail,
To fields where flies no sharp and sided hail
And a few lilies blow.

And I have asked to be
Where no storms come,
Where the green swell is in the havens dumb,
And out of the swing of the sea[1]

    – Father Gerard Manley Hopkins, S. J.[2]

And life is Colour and Warmth and Light
And a striving evermore for these;
And he is dead who will not fight,
And who dies fighting has increase.[3]

    – Captain the Honourable Julian Grenfell, D.S.O.[4]

Contents

Chapter 1

Happy Returns

Long experience had taught Rufus Wade that in order to bath, shave, dress, eat his breakfast in comfort and arrive at his office by nine-thirty, it was necessary to rise at not later than eight-fifteen. It was therefore his practice to wake at 8 a.m., decide that he could allow himself another ten minutes, go to sleep again until eight-thirty, and then arise, hurried and cursing.

On the first of February, however, he abandoned this simple scheme, and positively rose at eight o'clock. So that at half-past eight, when the little maid brought his breakfast, there was no need to put it in front of the gas-fire to wait for him, since Rufus himself had reversed the usual process, and had placed himself in front of the gas-fire to await it. Despite her surprise, the little maid bade him a cheerful good morning. She was a remarkably cheerful person, considering that she represented practically all the service of the four small service flats in the house. Moreover, she had a decidedly soft spot for Rufus. He might put ash on the floor and he might, by rising at eleven o'clock on Sundays, make it impossible to get him 'cleaned up' until inconveniently late. But Rufus seldom complained, which the occupants of the other three flats did incessantly; he was young, which the occupants of the other three flats were not; and further, in the opinion of the little maid, he was handsome and had a nice smile. So she beamed at him and said 'Good morning, Mr. Wade' very cheerfully, and Rufus, who knew all about his nice smile and its effect on small maids, employed it and said 'Good morning, Edna' in reply.

'You're early this morning,' said the service, archly, unloading the breakfast tray on to the table. 'And a lot of letters and parcels for you, too,' she added, glancing at the table with interest.

'That's *why* I'm early,' said Rufus. 'It's my birthday.'

'*Reely?*'

'Yes. Don't be so surprised, Edna. I'm twenty-one to-day.'

The little maid gave a faint giggle of disbelief.

'Many happy returns of the day, then, Mr. Wade.'

Rufus bowed solemnly. 'Thank you, Edna. When I'm twenty-two and really grown up, I'll take you to the pictures.'

He sat down as the door closed on another scandalised and delighted giggle, and surveyed the table. There were three parcels and three letters. Rufus glanced quickly at the handwritings and was faintly and foolishly disappointed to find that they were all known and familiar. He hesitated for a moment and then decided, in the best childish tradition, to have his breakfast before looking at the parcels. Slowly consuming his bacon and egg he speculated on their contents.

The letters were easy. One, in a rather shaky, but still beautiful copperplate, was Uncle Fred. It would wish him many happy returns of February 1st, and would remark sadly that time passed very quickly. Another was from an obscure cousin, whom he had not seen for at least a dozen years, but who always sent, on his birthday, a long letter giving detailed news of the doings of various members of the Family whom he had never seen at all. The third was Sally, who was the sister of a Cambridge friend and who kept a birthday-book. Rufus reflected with a shock of surprise that, since he was now twenty-nine, Sally must be nineteen, which was absurd. When last seen she had been fourteen and all leg and wing. He wondered idly, as he finished the egg, what sort of young woman Sally had become. Five years ago she had been a loud noise with dark red hair, freckles and a habit of standing on her hands in the drawing-room. Now, presumably—

He passed on to marmalade and the parcels. Mother and Auntie Rose would both be something to wear. Mother unexciting but at least wearable, Auntie Rose exciting, but impossible. Mother, judging by the flatness of the parcel, was handkerchiefs. Growing slightly metaphysical over the marmalade, Rufus decided that the parcel summed up his relations with Mother perfectly. Flat, and containing serviceable white handkerchiefs. To elaborate the pleasing conceit a little further, without frills or garish colourings, but plain, hemstitched, useful, and in the best of unimaginative good taste. He gave a little nod of satisfaction at the completeness of the parallel and, finishing his toast, glanced quickly at the other parcel, which was clearly the thing over which Marjorie had been undergoing agonies of secrecy for at least a fortnight. He found himself hoping that it wasn't something quite useless and ridiculously expensive and, rather appalled to find that this was his only emotion, hastily poured himself out a cup of tea and began the opening process.

The letters ran true to his expectations and, having skimmed rapidly through them, he tossed them aside with the churlish reflection that three people had expended three-halfpence[5] each to say something they did not particularly feel, and which he did not want. He opened Mother's parcel and discovered not handkerchiefs, but a white silk scarf; made a half-hearted effort to adjust the parallel of the handkerchiefs to this new situation; decided that he was a nasty young man; made a cursory examination of Auntie Rose's impossible reddish-brown pullover; and turned at last to Marjorie.

Marjorie's present was a small, hard parcel. Rufus stripped off the paper and saw, with a sinking heart, a box with the mark of the Goldsmith's and Silversmith's Company.[6] He opened it and sat for a moment frowning down at the handsome rectangular gold wrist-watch.

'Damn!' he said aloud, 'I wish she hadn't done that.'

He slowly extracted the watch and looked at it thoughtfully. Certainly, he decided, it could not have cost less than twenty pounds. Probably a good deal more. And Marjorie hadn't much money. That, however, was hardly the point. Presents to one's fiancé are not necessarily, or indeed usually, governed by what one can afford. Superficially there was no reason why Marjorie should not give him an expensive watch, even though she could hardly afford it, and though he already had a perfectly serviceable one. It was something more than that…

Rufus carefully replaced the watch in its case and, gathering up the litter of paper and string, rolled it into a ball and threw it carelessly down beside the gas-fire. The clock on the mantelpiece stood at a quarter to nine. For once there was a clear quarter of an hour to spare before he need start for the office. Flicking the ash from his cigarette, he strolled over to the window and looked out. A thick yellow fog covered everything, and the trees of Regent's Park, on the opposite side of the road, were only just visible. A bus nosed its way cautiously by, its side-lamps making queer rainbow-coloured globes in the fog. Rufus's brain automatically registered that this was a Baker Street and Tube morning, not a Regent's Park and bus—the alternative route to the office.

He turned away from the dismal outside world with a frown—a frown which was still present as he returned to the fire and caught sight of himself in the mirror. He remembered that he had now reached the age of twenty-nine, and thoughtfully examined the frowning reflection for signs of wear and tear. None were particularly apparent. His hair was still black and wavy. His eyes were still grey. His clothes were still the clothes of a young man who has to dress well and rather likes it, and his figure, unbowed by care, looked still the figure of a nice-sized Rugger forward; which it was. Rufus was annoyed to find that his scowl, instead of making him look worried, merely made his face sullen and discontented—an effect which was heightened by the fact that his big full lips were pouting a little… He hastily stopped scowling, grinned the grin beloved of Edna, just to see that it still worked, and then, abandoning the mirror, sat down by the fire, lit another cigarette and scowled again. Whether it was the fog, or the rather uninspiring collection of gifts or the peculiar uneasiness about Marjorie, or merely the shattering feeling that he was now in his thirtieth year, he could not tell. But he was conscious of an acute malaise—a discontented restlessness which left him appalled at the prospect of going to the office, and impatient of sitting idly by his fire.

He remembered a bygone habit of his schooldays—a sort of personal audit which he had made regularly upon his birthday, and which had consisted of general appraisement of the past and speculation as to the future. In those days the entries of successes and ambitions had usually been a whirl of house-games caps and school certificate examinations. How did the principle apply now?

Rufus glanced again at the clock and reflected that he must have been a rum, methodical sort of kid, and probably pretty intolerable. Still, there was something to be said for the system… He began a little self-consciously.

'Item,' he said aloud, 'I am exactly twenty-nine years old.

'Item, I am a copywriter in the employ of Messrs. Ritson and Partners, Incorporated Practitioners in Advertising, London, New York, Montreal, Paris and Timbuctoo.

'Item, I am generally admitted to be rather good.

'Item, despite which I am in receipt of a salary of only seven hundred a year, and if I want more I shall have to go to some bloody place like Gaskell's…'

His eye fell on the neat case of Marjorie's present. He frowned instinctively.

'Item, I am engaged to Marjorie, who is a very beautiful girl–'

Rufus paused and reflected. That seemed to sum up the house caps acquired so far. Now, presumably one came on to the future. He flicked the ash from his cigarette and stared thoughtfully into the brightly glowing gas-fire. The future seemed a little vague, somehow…

'Well,' he murmured almost defensively. 'Item, presumably I shall soon marry the aforesaid Marjorie, and I suppose Item, I shall go on writing bigger, brighter, and better copy, and–'

He paused and glanced out of the window at the depressing morning. Suddenly he threw up his head.

'Item,' he said defiantly, 'the whole bloody outfit bores me stiff. *Stiff*…'

Rufus stopped abruptly and guiltily, acutely aware that this was blasphemous, somehow, and ungrateful. He hastily and weakly made a mental reservation excluding Marjorie from the general condemnation, and did a little rapid moralising on the subject of people who didn't know when they were well off, and the horrors of want and unemployment. But there had been a satisfactory viciousness about the blunt statement which even telling the beads of one's blessings did not quite eradicate. Noticing that the clock now stood at two minutes to nine, he rose and, hastily donning his hat and coat, plunged out into the fog, pointing out to himself that when one got to the whining stage, a Spot of Work—

Had Rufus lived in Bloomsbury, and thus been able to reach his office quickly, and to plunge into the soul-cleansing bath of a Spot of Work, all might have been well. But Messrs. Ritson's offices were in Gargantua House, and Gargantua House lies just off the Strand. Rufus had therefore to face half an hour's rather complicated journey which included nearly ten minutes' walk to Baker Street Station, a quarter of an hour of crowded Bakerloo

Tube, and a final five minutes' bus or ten minutes' walk at the other end. On the way to Baker Street, therefore, he fell under the influence of the raw, depressing dampness of the foggy February morning and began a morbid analysis of the reasons for this sudden mood of discontent and restlessness.

Huddling his chin as far down into the collar of his overcoat as possible, he thrust his hands deep into his pockets and, carefully avoiding the subject of Marjorie, tried to consider Advertising and his own part in it as dispassionately as possible. There was nothing new, of course, in being fed up with Advertising. Everyone connected with the business was usually in a state of almost suicidal depression about it five times a week. That was a well-known phenomenon and part of the game. But this feeling was more than that.

Then again, there were the standard philosophical objections which he had argued out with vast solemnity with Ted Lewis— that the job was parasitic, fundamentally unproductive, and so on. But this, again, was something more than a mere philosophic objection… Rufus stopped thinking and, like a good Londoner, slipped quickly across the road, concentrating for the moment only on the preservation of life and limb. But on arrival at the other side, he suddenly realised, to his surprise, that advertising and its shortcomings were not the point at all, and that his feelings, vague as they were, were rather a hatred of London and fog and Gargantua House and offices and work of all kinds, than of any mere detail like writing copy for Custard Powder.

At first the realisation cheered him a good deal by its delightful broadness and absurdity. A dissatisfaction with one's job might possibly be entirely logical and demand action. But a thorough-going, all-embracing hate of this kind was too clearly the result of a disordered liver to be taken seriously. Rufus arrived at Baker Street grinning broadly, relieved to find that he had merely been making a fool of himself. He had feared something worse—that he might be right. And to be right is a disconcerting thing.

In the Tube, however, his troubles began again, in a slightly modified form. As usual, he found a seat at Baker Street, and equally as usual surrendered it to an indifferent typist at Oxford Circus. But this morning he resented the typist bitterly and, glancing round the crowded compartment, found with melancholy satisfaction that he resented all the other occupants as well. Apparently, London, fog, advertising and offices were now reinforced by the whole of the human race. There they were—thousands of them—all with newspapers and cabbage-like faces, going dutifully off in droves to do something they didn't want to do, in return for the privilege of going on doing it. There was one man whom Rufus selected as an arch type. Respectable, bowler-hatted, an umbrella leaning against his fat thigh. He wore horn-rimmed spectacles and his face was lined and yellow. He worked steadily through the *Daily Telegraph* and, when the train reached Charing Cross, he would fold the paper neatly under his arm and get out. And he would do this every day in exactly the same way for thirty to forty years. And then he would die and be buried in Honor Oak Cemetery...[7]

The train drew up at Piccadilly Circus. The bowler-hatted man folded up his paper and fought his way to the door. All right, thought Rufus sullenly. Have it your own way. Piccadilly Circus. *Not* Charing Cross. But it doesn't make any difference...

The train started again and, for some obscure mechanical reason, began to squeal in that ear-piercing torment which sometimes afflicts Tube trains. Rufus screwed up his face in agony and decided that the one *really* intolerable thing was noise. Struck by a sudden thought he glanced round the compartment. The indifferent typist was frowning in irritation, but she never raised her eyes from her Boots Library[8] book. On every other face was the same sullen, rather ill-tempered unconsciousness that he had seen before.

'Christ!' he murmured to himself, his voice inaudible in the agonising racket. 'They don't even notice it!' His eye caught an advertisement on the wall of the rocking carriage. It was an advertisement of the Underground Railways, for some country journey. The artist had drawn a country landscape in winter. Vague, geometrical, the impressionistic trees thrust out their bare branches, bending to the wind, to balance the curving rim of bare hill. He did not even see the caption beneath. But for one moment the geometrical trees were real trees, tossing and swaying in a tearing breeze, and he felt the buffet of the wind on his face and heard its blustering above the noise of the train. He looked for the last time round at the unconscious figures who sat and stood about him, and knew fatally and finally that he was right. And then the train was jarring into Trafalgar Square Station,[9] and he was moving to the door, drawing on gloves, clutching his paper, extracting his season-ticket from his breast pocket, and going through the whole cycle of complicated, civilised movements which long practice had made mechanical things, unbacked by, and not needing, thought, or calculation or intelligence.

Chapter II

Extraordinary Effect of Mr. Corder's Nails

As became one of the biggest advertising agencies in the world, with branches in four continents, J. Ritson and Partners occupied offices in one of the largest and most modern buildings in London. From the tenth floor of Gargantua House one could see almost to Greenwich. The shops and restaurants which occupied its ground floors and basements supplied almost every necessity from the cradle to the grave, and it was credibly reported that an executive, engaged in some mighty task, had once lived in Gargantua House for six months, without leaving it, emerging at the end of that time sleek and well-nourished by its restaurants, beautifully groomed by its hairdressers, attired in a new suit made by the expensive little tailor in the basement, slim from constant exercise in its squash-courts, and with a new set of false teeth supplied by its tame dentist. Alone almost amongst English office buildings, it had central heating which really heated, and lifts which were swift, plentiful and reasonably organised. Beside such advantages, the fact that its smallest suites cost four thousand a year, and that even in the height of summer it was necessary to work with the windows closed to make oneself audible above the noise of the traffic, paled into insignificance.

In such surroundings, J. Ritson and Partners Ltd. was in its element. 'Advertising' (it had been the original J. Ritson's favourite saying) 'Advertising isn't just a matter of writing a bit of copy and taking a bit of space. It's an attitude of mind.' J. Ritson was dead these fifteen years. But his photograph still hung in the managing director's office, and the lofty spirit which had built up the great agency still permeated Gargantua House. The offices themselves were an advertisement. The brisk young men in beautifully-cut suits who interviewed Messrs. Ritson's clients were living examples of advertising art-work. And if a Ritson representative took a client to lunch, the meal was always a perfect example of up-to-date, forceful, but well-bred copy. It was a well-known fact in the advertising world that no manufacturer, however case-hardened, could ever enter the offices of Messrs. Ritson without being assailed by an uncomfortable feeling that he was twenty years behind the times—a feeling only dispelled by the gentle and kindly assurance of Messrs. Ritson that for the smallest of small appropriations—say £100,000 in the first six months—he and his products could be Ritsonised into their proper place at the head of the march of Progress.

At nine-thirty on the morning of his twenty-ninth birthday, however, Rufus Wade was viewing Messrs. Ritson and Partners with a jaundiced eye. Unmoved by the massive outlines of Gargantua House, he saw in the buildings merely an attempt to hide a lack of imagination beneath a mask of simplicity. Unmindful of the fact that the air on the lower floors was ozonised to safeguard his health, he reflected that it smelled like the Tube. And when the efficient high-speed lift whirled him rapidly to the tenth floor, he merely cursed a state of society which made it necessary for a man to be thrown about like that directly after breakfast.

His temper was not improved by being temporarily unable

to find his own office. The ebb and flow of Messrs. Ritson's business involved a constant change in the provision of office accommodation. The firm rented a certain number of square feet of space but, within that space, walls and partitions might be arranged at will. Accordingly, about once a month, when a new account arrived, or when some fresh development made a change in grouping imperative, there was a sort of 'general post'.[10] With the tremendous verve and efficiency which characterised all its doings, Messrs. Ritson's moved old partitions, built new ones, or scrapped superfluous ones, overnight; and the fact of having left one's office, square, and next to the accountant, on Friday night, was no guarantee that by Monday morning it would not have become an oblong, next to the comptometer[11] section. Occasionally one was forgotten altogether, and Rufus had once descended wrathfully upon the secretary and pointed out that under the latest arrangement he was apparently expected to write copy on the window-sill.

On this occasion, however, he had not been forgotten. True, his office, which had previously been a small cell containing a desk, was now a desk surrounded by a hutch, but it was at least the *right* desk, which, after one of Messrs. Ritson's rearrangements, was rare.

Rufus had barely removed his hat and coat and seated himself when there was a perfunctory knock and Fines entered. Fines was a spectacled being whose age was pretty clearly somewhere between fifteen and fifty. He was in charge of the agency's research department, and was deeply interested in his work. Rufus sighed. Fines was a modest soul who believed in getting all the advice he could, and he supplied the office with a constant series of complicated queries as to the possible meaning of his results. From the far-away look in his eyes, some such problem was troubling him now.

'Morning, Rufus,' said Fines.

'Morning, George,' said Rufus.

'Are you busy?' inquired Fines, advancing into the room and seating himself on the tiny radiator. 'Blast!' he added, springing up again rapidly. 'Why the hell do they–?'

Rufus spread out his hands apologetically.

'Busy? I'm absolutely jammed up with stuff. This bloody Creamo thing ought to have been up–'

'Ah,' said Fines regretfully. 'Pity. I hoped you'd got a minute. We've just got out some stuff which I think'd interest you.'

Rufus shook his head.

'I'm awfully sorry but–'

Fines removed his spectacles and, holding them up to the light, produced a snowy handkerchief and wiped them carefully.

'It's like this,' he said. 'You know that stuff I've been doing on Calorine?'

'No,' said Rufus, firmly. 'I don't.'

Fines raised his eyebrows in surprise.

'Oh, you don't know about it? Well, then I shall welcome your opinion as––as a sort of impartial brain. It's like this…'

'Some other time,' said Rufus.

Fines replaced his glasses with a flourish.

'It's like this,' he went on gently, 'J.W. has been trying to get Simpson's to splash on Calorine and they've been standing out against really going into the National Press with the thing because they aren't sure there's a market for it…'

Rufus laid down his pencil with a sigh.

'What *is* Calorine?' he said, hopelessly.

'A health drink. Not the sort that fizzes and conquers constipation. The other sort––the sort you mix with milk that makes children popular at school––*you* know.'

'Yes,' said Rufus heavily.

'Well, at last J.W. got old Simpson to let me look into the market. All the usual stuff––sending women round to interview housewives and ask them if they drink a health drink or if they give it to their husbands or children, and how much they pay for it, and where they buy it and so on. All the usual how, when and why questions. *You* know.'

'Yes.'

'Well, I've done that on ten thousand housewives in London, Birmingham, Glasgow, Edinburgh, Manchester, Newcastle, Cardiff and so on. And we've just started to analyse the answers.' He paused.

'Well?' said Rufus drowsily.

Fines leaned forward.

'Well, *this* is where I want your advice. We've got some extraordinary results. In Cardiff and Birmingham.' He consulted a small slip of paper. 'In Cardiff and Birmingham ninety per cent of all the housewives drink this stuff.'

'Which stuff?'

'Calorine. And so do their families.'

'Really?'

'Yes. And in the other places nobody's ever heard of it apparently.' He shook his head with a puzzled frown. 'It's the most remarkable case of localised sales I've ever struck.'

'It *is* remarkable,' said Rufus.

Fines nodded.

'Yes, but that isn't all. They were asked when they drank it. And most of them said Breakfast. That is, they said Breakfast in Cardiff. In Birmingham they all said "For Tea."' He spread out his hands. 'Well, of course you're supposed to take it at night.'

'Do they *know* they're supposed to?'

'It says so on the tin.' Fines rose and ran his hands through his hair. 'But what's puzzling *me*, Rufus, is this. Calorine's never been advertised. *Why* is it so popular in these districts? And, anyhow, I always understood that the sales were very small—too small for this to be true. What's wrong?'

Rufus shook his head. 'What, indeed?'

'My own view,' said Fines in a low voice, 'is that Simpson's got dishonest travellers in those areas and that he keeps such bad check on stock that they can just sell the stuff and stick to the money. I can't think of anything else. Can you?'

Rufus slowly produced and lit a cigarette, and regarded Fines with a smile.

'Well,' he said slowly, 'there *is* another possibility, of course…'

'What?' said Fines, sharply.

'That your results are wrong.'

Fines frowned. 'You mean that that ninety per cent isn't true?'

'Yes. That's possible, isn't it?'

Fines smiled a trifle pityingly.

'Possible, but hardly probable. Surely the people know if they drink the stuff or not?'

'Probably. But you see they may not want to tell you. They might be pulling your interviewers' legs, or trying to get rid of them.'

'Nonsense,' said Fines brusquely. 'Why should they?'

'Or, alternatively, the Birmingham and Cardiff interviewers may have filled in the answers beside their hotel fires. *I* should if I were an interviewer.'

Fines flushed.

'That's a very serious suggestion,' he said. 'I'd trust my people with my life.'

'Quite,' said Rufus. 'But this isn't your life.' He gazed meditatively out of the window. 'Yes. On the whole, I back the wangling theory.'

'But isn't it patently obvious,' Fines waved his spectacles, 'that this is a simple case of localised strength?'

Rufus sighed.

'If you're a research man, I suppose it is. If you're only a poor bloody copywriter it's perfectly obvious that it's a case of localised laziness.'

Fines went a dull purple colour.

'I didn't come in here to be insulted,' he said with some difficulty.

'Well, what the blazes *did* you come here for?' rejoined Rufus irritably.

'For constructive comment and suggestion.'

Rufus picked up his pencil.

'Well, you've got it. Now for God's sake go away and let me work.'

He turned to his desk. Fines stood for a moment staring at him in speechless fury. Then he swallowed hard and over his face spread a faintly pitying smile.

'The inability of the average man to grasp a research problem is an extraordinary thing,' he said, and went out.

Left to himself, Rufus turned without enthusiasm to the sheets which lay before him. His desire to get rid of Fines had not really been inspired by a panting urge to get at his own work, but merely by a desire to be alone. There was, as he had said, a lot to do. The February fog hung thickly over London, but nevertheless it was highly desirable that all the main essentials of the Creamo Custard campaign for summer should be well in hand.

It was not an encouraging job. Billing's Creamo Custard had been before the public for a great many years, during which time it had made enormous fortunes for every member of the Billing family. The stuff was a household word, and it was fairly certain that everyone who had the slightest intention of using it would be doing so already. But nevertheless Billing's continued to spend a steady fifty thousand a year in advertising it. Its pack had remained the same for twenty years, and old Sir Josiah Billing would never listen to pleas for something a little more up-to-date. Its simple constituents were exactly the same as those of twenty competitors and its price was extortionately high. But it continued to sell steadily and well, and Sir Josiah steadily continued to spend fifty thousand a year on his advertising, whilst obstinately refusing to give Messrs. Ritson any reasonable opportunity to earn their money.

'If only you would let us repack it,' Mr. Winstrowe, the partner who dealt with Sir Josiah, had urged. 'Or do anything else that would give us a story to tell…'

But the old autocrat had remained immovable, and Mr. Winstrowe, who did not wish to lose a fifty-thousand-pound account, had not insisted.

Resignedly, Rufus picked up a scribbling-pad and began to jot down casual notes. Strictly speaking, it was not his job to have ideas—it was his job to express them in persuasive prose. But Winstrowe had handed the job on in despair.

'Get out something,' he had said, 'I said my last word about this muck in the first year after the War.'

Rufus lit a fresh cigarette and considered. Traditionally, one did not think of anything original for Creamo. One simply adjusted the fashionable advertising idea of the moment to fit in with the idea of custard. He could remember a long succession of campaigns run on this basis. When every advertisement had been a little play, there had been improbable conversations between members of the Everyman family about the virtues of Creamo. When the sole method of successful advertising had been to bribe Society women to say they used your product, Lady Powater and the Dowager Lady Smiles had been featured as enthusiastic Creamo users. When managing directors had first appeared, delivering little homilies on the virtues of their goods, Sir Josiah, from the pages of the *Daily Mail*, had assured the public that Creamo was absolutely pure. And recently, when every successful advertiser had been concentrating on strip drawings of the influence of their product on domestic crises, Creamo had been shown repeatedly saving the domestic, matrimonial, and social situation.

Rufus blew a thoughtful cloud of smoke towards the ceiling.

This year, humour was in. Everybody was going to exploit funny advertising. It had been clearly shown that people wanted to be *amused* by advertisements. It looked like the light fantastic toe for Creamo. Rufus picked up his pencil. Anyhow, humour was never too bad. It had the great advantage that the essential humorous content of the advertisement need have only the very vaguest connection with the subject advertised...

He hesitated a moment and then wrote rapidly.

'Series of humorous drawings. Must be by first-rate artist—' (He paused and underlined this heavily. The most shattering of all types of advertising was the unhumorous humorous drawing.) 'Say Bateman or Fougasse[12]—' He paused and chewed his pencil. 'Perhaps scenes showing humorously "Awkward Moments in the Home"—solved by C.

The unexpected guest.

Spring cleaning.

When John has had losses in the City...'

Rufus paused and shook his head. It wouldn't do. It was too old... Suddenly his brow cleared and he wrote rapidly.

'Why not guy the strip stuff? Everybody's tired of advertisements which show the home being saved from a break-up by soap or something. Why not a satirical series, *not* done as funny drawings, showing perfectly solemnly, Creamo saving the family from fire, bankruptcy, burglary, etc.? This might—'

He paused. He had been about to write, 'This might be good fun.' But would one ever get away with it? Or would it be too subtle? After all, if one had a satirical mind, most advertising was satire anyway...'

He threw down his pencil and gazed moodily out of the window. There was a tap and Fines entered. His face was triumphant.

'I thought you might just like to know,' he said coldly, 'that I have definitely proved that your preposterous theory about Calorine is wrong.'

'How?' asked Rufus.

Fines produced a sheet of paper and laid it before him.

'Because,' he answered with quiet pride, 'on looking into it, I find that there was a slip in the analysis figures. That figure of ninety per cent should be point nine per cent.'

He raised his glasses and regarded Rufus with a myopic gaze and a sarcastic smile. 'In the face of *that*, perhaps even *you* will admit that you were wrong?'

∾

At twelve-forty-five Rufus's internal telephone rang, and a diaphragm-shattering voice inquired if he had made any progress with the Creamo scheme. (Mr. Winstrowe, though a particularly gentle speaker in conversation, had 'hidden reserves', in the shape of a bellowing roar which he used exclusively for telephone conversation.)

'I haven't really got very far with it, sir,' replied Rufus, carefully manoeuvring the receiver mouth as far from his ear as possible. There was a violent uproar from the other end to the effect that Mr. Winstrowe desired progress to be made as rapidly as possible.

'I rather *thought* humour,' said Rufus diffidently when the uproar died down.

'Um. No good, I'm afraid,' rioted Mr. Winstrowe. 'Firm would never stand for it.'

'You don't think so?'

Mr. Winstrowe, 'blasting' badly, was sure of it. 'You'd never convince old Sir Josiah that there was anything funny about his damned stuff,' he roared.

Rufus frowned.

'No. I suppose not. But the idea I had was really more satirical than funny. A satire on–' He hastily shifted the receiver.

'Blur-r-ical?' Mr. Winstrowe was saying. 'Be yourself, Wade.

Surely you know by this time that blur-r-ical advertising is a blur-r?'

'There is that, of course,' said Rufus, feebly.

'Blur-r,' said Mr. Winstrowe firmly. 'Health and the children… blur-r. Blur-r it over this afternoon.'

There was a click and calm silence. Rufus slowly hung up and, turning, gazed at the half-dozen pages of rough notes on his desk. Then, with a sudden movement, he tore them into fragments and, seizing his hat, flung out of the office, crashing the door shut behind him. Ted Lewis was passing. Rufus caught him by the arm.

'Come and have lunch, for God's sake.'

Ted Lewis glanced at his watch.

'O.K. Half a mo while I dump these in my rat run.'

In the normal course of events, Rufus and Ted Lewis would have consumed an eighteenpenny lunch in one of the humbler of the many Gargantua House restaurants. To-day, however, as they stepped out of the lift, Rufus turned sharply towards the door which opened on to the roaring street.

'Come on,' he said, laying a hand on Lewis's arm. 'Let's go somewhere else and get out of this bloody place.'

'Righto,' said Ted, turning obediently, 'where d'you want to go? None of your five-bob touches, mind.'

'I don't care where we go as long as we get out,' replied Rufus, savagely.

They stood on the pavement for a moment and considered.

'How about the Raven?' said Ted. 'Bread and cheese and a pint? Or doesn't that fit in with the vibrations?'

Rufus nodded.

'That'll do.'

The Raven Inn was one of those odd places, found in large

numbers in the City, where business London throngs during the lunch-hour. In it, one fights a way through a large and motley crowd, ultimately acquires a glass of beer and a large portion of bread and cheese, and consumes both, standing, in considerable discomfort. Ted, who had fair claims to being the fastest buyer of drinks in a crowd in London, disappeared into the ruck, and emerged again, in a miraculously short time, with two tankards of beer. Rufus, in the meantime, had collected the bread and cheese, and two seats at a little table which, by a miracle of good luck, had been vacated under his very nose. Ted set down the beer with care and took the remaining seat.

'What have you done with the bodies?' he inquired.

'What bodies?' said Rufus.

'Of the blokes you had to murder to get these seats?'

'I didn't,' said Rufus. 'They went.'

'Oh,' Ted raised his glass. 'Well—cheero.'

'Cheero,' said Rufus, mechanically, drinking.

There was a long silence while both attacked the bread and cheese.

'How's Creamo?' inquired Ted at length with his mouth full.

'Bloody,' replied Rufus gloomily. 'J.W.'s just been howling about it on the phone. How the hell can anyone get ideas about that muck?' he added savagely. 'You might as well try to advertise—' He stopped, at a loss for a parallel.

Ted sliced a piece of rind off his cheese and nodded sympathetically.

'Played out, eh?'

Rufus did not answer.

'Added to which,' he said after a pause, 'I've now landed next door to Fines.'

'Christ!' said Ted.

'He pops in about every ten minutes,' Rufus added morosely, 'to ask if I don't think some of his results are funny.'

'Well, so they are,' said Ted. 'Bloody funny. Everybody knows that. The only trouble is that he doesn't see it.'

Rufus pushed away the remainder of his bread and cheese and fumbled for a cigarette.

'What are you on?' he asked abruptly.

'I am engaged,' said Ted solemnly, 'on a drawing of a leetle child. Very touching it is.'

'This Calorine muck?'

'God, no! Blenkin cigarettes.'

'But how does the kid come in?'

'Collects the fag cards. Family appeal, see?' Ted finished his beer. 'When coupons went out,' he said with a grin, Blenkin's were up a gum tree. Nobody in his senses would buy their damned gaspers to smoke. The only people who used to buy them before threw the cigarettes away and kept the coupons.[13] So now they're running kid appeal, hoping kids will bully the old man into buying the things.'

There was another long silence.

'It's my birthday to-day,' said Rufus suddenly.

'Birthday?' said Ted. 'Fine! Many happies. Have another on me?'

'No thanks,' said Rufus. He gazed listlessly round the crowded bar. 'Let's get out of here,' he said suddenly, rising abruptly to his feet.

'What for?' protested Ted. 'This is the only time in our lives we'll ever be able to sit down here.'

'Come on,' said Rufus, elbowing his way towards the door.

He stood for a minute outside the Raven, gazing gloomily across the road at the great mass of Gargantua House.

'What the hell's the matter?' said Ted, rather irritably, as he rejoined him.

'I can't stand the gabble in there,' said Rufus. 'Come on—let's go down by the river. I'm not going back yet.'

Ted demurred. 'Think I'll go and get a haircut.'

'No, you won't,' said Rufus firmly. 'You'll come with me.'

He took the unwilling Lewis by the arm and led him down the slope towards the Embankment.

'If I don't talk to somebody I shall step under a bus.'

The fog had lifted a good deal and, dimly across the river, they could see the huddle of assorted buildings on the south side. The tide was low and the buoys lay lopsidedly in a few inches of water. A tug going downstream hooted mournfully.

'God, what a mess!' said Rufus with distaste.

A dampish breeze blew keenly off the river. Ted Lewis shivered and turned up his collar.

'It's bloody cold,' he complained. 'Let's go back to the Raven and have another drink.'

'Damn the Raven,' said Rufus. 'I want to think.'

'Think? What about?'

'I tell you, it's my birthday,' said Rufus slowly.

Ted grinned.

'Well, it's no use worrying about that. You can't help it.' He turned and eyed his companion. 'What's up, Rufus?' he said more seriously.

Rufus took a final puff at his cigarette and flicked the stub out into the grey–brown mud.

'More or less everything,' he said thoughtfully.

'Fed up with Creamo, eh?'

Rufus nodded.

'And everything else,' he hesitated. 'It sounds damned silly, but at the moment I just don't see the point of—of carrying on at all. Not like this.'

'Oh, I don't know,' said Ted comfortingly. 'I don't see that there's much to complain about.'

'Complain about!' Rufus turned to him indignantly. 'How about this bloody job? *Creamo!* What the hell have I got to do with

Creamo? I don't care a cuss if they never sell another packet.'

'Well, *every* job's like that, o'man.'

'Rot,' said Rufus decidedly.

They walked a little way in silence towards Blackfriars Bridge.

'Here am I,' went on Rufus, indignantly, 'twenty-nine. For eight years I've been sweating away in that damned great ugly barn of a place, and at this rate I shall do it for another twenty-eight. Where does it get one?'

'Gets you bread and butter,' said Ted, 'which is more than most people can depend on nowadays.'

Rufus shook his head irritably.

'Oh, I dare say! But there's no point in living for the sake of going on living. It's a vicious circle.'

'Well, then, why don't you marry what's-her-name?'

'Marjorie? Because I don't think I want to.'

'Oh.' Ted reflected. 'Well, you wanted to like hell about a month ago,' he added.

'I dare say. But I don't now. Not if it means staying in—in *this*.' Rufus waved an all-embracing hand.

'You've got a liver,[14] o'man,' said Ted Lewis.

'Don't be a bloody fool.'

'Fact. I've often felt like this myself. I bet if you tried the little daily dose for a week it'd look all different.'

There was a long silence.

'Of course,' said Rufus thoughtfully, 'I could probably get another job.'

Ted nodded. 'Mm. As a matter of fact I know Gleason's want a bloke. Ideas man.'

Rufus shook his head.

'No—I don't mean another agency job. That wouldn't be any better. I mean another *sort* of job.'

They turned at the opening of Blackfriars Bridge and slowly retraced their steps.

'See here, Rufus,' said Ted suddenly. 'I don't quite get all this. What's biting you? Is there any more to it than a brute of a day and a bit of a liver and fooling around with Creamo?'

Rufus hesitated.

'Wait a minute,' he said thoughtfully. 'Just let me think it over for a minute so as to be sure I tell the truth.'

He gazed unseeingly out across the river for perhaps a minute. A police boat chugged rapidly by, leaving a long white trail in the depressing brown. A tram went booming and clanging past them.[15] Rufus turned suddenly.

'Yes!' he said with an emphatic nod. 'There *is* more to it than that. This is something fundamental that—that I've got to get right.'

'You mean you really are seriously fed up—with the job?'

'No. Not just with the job. The job's only part of it. I'm fed up with everything—with the whole way things are organised.'

'Life, in fact,' said Ted with a grin.

Rufus nodded solemnly. 'Yes. Life. At least, *my* life. It just isn't good enough.' He waved a hand. 'I propose to alter it.'

'How?'

'God knows,' said Rufus frankly. 'I haven't got as far as that yet. I only know that this *won't* do. What *will* do's another matter.'

Ted projected a tiny piece of tongue—a sure sign of scepticism.

'Rather a tall order,' he said dubiously. 'Jobs aren't exactly plentiful.'

'I'm not at all sure that I want a job.'

'Proposing to live on previously unsuspected private means?' said Ted sarcastically.

'No. I just mean that I'm not at all sure I want the sort of job you're thinking of.'

Ted Lewis turned and regarded him in silence for a moment.

'Rufus,' he said at last, 'as one working girl to another, what *do* you want? Because if it's one of those things where someone pays you a thousand a year without taking up your time and energy or interfering with you in any way, give it up, o'boy. We all want one of those, but there aren't enough of 'em to go round.'

Rufus smiled.

'No,' he said calmly, 'that isn't it at all. I can't tell you in detail what I want, but I can outline it.' He threw away his cigarette, and placed his foot carefully upon the glowing stub. 'I want,' he said slowly, 'a job which is worth doing, i.e., something which involves *making* something which has to be made or which ought to be made. Further, I want it to be a job in which I can be physically alive and in the air—not fugging about in a stuffy hencoop of an office.'

'Bricklayer,' suggested Ted, humorously.

'More that sort of thing,' agreed Rufus. 'And finally— and easily the most important of the lot—I want to get out of this—this bloody racket, and go somewhere where it's quiet, and where there aren't any people—or at least not many.' He stopped suddenly and stared at Lewis inquiringly. 'How long is it since you've seen any birds?' he asked abruptly.

Ted grinned. 'If I make the obvious quasi-humorous reply you'll be annoyed.'

'I shall,' said Rufus. 'Answer my question and don't be a bloody fool.'

Ted jerked a thumb towards the river.

'Plenty of birds there,' he said.

'No, no,' said Rufus impatiently. 'I mean *real* birds—rooks and things.'

'Seen them in Regent's Park,' said Ted defensively.

'He's seen them in Regent's Park!...' Rufus threw up his head in impassioned appeal to the universe. 'Christ!...'

'Well, see here, o'man,' said Ted reasoningly. 'I can see what you mean, of course. But where does all this get you? We all get like this at times—get fed up with the row and our jobs, and living in Town[16] and so on. But there's nothing to be done about it. After all, the simple life may be all right in its way, but I reckon it must be damned uncomfortable. I know a bloke who's got a cottage. Down on Dartmoor. Well, I go and stay with him sometimes. It's grand for a week or so. But to tell the truth, I'm always damned glad to get back to Town where I can get a decent hot bath.'

'God!' exploded Rufus, 'I talk about the present organisation of life and you talk about a "decent hot bath"! I suppose we've all go to stay and stifle in bloody towns because we must have electric light, eh?'

'Well, there's something in that,' said Ted with spirit. 'You try and manage without electric light and baths and things for a bit and see how you find it.'

'I will,' said Rufus, grimly.

'Oh, no, you won't. You'll do what everyone else does—stick to your bread and butter and grouse.'

'I don't think so.'

Ted shrugged his shoulders. 'We shall see. Well, from what I've heard of it, the job you'd like would be hoeing swedes on a desert island. That about fills the specifications you gave.'

'Exactly,' said Rufus calmly. 'It would do admirably.'

'Oh, go and climb a tree,' said Ted rudely.

It was four o'clock and Rufus, sipping dispiritedly at his cup of tea, was dismally regarding his latest efforts to produce a real sales story for Creamo, when his telephone-bell rang and a raucous clatter from the other end announced that Mr. Winstrowe required his attendance at once. Gathering up the scattered sheets of paper, Rufus walked through the buzzing and clicking main office, trying hard to think of some reason which Mr. Winstrowe would understand and appreciate for having made so little progress.

Mr. Winstrowe, however, did not wish to discuss Creamo. He was seated in close conclave with a rather elderly, thick-lipped, overdressed stranger who was introduced to Rufus as Mr. Corder. Rufus, after one look at his chief, decided that Mr. Corder was a prospective account. An old client might induce cordiality in Mr. Winstrowe. A new one might make him beam at Rufus in that affectionate way. But only a 'prospect'—and a prospect half hooked—could bring out that unique blend of good humour, charm of manner, and quick-fire efficiency.

'Sit down, Wade,' said Mr. Winstrowe cordially, and proceeded to confirm Rufus's analysis of the situation.

'Wade,' said Mr. Winstrowe, and the voice was as the baying of hounds who scent a kill, 'Wade—Mr. Corder is the managing director of Silton Proprietary, who, as you may know–'

'Gargazene,' said Mr. Corder briefly. 'He'll know that.'

Rufus nodded. It was difficult not to know all about Gargazene, that sovereign remedy for constipation. Rufus began to understand Mr. Winstrowe's excitement. Silton Proprietary spent at least two hundred thousand a year in advocating internal cleanliness. The famous slogan 'Better a dirty face than–' blazed nightly above Piccadilly.[17]

'He'll know our Gargazene stuff,' said Mr. Corder.

Mr. Winstrowe inclined his head.

'Quite, Mr. Corder.' He turned to Rufus. 'Well, Wade, Mr. Corder is thinking of launching a new campaign on a national basis, and having seen the work we've done for Oko–'

Mr. Corder leaned forward, and nodded his head at Rufus with emphasis.

'I liked your Oko ads,' he said. 'Understand from your chief here you wrote the story. Good stuff. Just the stuff *we* want.'

'I explained that you wrote the copy–' put in Mr. Winstrowe.

'So I thought I'd like a word with you about Bindax,' concluded Mr. Corder, unheeding.

Rufus blushed.

'Well, of course Oko was a reasonably easy story,' he said modestly.

Mr. Corder waved a hand.

'Don't you tell me. Easy maybe. But it was *noo*. It'd got punch. That's what we want—punch.'

'Mr. Corder particularly wanted to see you,' said Mr. Winstrowe, perseveringly, 'because–'

'I'll say this,' said Mr. Corder handsomely, 'when I read your last ad for Oko, I as near as nothing went and bought a bottle. And that, mind you, though I'm not rheumatic myself. *And* knowing it's only cinnamon and magnesia.[18] There isn't a man living,' said Mr. Corder, 'that could make me buy Oko, not knowing what I do. But I give you my word you had me wavering.'

'I told Mr. Corder–' began Mr. Winstrowe without conviction.

'Now, this is the proposition,' Mr. Corder leaned forward and spoke earnestly and confidentially. 'You know Gargazene's constipation?'

Rufus nodded.

'Well, I don't mind telling you that Gargazene's groggy. Constipation's been overdone, that's the trouble. Why, there was a time,' said Mr. Corder lyrically, 'when there wasn't a story that could hold a candle to constipation. But we've got to move with the times. Get me?'

'Of course there's a lot of competition in laxatives now,' said Rufus, wearily.

Mr. Corder smote the table with the flat of his hand.

'Competition!' he said. 'You've hit it. After all, there's only forty-nine million people[19] in these islands and their capacity for laxatives is limited. Mind you, Gargazene's held its own well, considering. But the trouble is it's an old-established line, and in this market people want something *new*—something they haven't tried before—something where they can have a bit of fun seeing what happens, see? Sort of spirit of adventure.'

'Mr. Corder therefore proposes–' said Mr. Winstrowe.

'So this is the idea, boy,' went on Mr. Corder. 'Let constipation go. See? Keep on with Gargazene, of course, but don't worry about it too much. And come in with both feet on the noo angle.'

'Which–' said Mr. Winstrowe.

'Which is this: everyone's taking laxatives, aren't they? Right. Well, too much laxative's bad. Lowering, see? Well, that's where we come in. "The modern curse, relaxed bowels. Take Bindax and feel bright." See?'

Rufus hesitated.

'You propose to market a—an anti-laxative?'

'Yes,' said Mr. Winstrowe, very quickly.

'Ex-actly,' said Mr. Corder.

There was a moment's silence.

'It's very ingenious,' said Rufus, slowly.

'You're saying so,' said Mr. Corder exultantly. 'Good stuff, eh? See it? Pep up Gargazene a bit, see? And then every bottle of Gargazene sells two of Bindax. It's a cinch. Noo. Out of the ordinary run. Fresh angle. There.' He threw himself back in his chair. 'Reckon you could get a story out of that, boy?'

Rufus hesitated. Mr. Corder was leaning back in his chair with an inquiring grin on his fleshy face. Rufus found his eyes irresistibly attracted by Mr. Corder's hands, which rested, short, square, and dirty-nailed, on his plump thighs. The room was very hot and Rufus was suddenly conscious of feeling sick. Mr. Winstrowe glanced at him with a prompting little cough. Rufus roused himself with an effort.

'What *is* Bindax?' he asked in a curious dry voice. He was playing desperately for time.

'You mean what's in it?'

'Yes.'

Mr. Corder shook his head with a grin.

'Never you mind. It's good wholesome stuff. Won't do anybody any harm, anyway.'

'I don't see—' began Mr. Winstrowe reprovingly.

'But will it do them any *good*?' asked Rufus with unexpected energy. Mr. Corder's smile vanished.

'How do I know? I aim to sell this stuff, not drink it. You aren't a public analyst, are you? The stuff's all right. All I want to ask you and Mr. Winstrowe here is—can you help me sell it?'

'I brought you in, Wade,' said Mr. Winstrowe, severely, 'to see if you felt that Mr. Corder had a—a good selling platform.'

'Oh, he's undoubtedly got *that*,' said Rufus with a sarcasm that amazed himself.

'All right, then,' said Mr. Corder, reassured. 'Then this is where you come in, boy. Get me out a sales line, see? Put me up some ideas. Same sort of thing you did for Oko, see? Recollect this is a noo angle. Get some snap in it.' He leaned forward and pointed a finger at Rufus. 'Recollect—it's up to you folks. There's the line. Sell it and—' He threw out his hands. 'It's a big account for you. It's what you make it, see?'

'You can rest assured that we appreciate that, Mr. Corder,' said Mr. Winstrowe cordially. He glanced at Rufus a little doubtfully. 'I don't know if there's any more you wish to say to Wade?...'

Mr. Corder shook his head.

'No. There it is. Now all I want's the goods. Put me up a proposition and we'll talk business. Just a line of talk, that's all.'

'Of course,' said Mr. Winstrowe gently, 'we don't actually do detailed speculative schemes...'

'Scheme nothing,' said Mr. Corder. 'I don't want a scheme yet. Just you set this boy here to do a think, and then we'll talk. See?'

'Very well,' said Mr. Winstrowe with some relief. He turned to Rufus. 'Then if you'll be getting out some rough ideas, Wade...'

Rufus rose mechanically to his feet. Ideas. Ideas for selling Bindax...

'And if there's anything you want to know,' said Mr. Corder, 'let me have a line, see?'

Rufus's eyes were on the window. Far, far below the white tops of the buses gleamed in the gathering dusk. It was raining, and the fog, which had lifted a little in the middle of the day, was gathering thickly over the river. His mind made itself up with a click—as though by an agency outside his volition. He turned suddenly and heard his voice, cool and steady, almost with surprise.

'You want ideas, Mr. Corder?' said the voice.

'That's it,' said Mr. Corder emphatically. 'I want ideas.'

'Very well, then,' the voice of Rufus went on. 'Here's one straight away–' He paused. Mr. Winstrowe was looking at him in surprise.

'I should recommend,' said Rufus coolly, 'that you should give up exploiting the public with your fraudulent dopes and do a little honest work. Further–'

'What the hell?...' said Mr. Corder inquiringly.

'Further,' said Rufus, 'I should recommend you to clean your nails. "Better,"' he added with relish, '"Better a dirty face than unclean nails."'

Mr. Corder had risen to his feet. His face had gone a deep mulberry red.

'Wade!...' Mr. Winstrowe clutched Rufus by the arm. 'Are you drunk or mad?'

'See here, boy…' said Mr. Corder, with violence.

'And kindly cease to call me "boy".'

Mr. Corder picked up his hat. 'All right,' he said in a suppressed voice. 'All right. If this is your idea of a joke, my lad, I reckon it's going to cost your firm a pretty penny.'

'Excellent,' said Rufus. 'The larger size,' he added a little hysterically, 'costs only half a crown and contains–'

Mr. Winstrowe, with a little whinny of pain, sprang across the room and intercepted Mr. Corder on his way to the door.

'Mr. Corder, please—allow him to apologise! Wade, what—'

'Apologise?' said Rufus, 'what for? His nails *are* dirty.' A curious exhilaration was sweeping over him. His voice rose almost to a shout.

Mr. Corder put Mr. Winstrowe aside and opened the door. He was regarding Rufus with interest.

'Cuckoo!' he said decidedly. 'That's what.' He turned to the agonised Winstrowe. 'You know your own business best, but I reckon you'd get more of it without him. 'Day.'

The door slammed behind him. Mr. Winstrowe gave a little yelp of dismay and turned furiously to Rufus.

'You damned young lunatic!' he roared. 'That's a hundred-thousand-pound account gone…'

'More than that,' said Rufus with satisfaction.

Mr. Winstrowe made an incoherent noise.

Rufus looked out of the window. It was still raining. He turned to Mr. Winstrowe.

'I shall go now,' he said gently. 'Cheerio, Winstrowe. You're wrong about Creamo. Humour's the thing. Series of drawings by Fougasse or any *first*-rate artist. Cheerio, Winstrowe.'

He nodded cordially and closed the door gently behind him. Going through the office he saw Mollie Bain. Rufus had always liked Mollie Bain. He chucked her under the chin and, going into his office, collected his hat and coat and fountain-pen. Then, humming a gay little tune, he walked briskly out to the lifts.

Chapter III

End of a Tiring Birthday

As Rufus passed under the great archway which spanned the
entrance to Gargantua House, and strode out into the foggy drizzle
of the February evening, he was conscious of a rapid draining of
the heady exhilaration which had marked his last minutes with
Mr. Winstrowe. Not that he regretted his action. That, in itself,
seemed merely an inevitable and logical end to an unsatisfactory
situation and, as such, neither particularly good nor particularly
bad. But with the cold damp touch of the night air on his face,
he found himself suddenly intensely interested by the realities of
the situation. His sudden action, consciously at least, had been
unpremeditated. But he was now face to face with a situation for
which his unconscious mind had long been preparing; and the
results were as fascinating as the practical fulfilment of a vivid
dream. Here were all the facts, just as in the dream. He had burned
his boats and was walking out of Gargantua House magnificently
free, magnificently unemployed. The dream had never got beyond
that point. It had never contained any clear emotional reaction at
all. Could the reality go farther?

As Rufus walked aimlessly down the Strand, he was reluctantly forced to admit that, so far at least, reality also was emotionally barren. Unemployment did not horrify, nor did Freedom incline him to throw up his hat and burst into song. Rufus sighed. The process of Awakening to a New Life—of Seeing Another Face in the Mirror—had always attracted him. He had awaited it hopefully after every landmark in his life—on leaving school—on attaining his majority[20]—on losing his virginity. Always it had been denied him. Always the face in the mirror had been distressingly the same. A little paler perhaps, or even a fraction more dissipated, but always the same in its essentials. Now, it seemed, a dramatic renunciation of his livelihood was to be equally disappointing.

At Trafalgar Square he paused and considered. To go back to his rooms seemed unnecessary and rather useless. At six-thirty he had arranged to meet Marjorie and to do a show[21] in honour of his birthday. Apart from which, Marjorie was clearly one of the matters which must be Cleared Up forthwith. He glanced at his watch and decided that a walk to Marjorie's home (Marjorie lived in Kensington) would dispose of an hour and provide an excellent opportunity to Think Things Out.

As he turned into Pall Mall, however, it gradually dawned upon Rufus that thinking things out was not as easy as he had supposed. It was one thing to be Free. It was quite another, in his present state, to think of any reasonable way of using one's freedom. Only a week before, he had received a covert offer of employment from George Gaskell's Advertising Service. But manifestly there was no point in exchanging the familiar frying-pan of Ritson and Partners for the unknown fire of Mr. Gaskell. On the other hand, he could not simply live in London and do nothing. His total assets, Rufus reckoned, were about one hundred and seventy pounds and an insurance policy of indefinite value. Moreover, the dramatic abandonment of his career called for an interesting—a definite—sequel. Otherwise his protest would have been in vain.

Clearly, he reflected, skilfully dodging a skidding taxi, clearly a good deal depended upon Marjorie. If Marjorie turned up trumps, and was willing to marry him whatever happened, then they could talk it over, and weigh the advantages and disadvantages of sweeping a crossing[22] and emigrating (steerage)[23] in calm confidence and mutual trust. If, on the other hand—

At Hyde Park Corner an unpleasant conviction was borne in upon him that Marjorie was going to be difficult; and as he neared Knightsbridge, it had become a certainty. The vagrant poverty idea, which had seemed logical and, indeed, desirable, in the Strand became almost a blasphemy in the shadow of Exhibition Road. And Marjorie, somehow, was closely connected with Exhibition Road…

Marjorie Weddle's father had been dead some years. She and her mother lived in a service flat near Barker's,[24] from which they issued severally, Marjorie to pursue a series of rather pointless lessons in singing and elocution, Mrs. Weddle to work with grim intensity at the dozen or so good causes which now occupied her whole life. Mrs. Weddle was an active person. In youth an ardent suffragette, she had once brought the vote considerably nearer by chaining herself to the rails of Hyde Park. On the outbreak of War she had converted her country home into a hospital which became famous throughout the country as a death-trap for delicate V.A.D.s.[25] And recently, when the death of her husband had left her with depleted means, and peace and Mr. Baldwin[26] had deprived her of her vocations, she had turned indefatigably to work on Temperance, Girls' Clubs, Blood Sports, Anti-Vivisection and Spirit Healing.

Privately, Rufus found Mrs. Weddle a little difficult. True, she had placed no obstacle in the way of his engagement to Marjorie. But she had an awkward habit of demanding to know his views on controversial matters without revealing her own. Rufus remembered with pain the occasion on which, knowing Mrs.

Weddle's views on blood sports and vivisection, he had cheerfully pronounced himself an extreme pacifist, only to find that Mrs. Weddle was a staunch believer in International Blood Sports in their most advanced form. The great advantage of Mrs. Weddle, however, was that she was nearly always out. And this evening she rang true to form. But Miss Marjorie, the maid informed him, with a confidential smirk, was in the lounge.

Marjorie greeted him with some surprise. Rufus, as she rose, felt the familiar thrill of sheer surprise which her loveliness never failed to wake. One knew—one had always known and always boasted—that Marjorie was pretty. But in her presence it was always more than that—more than one had expected or remembered.

'Darling!' She came across the room and took both his hands. 'I didn't know you were fetching me. I thought–'

He kissed her, noting the faint, familiar smell of Verbena.[27]

'I left the office early,' he said. With one arm still round her, he led her back to the fire.

'But aren't we changing?' asked Marjorie in surprise.

Rufus looked at her. She had dressed already, for their meeting. The slim lines of the simple black evening gown set off perfectly the white neck and throat, the big, forget-me-not eyes, and the wavy gold hair.

'You look marvellous, sweet,' he said quietly.

'Nice, isn't it?' Marjorie pointed a toe. 'Specially for the occasion. Smart, I feel, but refeened.' She dropped into a chair. 'But look here, I'm not going to go out like this with a man in his dungarees. This frock requires tails. *Definitely* tails.'

Rufus sat down and slowly extracted his cigarette-case.

'Smoke?'

'No, thanks.'

He lit a cigarette. 'I was going to change—but—well, several things have happened and I rather want to talk to you first—

before we go.' He hesitated, gazing into the fire.

'Oh—by the way—many happy returns, Rufus,' said Marjorie, suddenly.

'Thank you,' he said abstractedly.

There was a moment's pause.

'Did you like it?' said Marjorie, with a rather disappointed little smile.

'Like it?' Rufus glanced up. 'Oh—the watch. Darling—I am an ungrateful beast. Of course. It was lovely. The nicest one I've ever seen. But you shouldn't have–' He trailed off into silence. Marjorie looked at him keenly for a moment.

'Rufus, love.' She leaned forward and took his hand. 'Is there anything wrong?' Rufus raised his head and met the puzzled blue eyes.

'Wrong?' he said with a little smile. 'Why, no. There's nothing wrong. In fact everything is extremely right… I think.'

'But something's happened?'

'Yes.' He hesitated for a moment and flicked the ash from his cigarette. 'I've chucked up Ritson's,' he said quietly.

'Chucked up–'

'Yes. Told them just want I think of them and advertising in general, and walked out.'

'But why, Rufus?'

He shrugged his shoulders.

'Just couldn't stand it any longer.'

Marjorie was gazing at him with a puzzled frown.

'But I thought you liked it?'

'Did you?' said Rufus rather bitterly.

'You always seemed to. What happened? Were they beastly to you or something?'

Rufus shook his head.

'Oh, no. It wasn't really anything to do with them at all. It was just the job.'

Marjorie hesitated. 'Well, of course, darling, you know best. If it was beastly there wasn't anything else you could do.'

'No.'

'But it's rather a curse,' said Marjorie pensively. Rufus looked up quickly.

'Why?'

'From our point of view, I mean.'

'Why?'

'Of course it is,' said Marjorie rather impatiently. 'It means we can't get married, doesn't it? At least, not until you've got another job?'

Rufus was gazing into the fire again.

'That's what I wanted to talk about,' he said slowly.

'What—about our getting married?...' Marjorie glanced at him sharply. 'You—you're not trying to tell me gently that?–'

Rufus raised her hand to his lips and kissed it rather abstractedly. 'Don't be an ass,' he said gently. 'No. About this other job business.'

There was a short silence.

'Can you get one, do you think?' asked Marjorie. 'Reasonably easily, I mean?'

Rufus nodded.

'Very easily—if I want it. I was offered one last week.'

'As good?'

'Probably better.'

'Darling! Really?'

'Yes.' Rufus threw away his cigarette. 'If, as I say, I want it...'

'Well, surely–'

'That's what I want to talk about,' said Rufus.

Marjorie shook the golden head irritably.

'You're being very mysterious and extremely irritating,' she said rather crossly. 'Isn't it a good job really or what?'

Rufus hesitated and ran his fingers through his thick black hair.

'It's a bit difficult to explain,' he said slowly. 'You see, for several months now, I've been feeling… well, fed up.'

'With advertising?'

'Yes. But not only that. With work in general.'

'Well–' began Marjorie with a laugh.

'Oh, I don't mean what you think.' Rufus shook his head. 'I mean fed up with work in an office—in London. Work that isn't any *good*—that doesn't really get anyone anywhere.' He took another cigarette and, lighting it, gazed thoughtfully at its glowing tip.

'Don't you see what I mean? I'm tired of messing about in an office from nine-thirty till six. After all—one hasn't got long to live, really. And somehow it seems such a complete waste of time…'

'Well, what do you *want* to do, then?' asked Marjorie impatiently.

Rufus shrugged his shoulders.

'There you are. I don't *know*. That's the trouble.'

'Then–'

'But it's something—quite—quite *different*.'

There was a moment's silence.

'Well, frankly, my dear, I think you're talking rot,' said Marjorie decidedly.

'You would,' said Rufus, unthinkingly.

Marjorie flushed slightly.

'What exactly do you mean by that?' she said sharply.

Rufus looked at her. How lovely she looked with that angry little flush and her head held so proudly and indignantly! Far away, detached and impersonal, he looked at her, like a connoisseur at an exhibition.

'Because,' he said slowly, 'it's what all the reasonable people do think. Ted Lewis was just the same.'

'I'm glad to find that I'm reasonable at least,' said Marjorie, sarcastically.

Rufus nodded. 'Oh, yes. You're reasonable all right. That's the damnable part of it.'

For a moment she was about to reply angrily. Then she hesitated.

'Rufus,' she said in a low voice, 'do you realise that you're being very rude?'

'I'm sorry,' said Rufus sincerely.

'Rude and rather unfair. You don't explain, and then you're rude because I don't understand.'

'But don't you? I–'

'No. I don't. I don't believe you understand yourself. As far as I can see all you've said is that you've thrown up your job, don't want another like it, and don't know what you do want. It isn't sense.'

'Of course it isn't.' Rufus smiled a little wryly. 'It isn't supposed to be. Life's a damned sight too reasonable and sensible, and I'm trying to get away from it a bit, that's all.'

'Oh, for God's sake, Rufus!' Marjorie burst out angrily, 'stop being a fool, and say what you mean!'

'All right.' Rufus leaned back in his chair and regarded her with a slight smile. 'Do you love me?'

'Love you?' Marjorie looked at him in puzzled irritation. 'Of course I do. You know perfectly well.'

'And we want to get married, don't we?'

'Well, if–'

'Right. Well, now about what income do you think we need to get married on?'

'I just *don't* see what you're talking about,' said Marjorie hopelessly. 'What's it got to do with it?'

Rufus spread out his hands.

'But surely, everything! Do you think six hundred a year would be enough?'

Marjorie hesitated.

'Yes, I should think so. It all depends.'

Rufus nodded.

'Quite. Well, now supposing I told you that I was going to leave London and go and be a—a farm labourer or a bricklayer or something like that, on two pounds a week, what would you say?'

'Rufus—is this your idea of humour?'

'No. That's the sort of thing I mean by something quite different. Something *physical*. Something *closer* to—to things. That's the sort of job I want. What do you say?'

Marjorie hesitated. 'You can't really expect me to say anything,' she replied coldly, 'except that you seem to be slightly mad.'

'Why mad?'

'Well, why *should* you? Why should you suddenly throw up a perfectly good job, and start talking nonsense like this? It's—'

'Why should I? Because I want to. Because I've only got one life to live and I don't propose to spend it helping Ritson's to help someone else to sell something I don't care a damn about. I want to be alive—physically alive. Not a respectable cabbage in a bowler hat.'

'And your idea of being alive is to be a bricklayer?' said Marjorie icily.

'I don't know,' said Rufus frankly, 'but I'm willing to try it. At least it's a job in the air.'

'And that's all you care about?' said Marjorie quietly. 'Just the little-boy pleasure of doing what you like whatever happens?'

'That's all any of us care about really,' said Rufus, bluntly.

'I see,' Marjorie's voice rose a trifle. 'Then you don't think I—I'm worth working for?'

'You?' Rufus looked up in surprise. 'Of course. That's the whole point. Worth *working* for.' He leaned forward. 'Look here, sweet—if you'll come with me—just on trust—just to see if I'm right—I'll work for you or—or anything. But don't you see it's no good spending our whole lives vegetating like this? Supposing I go and take that job and we just get married. Where does it get us? We can settle down and be respectable and have a family and live in a nice little flat and—Oh, can't you see?'

Marjorie's eyes were hard.

'I see. So you want me to come and help you lay bricks?'

Rufus rose suddenly to his feet.

'You don't see,' he said slowly. 'You don't see at all. I was afraid you wouldn't.'

'Well, do you wonder?' rejoined Marjorie with a short laugh. 'Did you—'

'What you want,' went on Rufus, unheeding, 'is to settle down and marry a promising young business man with prospects. Live in Kensington. Have perhaps two children and go to Brittany for a fortnight in the summer…' He paused and regarded her thoughtfully. 'Has anyone ever slept with you?' he asked suddenly.

Marjorie rose to her feet. Her face was flushed.

'I think you'd better go,' she said dangerously.

'As I thought,' said Rufus. 'Well, look at yourself.' He caught her suddenly by the shoulders and swung her round so that she saw her reflection in a long slim mirror. 'Look at yourself! Twenty-three—looking like that—and no one's ever had you!'

'You beast!' With a wrench she tore herself free.

'Exactly!' said Rufus. 'A beast. With a body. That's what I am. And I want to know what it feels like to be a cold beast and a warm beast and a hungry beast and an amorous beast. But you don't. You just want to be a well-warmed, well-fed vegetable with a respectable husband and—'

Suddenly, without warning, he caught her in his arms and began to kiss her violently. Too violently for accuracy. The first three kisses before Marjorie had recovered from her surprise crushed her lips painfully. But the last, as she wrenched herself free, landed somewhere behind her left ear. Instinctively, defensively, she struck out at his face. Rufus staggered back, his eyes watering.

The blow had caught him full on the bridge of the nose. Blinking hard, he turned. Marjorie was standing with a hand on the bell.

'Now,' she was panting a little, 'will you go or shall I–'

Rufus reflected.

'I'll go,' he said at length.

'Right,' Marjorie drew his ring from her finger and tossed it to him, 'and don't come back. Ever.'

'I shouldn't think of it,' said Rufus with dignity, blinking away tears and placing the ring in his waistcoat pocket. 'Good-bye.' He bowed stiffly and walked towards the door. Marjorie turned her back without reply. As he blundered out he passed the little maid. The maid said 'Good evening, sir,' but Rufus did not reply.

'An' I *know* they was goin' out,' said the little maid later. 'Been 'avin' a row, I reckon. There was tears in 'is eyes.'

'Sort of lovers' tiff,' said the cook.

As he emerged into the street, Rufus suddenly began to laugh. It had just occurred to him that if he had refused to go Marjorie would have called the police and given him in charge. The idea of being arrested for kissing his own fiancée amused him.

'What *she* wants,' he muttered to himself vindictively, 'is six months on a desert island with a buck navvy.' It was his invariable prescription for coldness in the young female.

Greatly to his annoyance he found that the encounter had left him with a peculiar sense of weakness about the knees. His head was aching slightly and, despite his heavy overcoat, he was shivering. He realised suddenly that his underclothes were soaking with perspiration. 'Damn women!' said Rufus viciously.

Passing a narrow turning he noticed the illuminated sign of a small public-house. He glanced at his watch. They would be open now. 'A drink,' he said aloud. An elderly woman who was passing gazed at him curiously and disapprovingly. 'A drink,' repeated Rufus, unheeding, 'after the stress of the day.' And walking down the cutting he turned into the bar.

The bar of the Hen's Roost was unusually small, but in other respects it was very like the bar of any other English public-house—dull, drab, faintly beery, and furnished with almost studied discomfort. But to Rufus it was a warm haven of refuge after the cold clamminess of the outside world.

There were only three other people in the bar—a tall, lank individual in a bowler hat several sizes too small, a tubby little man with a red face and a jaunty cap, and a youth in a sports coat and flannel trousers. The tall man and the tubby man were engaged in vigorous argument, involving much tapping of one another on the chest and significant shaking of the head. The youth in the sports coat, leaning back in his chair with a patronising smile, was constantly winking and smirking at the barmaid, as though to emphasise his own amusement at, and detachment from, the antics of his companions. They glanced up as Rufus entered, but took no further notice of him.

The barmaid, who had been leaning on the bar, apparently umpiring in the controversy, reluctantly left her post and greeted Rufus with a professional and false-toothed smile.

'In 'undreds,' the tubby man was saying. 'Not jes' one or two. In 'undreds.'

'Not on yer life,' said the tall man in the bowler, with scornful scepticism. ''Cause why? 'Cause they ain't *got* 'em.'

The barmaid deftly measured out Rufus's double whisky and, pushing a half-empty siphon towards him, returned to the umpire's chair. Rufus splashed a little soda into his drink and sat down near the fire.

'Well, I reck'n they *'ave*,' said the tubby man. 'I reck'n if we only *knoo—*'

'The *Daily Post*'s correspondent says they've got secret

underground aerodromes,' said the youth in the sports coat, winking at the barmaid.

'Aw, the papers–' The lanky one spat disgustedly. 'I tell you what it is,' he leaned forward and poked a dirty finger into the tubby man's chest. 'If there's ever another war, an', mind you, I'm not sayin' there won't be—it'll be the papers what start it.'

'That's right,' said the barmaid, picking up a mug and giving it a desultory polish, 'so it will. Always lookin' for trouble so as to give theirselves somethin' to talk about.'

The tubby man finished his beer and set down his mug. 'Ah, well,' he said with a shake of the head. 'I'm not talkin' about what'll *cause* it. I'm talkin' about what'll *'appen.*' He caught the barmaid's eye and pointed silently at the mugs. 'London's defenceless,' he added with relish.

'So's Berlin,' said the tall man cunningly.

'Well, maybe it is or maybe it isn't. But 'ow's that goin' to 'elp you an' me?'

Rufus gulped down a mouthful of his whisky and closed his eyes. Possible careers. (1) The army. Join the army and see the world. There's room for you. Possible, but–

'Armies and navies,' said the tubby man, 'is finished. The nex' war will be in the air.'

Rufus sighed. That apparently disposed of the army. Or did it? Surely the safest place to be in the next war would be the army, which would do nothing? He finished his whisky and, depositing his glass on the counter, held up a finger.

'Same again, please.'

'I don't reckon so,' said the tall man firmly. 'I don't reckon they got aeroplanes good enough yet. Bit o' fog, and they're finished. Can't see to steer,' he added explanatorily to the barmaid.

''Ow about Scott and Black?'[28] said the man in the cap.

'They might navigate by wireless beam,'[29] said the youth encouragingly.

The tubby man took a pull at his beer. 'An' not bombs either,' he said inconsequently, 'not like it was before. Germs. In the reservoirs. P'ison the water.'

'Oh, be quiet,' said the barmaid with a shudder.

'Then we'll all 'ave to drink beer,' said the youth humorously.

The long man seemed much amused by this suggestion and laughed uproariously. The tubby man seemed to take his laughter as a personal affront.

'Ah, it's bloody funny, ain't it?' he said bitterly. 'But it won't be so funny to 'ave us all wiped out wi' p'ison-gas.'

Rufus finished his second whisky and meditated. A pleasant warmth enveloped him. Quite clearly there was always the business of war to be reckoned with——a silly affair in which one was completely uninterested, coming in and upsetting everything… He laid his glass on the bar and raised his finger. The barmaid's nails were blood-red and upon her engagement finger was a glittering diamond ring. He felt through the material of his waistcoat the hard outlines of Marjorie's engagement ring. Of course the end of the engagement would have to be announced. But who should do it? Himself or Marjorie? Presumably Marjorie. He raised his glass and drank a silent toast to his freedom.

'Oh freedom is a noble thing
Freedom makes men to have liking.'[30]

Criticised, one remembered, by Quiller Couch[31] because it merely repeated a platitude twice.

'The League of Nations,'[32] said the tall man.

'League of Nations, me foot,' said the tubby man. 'What you say, miss?'

'All afraid of one another,' said the barmaid.

But seriously, Rufus reflected, setting down his glass, seriously, this matter of war… One could emigrate, of course. Emigration is the sincerest form of flattery.[33] But where? The trouble about war was that it *caught* so nowadays.

The youth was going.

'Cheerio. Going to get some food.'

Rufus glanced at his watch. Half-past seven. He suddenly realised that he was hungry. He rose and walked to the bar. The warmth and three double whiskies were making things a bit difficult to focus. Rufus pointed to some ham sandwiches nestling under a glass cover.

'I'll have two of these, please, miss.'

The barmaid lifted a couple of sandwiches delicately on to a plate with a pair of little tongs.

'And another double?'

Rufus hesitated. 'Yes, please.'

He took the plate and his glass and returned to his table. The two other occupants of the bar, lacking the encouragement of the youth, had abandoned war and were sitting with their heads close together, talking in confidential undertones. Rufus thought of asking them to go on and tell him more about the decimation of London but, before he could do so, they rose, said 'Good night' to the barmaid and went. Rufus closed his eyes again and, munching a mouthful of sandwich, tried hard to concentrate his thoughts on the future. He still felt strongly the absence of a programme. Marjorie and advertising were lying forlornly together on the scrap heap, (No, not together. Nothing ever lay with Marjorie. He chuckled silently and appreciatively at his witticism…) were both on the scrap heap. But what was to take their place? Deserted by the debate on Wars of the Future, the barmaid had produced some knitting in a brilliant green wool, and was regarding Rufus with more interest.

'Nasty night,' she said conversationally.

'Foul,' agreed Rufus. In the rather hazy glow of his fourth whisky, he noted with appreciation the ample curve of the barmaid's bosom beneath her tight black satin dress.

'Knitting yourself a jumper?' he inquired archly.

'That's right,' said the barmaid.

'Ought to suit you, that colour.'

'Think so?' The barmaid held the long slab of knitting up under her chin and gazed down at it appreciatively.

Rufus nodded and lit a cigarette rather inaccurately.

'Green's a good colour for blondes.' Suddenly he fumbled in his waistcoat pocket and produced the glittering emerald ring. 'Go well with this.'

'Ooh!' said the barmaid. 'Can I look?' she added doubtfully, as he extended the ring towards her.

'Help yourself,' said Rufus vaguely.

The blonde barmaid took the ring and examined it reverently.

'This for the girl friend?' she inquired coyly.

Rufus gave vent to a Homeric laugh.

'It *was*,' he said with a shake of the head. 'But it isn't any good now.'

The barmaid made a rapid calculation in double whiskies and drew her own conclusions.

'What, all off?' she said in shocked tones.

'All off,' said Rufus solemnly.

'Thrown you over?'

'Certainly not,' replied Rufus with marked indignation. 'I threw *her* over.'

'Ah, well,' said the barmaid, returning the ring, 'I reckon she deserved it, didn't she? Didn't appreciate you, eh?'

'No,' said Rufus, 'she didn't. I'd been nice to her too,' he added almost tearfully.

'Of course you had,' said the barmaid consolingly. 'Anybody could see you would be.' She knitted a rapid line of purl and looked at Rufus with compassionate interest.

'I was always brought up to be nice to women,' said Rufus. 'I think I'll have another drink.'

The barmaid laid down her knitting and measured out the whisky.

'I'll tell you something,' said Rufus confidentially. 'I haven't told anyone else. I've thrown up my job too.'

'Is that really so?'

'Yes. Threw it up this morning[34] and walked out. Threw *her* up this evening and walked out.' He picked up his glass and shook his head reflectively. 'I've been walking out of places all day,' said Rufus plaintively.

The barmaid looked at him with considerable admiration.

'Had a big day, haven't you?'

'Big day,' said Rufus indistinctly. 'Big as that.' He made a fisherman's gesture.[35] The barmaid returned to her knitting.

'An' what are you goin' to do now, lovey?'

'Kiss you,' said Rufus hopefully.

'I don't reckon I'd do that, lovey,' said the barmaid calmly. ''Cause then I'd have to turn you out, see? An' it's cold.'

'So it is,' Rufus agreed. 'And anyhow I don't want to.'

''Course you don't,' said the barmaid, casting off. 'I s'pose you'll have to look for another job?'

'Damn jobs!' said Rufus. He leaned forward and regarded the barmaid with a glassy eye. 'Do you know what life is?'

''Pends what you mean,' said the barmaid cautiously.

'Life,' said Rufus firmly, 'is change.'

'That's true, lovey.'

'Look at the bank rate,' said Rufus with passion, 'dead. Just dead. Day after day, no change.' He finished his drink. 'I propose to seek life,' he said, pushing forward his glass. 'Let's have another.'

'I wouldn't have any more if I was you, lovey,' said the blonde.

'Why not?'

'You'll like it better if you don't have another now.'

'That's not logic,' said Rufus. He banged his hand loudly on the counter. 'More!' he said violently.

'Quiet now!' said the barmaid with gentle menace. 'How about a nice tonic?'

'Just whatever you say,' said Rufus with a catch in his voice. 'You're very lovely and you understand these things.'

''Course I understand,' said the barmaid.

'I put myself in your hands,' said Rufus, 'un—unreservedly.'

He sipped the bubbling bluish drink without enthusiasm.

'D'you live far away?' asked the barmaid suddenly. Rufus chuckled.

'I don't live anywhere,' he said gleefully. 'That's what's so bloody funny.'

'Oh, come, lovey—you must live somewhere?'

'No,' said Rufus with decision, 'a wanderer. The foxes have holes and the birds of the air have nests. But I go to see a noise that I have heard. Get me?'

'Sure, lovey,' said the barmaid rather absently.

Rufus rose from his seat.

'The world,' he said oratorically, 'has pressed upon me— caged me—ground me down. I discard it. See? Utterly. I give up all and go forth in search of the grail of Life. He either fears his fate too much or his deserts are small who dares not put it to the touch to win or lose it all.[36] Explain,' he added, 'with reference to the context.'

'Is that Shakespeare?' said the barmaid.

'*Nein, nein,*' replied Rufus, 'Montrose. That's me too. He was a great fellow Montrose.' He brandished his tonic water. 'God bless the king, the nation's great defender. God bless (no harm in blessing) the Pretender. But which Pretender is and which the king, God bless us all, that's quite another thing.'[37] He drank the toast with solemnity. Two men entered the bar. 'Enter murderers,' said Rufus, and sat down clumsily.

It was a grotesque description of one at least of the new-comers—a little man with a completely bald, egg-like head and a queer incongruous hook-nosed face like that of a merry cardinal. The little man beamed around with a delightfully comprehensive cheerfulness at the barmaid, the bar, the fire, Rufus, and his tall, scraggy-moustached companion.

'Two pints, please, miss,' he said, advancing to the bar. 'And thank Gawd fer a fire.'

'Nasty night,' said the barmaid, drawing the beer.

'Ah,' said the cardinal brightly, 'so it is. But there—makes you all the 'appier to be in out of.' He turned to his tall companion. 'Come on, Bert,' he said encouragingly, 'sit down and make yerself a bit comfortable.'

The tall man slowly seated himself. He made no reply, and seemed to be labouring under a burden of sorrow.

''Ere you are,' said the little man briskly, placing his mug before him. 'You get a drink o' that in you and you'll feel better.' He beamed at Rufus in a friendly way. 'Bert don't like the cold,' he said explanatorily.

Rufus nodded sympathetically.

''Tain't so much the cold,' said Bert suddenly, 'as the ruddy fog.'

'But there isn't much fog,' said Rufus.

Bert shook his head. 'There'll be plenty out on the road,' he said darkly, plunging his moustache into the mug.

'Well, never mind,' said the cardinal consolingly, 'we ain't on the road yet and we needn't be fer two hour. Give it time to clear.'

Bert set down his mug.

'*Clear!*' he said bitterly.

'Where is it this time, then, Charlie?' said the barmaid.

'St. Ives,' replied the cardinal.

'Long way for you.'

'I bin plenty longer,' said Charlie philosophically, setting down his beer and producing a short black pipe.

'Ah, I dare say you have.'

Under the influence of the numerous double whiskies, Rufus was no longer a really good listener. Clearly, he felt, the conversation needed the stimulant of a fresh point of view.

'Last time I went to St. Ives,'[38] he remarked, 'there were people with wives about all over the place.'

'Reely?' said Charlie, polite, but clearly rather puzzled.

'And truly,' said Rufus firmly.

Charlie shot an inquiring glance at the barmaid. The barmaid said nothing, but apparently Charlie gleaned what information he required. He turned back to Rufus with renewed interest.

'Wives, eh?' he said cordially.

'Seven,' said Rufus, 'each with a knap-cat and a sack—no, a knap–' He paused and laughed immoderately. 'That's a damned difficult thing to say,' he gurgled. '*You* try.'

'Knap sack and cat,' said Bert glumly.

'Exactly,' said Rufus. '*You're* going to St. Ives, aren't you?'

'Ah,' said Charlie.

Rufus shook his head. 'Well, of course the chap was coming away. That's the whole point. Only you don't see it. You think *he* was going to St. Ives. See? Have another?'

'I don't mind if I do, sir,' said Charlie.

'What are you going to St. Ives *for?*' asked Rufus as the barmaid refilled the mugs.

'Goin' wiv a load,' said Charlie briefly.

'What of?'

'Load o' stuff. Furniture.'

'In a plain van?' asked Rufus hopefully.

Charlie roared with laughter.

''Ear that, Bert? Gent wants to know if we've got a plain van?'

Bert was understood to say that the van, far from being plain, was bright red in colour.

'I envy you,' said Rufus fervently. 'Fancy driving to bloody St. Ives in a bloody van! *I'd* like to.'

'Awright, mister,' said Bert bitterly, 'you go instead of me. You're welcome.'

'Bert don't like the fog,' said Charlie apologetically.

'I envy you,' repeated Rufus. A great sense of the injustice of things was welling up in him. 'Why the hell shouldn't I drive a lorry to St. Ives with a load of stuff?' A tear rolled down his face. 'It isn't fair,' he said brokenly.

'Here, come, matey,' said Charlie in shocked surprise.

'Don't you take on, lovey,' said the barmaid. 'He's had a hard day,' she added to Charlie, 'lost his job and his girl both together.'

'Reely?' Charlie gazed at Rufus compassionately. 'Come on, chum,' he said, laying a hand on Rufus's shoulder, ''old up. There's always a silver linin' after all.'

'Ah, so there is,' said Bert unexpectedly, 'and ye're prob'ly best off wivout 'er,' he added comfortingly.

'Jes' what I been saying,' said the barmaid.

Rufus looked up with tear-filled eyes. 'You're all very nice to me,' he said chokily, 'you're the only people who've ever really been nice to me.'

'That's all right, chum,' said Charlie, winking at the barmaid.

'Pardon these tears,' said Rufus with dignity. 'I've been drinking. Fourteen double whiskies. Will you take me with you to St. Ives?'

'I wouldn't come to St. Ives if I was you,' said Charlie gently. 'If I was you, I'd go 'ome. Straight I would. Go 'ome and 'ave a rest.'

'I haven't got a home.'

'That's too bad,' said Charlie. 'Where is it? Ealing?'

'Regent's Park,' said Rufus vaguely.

'Regent's Park, eh?' Charlie thought rapidly. 'I reckon you'd best 'ave a taxi, chum. Got any money?'

'Ten pounds,' said Rufus. 'Got it yesterday. Do you want it?'

'No, no,' said Charlie soothingly. 'You just keep it and go and get a taxi—'Ere—I'll get it for you. Come on.'

He rose to his feet and, taking Rufus gently by the arm, raised him from his chair.

'That's right,' said the barmaid. 'You see to 'im, Charlie. 'E ain't fit, poor lamb.'

As they neared the door, Rufus paused.

'I'll tell you what,' he said, 'I'll give you a quid each to take me to St. Ives with you.'

'But you don't wanta go to St. Ives, chum,' reasoned Charlie. 'You–'

Rufus shook off the little man's restraining hand impatiently.

'But I *do*,' he said exasperatedly. 'I want to go to—to the country. And St. Ives'll do as well as anywhere.'

He placed a hand on a table to steady himself, and waved an emphatic hand in Charlie's face.

'Look here—you think I'm tight. Well, so I am. Damned tight. Tight as a lord. But I want to go to the country. Honest Injun. An' if you won't take me—I shall go by train to-morrow.'

Charlie hesitated, gazing at him in perplexity.

'Ah,' said Bert morosely, 'an' if we takes you you'll wake up to-morrow mornin' 'bout at Andover and give the pair of us in charge fer kidnappin'.' He picked up his mug. 'You go 'ome,' he concluded, draining the remainder of his beer.

'Two quid each,' said Rufus.

There was a moment's silence.

'More'n our job's worth,' said Charlie feebly.

'Five quid between you,' said Rufus.

Chapter IV

On Going to St. Ives

Rufus awoke the next morning by degrees. His first sensation was one of a peculiarly numbing coldness and stiffness, which suggested that he had been cold and stiff for a long time without noticing it. Reaching the state of opening his eyes, he was horrified to find himself staring into the glassy orbs of a large and very truculent-looking eagle. And finally, as full consciousness returned with a rush, he sat up to find the cardinalesque face of Charlie gazing at him with a rather nervous smile.

''Ullo, mate!' said Charlie rather doubtfully. 'Awake then?'

'Morning,' said Rufus. He rubbed a hand over his eyes, which felt curiously tight and inflated. 'Christ!' he added, 'that damned thing gave me a turn!' He looked with bleary indignation at the stuffed eagle.

'Wonder where you was?' asked Charlie.

'For a moment.' Rufus glanced round as if to make sure that his final conclusion as to 'where he was' was correct. The inside of the huge van was moderately full of furniture, looking as motley as only furniture in the process of removal can look. He had been lying on an improvised bed of rugs, curtains and blankets, and

Charlie, as bald, egg-like and cardinal-like as ever, was grinning down nervously from over the side of an upright piano.

''Ead awright?' asked Charlie. Rufus shook his head experimentally.

'Fairly,' he said, without conviction. He rose rather stiffly to his feet. 'Where are we?'

'Jes' outside Andover,' said Charlie. 'Stopped fera bite o' food. 'Course the fog 'eld us up a bit.'

Rufus glanced at his watch. It was nearly eight o'clock.

'Me an' Bert wondered if you'd like a cup o' coffee,' said Charlie.

Rufus became aware of a violent and foul-tasting dryness in his mouth.

'Good idea,' he said.

He nearly fell as they jumped down from the back of the van and the drop stung his numbed feet painfully.

'God, I'm stiff!' he said, stamping vigorously. The air was damp and piercingly cold, and he shivered as they walked across to the little wayside shanty. 'Good pull-in for Carmen,' said the rudely-chalked notice.

'Come on in by the stove,' said Charlie.

Bert was sitting beside an oil stove inside, talking to the proprietress of the good-draw-in—an immensely fat woman with pendulous dewlaps. The stove scented the hut unpleasantly, but it was gratefully warm.

'Mornin', sir,' said Bert rather doubtfully.

'Morning,' said Rufus.

''Nother two coffees,' said Charlie.

There was a moment's silence.

'Well, 'ere we are on the way,' said Bert.

Rufus nodded. 'Yes. Not bad going if you had fog.'

The reply seemed to relieve Bert. He glanced at Charlie and a certain stiffness went out of his manner. Rufus looked from one to the other as he paid for the coffee.

'What the hell's the matter with you two anyway?' he said with a smile.

Charlie's incongruous features broke into an impish grin.

'Well, y'see, t'tell the truth, we was wonderin' jes' how you'd feel wakin' up and findin' yerself out in the middle of nowhere, so to say.'

Rufus grinned.

'Y'see,' Charlie went on, 'night's one thing and mornin's another if you take my meanin'. An' several times we bin wonderin' whether we ought to 'ave took you at yer word like we did…'

'You took a hell of a lot of persuading,' said Rufus.

'We-el–' Charlie spread out his hands. 'After all, you *'ad* 'ad a drink or two, and you wantin' to come wivout any luggage nor nothin'…'

'Thought perhaps you'd turn funny, see, when you found you was 'ere,' said Bert, taking a large bite of a slice of bread and butter. Rufus sipped the hot, harsh coffee and smiled.

'You thought I was tighter than I was,' he said with a grin.

'Well, you'd 'ad one or two,' said Charlie. 'Still,' he added, 's'long as you're satisfied…'

Rufus put down his coffee and drew his chair nearer to the fragrant stove. 'You bet I am,' he said quietly. 'Where are we making for now?'

'Salisbury, Wincanton, Exeter,' said Charlie. ''Ave a bite o' this.'

'Thanks,' said Rufus. The bread and butter tasted very different from ordinary bread and butter.

Nine o'clock found them lumbering heavily along the road to Salisbury. Bert, a yellow stump of cigarette attached to his tongue, hung grimly and silently on the wheel of the huge lorry.

Charlie and Rufus sat beside him on the wide front seat. Rufus felt extremely happy. He had resolved to send a telegram from Salisbury explaining to the resident owner of the flat that he had been called away on urgent business, that he might be away for some time, and that he would send for anything he required. The rent was paid for a quarter and he felt that this was the easiest way to overcome the difficulties arising from his rather hurried departure. And now the steady rumble of the van and the slowly uncoiling road before them seemed every moment to be putting unmeasurable leagues between himself and the past. Creamo, Ritson's, Marjorie, London—the passing landscape bore them steadily away. The need for a programme disappeared in the complete relaxation and satisfaction of the present. The past was already out of sight and the future was the next bend in the road. He leaned back, lit a cigarette and, giving himself up to the new and magnificent thrill of complete improvidence, listened to Charlie's steady flow of reminiscences. Starting from the focal point of the stuffed eagle, Charlie was discoursing on queer cargoes.

'Ah,' the little man was saying, 'I've often said, if one of us chaps could write a book, we could write a good 'un. What you say, Bert?'

Bert grunted assent.

'All 'cept nobody wouldn't believe it,' Charlie went on. 'Not only furnitoor, mind you, but general 'aulin'. I reckon there aren't many things I 'aven't 'ad a 'and in 'aulin' one time and another. Rec'lect the tiger, Bert?'

'*Tiger?*' said Rufus incredulously.

'Ah, tiger. Gawd, that was a set-out, that was,' he shook his head reminiscently. ''Twasn't a full-grown one, o' course. Leastways, they *said* it wasn't. 'Alf-grown like—ah—thank 'ee.' He took Rufus's proffered pouch and began to stuff tobacco into the little black pipe with a gnarled forefinger. 'It were back—ah, must 'ave bin fifteen year ago, eh, Bert? We was movin' an old gent by the name of Gadby. 'E'd 'ad a big place down in Devon, and 'e was givin' it up an' comin' to live in London.' He struck a match and applied it to the pipe. 'Well, it seems,' he went on between puffs, 'that the ole cove 'ad bin out in foreign parts, and fer some reason or another 'e'd brought this tiger back wiv 'im—it being just a cub then, see? Well, 'course, when 'e come to move up to London 'e found 'e weren't goin' to 'ave room fer a thing like a tiger, not in London. Mind you, it was a sizeable thing this tiger was. Growed up, see, since 'e'd 'ad it. 'Bout the size of a big dog, weren't it, Bert?'

'Ah,' said Bert, ''bout like a big mastiff dawg.'

'That's right,' said Charlie. 'Well, this ole cove were very attached to this tiger, see, but 'e knoo 'e couldn't keep it. So 'e says 'e'll give it to the Zoo. Sort o' presentation like, if they'd give it a good 'ome.' He paused and shook his head with a smile. 'Well, o' course, me and Bert goes down there, thinkin' it was an ordinary move like, and when we'd got the stuff on board this old bloke comes out and says, "'E're" 'e says, "I want you to take a tiger for me and drop it in at the Zoo."

'"Tiger?" says Bert.

'"Ah," 'e says, "they knows you're bringing it."

'"Then they bloody well knows wrong," says Bert. "We ain't a ruddy circus. Send it by post," 'e says. "Tigers ain't my work."

'Well then the ole bloke 'e pulls out 'is note-case and starts sayin' as 'ow 'e particularly wants this 'ere tiger 'andled gentle, and 'e'd got 'im all done up ready and so on, and the long and short of it was we 'oists this tiger up in the back in a ruddy great crate and off we starts. "'Ave it in the back," the old bloke says, "so's they kin get it out easy the other end."'

Charlie paused and pulled vigorously at the short pipe. Over the saturnine face of Bert a far-away smile was flickering, but his eyes never left the road.

'So off we starts,' continued Charlie, 'jes' as we might be now. Well, the old van we 'ad then 'ad two big doors at the back much the same as this un. We was jes' comin' along a bit o' road out by Basin'stoke—lonely place it is too—when we goes over a bit o' loose road metal, see? Well, a bit after that I suddenly 'ears a 'ell of a banging, and I looked back and there was the doors swingin' wide open and the ruddy crate and the tiger and all was gone.' He grinned impishly at Bert. 'So we stops and I looks at Bert and 'e looks at me.

'"Where's the tiger?" I says.

'"Fell out," says Bert, "that's what."

'"Well, then, we'd better go back," I says.

'"Not much," says Bert, "if the crate's fell out it's busted itself."

'"But that tiger's a valyable animal," I says.

'"Maybe," says Bert, "then let someone pick it up and get a nice reward."

'Well, we stands there fer a bit arguin' and then we thinks per'aps the crate ain't broken, and we walks back round the corner, pretty careful, as you kin imagine. An' jes' as we gets round the corner we sees the crate lyin' all but t'pieces, an' the tiger lyin' beside it, fer all the world like a big cat, wiv' 'is tail wrapped round 'im like cats do. Well, we looks at the tiger and the tiger looks at us, and then we starts to go back to the lorry quiet like. An' all of a sudden the tiger gets up and stretches 'isself and yawns and starts t'walk after us. So we walks backwards and I says to Bert, "Don't run," I says, "or we're finished." An' so we goes on walkin' backwards as fast as we can, and the tiger walkin' after us jes' about three yards be'ind. "Puss, puss," says Bert, friendly like. But the tiger jes' went on follerin'. So at last we gets back to the van an' stops an' the tiger stops too. "Shall we 'ave a dash for it?" Bert says to me out of the corner of 'is mouth. "No," I says, "otherwise 'e'll spring. So I thought I'd try somethin', so I pats the floor o' the old van and says, "Up!" I says, "good boy! Up!" An' if you believe me that tiger jes' looks at me an' gives a bit of a lep an' up 'e goes an' sits 'isself down inside like a retriever dawg.' Charlie paused and shook his head thoughtfully. 'So, o' course, you kin bet we slams the door shut pretty quick and jumps up and drives like 'ell. And we never stop agin, not till we get to the Zoo. An' when we got *there*'—he chuckled—'we tells 'em we got a tiger inside from Mr Gadby. "O ah," they says, "we knoo it were comin'." "Well, it's come," I says, "p'raps you wouldn't mind takin' it out while we 'as a drink?" And we legged it.'

'How did they get it out?' asked Rufus.

'Jes' opened the doors and it walked out,' said Charlie. 'Good as gold that tiger were. But o' course, see, Bert and me wasn't to know. They was a bit surprised and asked where its crate were when we come back. "Crate?" I says, "what you want a crate for with a tiger like that? That tiger," I says, "is as tame as you or me." An' we come away.'

A faint sound came from Rufus's right. Bert, his eyes still fixed on the road before him, was giving vent to that rare sound, his abdominal chuckle.

They lost their way in Salisbury. It was not easy to find a post office and, when a post office had been found and Rufus's telegram dispatched, their sense of direction had disappeared. Charlie, supported by signposts and a rather vague yokel, was all in favour of turning to the left. But Bert, without deigning to argue, swung the big lorry to the right as they left the city and set them switch-backing merrily over the rolling downs.

'Too far north,' said Charlie decisively. 'You go on this way and you'll 'it Bath, not Exeter.'

'Ah,' said Bert non-committally.

'Further round, Bert,' said Charlie.

'Better road,' replied the taciturn pilot.

'Ah, well, so it is,' said Charlie reasonably. 'Nice drivin' road,' he added to Rufus.

Rufus nodded. A nice driving road that swept up and down amid the great bare sweeps of Salisbury Plain… He drew a deep breath. To the left the brow of a hill mounted sharply only a hundred yards away. But to the right there was nothing. Nothing but bare green downland and far-away sky. The sun had come out and was shining brilliantly in a sky full of heavy, fleecy white clouds which cast quick-moving changing shadows over the close-cropped, rabbity turf.

'Might be spring,' said Charlie appreciatively. 'We ain't far from Stone'enge now. Ever bin there?'

Rufus shook his head.

'Nothin' much to see,' said Charlie. 'The stones is *big*, mind you, but I don't see much in it meself. Not seein' 'ow it's cracked up.'

'It's gorgeous country this,' said Rufus almost to himself.

'Think so?' Charlie sounded rather doubtful. 'I like a bit more t'see meself.' He put an arm out of the window and tapped his pipe out against the lorry door. 'I was at Bulford Camp[39] in '14. That ain't far from 'ere either.' He shook his head. ''Cod, that were a spot. *Cold?* Winds fit ter take the 'ide off yer.'

Rufus gazed out at the rolling downland and sighed. One could hardly ask the stolid Bert to stop the lorry and wait whilst one ran and shouted across that sunny grass…

'There's an 'are,' said Charlie suddenly.

It was about seven miles from Salisbury that the journey came to a sudden end. For some time the interior of the lorry had been getting hotter and hotter, until the metal-plated footboards were almost painful. Steam was pouring from the radiator-cap, and Bert's violent, rasping gear change had become necessary on the slightest of slopes. Charlie, apparently quite used to this gradual phenomenon, had paused once in his recital of the horrors of Bulford to remark that 'the ole cab was over-'eatin' again', and Bert had once shaken his head ominously when a very slight hill had demanded the lorry's three mile an hour bottom gear. But neither made any move to put matters right, and when at last the lorry's engine note dropped lower and lower on a slight upward gradient, and finally chugged to a shuddering halt, Bert climbed from his seat, took a fresh Woodbine from a battered paper packet, and sat down on the running-board without a word.

'What's up?' demanded Rufus.

''Ave to wait,' said Bert briefly.

Charlie jumped down from his seat. 'She over-'eats,' he explained. 'Over-'eats something crool. Allus does it if you gets a few bits of 'ills.' He took the short pipe from his pocket and gazed meditatively down the road.

'Isn't there anything you can do?' asked Rufus, surprised at this attitude of calm acceptance.

'Ooh, she'll be all right,' said Charlie reassuringly. 'Give 'er a minute or two to cool down, see, and she'll get 'er breff like.' He glanced quickly up and down the road and disappeared behind a near-by bush. Rufus sat down beside Bert.

'How do you manage down in Devon?' he inquired. 'I should think she over-heats pretty badly there, doesn't she?'

'Ah,' said Bert briefly.

They sat for a moment in silence. Then Rufus rose to his feet and, jumping the narrow ditch at the side of the road, walked out on to the smooth springy turf. A fair wind was blowing from the West. He turned his face to it and, opening his mouth widely, took in great gulps of the clear, sharp air. Charlie re-emerged from behind his bush.

''Bout ten minutes and she'll be awright,' he called.

Rufus nodded and, turning, gazed at the vast expanse before him. A smooth green road, clearly marked against the more sombre green of the downs, curved away from where he stood, and vanished behind a clump of trees half a mile away. What was it, and where did it go? Rufus hesitated and glanced back at the lorry. Bert had risen and had thrown up the bonnet, presumably to aid in the cooling process. Charlie was dabbing a hand tentatively against the hot radiator. Rufus made up his mind quite suddenly not to go to St. Ives, but to see where the green track went. He went back to the lorry.

'Look here, Charlie,' he said, 'I don't think I shall come any further. I rather like this place.'

Charlie looked up in surprise.

'You goin' to stay *'ere?*'

'No. But I shall walk on over the downs.'

Charlie pursed his lips.

'Long way from anywhere,' he said doubtfully.

'How far?' asked Rufus.

'Matter o' seven mile either way,' said Bert.

'Well, that's all right,' said Rufus with a smile. 'Seven miles isn't so very far.' He felt in his breast pocket and produced his note-case. 'Let's see, what did we say the fare was to be after all? Five quid between you?'

Charlie drew back hastily as though something had stung him. 'But you don't 'ave to pay us nothing,' he said. ''Twasn't 'cause o' that we wouldn't bring you. Was it, Bert?'

''Course not,' said Bert solemnly.

'It was only 'cause we didn't think you *reely* wanted to come, see?' said Charlie. 'We bin glad to 'ave you. Ain't we, Bert?'

'Ah,' said Bert.

'Rot!' said Rufus. 'We agreed on the fare before we started.' He opened the case and took out five one-pound notes.

'An' anyway,' protested Charlie, still retreating, 'you ain't come 'alf the way, chum. Not more'n 'undred mile all told.'

It took him some time to get them to accept a pound each.

The lorry's engine had 'got its breff' by now, and Rufus, standing by the roadside, watched the huge vehicle move slowly up the slope and disappear over the brow. A handkerchief fluttered from the window, and he waved his hand in return. And then the lorry and Charlie and Bert were a tiny shape rolling rapidly down the grey ribbon of road and out of his ken, and he turned and strode off to see what happened to the green road behind the clump of trees.

Nothing did. As he rounded the beech-clump, he saw it still, curving away for fully a mile, and vanishing over the brow of a hill. He laughed as he saw that. It had deceived him—by that ruse of the trees—deceived him and led him to follow it, in the hope that it did something exciting. And now it was playing the same trick again, and pretending that, over there on the crest of the hill, it would reveal its secret. 'Go on,' he said aloud. 'I'll buy it. Where *do* you go?' He walked on rapidly. Sometimes he broke into a run, and ran until he had to pause and gasp for breath in the tumbling wind. He was nearing the brow rapidly now. Rufus smiled happily. 'Over that brow,' he said to himself, 'is precisely nothing, except the road running across the down. But about two miles further on it disappears over another hill in a most exciting way…' He broke suddenly into a run, and bounded up the last hundred yards of the slope to the brow. He stood there gazing eagerly before him, hat in hand, with the wind fluttering his black hair. Looking, he threw back his head and roared with laughter.

'I knew it!' he cried, 'you devil!'

Chapter V

Country Matters

There may have been inhabited places within seven miles of the spot where Rufus left the lorry, but the green road did not lead to them. It was ten o'clock when he set out and in the buoyant air he walked briskly. But for all that his watch showed nearly one when he came down the steep chalk road and tramped into the main, and indeed only, street of Leaford St. Michael.

Rufus had left the green road half an hour before with mixed feelings. Untired by his walk, he was still intoxicated by the sheer grandeur of space and silence through which he had passed. He had walked for nearly three hours and had seen no human thing. There had been two or three distant outlying farms, and twice there had been men and horses moving, pygmy-like and slow, over vast expanses of brown earth. He had heard a dull far-away booming and had seen the weather-worn notices warning the passer-by from artillery ranges. There had been a distant patch of white, moving sheep, with one tiny figure which was the shepherd, and a frisking, busy, brown fleck which was his dog. But none of these things was human. They were lay-pieces—mere scenery, which emphasised and intensified the silence and loneliness of the serene rolling countryside.

But he turned aside from it all at last and took the narrow chalk road to the village. For the sun had disappeared, and the immense stretch of sky above him was a uniform, dull, threatening grey. And he was hungry with a curiously intense hunger which was quite unlike the rare hunger one felt in London.

He was delighted with Leaford. He was in the mood to be delighted with anything. The searcher after rural beauty would have complained of the absence of picturesque thatched cottages, at the long straggling street of rather dull houses, at the very mixed-period manor-house, and at the large hoarding with its glaring posters which some enterprising firm had installed midway down the village street. But in his present mood these things pleased Rufus. In his heart of hearts he would probably have liked to find the perfect village, with half-timbered houses, and village worthies in white smocks. But in their absence he merely decided that Leaford was delightfully unselfconscious about its picturesqueness. It was enough for the moment that one could walk up the middle of the village street, and even feel mild indignation when the occasional motor car forced one to use the pavement.

Rufus had lunch at the Angel Inn. He thought at first of demanding cooked food, but the sight of the soapy yellow cheese and the white bread in the bar was too much for him, and he sat down in the musty little room and ate ambrosial[40] bread and cheese and drank nectar in the shape of rather flat, strange-tasting, heavy beer.

The landlord, a tall, bald, well-spoken man, leaned on the counter and talked to him as he ate. The landlord was interested to hear that Rufus had come from London. He himself was a Londoner.

'Have you been here long?' inquired Rufus, rather disappointed.

'About two years,' said the landlord. 'Too long for my better half,' he added with a rueful smile.

'Doesn't she like it?'

The landlord shook his head.

'Too quiet,' he said.

'I should have thought that was a good thing,' said Rufus. 'That's partly why I've come away from London—because of the row.'

The landlord smiled.

'Ah, yes, sir, it's all right for a *bit*. But it gets very dull when you've got to live here. Particularly for a woman, see, sir.' He glanced at Rufus inquiringly. 'I suppose you'll have come down by car?'

Rufus hesitated. 'Well,' he said at last, 'I came to—to just beyond Salisbury by—by car. Then I walked.'

'Walked?' said the landlord in surprise. 'From Salisbury?'

'No. From a few miles this side of it.'

'That's a tidy step.'

'It was a grand walk,' said Rufus thoughtfully. He drank the last of his beer and lit a cigarette. 'By the way,' he added, 'have you any rooms here?'

'Rooms?' said the landlord inquiringly.

'Where I can stay? Can you put me up?'

The landlord rubbed his nose. 'Yes, sir. We've got a room you could have. He hesitated. 'Would it be just for the night?'

'I don't really know,' said Rufus. 'Probably.'

'Yes, that'll be all right, sir.' The landlord peered vaguely round the bar. 'Have you got any—any luggage?'

'Not a thing,' said Rufus. 'In fact, I shall have to go out and buy some pyjamas and a toothbrush. Is there anywhere here I can get them?'

The landlord rubbed his nose again thoughtfully. 'You can get the toothbrush,' he said, 'but I don't know about the pyjamas. There's a place just up the road—Sim's—where they *might* have 'em. But–'

They sold toothbrushes and pyjamas at Mr. Sim's. In fact, there seemed to be nothing they did *not* sell. Rufus selected a red toothbrush and a homely suit of pink-and-white striped union-flannel[41] pyjamas and, having deposited this gear at the Angel, wandered out again into the village street. Leaford lay, apparently, on the very edge of Salisbury Plain. North, south, and east, the Plain surrounded the village like the rim of an enormous cup and, away in the distance, Rufus could see the white, ribbon-like chalk road by which he had descended. The sky was still leaden and it was much colder, but the wind of the morning had died away. The village stopped abruptly some three hundred yards beyond the Angel Inn, and Rufus, after a moment's hesitation, turned down a lane to the left and made again for the hills. He liked Leaford. He liked it very much. But it inspired a curious loneliness which vanished as soon as he left the houses behind him. Rufus, plodding happily away down the narrow, high-hedged lane, decided that loneliness must be a function of human beings and that the completely solitary man could no more be lonely than he could be self-centred.

Pondering this pleasing, if not startlingly original paradox, he left the lane and walked on up the sweeping hillside. The ground to left and right was arable, and the narrow grassy track up which he walked was one of several which intersected and divided the sloping brown plough. The path was steep, and his quick breath smoked in the cold air. How long would it be, he reflected, before the last traces of smoke and dust were blown from his lungs, and he could climb steeper paths than these with steady heart and unlabouring breath?

They were ploughing at the top of the hill. Abruptly the slope flattened out, the pathway ran into a wide track and, in the big field before him, were two ploughing teams. He stood and watched, fascinated. From some remote distance of time and space he remembered that when land was heavy they used three horses. Where light, two. This was light land, then.

The headland[42] was just in front of him. The two big black horses were walking in step. He could see the taut muscles of the forearm as the ploughman drove his furrow—hear the faint sound as the brown soil slid backwards over the shining mould-board.[43] They reached the headland, and horses, plough and tensing man swung in a wide half-circle, scratching on the ground one more semi-circular mark.

'Harry Ploughman,' he said aloud.

'He leans to it. Harry bends, look. Back, elbow and liquid waist
In him, all quail to the wallowing o' the plough...'[44]

He stopped with a frown. Partly because he could not remember any more. Partly because he suddenly found himself disagreeing violently with Father Hopkins's attitude. The ploughman was a small man with a foolish, vacant face. To talk about his 'liquid waist' was nonsense. But it didn't matter. The man was nothing. He was no more human than the more distant figures on the landscape of the morning had been human. He, the horses, the plough, the land they tilled—they were all one and therein lay their strength. Elsewhere a little man with a foolish face was a rather deplorable human unit. Here, on this great brown stretch, he was part of something—superhuman?—sub-human? No matter. He was part of it, in it, and of it, like a block of stone in the towering wall of a cathedral...

A wild, unreasoning envy swept over Rufus as he watched. A sudden intense hatred of standing outside on the green pathway, a spectator. Why could one not step on to the yielding brown space, and lose this intolerable itch—this awful consciousness of self—in the calm unity of it all? To stop thinking, save of the straightness of the furrow. To stop feeling, save the strained tenseness of the

muscles. To stop seeing, save the distant mark of the headland...
Saul Kane had concluded the Everlasting Mercy[45] by jumping
the ditch and taking over the plough from the (apparently) willing
farmer. One could hardly do that, clearly. But was there any hope
that either of these inhuman ploughdrivers would accept half a
crown and let one?...

His train of thought was interrupted by the arrival of a man
on a horse—a big man in old breeches and a seedy brown cap,
who came cantering gently along the green track from the left. He
drew rein some twenty yards away and, swinging himself to the
ground, threw the reins carelessly on his horse's neck and struck
out towards the ploughman. The horse turned quietly away and
cropped, with a faint jangle of bit, at the grassy track.

Rufus noted the tall, rather ungainly figure in breeches with
interest. He had paused to talk to one of the ploughmen. Clearly
the farmer, thought Rufus. Or perhaps a bailiff. He lit a cigarette
and, leaning against a fencing-post, watched the distant figures. A
half-formed resolution was burning in him as he saw master and
man talking and gesticulating together. The conversation was soon
over. The tall man stood for a few moments watching the steady,
plodding teams. Then, turning abruptly, he walked briskly back
towards his horse. Rufus saw his face. It was a good face. Quite
young—younger than his slightly stooping figure—tanned and
blue-eyed. Rufus made up his mind. He threw away his cigarette
and stepped forward.

'Good afternoon,' he said, as the tall man approached.

The farmer looked at him curiously.

'Good afternoon, sir,' he replied with the pleasant Wiltshire
burr.

Rufus hesitated. The 'sir' had rather disconcerted him. He
did not recognise it as the farmer's typical courtesy to the stranger.
The tall man clicked his tongue gently. The horse, still cropping
busily, came slowly towards them. Rufus took the plunge.

'Is this your land?' he asked suddenly.

The farmer looked up quickly, his hand on the loose hanging rein.

'It is,' he said questioningly.

Rufus took a deep breath.

'Well, do you want a man?'

The farmer frowned. 'A man?' he said in perplexity. 'What sort of a man?'

'A—a workman.' Rufus threw out his hand towards the ploughing teams. 'To work on the land. Because I want a job.'

There was a moment's silence. Then the farmer's perplexed frown gave place to a broad and charming grin.

'What—you want a job o' *that* sort?' His twinkling eyes were taking in the details of Rufus's well-cut overcoat.

'Yes—why not?'

'Bit out of your usual line, wouldn't it be?' said the tall man with a smile.

Rufus nodded.

'Yes. That's why I want it. I don't suppose I should be much good,' he added hastily, 'I mean, I can't plough or anything. But there must be something I could do.'

The tall man was gazing at him with a quizzical smile.

'Want to try working on the land as a sort of holiday? Bit of a change like?'

'That's it,' said Rufus, smiling. 'I usually work in London and I want a change—want to get out in the air.'

The farmer nodded slowly.

'I reckon I should want to if I was in your place,' he said thoughtfully.

'Well—will you take me on?' asked Rufus, more confident in the face of this understanding. 'I don't care what you pay me.'

The tall man's bright-blue eyes were on the distant ploughing teams. He slowly shook his head.

'I'd have liked to oblige you,' he said gently, 'an' I would have if I could. But there's nothing I could use you for, see. I'm layin' men off already.' He threw out a hand vaguely. 'I've got eight men working for me, sir. I could do with six. I keep the other two on just because I don't want to throw them on the parish.'[46] He shook his head slowly. 'There aren't many in farming that are taking men on nowadays.'

Rufus looked at him for a moment, and suddenly the plight of agriculture was no longer a leader in a London paper, but was something in this man's voice, and in the faint greying of the hair round his temples.

'I'm sorry,' he said quickly, 'I never thought of that. Of course, you can't afford fools of amateurs nowadays.'

The tall man shook his head again.

''Tisn't that I won't,' he said, 'it's that I *can't*.'

He hesitated for a moment and then, turning away, swung quickly into the saddle. 'Mind you,' he added, 'there's some who *are* making money. Maybe one of them—'

Rufus looked up sharply.

'Is there anyone about here?'

The man on the horse smiled a little crookedly.

'There's Mr. Christianson up at Top Land. I reckon he does all right.'

'*How* does he?' asked Rufus inconsequently.

The farmer swung his horse's head towards the village.

'Mr. Christianson takes what his land'll give him,' he said slowly. 'But he doesn't give anything back.'

'And you think he might take me?'

'Maybe.' The farmer shrugged his shoulders. 'I know he's had young gents there before.' He shook the reins. 'Good day, sir.'

Rufus watched him out of sight. He was disappointed, but the disappointment had no edge. 'There aren't many in farming that are taking on men now—' He turned and took the path towards the village. Somehow he felt like a man who has driven a small motor car, hooting egotistically, through the mourning of a stately sad procession.

At nine o'clock that evening, Rufus left the Angel Inn and set out for the village school. As he descended from the hill he had seen a hand-printed notice announcing a Select Dance, and had resolved, if the bar of the Angel did not prove very entertaining, to have a shilling's worth of selectiveness. The bar had proved a disappointment. He had sat for an hour and a half over a pint of the flat, heavy beer, but the half-dozen customers had been uniformly uninteresting. Two passing motorists had stopped for a drink, and had talked volubly about racing. A silent, respectable man had come in, consumed a pint of stout and departed without a word, and three 'regulars' had arrived at opening time and were still there when he left, playing desultory bagatelle. But there had been nothing save the queer, broad accent to distinguish them from the *habitués* of any inn from London to Liverpool.

Had he but known it, Rufus had happened on a time when the flatness of the beer had made the Angel Inn unfashionable, and he would have found a much more truly representative company down the road at the Bell. Not knowing it he left the Angel with some relief, more than ever convinced that the life and inhabitants of Leaford did not come up to the promise and appearance of its surroundings.

The Select Dance had been billed to start at 8 p.m. and Rufus, arriving just after nine, had every reason to suppose that it would be in full swing. In point of fact, however, having paid his shilling and passed into the big shabby room, he found not more than twenty people present. The caretaker, mounted on steps in the middle of the floor, was attending to one of the big oil lamps which hung from the roof, and the band, sitting grouped in a corner, round the piano, showed no sign of action.

Somewhat puzzled, Rufus sat down on one of the long forms which ran round the walls and, lighting a cigarette, looked around him with interest. The long, rectangular floor space had clearly been obtained by removing a partition which normally divided it into two schoolrooms. On the peeling, distempered walls were a number of water-colour and pastel drawings, presumably the work of pupils. A blackboard which leaned against the wall behind the band still bore in a neat, precise hand, the statement 'The oak and the Beech lose their leaves in the Autumn—*Deciduous*'. He glanced down at the floor. It was worn and rather knotty wood blocks. As he looked, the caretaker, having dealt with the lamp, was walking round scattering white powder on the surface out of a large packet.

A single, repeated tuning note from the piano turned his attention to the band.[47] He had been surprised to see from the notice that a band would be present, and it was even more surprising to find that it consisted of five men, who, with one exception, wore dinner jackets. Rufus frowned slightly. Surely, at a shilling dance in an obscure village, one had the right to expect a simple piano, plus perhaps, one local worthy with a violin? But here were five men, complete with drums, saxophone, trumpet and fiddle, for all the world as one would have expected to find them in a London night club.

The preliminary tuning noises ceased. The pianist stamped loudly three times, and the band burst into full blast. Rufus was surprised to experience a feeling of positive relief at the fact that they were not very good. Somehow, perfect time rhythm, and intonation, would have made the evening hopeless from the outset. But the drummer and the pianist seemed to have found no common ground about the time, and the saxophonist in mufti hooted like a soul in faultily-intoned agony. Rufus, forgiving them their distressingly sophisticated appearance, could turn his attention more happily to the dancers.

Despite the lateness of the start, there was no rush to take the floor. The band had rioted on for several minutes before a tall, solemn man in a brown suit, and a rather plump middle-aged woman, rose and began to circle the room with expressions of gloomy concentration. It was only after nearly ten minutes of *fortissimo* perseverance, that the band, having persuaded six couples on to their feet, stopped with a loud clash of cymbals, and rapidly turned over its music, while the twelve dancers gently and decorously clapped for more.

Rufus rose and walked over to the man at the door.

'Not many here,' he said reproachfully.

'It's always like this,' said the man. 'They'll come in after ten, see?'

Rufus nodded gloomily. The band had begun again, and so had the decorous walking. He looked at the formal circling figures, and suddenly realised that he had seen them all before, in slightly different clothes and a different setting, but with the same expression on their faces, at Pancho's Club in Villiers Street,[48] just a month before.

The man at the door was quite right. By half-past ten the original twenty had swollen to nearly a hundred, and the schoolroom, if not full, was no longer disconcertingly empty. Rufus, fox-trotting mechanically with a plump, fair-haired, pretty little girl in a pale green velvet frock, was trying to decide whether to go back to the Angel and bed, or to persevere with this rather dull amusement. He had a curious resentful feeling of having been cheated. First there had been the surprising band. Too good to be funny or interesting and not good enough to be pleasurable. Then the people. He had hoped that they in turn might be amusing or interesting, or at least, different. But after an hour and a half's solid dancing with as wide a variety of partners as he could select, he was left unsatisfied. True, they were shy with him and rather silent. Equally true, few of them could dance, and most of them wore queer home-made-looking clothes. But Rufus realised with something approaching bitterness that no characteristics he had encountered so far differentiated them from the young women one would expect to meet in the most ordinary of lower middle-class dance-halls. What he had expected to find he did not know. But the fact remained that to find a shilling dance in Leaford village schoolroom so exactly like a shilling dance elsewhere, was a peculiar and rather inexplicable disappointment. He had ridden away from the boredom of ordinariness in a furniture van and had walked away into the unknown. And here was ordinariness slightly more drab, slightly cheaper and less intelligent, waiting for him at the end of the journey. So might the intrepid explorer of the African interior have felt if the cannibal chief had worn a dickey[49] and given him a cheap cigar after dinner.

The dance ended, and Rufus, finding a chair, deposited the plump, fair, pretty little girl and excused himself. The green velvet frock, he reflected bitterly, was not even home-made. It had almost certainly cost twenty shillings and she had bought it by post from a shop in Kensington. (In point of fact the plump girl was the daughter of Mr. Sims, who sold toothbrushes and pyjamas, and the frock had cost twenty-five shillings at a shop in Salisbury. But this would have comforted Rufus very little.)

He sat down in his original corner and lit a cigarette, resolving to sit out the next dance and then go home. A few moments later the roar of conversation was interrupted by a series of crashing discords from the piano. The leader of the band was calling for silence by the simple method of jabbing the flat of his hand hard on the keys. The roar died into an expectant silence. The leader of the band looked round with the confident smile of one who realises that he is a 'popular favourite'.

'Ladies and gentlemen—the next dance will be a fox-trot. *Ladies' Choice!*'

There was a roar of approval mixed with a few modest feminine squeaks. The leader of the band grinned round archly and, picking up his fiddle, led his band into a quick fox-trot. Rufus looked on with amusement. Whatever else there was against them, the young females of Leaford were not coy. The floor, if anything, filled up more quickly than usual. Rufus wondered for a moment if the plump little girl would ask him to dance, but she was already whirling round in the arms of a short youth with heavily watered hair.

Rufus flicked the ash from his cigarette and gazed round the room. There were few wall-flowers. The only notable ones were two girls who had arrived only a few minutes before. They sat together on the opposite side of the room, looking on at the dancers with an air of tolerant contempt. Rufus, who had been dancing as they entered, looked at them with interest. Both were tall and dark, with the same rather discontented mouth and small chin. But like many sisters they seemed to be examples of a similar art in a good and bad period. One, whom he judged to be the elder, had a peculiar coarsening and hardening of the facial lines which made the effect rather horsy and unpleasant. The other was almost beautiful.

She looked quite young—twenty-three or -four, he guessed, and the dead black of her hair contrasted sharply with a creamy-white skin. It was only when she turned to speak that the lines of her face seamed and altered and the same peculiar horsiness appeared. Rufus, watching, shook his head. 'She shouldn't open her mouth,' he murmured, 'then she'd be rather charming.'

He found himself wondering who they were. Clearly, they were a cut above most of the company. Both were well dressed— almost too well for the circumstances, Rufus felt, and their make-up was careful and sophisticated. He decided that they must be visitors. Those were certainly not village frocks. Nor village shoes. Nor, for that matter, village faces.

At the end of the dance, Rufus decided that he would give it another quarter of an hour and then go.

The band played waltzes better than fox-trots, chiefly because the erratic drummer abandoned his drums for them and became a mercifully inaudible cellist.

'Do you live here?' inquired Rufus, swinging the dark girl in a wide half-circle.

'Yes, worse luck,' she said, almost viciously. She threw back her head and gazed up at him with the challenging dark eyes. 'You come from London, don't you?'

'How do you know?'

The dark girl smiled.

'I guessed you did.' She looked round the room disparagingly. 'You're lucky.'

Rufus smiled.

'*I* don't think so. I'd rather live here.'

'Here?' She gazed at him with a frown. 'What for? It's as dead as… as–'

'I'd like to live somewhere quiet.'

She gave a contemptuous little grunt. 'There's nothing to do.' She smiled reminiscently. 'I love London.'

'Know it well?' asked Rufus curiously.

'I go there quite a lot,' said the dark girl rather doubtfully.

'I live near Regent's Park,' said Rufus.

The dark girl nodded.

The saxophonist wailed out the treacly melody.

'Isn't this band ghastly?' said the girl. 'Rita and I only came to see what it was like. I think it's awful.'

'Is Rita your sister?' asked Rufus, gently piloting her past a bad traffic block.

'Yes. She's married. But her husband doesn't dance.'

'Pity.'

The dark girl shook her head. 'I could *never* marry a man who didn't dance.'

'It's awfully lucky you were here,' said Rita. 'Ruby didn't want to come because there wouldn't be anyone to dance with. Poor kid, she doesn't have much of a time here. There isn't anyone for her, you see.'

'I suppose not,' said Rufus.

'Of course, it's different for an old married woman like me,' said Rita.

The clock stood at ten minutes to one.

'Well, there's no need for you to come, Rube,' said Rita. 'But I must go. Jack's coming part of the way to meet me.' She rose. 'Good-bye, Mr. Wade. It's been awfully nice to meet you.'

Rufus turned to Ruby as Rita disappeared.

'Will she be all right going home by herself like that? It's pretty dark.'

'She doesn't mind,' said Ruby. 'We often don't–' She paused…

'Shall we dance again?' said Rufus.

Half an hour later, Rufus found himself the playground of a peculiar and not unpleasant mixture of sensations. Physically, he was dead tired. A fifteen-mile walk[50] in cold blustering air, a further walk in the afternoon, and several hours' dancing on an indifferent floor, were making his legs heavy and painful. But whereas two hours ago he had felt sleepy, he was now possessed by an almost unnatural wakefulness—an exhilaration like the first effects of alcohol. He talked and laughed loudly and cheerfully, and once, in the midst of a fox-trot, insisted on experimenting with a new and intricate step which nearly deposited him on top of Ruby on the floor.

The chief effect, however, was a rapidly increasing physical perception of the dark girl. He no longer looked at Ruby with an interested appraising and speculative eye. As he mechanically circled the room, the slender form clasped in his arms, he felt only the warmth and softness of her body against him, the gentle touch of her thigh against his own, and the faint quiver of response as he tightened his encircling arm. The prattle of his own voice and her occasional replies was going on in some distant outer darkness. The true conversation, perfectly understood by both, was carried on in silence.

'I'm *glad* Rita went home,' he heard himself saying in the peculiarly emphatic voice of the drunken man. 'I *like* Rita. I like her very much. But I'm *glad* she went home.'

The soft warmth was pressing a fraction closer.

'Why?' asked Ruby, smiling at him with the dark challenging eyes.

'Because,' said Rufus firmly, 'when I take people home, I like to take them one at a time.'

'Is going home with you as exciting as all that?'

Rufus bent his head until his lips were close to one small white ear.

'Wait and see!' he murmured secretively.

The church clock was striking two as they turned off the main street and struck out across the field pathway which Ruby had indicated as 'the quickest way home'.

'Gosh, it's dark!' said Rufus. 'You'll have to lead me. I can't see a thing.'

'It's all right,' said Ruby, reassuringly. 'We just keep to the path.'

They walked on slowly in silence.

'Not very cold, is it?' said Rufus, thoughtfully.

Ruby hesitated.

'No, not very,' she said at last.

'Not *too* cold?' said Rufus, smiling to himself in the darkness.

'I don't know what you mean,' said Ruby primly.

'Liar!' said Rufus, bending and implanting a kiss at random on the white face glimmering in the darkness. The hand that clasped his arm tightened sharply.

The pathway led past a spinney. Blacker still in the blackness, the gaunt winter trees loomed up beside them as they walked.

'Christ!' said Rufus softly. 'What a gorgeous place!'

'There's supposed to be a ghost here,' said Ruby.

'I should think so. I've never seen a more desirable freehold residence for a ghost in my life.' He slipped his encircling arm upwards till his hand rested on the firm pneumatic roundness of her breast. 'Do you come home past here by yourself?'

'No, I *don't*,' said Ruby decidedly. 'I go by the road.'

'I don't blame you.'

'It isn't that I care about the ghost,' said Ruby, 'but it's too lonely.'

'Afraid someone might jump out at you?'

'Well, you don't know about here—'

There was only about twenty yards of the spinney. Rufus paused.

'If anyone *did*,' he said thoughtfully, 'he'd probably do *this*.'

He seized her firmly in his arms and kissed her vigorously.

'Darling!' he said foolishly.

Ruby clung to him tightly.

'My love!'

'God, I want to make love to you,' said Rufus rather hoarsely five minutes later.

'Well, do then,' replied Ruby with almost flattering readiness.

'But won't you catch your death, love?'

'Well, I shan't strip myself naked, silly.' She took him by the hand. 'Come on. It's nice in the spinney. Lots of dead leaves.'

They lay down on the crackling ground.

'What damn silly things suspenders are,' said Rufus, busily.

Chapter VI

Winter Sports

It was ten o'clock before Rufus awoke the next day, and even then only repeated hammerings on his bedroom door roused him from heavy sleep to stiff-limbed, heavy-headed consciousness. Nevertheless, by eleven-thirty he had eaten his breakfast and paid his modest bill and was walking rapidly down the village street. He walked, despite his stiffness, with furious energy. Ostensibly he was heading for Top Lands Farm, to interview Mr. Christianson. But in his mind Top Lands and Mr. Christianson were secondary considerations beside his desire to put behind him Leaford and all its works. No disgusting morning head—no foul furred tongue— which had ever followed a riotous night could compare with the dirty mental taste of his adventure with Ruby. Rufus had never been a Saint Anthony. The extreme propriety of his relations with Marjorie had been a unique exception in a life of occasional and rather pointless sexual experience with willing young women. So far the incident with Ruby had been nothing to cause this violent revulsion of feeling. But now, in the absence of that heady physical exhilaration, he saw in it a deep and damnable significance. He had come seeking a physical life. He had found a place

91

where the sheer power and glory of physical existence seemed overwhelmingly beautiful and magnificent. And then, when it caught him and overwhelmed him and seemed about to make him part of itself, he had proved cheap and nasty. The Plain had done its best for him. It had awakened in him a glow of physical power and relaxation such as he had never known before. He had made the absurd, the childish mistake which showed him in his true colours. At the time it had seemed so completely necessary that he should have Ruby—in the night, in the cold, in the intense blackness, on a bed of dying leaves. But the awakened animal had proved to be only a conventional young business man, who had chosen as his wild mate a dissatisfied little amateur prostitute who painted her lips and wished she lived in London, and the mating which was to be a realisation of a new physical life had been a bungling affair of suspenders and contraceptives. Cheap and nasty, he reflected bitterly. One had fled from Marjorie and all her works. And one had chosen, as the symbol of one's freedom, the nearest thing to Marjorie that Leaford could provide.

'God damn it!' he said aloud. 'What's the matter with me? I get fed up because things here aren't different enough and then I go hard after a bad imitation of a Jermyn Street whore.[51] Why the hell didn't I go for one of the village girls, shiny nose and all?'

'The true explanation,' he reflected, as he left the village behind him and plodded on up the gradually steepening hill, 'must be that I've got this all wrong. The place is all right, but the people aren't. It wasn't because their noses were shiny that I couldn't do with those females. It was because they were cabbages—dead—boring. They live in this place but they might as well live in Ealing for all it's done to them. And if I'd got to have one of them, and it was going to be an ordinary show, anyhow, that girl was most like the genuine Ealing article. The only snag is that I didn't realise that. I was trying to pretend it *was* new…'

He looked round at the great rim of the Plain, towering now

close above him. The sky was the same leaden monotonous grey, and it was bitterly cold. He remembered with ironic amusement that Ruby had been the possessor of unexpectedly sophisticated underclothes. He smiled ruefully at the barren wind-swept slopes.

'Sorry,' he said in sincere apology, 'I seem to have got things in a hell of a mess. But it takes time, you see.'

Top Lands Farm was in a position which a house agent would probably have described as 'secluded but not isolated'. The farmhouse stood only a couple of hundred yards from the road, some mile and a half out of the village. A tractor was humming busily in an enormous field close to the road, and in the distance Rufus could see two men with horses engaged in some hauling operation. Otherwise the big stretches of land were empty. The farmhouse itself, a small and not very romantic building of lichened brick, stood in the midst of a heterogeneous collection of barns and stables, together with three or four small cottages. A large half collie half sheepdog ran out barking furiously as Rufus picked his way through the mud to the farmhouse door. But there was silence and a curious air of desolation about the empty farmyard.

A fat, rather pleasant-faced woman answered the door to Rufus's knock. Rufus removed his hat politely.

'Is Mr. Christianson in?' he inquired.

The woman looked at him with some curiosity.

'I'm afraid he isn't. Is it anything I can do? I'm Mrs. Christianson.'

Rufus hesitated. 'I'm afraid not,' he said. 'I rather wanted to see him himself.'

'I see. Well I'm expecting him back any minute now. He's down in the field with the tractor. I expect you saw him as you came by.'

'Oh–' Rufus's eyebrows rose slightly. 'That was Mr. Christianson, was it?'

'Yes.' The fat woman nodded. 'Why don't you walk down that way? I expect you'll meet him coming up.'

Rufus bowed. 'Thank you. I think that's what I'll do.'

He replaced his hat and picked his way carefully back past the still-barking mongrel. It was rather surprising to find that the figure on the tractor had been Mr. Christianson himself. Rufus had never visualised a farmer as *doing* anything. Half-way down the road from the farm he duly met Mr. Christianson. The farmer was a middle-aged Dane with sandy hair, watery light-blue eyes and an explosive manner. He returned Rufus's greeting cordially enough and listened politely while Rufus plunged into the matter of employment.

'I met a man yesterday who told me you sometimes took people like me on here, Mr. Christianson.'

'Yas. I do,' said the Dane, eyeing him with interest. 'I show them how to farm like we do in Denmark. Yas.'

Rufus nodded. 'Well, I wondered whether you'd take me on?'

Mr. Christianson hesitated and looked him up and down.

''ow long for?' he said at last.

'I don't know quite. Perhaps indefinitely.'

'You 'ad any experience, yas?' inquired the Dane.

'None at all.'

To his surprise the farmer nodded with great satisfaction.

'That good. You start right, yas?' He held up a hand. 'I 'ave three four young gents come 'ere. None of them knew *nothing*. They all got good jobs.'

'Really?'

'Mind you,' Mr. Christianson shook his head, 'you 'ave to work like 'ell. That's why I do all right, see? I work.' He jerked a thumb contemptuously over his shoulder. 'They—those others— they don' work, see?'

'I was surprised to see you driving the tractor,' said Rufus.

Mr. Christianson smiled.

'I only got three men—four men,' he said. 'You come I get rid of one, yas.'

Rufus frowned.

'But you can't sack a man to take me on,' he protested.

'Yas,' said Mr. Christianson with an emphatic nod, 'you betcherbloodylife. Yas.'

'But why?'

'Better business,' said Mr. Christianson calmly.

'You mean I shouldn't cost so much?'

The Dane shook his head.

'Yas. I pay you ten shillin'—fifteen shillin'. They make me pay 'im thirty-two shillin'.'

'You'd only pay me fifteen?' said Rufus, rather taken aback.

'Maybe,' said Mr. Christianson.

'It isn't much, I mean, even if–'

'Ah, but you learn a lot, yas? You get a job anywhere if you bin with me. My young gents they get the good jobs, yas.'

'But could I—could I *live* on fifteen shillings—even down here?'

Mr. Christianson frowned.

'Live?' he said in surprise, 'you live at the farm'ouse. Mrs. Christianson, she look after the young gents fine.'

'Oh, I see,' said Rufus. 'What an odd arrangement.'

Mr. Christianson laid a hand on Rufus's breast.

'No, no,' he said. 'Listen. You come 'ere and I train you, see? You 'ave to work like 'ell, but we treat you good. You live with us and Mrs. Christianson she look after you. Then in a year—two year—you go an' get a good job.' He paused and looked at Rufus thoughtfully. 'I like you,' he said at length.

'It's very good of you to say so,' replied Rufus.

Mr. Christianson nodded emphatically.

'Yas. I like you. I only charge you three 'undred pound. Usually four 'undred pound.'

Rufus looked at him with a puzzled frown.

'I don't understand.'

'I only charge you three 'undred pound premium instead of four 'undred pound,' repeated Mr. Christianson patiently. 'Because I like you. Yas?'

'*Premium?*'

'Yas. For your keep and teachin' you, see? Cheap,' added Mr. Christianson. 'All my young gents they get good jobs, yas.'

Rufus hesitated.

'I'm afraid you've misunderstood me. I don't want to be a—a premium pupil.'

The cordiality died out of Mr. Christianson's face.

'Then what you want?' he inquired shortly.

'I want a job. On the farm. As a labourer. Ploughing and so on. I shouldn't think of paying a premium.'

For a moment Mr. Christianson gazed at him in astonishment. Then his face slowly reddened and the storm broke.

'An' you stop me, an' you talk to me, an' you waste my time, an' you keep me from my dinner, an' you think I 'ave the time, yas, to waste on bloodyfooltalk yas, what you think I am, eh, I don' want–'

Rufus looked at him with interest.

'We have been at cross-purposes,' he said. 'Good day.'

Somehow Mr. Christianson was the last straw. As Rufus walked quickly down the farm track, he was conscious of one desire and of one desire only—to get away from the people, the men and women who were proving so uniformly disastrous and disappointing, and to recapture the tremendous serenity of his first long walk over the downs. It was only yesterday morning that he had waved good-bye to Charlie and Bert and stepped into the new life. Yet already the memory of it was fading—was being thrust out by the squalid ordinariness of the last twenty hours. And soon, unless he took some steps to renew it, that first ecstasy would fade out like a momentary fire and be lost for ever.

He paused as he reached the road. A white signpost stood at the junction. A finger pointing to the farm said Top Lands Farm. Another pointed back down the road to Leaford. The third, pointing in the opposite direction, said Salisbury fifteen miles. Rufus shook his head. He did not wish to go to Salisbury. Still less did he wish to go to Leaford. He made up his mind quickly and, crossing the road, took an unsignposted rutty track that led away through the ploughed fields. The signpost ignored the track. Therefore there was a hope that, like his green road, it led nowhere at all, save into the great bare space of the Plain where he could be alone.

For about a mile he followed the track with cultivated land on either side. Then it joined another and he saw in a depression, a few hundred yards away, the typical group of scattered buildings and the tall windbreak of trees of an outlying farmhouse. And beyond the farmhouse the ploughed fields ended, and there was nothing but the great stretches of grey-green grass which he sought.

He turned down towards the farmhouse with a sigh of relief. He no longer considered the possibility of finding a sporting farmer who was willing to employ a novice farmhand. He simply wanted to be out on the lonely sweep of the downs beyond that farm. There were a few rusty old implements in one of the open barns, but the farmhouse was empty. He wandered idly into the farmyard, and peered in through the broken, boarded windows. The rooms were small and dust and fallen plaster were thick on the floor. The barns were in fair condition, but they too were empty, and in one, as he looked in, a huge rat scuttled quickly along the side of a manger and vanished.

He looked at the barns with a speculative eye. One might well go for a walk on the downs and then return to sleep in one of them, rats or no rats. He pushed open the broken wooden gate of the farmyard and set off up the track into the downs. In ten minutes he had passed the brow and the farmhouse had sunk into the depression and out of sight.

Half an hour's walk brought him to a strange and fascinating place. The track no longer ran along the surface of the downs, but was a sunken cutting between two gentle hillsides. Rufus decided that it could not be a natural road. Roman, or perhaps an old coaching track. It led him gently downwards and finished in a curious grassy arena, from which no less than four tracks radiated. A clump of trees marked the junction, and beside them a small pond. The place was a long way from any farm, but people came there, for there was an iron lid in the ground that looked like the site of a water hydrant. Rufus sat down on the ground and lit a cigarette. The scraping of his match sounded oddly loud in the silence. He looked around him and sighed thankfully. It was all right. The silence and the calm and the solitude were there. One had only to walk for an hour to reach them.

Rufus was awakened from his reverie by something soft and cold alighting on his cheek. He started and gazed round. A few slow white flakes were drifting languidly in the air. He glanced up at the yellowish leaden sky.

'Snow!' he said delightedly. 'And it looks full of it.'

He scrambled to his feet. The wind had dropped almost completely.

'God!' he said aloud, 'what will this place be like under snow?' Another flake landed on his coat. He watched the delicate exquisitely-fashioned thing shrivel and melt and vanish.

'Ensculptured, embossed
With his banner of wind
And his graver of frost...'[52]

He stood hesitating for a moment and then, turning his back on the way he had come, set off once more on the centre track of the other three.

Some time later he glanced at his watch and paused. It was half-past two, and he was extremely hungry. The snow was falling thickly now. The front of his overcoat was white, and already a thin crisp layer covered the shorter grass of the track, for the ground was dry and cold, and it was lying almost at once. Rufus considered. His impulse to leave civilisation behind him had caused him to set out with no definite programme. Clearly there was no point in going back to Leaford, for, apart from the hatred which he now felt for the place, it must by this time be six or seven miles away. Quite probably he was close to somewhere. But on the other hand the nearest place other than Leaford might be ten miles away. After a moment's thought he decided to go on. After all, the track must eventually go somewhere, and in the meantime one must just go hungry. He turned and plunged on into the white curtain. The wind had risen again a trifle, and he could see no more than a dozen yards through the thickly whirling flakes. He plunged his hands into his pockets and retired within a glorious inner warmth, from which he looked out at the snow as from the window of a cosy room.

It was half-past three precisely when Rufus decided to turn back. For some time now the visibility had been only a few yards, and the snow under foot was already so thick that he could no longer be sure whether he was on the ill-defined track. Moreover, the snow was caking on the heels of his shoes in thick icy lumps, making walking difficult and uncomfortable.

For an uneasy moment, as he stopped and gazed around him at the whirling whiteness, he wished he had returned half an hour before. But the sight of his own footmarks showing clearly behind him was reassuring. They would lead him back to the junction of the tracks and then, presumably, there would be nothing else to do but go ignominiously back to Leaford and spend another night at the Angel. He started to plod back rather resentfully.

Half an hour later his footmarks were no longer visible in the gathering darkness.

At 4.15 p.m. Rufus paused rather wearily and reflected that this was really too damned silly. He had walked for an hour and a half[53] and still around him there was nothing but, dimly seen through the thickly whirling flakes, a white expanse. He kicked once more at the uncomfortable icy clods which clung to his heels, and tried a little mental ridicule at the expense of the uncomfortable feeling in the pit of his stomach. True, it was still snowing hard. Undeniably it was rapidly growing dark, and equally undeniably he had no idea where he was. But one could not, he reflected, one *could* not be lost in a snowstorm on Salisbury Plain. In the Alps—in Canada—the situation would have been conceivable and definitely worrying. But to be caught by a snowstorm and to face the prospect of a night of wandering on Salisbury Plain, when one could not possibly be more than a few miles from civilisation, was altogether too like being drowned in six inches of water. He brushed the crisp powdered snow from the front of his overcoat and laughed.

'A traveller by the faithful hound
Half buried in the snow was found…'[54]

And instead of 'Excelsior' you said 'Bottom Upwards' and that was funny…

He set off again more rapidly. He had paused just below the brow of a slight rise and, as he topped it, he saw the clump of trees he had left two hours before, lying a quarter of a mile below.

'Thank God!' he said aloud. 'This was rapidly ceasing to be funny.' Now that it was all right one had to admit that it had been frightening.

The trees before had been beeches and these were beeches. But there was no pond and there was no sign of the deep cutting. He would not believe it was not the same for a while, and plodded on for a couple of miles, looking for the farm. But it was not there and after a while he stopped. It was dark now and his legs were very tired. There was no sound save the rapid thumping of his own heart and the quick sound of the breath in his nostrils.

'If I keep on walking in a straight line,' he said, 'I must hit something soon.'

It was very hot in the ballroom—a queer glowing, centrally-heated feeling. Marjorie was talking rapidly, but he could not catch what she was saying. For some reason it was quite out of the question to tell her so. He was laughing and nodding as though he quite understood. Suddenly he saw a girl. She was standing in the middle of the floor. She was dark and very beautiful, and he realised that he had asked her for this dance. He rose and bowed to Marjorie, saying very solemnly, 'Excuse me, but I have a lateness at the office.' Marjorie did not reply but went on talking.

He was dancing with the dark girl, and he realised with a thrill that she was naked. He put his hand on her naked breast and she laughed—a rather unpleasant laugh which scared him. He remembered that someone had told him she was mad.

They were quite alone on the floor and people were standing round the walls throwing streamers. The streamers were curving towards them like live things, and he knew they must avoid them at all costs. Once he only just pulled his partner aside as one glided past their feet. 'Look out!' he said warningly. 'If they touch us life won't be worth living.'

The floor was thick with the uncoiled streamers now. He could hardly move for them. The dark girl was laughing; everyone was laughing. Everything was one great shout of laughter about his ears. Desperately he strove to kick them aside, but they coiled and coiled about his ankles. He gave one last desperate plunge, lost his balance, and found himself falling—falling—

The shock roused him. He had plunged into a shallow drift and the snow was cold against his face. He staggered bemusedly to his feet and peered into the thick, gently stinging blackness.

'I mustn't do that,' he said reprovingly, 'or I shall go to sleep. You always want to go to sleep. It's the one thing to avoid.'

He kicked once more at his heels, but the shoes were curiously heavy—too heavy to be lifted in comfort. And besides it was too much trouble. He began to plod slowly forward. Something to do. Something physical to keep one awake…

'In dulci jubilo
Now sing we all Io…'[55]

But singing took a lot of energy and he soon fell silent, listening with foolish interest to the quick gasping of his own breath.

Humour was undoubtedly to be the thing this year. A series of drawings by Fougasse or any first-class artist… He walked to the window and looked out. The Strand did not look like the Strand, but it was. People were decorating the streets and cheering. He saw a man throw up a hat and noticed that he still had a hat on. He remarked on this to Charlie. He thought it was funny. But Charlie shook his head and said it was a secret and he couldn't explain. Rufus was very hurt by this.

Ted Lewis was addressing a golf ball. He looked very smart in plus-fours.[56] New plus-fours. He swung at the ball, but then, instead of watching the flight, continued to swing to and fro like a pendulum, saying, 'Tick tock! Tick tock!' Rufus was annoyed and pointed out that there were only twenty-seven hours in a day. His mother stroked the tiger, which was very small—barely the size of a cat. He knew it was vicious, but he could not tell her. He knew she would not understand. But it was very warm and comfortable and everything was soft.

Chapter VII

Three Trees

Rufus found the faint chipping noise extremely irritating. Several times it stopped, but always before he could quite escape it began again. For a long while it did not occur to him to do anything about it, but at last he realised with a start that it was a chipping noise and that he was listening to it. He opened his eyes and was immediately very awake indeed. The chipping noise was being made by a man who was sitting a few yards away.

'Hello,' said Rufus, sitting up, 'how did you—'

The man looked round sharply and then smiled.

'Awake, then? How do you feel?'

Rufus swung his legs off the long settee on which he had been lying and noted simultaneously that the said legs were stiff, that he wore pyjamas and a dressing-gown, that he had been lying warmly in a comfortable improvised bed of cushions and blankets, and that the man had blue eyes.

'Quite all right, thanks,' he said. 'Legs are a bit stiff, that's all.'

'Good,' said the big man with blue eyes, laying down a chisel and rising. 'You've had a long nap. Find it a bit difficult to get your bearings?'

'I am a bit in the dark,' Rufus confessed. 'What's the time, and which day?'

The big man with blue eyes and the mop of yellow hair shook his head. 'Afraid I don't carry a watch. But I think it's now just after ten o'clock and I expect you'd call it to-morrow. Anyhow, it was last night we found you.'

'You found me? I didn't get here by myself?'

The big man grinned a white-toothed grin.

'You were fast asleep just about thirty yards from the door. Luckily for you, on the track. I fell over you, as a matter of fact.'

Rufus reflected.

'It seems to me that I've been pretty lucky,' he said thoughtfully. 'Would it have finished me off if you—'

The other shrugged his shoulders.

'I really don't know. Probably. Actually, you can only just have stopped when we found you. You were quite warm. Don't you remember half waking up when we undressed you?'

Rufus wrinkled his brow.

'I don't know,' he said helplessly, 'now you mention it, I do remember something, but—'

'As a matter of fact you were quite tired out, and would go to sleep. That was all that was the matter. So we dumped you there and let you. We thought of taking you upstairs, but you're no light weight and they're very narrow.'

The yellow-haired man produced a cigarette-case and proffered a cigarette. Rufus took one and, lighting it, inhaled thankfully.

'God!' he said, 'you seem to have been the Good Samaritan all right…' A sudden thought struck him. 'By the way—where *is* this anyhow?'

'Well, this is actually Three Trees Farm, but I don't suppose that conveys much. We're right in the middle of nowhere. The nearest place is Leaford. That's about two miles away down the track.'

'Leaford? Two miles?' Rufus sat bolt upright. 'You mean to tell me that after all that I'm only two miles from that wretched hole? Why, I walked at least twenty miles.'

The big man looked at him curiously.

'How long had you been out on the Plain then?' he asked.

'Since about one.'

'One?' The other looked at him in astonishment. 'But, my dear man, when did you eat last?'

Rufus smiled.

'Breakfast yesterday.'

'Good Lord, I'd no idea! Half a minute–'

The big man rose and went quickly into the kitchen. When he returned he carried a loaf, butter and cheese.

'Here, have a hunk of this to carry you on. Ruth will be back soon and we'll feed you properly.'

He cut a large crust of bread and cheese and sat watching in silence whilst Rufus dutifully ate. Curiously enough, he did not feel hungry and it was with difficulty that he finished the slice.

'More?' inquired his host.

Rufus shook his head.

'No, thanks. I shall be quite all right now. By the way,' he added, 'what time did you find me?'

'About nine.'

Rufus shook his head helplessly.

'I must have walked round in circles,' he said.

The big man nodded.

'People always do on the Plain.'

'This has been done before?' said Rufus with interest.

'Oh, Lord, yes. The Plain can be very awkward when it snows. And even worse when it's foggy. I've lived here for years and I can't find my way about it in a fog. You see there aren't any near landmarks.'

Rufus grinned.

'Well, that's comforting anyhow. My last recollection is of feeling an abject fool at losing myself in an ordinary bit of English country.'

A sudden thought struck him, and he reddened slightly.

'By the way,' he said quickly, 'I'm being extremely rude and ungrateful. I haven't even said thank you yet, for—for—'

The big man smiled quietly

'My dear chap, there's nothing to be grateful about. We were terribly bucked at finding you. Purely selfishly. It isn't every night that we pick exhausted travellers out of the snow. Ruth was thrilled to the marrow.' He caught Rufus's questioning glance and grinned. 'Perhaps we'd better do a sort of "Dr. Livingstone, I presume?" thing. It'll get things straighter for you.' He leaned back in his chair and flicked the ash from his cigarette. 'My name's Mendel. Philip Mendel. Ruth is just Ruth and she lives here with me. She's gone down to the village at the moment, but she'll be back presently. This, as I say, is Three Trees Farm, so called because there are at least twenty large trees round it. It isn't a farm any longer, though there are still lots of very nice and entirely useless barns.'

Rufus glanced round the room. It was a large and low-ceilinged room, with big black naked beams and a large open fireplace.

'It's a gorgeous place,' he said enviously.

'We like it,' said Mendel indifferently. 'But go on—that's all about us. Now you tell me how you came to be wandering about Salisbury Plain—particularly in the very unsuitable clothes you were wearing?'

Rufus glanced at him and noticed for the first time that he was wearing an extremely disreputable old pair of flannel trousers and a tie from which the stuffing was escaping. Mendel laughed and ran a hand through the mop of yellow hair. 'You needn't tell me if you're an escaped convict or a fugitive from justice or anything,' he said.

Rufus shook his head with a smile.

'No,' he said slowly, 'I'm afraid I'm nothing as exciting as that. I suppose I am a fugitive in a way, but not from justice.'

Mendel nodded slightly without reply.

'My name's Rufus Wade, and I'm—or rather I was—in advertising. For—for various reasons I got fed up with the job and London and so on, and came down here.' Rufus frowned slightly. 'It's rather difficult to explain.'

The curious light-blue Norseman eyes were looking at him with interest.

'Well, it's quite unnecessary,' said Mendel quietly. 'I only asked in case you were trying to get somewhere, or wanted anybody to be told you're here.'

Rufus shook his head.

'No. I wasn't going anywhere. And the last thing I want is to tell anybody where I am.'

Mendel nodded slightly. 'Fine. Then that's that.' He rose to his feet, bringing the thick mane of yellow hair within a foot of the ceiling. 'How d'you feel now? Any ill effects?'

'None at all. Except that my legs are stiff.' Rufus rose also. 'I should think I'd better get dressed.'

Mendel glanced at him thoughtfully.

'There's no need, you know, unless you want to. Why not just stay by the fire?'

'But I'm quite all right,' Rufus protested. 'And really I'd rather.'

Mendel hesitated.

'All right. I'll get your clothes. I think they're dry.'

He threw his cigarette into the fire and went out. Rufus pulled the dressing-gown about him, strolled over to the window, and stopped with a sudden sharp little intake of the breath. It was still snowing a little, and the sky had not cleared. But the flakes now were few and lazy. Before his eyes there stretched a great mass of dazzling whiteness. In the foreground a big thatched barn stood snow-capped like a giant cake. And beyond it a sheer hillside, dazzlingly carpeted, rushed up like a rampart into the leaden sky. Running away to the left he could see some traces of a track, and on it a single trail of new clear footmarks. But though the swell and hollow of the downs could still be seen, all was levelled and indefinable beneath the huge white carpet. Only an occasional tree and bush stood out in gaunt and silent contrast.

Rufus turned as Mendel re-entered with a pile of clothes thrown over his arm.

'God! This is a magnificent place!'

Mendel glanced casually out of the window.

'Yes. It always looks rather magnificent under snow.' He looked thoughtfully at the sky. 'I should think we had about six inches last night. But it's always difficult to tell up here. It drifts so. There's more about too, from the look of it.'

He turned away and laid the clothes on a chair.

'Look here, I think everything's dry, but your things are in a bit of a mess, so I've brought you some old things of mine for the moment. Hardly classical, but they'll cover you. What size do you take in feet?'

'Nines,' said Rufus.

'Well, these may be a bit big for you, but I think they're probably wearable.' He put down a pair of thick brown brogues, a vest, a shirt, an old pair of flannel trousers and a tweed jacket. 'I should dress down here by the fire, if I were you.' He turned with a questioning smile. 'You don't mind dressing with me here?'

'Good Lord, no!' Rufus threw off the dressing-gown and pyjama coat and picked up the vest. 'God, I envy you this place!' he said with a sigh.

'Here's Ruth,' said Mendel an hour later. Rufus walked over to the window. Far away a small black figure was moving over the white expanse towards the house. Mendel threw open the window and sent a gigantic roar echoing across the icy stillness. They saw the small figure raise its head, and the distant flutter of a hand in reply.

'I should think she'll have had a nice walk,' said Mendel with a grin. 'There'll be some pretty good drifts between here and the village.'

'Where has she been?' asked Rufus.

'To Leaford. Getting food. We always stock up if it snows, because if we don't it always drifts and cuts us off. We lived for two days on an ancient loaf and a tin of beef once,' he added, 'before we got to know its little ways.'

'She seems to be carrying rather a lot,' said Rufus, peering into the dazzling distance. 'Hadn't we better go out and help?'

Mendel smiled.

'I doubt if she would thank you,' he said. 'Ruth rather dislikes being looked after.'

Twenty minutes later Ruth arrived, manfully ploughing through the deep crisp snow and lugging an enormous basket. At first glance Rufus thought she was very beautiful. A close-fitting black woollen cap and the big black coat buttoned up to her chin set off the bright pink glow of her cheeks and the whiteness of her teeth as she grinned cheerfully at the two faces at the window. But when, after a moment's parley outside, Mendel brought her into the big low room, he saw that beautiful was the wrong word. She had pulled off the cap, leaving bare the sleek dark head with its boyishly short hair, and Rufus saw that she was very dark— so dark that he could hardly believe her English. The coat was thrown open, and he saw beneath it a bright scarlet jersey and a short grey skirt. Her features were not classical. The nose was short and upturned, and the mouth large and full-lipped. But the most startling thing about her was her eyes, which were that very rare thing, a brown so dark as to be almost black. The warm glow was still in her cheeks, but Rufus could see that the snow alone was the cause. Normally he judged, her face would be almost dead white. Not beautiful, he thought. Too odd and startling for that. But God! how effective…

Mendel's hand was on her shoulder as they entered.

'Behold the corpse,' he said, throwing out a hand towards Rufus. 'His name is Rufus Wade, and he was going from Leaford to nowhere in particular, and lost his way.'

Rufus shook hands with her. The small hand was very cold.

'Do you feel all right?' she said. 'Pip, he oughtn't to have got up and dressed.'

'But I'm quite all right, really,' said Rufus. 'Only a bit stiff. I haven't even got a cold.'

She looked at him thoughtfully with the bright dark eyes.

'Well, you *look* all right,' she said at last, with a smile. '*I* was afraid you'd have pneumonia or something, but Pip said you wouldn't.'

'I wouldn't have guaranteed it if you'd been out another half-hour,' said Mendel. He produced his cigarette-case and handed her a cigarette. 'Well, have you bought a lot of food?'

'I have bought enough food,' she said between puffs, 'to last an army corps between three weeks and a month. It cost one pound four and eightpence, which you now owe me, and it nearly broke my arms carrying it up here. So if we starve now I can't help it.'

'You should have let me go,' said Mendel with a grin.

She shrugged her shoulders and, stripping off the big coat, threw it carelessly on a chair.

'I did my best, you lazy lout. You know perfectly well that if you'd suggested it *once* more I should have let you.'

Mendel chuckled.

'Never mind. Let's eat. I'm hungry and Wade hasn't had any food for about twenty-four hours apparently.'

They refused to let Rufus help with the washing-up, but quarrelled and clattered noisily in the big flagged kitchen, while he smoked a moody cigarette before the fire. He found himself sharply and furiously envious of them. They were so obviously together—so obviously completely at peace—the big yellow-haired man and the small, dark, short-haired girl, in the midst of this glorious quietness and desolation. He reflected bitterly that he must go soon. Where, he had no idea. But clearly one could not stay on, an uninvited guest, intruding into a private life so very intimate and *à deux*. He glanced round the room, and his eye caught the work on which Mendel had been engaged that morning. It was a partially finished carving[57] in a curious, hard, black wood. A negress, it seemed, from the thick pouting lips and sharply sloping forehead. He turned back to the fire with an impatient frown. Some people had all the luck.

It was Ruth who proposed the tobogganing expedition—or rather Ruth who wistfully remarked that it was a good day for tobogganing. They were doubtful at first if Rufus should venture out, but when he assured them that he felt perfectly fit and suggested that they should go alone and leave him, they would not hear of it.

'It's much better,' said Mendel firmly, 'to have three if you *can* come. Partly because it's much less fag pulling the darn things up the hill. Partly because the more people you have the more pace you get. And partly because you must have someone to get stretchers if two of the party break their necks.'

They set off about half-past two. Mendel had donned thick flannel shorts. Rufus still wore the old flannel trousers and ancient tweed jacket that Mendel had lent him that morning. There were two toboggans—beautifully made Canadian affairs which slipped along easily even over virgin snow. Mendel insisted on pulling one by himself, leaving the other to Ruth and Rufus.

'Pip made these,' said Ruth, as they trailed out of one of the barns from which the toboggans had been unearthed. 'Soon after we came here there was snow and we wanted to toboggan and hadn't any. We tried using tea-trays, but they weren't very good. So he did these.'

'How long have you been here?' asked Rufus with interest. A slight frown puckered her face.

'Three years,' she said briefly. 'Come on—it'll be less bumpy over here.'

They walked for about half an hour. Rufus's arms ached from pulling the toboggan over the steep and bumpy slopes, and he was panting hard. Several times he called out to Mendel as they passed a steep hill which looked an ideal run. But the big man just shook his head contemptuously and strode on, dragging his toboggan behind him as if it weighed a few ounces. Rufus had tried to ask Ruth about their life at Three Trees, but she answered briefly and rather vaguely, although she talked readily enough about other matters. He gave up at last and saved what little breath he had. It was annoying to find that not only Mendel, but Ruth as well, was still breathing easily and quietly while he panted in distress. On and on they plodded, until Rufus could see bright lights floating before his eyes, and felt that in a few moments he would be forced shamefully to demand a rest. But at last, before this crisis was actually reached, he saw with relief that Mendel had halted some twenty yards ahead.

'I think this is the one I thought would be good,' he said, as they thankfully dropped the rope. Rufus walked rather unsteadily forward and looked. Unlike most of the down slopes, the hill before them dropped away sheer and sudden from a definite edge. Immediately below them the slope seemed almost vertical. Down, down it went, a tremendous drop of four or five hundred feet, before it slowly flattened out and slipped again into the gentle undulations around.

'I noticed this last summer,' said Mendel. 'Ought to make a grand run when we get it worked down.'

'Is that Three Trees?' asked Rufus, pointing to a dark patch in the whiteness far below them. 'I should have thought we'd come further than that.'

Mendel smiled.

'It's about two miles,' he said. 'Things always look nearer than they are on the Plain. And we've come round the edge.'

Ruth was examining the slope with an expert eye.

'This is going to be a fast run,' she said. 'How about bumps, Pip? And wire? You can't see it against the snow.'

'I don't think there's any,' said Mendel, dragging his toboggan forward to the edge, 'but the best thing is to go down and see. I'll go down and if you see anything violent happening you'll know that there are bumps or wire or both.'

'Oh, no, look here, Pip!' Ruth caught him by the arm. 'Fair do's. Let me come down too, the first time. Going down without knowing what's at the bottom is half the fun.'

Mendel hesitated.

'All right,' he said at last. 'I suppose we may as well break both our necks—'

'Can I come too?' asked Rufus.

'Of course,' said Ruth cheerfully. 'We'll *all* go on one. Come on.'

She pulled the toboggan forward and sat down astride it.

'All right,' said Mendel. 'I'll go in front and we'll have you between us. And if we *see* any wire coming we must just capsize her,' he added, as they squatted down. 'Not that one ever sees much while the snow's loose.'

They worked themselves gingerly towards the edge.

'Now hang on tight.'

Rufus gripped the girl's slim shoulders firmly and gave a final push off with his feet. Despite the sheer slope, the toboggan started slowly on the soft virgin snow. Then gradually it gathered speed.

'We're off!' shouted Mendel, and suddenly they were flying at breath-taking speed through a dense and blinding curtain of upflung snow. Eyes and nose filled, Rufus let out an involuntary shout at the terrific exhilaration of the downward rush—a shout that was curiously broken as they passed over a ridge with a jarring bump. He grabbed at Ruth's shoulders and just saved himself from being flung off. Faster and faster, breathless and blinded, the snow stinging the face like wasps. He heard a squeal of delighted terror from Ruth, and saw Mendel lean sharply to the left with a yell of 'Whoops!', and then suddenly something like the talons of a huge cat was tearing his legs, and he pitched forward on top of Mendel and Ruth with a jar which shook the small remainder of breath from his body. For a moment he lay dazed by the shock. Then, as he brushed the snow from his face and staggered to his feet he saw the cause of the disaster. The toboggan had ploughed straight into and through a wild rose bush, crushing it flat, and its branches, coming up on either side, had been the talons that had torn his legs. Mendel, with blood streaming from his face, was hopping round and round in agony, clasping his right knee, and Ruth, shouting with laughter, was just rising from the other side of the toboggan.

'God damn and blast it!' Mendel was shouting. 'The only bloody rose tree for miles and we hit it!' He put his foot to the ground and limped painfully round, cursing.

Rufus became aware of an acute pain in his thigh, and pulled out a thorn half an inch long which was nailing his trousers to his leg.

'I couldn't see a thing!' said Ruth. 'We might have been running into a brick wall for all I knew. Thank goodness it wasn't wire!' She turned to Mendel. 'Pip—are you all right?'

'No!' said Mendel emphatically. 'I'm badly injured, blast it!'

They took stock of their injuries. Mendel, in front, had undoubtedly borne the brunt. Before it was flattened out, the thorns of the rose bush had made several long deep scratches in his face, and there was a deep cut in his lower lip, which was bleeding profusely. In addition, he had wrenched his knee in falling. Ruth and Rufus had come off comparatively lightly. Ruth's stockings were torn to shreds and her legs were bleeding. Pulling up her skirt, she began calmly and methodically to pick the big thorns out of the bare bit of thigh between knickers and stockings. She had suffered no other injury. Rufus was badly scratched, but his trousers had saved him to some extent. Otherwise he was intact save for a swollen mouth which had come in contact with Ruth's shoulder as they fell. Mendel dabbed hard at his cut lip with a handkerchief.

'Might have been much worse,' he said philosophically. 'If there *had* been wire we should have broken our necks.'

'It's a marvellous run,' said Ruth, looking appreciatively back up the hillside. 'Quite the best we've found, Pip. When you think we got up *that* pace over loose snow…' She abandoned her thorn extracting and, seizing the toboggan by the rope, heaved it clear of the rose bush. 'Come on. I'm going down again.'

For an hour and a half they alternately tore breath-takingly down and toiled breathlessly up. About four o'clock the dull day gradually merged into dusk, but they did not stop until hunger and fatigue had made the long climb too big an effort, even when rewarded by the thrilling downward rush. The blood from Mendel's torn legs had frozen, and from the waist downwards he looked like a butcher's shop. He liked best to take a toboggan down by himself, lying face downward on it and steering with his feet. Rufus did the same and found it at once exciting and entirely safe. They went down backwards, lying face upwards on the toboggans—a terrifying thing—and once Mendel made a brief attempt to do down standing. The attempt ended in himself and his toboggan rolling over and over down the last thirty yards of the slope.

'I'll tell you what,' said Ruth breathlessly, as she and Rufus reached the summit after a run, 'let's try horses. You lie down and I'll sit on your back.'

'All right,' said Rufus, delighted.

He lay down and she perched herself astride his back.

'Hey, look out…' they heard Mendel shout as they passed him toiling back up the hill, but they were going too fast to hear the rest of the warning. The run was a complete success until, almost at the bottom, they crossed the treacherous bump, and then Ruth was shot suddenly into the air, and descended with a bump which almost winded her unfortunate horse.

'Rufus—did I hurt you? My dear, I'm awfully sorry. I came down on you with an awful crash…'

'Asses!' said Mendel, 'I knew that would happen. It's an old fool trap. Are you all right, Rufus?'

'Quite,' said Rufus. He was feeling slightly drunk and incredibly happy.

'Come on, Ruth, my blossom, let's try it again with you further back.'

He put his arm round the slim waist and led the way to the toboggan.

'Can you hang on to me with your knees? Hoick your skirt up. That's right.'

The walk back to the farm through the dusk was strange. Rufus, struggling along through the snow, was acutely aware that he was dog-tired, that his arms ached from pulling the toboggan, that his scratched legs were sore and burning, and that his clothes, soaked through, were quietly freezing on him. But withal he felt extraordinarily well and happy. The physical sensations of weariness, aching and soreness were in themselves delightfully acute. He could feel his body—feel its good-natured protests—feel the ache and heaviness of each limb, and the piercing cold which battered unsuccessfully against the delicious internal glow. He was alive—an animal struggling through the snow aware that each muscle, though weary, would do its part—aware of their smooth interplay.

And there was more than that. They had gone out together and taken him with them. Because they had found him lying in the snow at their very door, and had been forced to take him in as an unescapable guest. But it was different now. The ragging was triangular. The calculated insults were thrown to and from three pairs of hands. Mendel sought him as an ally against Ruth; and better still, Ruth made common cause with him against Mendel. They liked him now. And he—he more than liked them, for they had given him something of what he was seeking.

The wind had whipped the snow into strange points and curves. Like stiffly-whipped cream, it hung on the crest above the farm.

'Do you think,' said Ruth thoughtfully, 'do you *think* we could toboggan down without hitting the wire? We could dig our heels in and stop just before it.'

'We do *not* think so,' said Mendel firmly.

'Funk!' she said, with icy contempt.

'You can if you like,' said Mendel. 'Rufus and I will pick up the bits.'

They stowed the toboggans in the barn and went thankfully into the pleasant warmth.

'Now I suppose you want to wash by the fire and I shall have to go upstairs in the cold,' said Ruth bitterly.

'Don't mind us,' said Mendel, stripping off his jacket. 'I dare say Rufus knows what little girls are like underneath.'

'I don't *know*,' said Rufus reprovingly, 'but I can *guess*.' For a wild, foolish, adolescent moment, he desperately wished her to undress with them. She hesitated.

'No,' she said with dignity. 'That would *not* be proper. Rather a chilly bedroom than—er—dishonour.' She went out and shut the door.

'The curse of this place,' said Mendel, 'is washing. Luckily Ruth put on a couple of kettles before we went.'

He went into the kitchen and returned lugging a large tin bath and, dumping it by the fire, went back to fetch the enormous black iron kettle. 'Ruth's going to do indelicate things upstairs with the hip bath,' he said, splashing out the boiling water. 'Get the cold, will you? There's a can of it out there.'

Rufus went stiffly into the kitchen and returned with a large watering can of cold water.

'Well, I'm damned,' said Mendel, 'look!' He had removed his bloodstained shorts. They were standing up by themselves, frozen quite hard.

It was six o'clock and they had finished tea before Rufus realised that he was prolonging his stay without a shadow of justification. He glanced at his watch and heaved an inward sigh.

'Well,' he said as cheerfully as he could, 'I suppose I must be making a move.'

Mendel looked up with raised eyebrows.

'A move?' he repeated.

'Yes. I think I'd better go back into Leaford and put in another night at the Angel. It isn't a bad pub.' He rose to his feet. 'It's been very good of you to… to—'

'But why?' asked Mendel with a frown. 'Why go?

You said you weren't going anywhere in particular?'

A great hope leaped up in Rufus, but he shook his head with a smile.

'But, my dear man, I can't inflict myself on you for another night. There's no possible excuse for it.'

'What on earth's that got to do with it?' said Ruth, almost irritably. 'You like it here, don't you?'

'Of course, but—'

'Well, then, don't be so damned polite and social. What on earth sense is there in going off if you'd like to stay here?'

Rufus hesitated. 'It's awfully good of you to put it like that,' he said, 'and, to be frank, I should love to stay. But—well—it isn't fair to you.'

Mendel grinned. 'Well then, let's put it like this. We'll give you our word that when we want you to go we'll tell you. Until then stay here, unless you *want* to go.'

Rufus looked at him for a moment in silence and then dropped heavily back into his chair.

'You don't understand the situation,' he said. 'Naturally, because I haven't told you. But if you did you wouldn't be making casual offers like that.'

'All right,' said Ruth, smiling up at him from the stool on which she was crouching. 'Tell us all about it and then perhaps we'll throw you out.'

Rufus lit a cigarette and pitched the match idly into the fire.

'Well,' he said slowly, 'it's like this. Until a day or two ago I was working in London. In an advertising agency. It was quite a good job—as a matter of fact, it was quite fun sometimes. And I was engaged.'

'You mean to a girl?' said Ruth.

'No, ass. To a duck-billed platypus,' said Mendel softly.

'Well, he *might* have meant engaged in doing something,' said Ruth defensively.

'Dry up,' said Mendel. 'Go on, Rufus.'

'She was a very beautiful person, was Marjorie,' said Rufus reflectively. '*Is* a very beautiful person—I'm talking as though she were dead. And she was respectable,' he added viciously, 'with a respectability passing belief.'

'Meaning she wouldn't sleep with you?' said Mendel with a grin.

'I never asked her,' said Rufus frankly. 'The idea never entered my head. At least, I mean, one couldn't sleep with Marjorie before being married to her. We weren't on those sort of terms.'

'Sounds a passionate romance.'

'Well, as a matter of fact, it was a good deal more passionate than it sounds, really. But anyhow that's beside the point. What happened was that a few days ago I had a birthday and—well, it sounds damned silly, but you know how odd it always seems to be a year older; and I started to think it over—about the job and Marjorie and so on—and I decided that it wasn't good enough.' He paused and blew a reflective cloud of blue smoke. Mendel nodded slightly in silence.

'Well, the upshot of it was,' Rufus went on, 'that I *could not* find a logical justification for it at all. I couldn't see the *point* of it. There was I, sitting on my bottom in a stuffy office in London, and likely to go on doing so, and for eighty per cent of my life not doing nor seeing nor hearing any of the things I liked. I just wasn't alive at all—not physically alive. I was a cabbage. And… well, I didn't like the idea of being a cabbage.'

'Go on,' said Mendel quietly. 'This is interesting.'

'So to finish up with, I threw up my job. I was very childish about it, and was quite unnecessarily rude to several people who had been very nice to me. And then I went along to see Marjorie and put the whole thing to her. Asked here if she'd take a chance and come away with me and look for a job where—where we could be alive.' Rufus smiled reminiscently. 'Of course she didn't see the point. You couldn't expect her to. According to her lights,[58] I was just mad. Anyhow, we had a row and that was that.'

'Of course,' said Mendel reflectively, 'if you hadn't said anything to her before, it was rather—'

'Oh, it was damned silly!' said Rufus. 'I know. But anyhow I wasn't sorry in the least.' He grinned broadly. 'Then I went into a pub and got rather tight.'

'The obvious step,' said Ruth.

'Quite. Well, while I was in there, two sportsmen[59] came in who were just starting off with a furniture van to St. Ives. It struck me that St. Ives was a nice long way away, so I tipped them to take me.'

'In the van?'

'In the van. I slept next to a stuffed eagle. Well, a few miles out of Salisbury the van broke down, and I thought the downs looked nice, so I left the van and set off on foot. Not making for anywhere. Just vaguely. I landed down in Leaford, and spent a night at the Angel and went to a dance—' he hesitated and glanced at Ruth, 'after which,' he said defiantly, 'I seduced a young woman.'

'This is all drink and women,' said Ruth in scandalised tones.

'Shut up!' said Mendel. 'Yes?'

'Then next day I had a shot at getting a job on a farm, but of course it was hopeless.'

'Mr. Christianson, yas?' said Ruth.

'Exactly. Mr. Christianson, yas.'

'God, how I loathe that man!' said Ruth feelingly.

'He is nasty, isn't he?' said Rufus. 'Anyhow, of course I couldn't get a job and, what with one thing and another, I got very fed up with Leaford, and just went for a walk on the downs to get the taste of it out of my mouth. Then it snowed, and then of course I, like a fool, went plugging on simply because I didn't want to go back to Leaford and because—well, I liked it.' He paused. 'That's all.' He concluded rather lamely.

There was a long silence.

'Well, I don't see that you've produced any reason why you shouldn't stay here,' said Ruth. 'Do you, Pip?'

Mendel slowly shook his head. He was gazing thoughtfully into the fire.

'On the contrary,' he said quietly.

'But don't you see,' said Rufus, 'this is so exactly the sort of place and this afternoon was so exactly the sort of thing I—I meant, that–' He shook his head helplessly. 'Well, you can't just walk in on people's lives as I've done, and… and–'

Mendel raised his head.

'What do you want, Rufus?' he asked suddenly.

Rufus hesitated.

'That's half the trouble,' he said slowly. 'I don't think I really know.'

'I mean, do you just want to be quiet, and potter around gently, and be lazy and lotus eat,[60] so to speak? Or is it more than that?'

Rufus frowned thoughtfully.

'I think it's more than that. It isn't just—just *negative*. There are an awful lot of quite definite things—physical things—I want. Like feeling tired, and feeling hungry and feeling cold. I don't think I'd really felt any of those things for years until a day or two ago. A lot of me is dead—or asleep. The whole animal part. And I want to give it a chance.'

'I see,' Mendel nodded. 'Have you got any money?' he asked after a moment's silence.

'About two hundred pounds in the world.'

'And is there anything you want to do with your time? Write, or paint, or anything?'

'I don't know. I don't think so. Not much, anyhow.'

'Really?' Mendel seemed surprised.

Rufus shook his head.

'That's odd,' said Mendel, 'and rather unusual too. Usually even if people just want to be lazy, they *think* they want to write or something.' He ran a hand through the thick yellow hair. 'In your ideal life, then, how would you want to spend your time?'

'How do you spend yours here?' countered Rufus.

'I? Well, I've got a sort of workshop fixed up in one of the barns. I spend a good deal of time making things—most of them quite useless. Then I chip about at blocks of wood like that thing there,' he pointed to the unfinished carving. 'I walk about a lot on the downs, I read, I occasionally write things, and tear them up—' He paused and smiled down at Ruth. 'And the rest of the time I spend making love to that.'

Rufus grinned.

'Sounds quite perfect,' he said.

Mendel spread out his hands.

'Well, there's no reason why you shouldn't try it if it attracts you, as I say.'

'Ah,' said Rufus, 'but you forget that there would be no way for *me* to spend "the rest of my time".'

'What, you mean making love to *her?* Well, you could borrow her off me. Be a nice change for her, wouldn't it, sweet?'

'Years ago,' said Ruth, looking at him with distaste, 'a mutual friend warned me that you had an "oriental attitude towards women". I fear—'

'But that isn't oriental,' said Rufus. To his fury, he felt himself blushing. 'If it's anything it's Eskimo. Surely they're the people who lend their wives to visitors? But seriously,' he added, turning to Mendel, 'it sounds very perfect.'

Mendel was regarding him thoughtfully, with the queer, long-distance eyes.

'I wonder,' he said half to himself. He lit a cigarette, and gazed closely at the glowing tip. 'You see, Rufus, it isn't everybody who *can* live this sort of life. I suppose almost everybody wants to at some time or other—when they get fed up with living in a town, and working from nine till six in an office. But one's got to face up to the fact that this sort of life—the sort of life I lead—is completely non-productive. Or almost so. I'm not *making* anything—except a few things in wood. Judged by the usual standards, I'm not justifying my existence at all. It so happens that *I* don't think any particular justification necessary. I prefer just to live as I like. But it doesn't "get you anywhere", as people say. And if you wanted to get somewhere—if you wanted constant change and progress, in the sense that people usually mean, or if you had any sort of ambition, then it would be hopeless.'

Rufus nodded.

'Yes, I can see that.'

'What I'm wondering,' Mendel went on, 'is this. Do you really want this sort of thing as a life? Or as a—a holiday? Do you see what I mean? You say this life sounds perfect. So it is, to me. But I wonder how long you would go on thinking so. Whether after a bit you'd be driven back by this extraordinary urge which people have to *do* things?'

There was a long silence.

'It's awfully difficult to say,' said Rufus at last.

'Of course it is. I didn't expect you to tell me. I was only wondering. Anyhow, it doesn't affect the immediate point, which is that you're more than welcome to stay here and see how you like it.'

Rufus shook his head in exasperation. 'It's terribly good of you, but don't you see I *can't?* I'd love to but it wouldn't be fair.'

'Why not?' asked Ruth.

'(a) because I obviously can't sponge on you, and (b) because this is your life—you two. And I might spoil it for you completely.'

'How?'

'Simply by being here.'

Mendel smiled. 'Well, we've already told you that we'll kick you out the moment we don't want you. And as far as sponging goes, if that worries you, you can pay. We haven't got much money, but there isn't much to spend *on* down here. And as far as I know it won't cost much more with you here than it did before.'

Rufus hesitated.

'It's a frightful temptation,' he said at last with a smile.

'Yield,' said Ruth. 'What was it Oscar Wilde said?'[61] She rose and walked over to the window, threw it open, and looked out.

'You're *sure* you wouldn't mind?' said Rufus.

'I really should like it,' said Mendel with a grin, 'for purely selfish reasons.'

Ruth closed the window with a bang.

'The good Lord has settled the matter,' she said cheerfully. 'It's snowing Heaven's hard. And if I know anything about this place, people who *do* want to leave it won't be able to for a couple of days, let alone people who don't.'

Chapter VIII

Curious Occurrence in Eden

The next few days were absurdly idyllic. The snow, as Ruth had prophesied, deepened and drifted until it was difficult to wade across the farmyard. And then the dull yellow cloud cleared away, and the sun shone brightly, so that the dazzling white carpet was painful to the eyes.

Rufus found himself falling with extraordinary readiness into the queer, casual, secluded life. It was as though he had put off with his well-cut lounge suit the whole of the strenuous, noisy worrying life he had known, and stepped, in Mendel's scarecrow garments, into another.

Three Trees was a small but solid old farmhouse. They lived in the big, low, beamed room with the open fire or, when assisting Ruth with the cooking, which was carried out on a big oil stove, in the large picturesque and hideously inconvenient flagged kitchen. The other downstairs room was small and little used, containing nothing but a chair, a table, and a confused mass of books, tools, pieces of wood, and old curtains, strewed vaguely on the floor.

Rufus's bedroom looked out on the big square farmyard and

the encircling hill. From his window, as he lay in bed, the sharp, perfectly-curved rim stood out clearly against the sky. Beneath, nestling close against the house, was the large thatched barn which Mendel had converted into a carpenter's shop. In the other side of the farmyard were other barns, but their thatch was green with moss and falling in, their doors were broken, and inside they were damp, derelict and useless.

Rufus found that time passed remarkably quickly. It was almost a fetish of Mendel's to pay no regard to the hour. There was no clock in the house, and although Ruth had a wrist-watch, Mendel himself never carried a timepiece of any sort. It was partly this fact, and partly the complete absence of any routine of life, which made days and evenings so ridiculously short; but more particularly, perhaps, the complete absence of those dull moments of waiting for the appropriate hour, or wondering what to do next. With the exception of a very few simple tasks, there was almost literally nothing which *had* to be done. And with the disappearance of things which had to be done, came the realisation of the thousand little things which *could* be done, which made the days all too short and densely crowded.

They rose early as a rule. If one wanted food, one went and took it, but there was no formal breakfast. Thereafter there was no morning or afternoon, or lunch or tea, beginning and ending and forming milestones to the day. There was simply a period of light to be disposed of in large or small sections, followed by a period of evening which might be short or very long, depending upon how soon one felt sleepy. Rufus, who at first could not shake off the bondage of time, noticed with surprise that although one day might last from six in the morning until three the next, and another from 8 a.m. until nine in the evening, it did not seem particularly strange. Nor, after a while, did it seem odd to have three meals in a day—at, say, 11 a.m., 3 p.m., and 8 p.m. There was only one time for going to bed—when one was sleepy. There was only one reason for a meal—that one was hungry. After a couple of days he seldom wore his watch, although he wound it carefully at night.

Occupation was equally casual and irregular. Rufus spent much time with Mendel in the improvised workshop. Mendel had plenty of tools and a great deal of excellent timber, of which he imported a cartload once a year. He had made most of the furniture in the house, and was engaged in making a large oak wardrobe. 'Not,' he remarked, 'because we've got any robes worth speaking about. But I like doing *big* things.' There were few days when they did not spend some hours sawing and planing in the big sawdusty room with its pleasant whitewashed walls and brick floor. Sometimes Mendel would spend a desultory hour at his wood carving.

For the rest one walked or read, or played curious improvised games. Mendel had a chess-board and proved a good deal too good for Rufus. But apart from this concession, the amusements of Three Trees were mostly original. There was, for example, a grand game played in the farmyard,[62] with a tennis ball, which had to be thrown on to the sloping roof of the barn and caught, despite hazards, before it fell to the ground again. The rules were complicated and variable. When Rufus arrived the horse-trough was a let. But soon after it was filled with clean water and became a hazard... Once, going to bed, Rufus noticed with surprise that it was after two, and found himself wondering why the day had seemed so short. He lay in bed thinking about it for some time, and finally decided that it was because one had been so busy. He was very nearly asleep at the time and the conclusion seemed perfectly justifiable.

With a quick movement Mendel removed the shining, freshly-planed piece of wood from the vice and, straightening his back, sniffed suspiciously.

'I've never been quite sure whether that oil stove was a good thing,' he said thoughtfully. Rufus looked up from his measuring and glanced at the black tin stove.

'Be mighty cold without it,' he said.

'I don't know. Perhaps it would. But wouldn't it be better to be cold and fragrant than warm and smelly?' He strolled over and rested a caressing hand on Rufus's big plank. 'How are you getting on?'

'I've got it all measured up,' said Rufus. 'I'm just going to begin sawing.'

Mendel nodded. 'It's darned good timber this,' he said thoughtfully, 'but it's vicious stuff to work in. Takes the edge off anything.'

He turned away and applied a square to the piece of wood he had been planing. Rufus placed his plank across the trestles and, picking up a saw, began to rasp slowly and carefully along a pencilled line. He could split a line now with a saw. His cut no longer swerved drunkenly from one side to the other as it had done at first. A last long stroke and the halves of the plank clattered on the floor. Mendel threw down his square and lit a cigarette.

'Interval,' he said, seating himself on his bench. 'Rest pause.'

Rufus nodded and, laying down his saw, sat down on one of the sawing trestles and produced his cigarette-case.

'You know this is extraordinarily good fun,' he said, carefully replacing the spent match in its box.

Mendel glanced at him with the distant blue eyes.

'You're enjoying it?'

'Immensely. It's absolutely *right*. How long have I been here? A week to-day, isn't it?'

Mendel nodded.

'It's an odd thing,' said Rufus, 'but it seems much longer. I feel as though I'd been here years. And yet the time goes frightfully quickly.'

Mendel glanced out of the window without reply.

The converted barn looked out on to what had once been the farmyard.

'What a pity it is that snow can't just disappear without all this slushy mess,' he said thoughtfully.

'Yes,' said Rufus absently. He was in a conversational mood, and he wanted above everything to make Mendel talk. His week at Three Trees had been satisfactory in every respect but one—he had never succeeded in making Mendel or Ruth talk about themselves. Always, if he tried, the conversation wandered away into something else, just as it was wandering away now to the subject of snow.

'Pip,' he said suddenly, 'I've been meaning to ask you for a long time. How did you and—and Ruth come to be here in the first place?'

Mendel looked up with raised eyebrows, and remained silent for a moment. Rufus suddenly felt acutely conscious that the question was in bad taste. 'I know it's nothing to do with me,' he said hastily, reddening slightly. 'I was just idly curious, that's all.'

Rather to his relief Mendel smiled quietly.

'Oh, that's all right. There's no mystery about it.' He paused and gazed thoughtfully at his cigarette. 'In fact, it's a very ordinary story, really. I was married to a woman who was—well, rather like your Marjorie, I should think. Then I met Ruth and—' he shrugged his shoulders, 'we found we had approximately the same views. Or rather, she had very few views of any sort and was prepared to accept mine. So we cleared out and came down here. I happened to hear that the place was for sale. It was quite useless to most people, of course, and I stepped in and bought it for a song. He smiled his sudden charming smile. 'That's my everyday story, as the Salvationists[63] say. We've got just enough to live on down here, so it's all right from that point of view.'

Rufus nodded.

'I only asked because you seem to me to have made such a very good job of your lives, both of you.'

Mendel frowned slightly. 'Why?'

'Well, you seem to—to suit one another awfully well. And you're the only people I know who seem at all—at all free.'

'I've never yet defined freedom,' said Mendel with a quiet smile.

'But you see what I mean?'

'Yes. I doubt if you're right though.'

'But surely,' Rufus protested, 'surely you'd agree that you and Ruth are extraordinarily happy? Far happier than people usually are?'

Mendel shook his head.

'I don't know. It's impossible to say. Happiness is purely subjective after all. I can't compare a subjective state of my own with the subjective states of other people. I just don't know them. All I can say is that I am probably happier in my present state than I should be in theirs. But even that's only a guess. I haven't tried their states so I don't really know.'

'You're splitting hairs,' said Rufus, almost irritably. 'You know perfectly well what I mean.'

'Broadly, yes. But what I'm trying to do is to stand up against your desire to make Three Trees into a sort of Garden of Eden with myself and Ruth as Adam and Eve. You'd like to think that, because this is rather the sort of thing you've been looking for. But it's wrong. Completely wrong. Practically all the features of the Garden of Eden are lacking.'

'What features?' said Rufus argumentatively.

Mendel shifted his position slightly and kicked gently at the leg of the bench.

'In the first place, your true Eden could not exist without absolute simplicity—simplicity of character, I mean. And neither Ruth nor I are particularly simple.'

'But—'

'Secondly, I'm convinced that Adam worked. I know it doesn't actually say so in Genesis—not in the Garden anyhow. But of course he did.'

'But so do you,' Rufus threw out a hand. 'Look at all this.'

'Ah, yes, but Adam worked because he had to. He had all the excitement of taking on Nature barehanded and winning. I merely make a pretence of working to fill in the gap which civilisation has made in life. If I were the true simple lifer I should grow my own corn—make my own bread, and so on.'

'But that's purely a matter of choice,' said Rufus.

'No. Not quite. It's simply that I'm far too lazy to be an Adam.' He flicked the long ash from his cigarette. 'And finally, the relations between Ruth and myself are not in the least Adam and Eveish. They are altogether too complex and psychological.' He grinned gently. 'As far as I can make out, most of my feelings for Ruth and her feelings for me were only invented fairly recently—by the psycho-analysts. I'm sure they didn't exist in Eden.' Mendel shook his head. 'You see, Rufus, you've forgotten the bit about eating the apple. The knowledge of good and evil and so on. *That's* what makes Eden an impossibility nowadays.'

Rufus shook his head obstinately. 'You don't know when you're well off,' he said. 'Eden or no Eden it seems to me that you're nearer happiness—nearer having the fundamentals right—than anyone I've known.'

'That's merely by contrast with your own experience,' said Mendel.

'Well, mine was fairly representative.'

'On the contrary. To a vast majority of people life here would be intolerably dull. You just happened to be an instance of a strongly physical person who woke up one day to find himself physically moribund. But most people are so completely lacking in the craving for physical things—things for their eyes and ears and hands and stomachs—that they never notice that anything's missing. You see, most of them have been civilised and urbanised until food is a thing you get in a Lyons's restaurant;[64] air is the stuff you breathe; beauty is a film star; cold is what you feel when you move away from a gas-fire; and physical love a routine indulged in once a week for a quarter of an hour, if at all.'

Rufus nodded in silence. Mendel ran a hand through his yellow mane.

'It's this craze for *doing* things, you see. The queer feeling that life must have an "object". This delusion of "progress" and movement. I suppose it all goes back to the parable of the talents.[65] See how it comes out there. The people who were commended had all *done* something. They had all made progress. But Christ never meant "progress" in the sense we interpret it. Otherwise, how do we square the parable talents with the business of the lilies of the field?[66] People think that as long as they're rushing round making money or writing books or promoting companies, or giving themselves up to good works that they're "justifying their existences"—being the good chaps in the parable. But of course they're not. The operative word in the description of the man who hid his talent is that he was *afraid*.[67] And that's just what all these energetic people are—afraid.'

'I don't quite see that,' said Rufus with a frown.

Mendel carefully crushed out his stub of cigarette.

'Well, it's like this. We've all got a certain short time in which to live—to live our physical and mental lives. We all have talents. (Remember, by the way, that those talents were money—purely a symbol. Not the "ability" sort of talents.) Well, the talents with which we're all born are our senses—our eyes—ears—noses— touch sense—and all the things which develop out of them—all our sensual life. If we are going to cultivate them properly—to make them really acute and perceptive—it's pretty well a full-time job. There's a life-object if you like. We start off, small, undeveloped animals, and we work to become perfect animals. But the majority of people won't accept that as a life-object. It's too natural, and natural things are always difficult. So they're like the man in the parable. They take the sensual life and dig a deep hole and bury it. And then they rush off and spend the rest of their lives "justifying their existence"—when they've already taken darned good care not to have an existence. Usually they seem to expect God to be pleased. Personally I prefer to think that God probably knew his own business best when he gave us a sensual life in a sensual world.'

'But you're assuming that sensuality is the only object of life,' protested Rufus. 'I agree that it's frightfully important, but I wouldn't go all the way with you.'

Mendel smiled. 'That's simply because nowadays people have reached the stage where they define sensuality as a sort of refined lecherousness. I don't mean sensuality in that limited sense at all. I mean all the things which are directly concerned with the senses— things which can be appreciated by the body without immense intellectual and mechanical complications. Look here—this is the sort of thing I mean—you'll agree that to a person who's hungry eating is a sensual pleasure—a simple one?'

'Yes.'

'Well, what I mean is that nowadays to eat because you're hungry is rare among a lot of people. The simple, *primary* sensual pleasure's gone. And if there is any pleasure left in food for them, it doesn't come from eating but from going to the Ritz[68] and spending money and showing off to other people, or something like that. Running is a simple sensual pleasure. But the only running the average man does is to catch a train so that he can get to the office quickly and get on with justifying his existence. That's the basis of the trouble—this urge for some complicated aim and object. People can never think of life as sufficient object in itself. They want something simpler—something more concrete and less frightening. You remember Maeterlinck's saying[69] that an old man sitting before the fire with the wind blowing outside seemed to him the essence of drama? That's the apotheosis of sensuality. But nowadays we want a murder in the first scene, adultery in the second and noble self-sacrifice in the third, or else we say the things is objectless.'

There was a long pause.

'But I can't see the whole of mankind–' began Rufus.

'I am not in the least interested in mankind,' said Mendel shortly. 'It's only when people are completely incapable of working things out for themselves that they start rushing about theorising and legislating for others.' He rose and picked up his piece of wood. 'I have plenty to interest me in trying to work out my own salvation.'

'And Ruth's?' said Rufus, rising also.

Mendel frowned slightly and hesitated.

'And Ruth's in so far as it affects me,' he said coldly, fixing his wood in the vice and picking up his plane.

Rufus had been at Three Trees a fortnight before he saw them quarrel, if quarrel it could be called. As he learned afterwards this was almost a record. Apparently at this early stage his presence was a pacifying influence.

It was undoubtedly Mendel's fault, and the subject was an absurdly undignified one. The household supply of milk could only be obtained by walking about a mile and a half over the hill to another outlying farm. Usually somebody made this expedition every other day. On this occasion, however, Ruth found that she had used more milk than usual for cooking purposes and, coming into the barn, she asked Mendel to go and fetch more.

The result, to Rufus, was astounding. It was not even as though the big man was merely irritated or angry. But for some reason he seized the opportunity to be bitterly unkind to her. Calmly, and with a queer, calculating cruelty, he passed from milk to organising ability, from organising ability to general usefulness, from general usefulness to brains, and so on. It was in vain that the wretched Ruth apologised and offered to go herself. It was in vain that Rufus offered to go. Rather to Rufus's surprise, Ruth did not defend herself, or lose her temper, or even go away. She simply stood meekly before him, lips trembling a little, while he worked the absurd triviality up into a subject for the bitterest taunts he could utter. At last he took the can and went striding away up the hill, leaving Rufus horrified and astounded, gazing after him with wide-open eyes. Ruth had returned to the kitchen, and Rufus instinctively followed her, with some wild, half-formed idea of apology for Mendel. She was peeling potatoes, and quite clearly and definitely crying. Rufus, as he looked at her, felt very angry indeed with Mendel. She looked up at him and then looked hastily away, blinking vigorously.

'Hullo,' she said with a rather pathetic attempt at cheerfulness.

'Look here, Ruth,' said Rufus, 'don't cry. He didn't mean it. He must have got a liver or something.'

She peeled a long brown ribbon without reply. A sudden thought struck Rufus.

'He—he isn't *often* like that, is he?'

She hesitated. 'Fairly often,' she said at last, looking up at him with tearful dark eyes and a rather bitter little smile.

'But why? You hadn't done anything. Damn it, I would have gone. I told him I would.'

Ruth shook the boyish head impatiently.

'Oh, it isn't anything to do with that—not the business about the milk. If it hadn't been that it would have been something else.'

'You mean he's just in a bad temper?'

She shook her head. 'Oh, no. He wasn't angry. He–' she hesitated, 'he just wanted to hurt me, that's all.'

'But why?'

'I don't know.' She shrugged her shoulders. 'Sometimes when he's annoyed with me he––he likes to.'

'Was he annoyed with you then? About something else?'

'Oh, not about anything in particular,' she shook her head wearily, 'it's just that he––he hates me rather at the––the–' She choked suddenly and, turning away quickly, fished in her pocket with a damp hand and produced a handkerchief.

Rufus's heart melted.

'Oh, look here,' he slipped a protecting arm round the shaking shoulders, 'it isn't as bad as all that. You know he doesn't hate you, don't you, you old ass?'

She shook her head in mute disagreement. He saw that the only thing to do was to let her cry in peace, and for a few moments he stood in silence with the encircling arm tightly clasped. Then, quite suddenly, she ceased to sob and, dabbing at her eyes with the handkerchief, blew her nose vigorously, and brushed back a strand of hair which had strayed across her forehead.

'That's better,' said Rufus, 'now come on––tell me. What have you been quarrelling about?'

The tearful black eyes looked up at him in genuine astonishment.

'Quarrelling? We haven't been.'

'But you said–'

She turned away and picked up her peeling knife.

'You don't understand Pip,' she said in a low voice. 'He doesn't quarrel with you and get angry––not *about* something.'

'Then why was he like that?'

'Because,' she said wearily, 'because sometimes he gets a fit of—of not liking me. Not because of anything in particular. He just hates the sight of me. And—and then he does—that.'

Rufus shook his head with a puzzled frown. 'I don't understand it.'

Ruth smiled a rather crooked smile. 'Nor do I, Rufus. 'I don't think he does. But there it is.' To his surprise she laid her hand on his and squeezed it hard. 'I shouldn't worry about it, my dear, if I were you. He'll be all right when he comes back.'

'But I hate seeing you cry,' said Rufus.

'It is a nasty sight,' said Ruth, with something like her usual grin, 'but I should have had hell till I did, so it's just as well.'

'You mean he *wanted* to make you cry?'

She nodded. 'Yes. Once he's done that he's satisfied.' She shook her head thoughtfully. 'I suppose if I'd got a grain of sense I should start to weep copiously as soon as he began. But somehow I always have to try not to, and that only makes him go on. I had a particularly good day once,' she added, with a smile, 'and just sulked for about three hours. It took him a long time to forgive that.'

Rufus turned away and shook his head bemusedly.

'But the whole thing's so *unlike* him. After all, he's desperately in love with you—anybody can see it...'

He turned sharply as the knife clattered into the bowl, but she had not moved.

'Yes,' she said.

Chapter IX

Patron das Macht der Wind

Ruth knew her man. When Mendel returned an hour later he was in his most charming mood—the mood of gentle affectionate chaffing. He completely ignored the incident and Ruth, for her part, neither sulked nor showed any sign of resentment. The situation, Rufus reflected, was clearly well understood by both.

After the meal Mendel proposed a walk. The snow had vanished now and the white carpet had given place to the dull olive green of the winter grass, alternating with the deep sombre brown of the plough. Only in isolated spots a few flecks of dirty white still remained, preserved by the icy wind that blew strongly from the north-east.

Rufus had abandoned his own clothes completely. Mendel's wardrobe apparently contained a vast stock of comfortable, disreputable garments, which ideally suited the life at Three Trees. Rufus was big but, even so, Mendel's garments hung about him in folds, and he had been mortified to find that the big man's jacket could be made to produce an almost double-breasted effect even over his big chest. He had retained only his own overcoat, and as they set out he caught sight of himself in a mirror—a queer, incongruous bare-headed figure in the smartly-cut town overcoat, with the tramp-like collar and rag of a tie, and the ancient flannel trousers hanging in festoons over the borrowed thick brown shoes. He was still laughing at the sight as he joined the others.

'What's up?' asked Ruth inquiringly.

'I was just thinking what a weird object I looked in this outfit,' said Rufus.

Mendel looked him over with a grin. 'In the days when I had a tailor,' he said, 'he always used to tell me that anything he made for me looked "very dressy". That, I think, sums you up. *Very* dressy. Particularly the trousers.'

'As a matter of fact,' said Rufus frankly, 'you don't look exactly Savile Row yourself. In fact, the only respectable member of the party is Ruth.'

Mendel looked at her for a moment in silence. She was dressed as she had been the day Rufus had first seen her, in the big black overcoat and the small wool cap.

'Respectable!' said Mendel. 'That's it! That's exactly the right word.' He stared at her fixedly for a moment with the queer light-blue eyes, a grin showing his big white teeth. She met his eyes but Rufus sensed in her face a curious fear.

'Respectable!' said Mendel with gentle mockery. 'You can take women into the middle of the Sahara. You can take away their virtue. You can take away their money. You can take away their clothes. But that's a thing you can never take away.' He paused and the grin widened. 'An innate respectability.' He raised the thick ashplant[70] which he carried and tapped her very gently on the buttock. Gently and experimentally, like a man seeking to goad an animal into movement. '*Respectable*, Ruth, my sweet!' The black eyes never left his face. Rufus saw her throat contract as she swallowed, but she neither spoke nor smiled.

'Come on!' cried Mendel, turning suddenly. 'Let's go along the top track!' Without another word he went striding off up the steep hillside which led to the rim of the downs.

It was unusual to meet any human soul in an hour's walk in the direction they had chosen, but to-day there were two figures on the smooth grassy footpath.

'Glory!' said Mendel, as they came in view. 'I believe that's the Owner himself, isn't it?'

'Looks like him,' said Ruth. 'What are they doing?'

'More wire, I expect,' said Mendel rather bitterly.

'Who's the Owner?' inquired Rufus as they walked quickly towards the two absorbed figures.

'The local God Almighty,' replied Mendel. 'In the last century, I suppose, he would have been the squire. Anyhow, he owns most of the district.'

'Does he live here?'

'Oh, on and off. The Manor House wasn't big enough for him, so he built himself a whacking great place just the other side of Leaford. He comes down about once a month. Paradine's his name. I believe he's something in the City. Tea or rubber.'

'Paradine Ward's?' hazarded Rufus, 'the tea people?'

'Probably. Anyhow, he's a nasty bit of work, and the folks about here loathe him. Apparently he's the world's worst landlord and he goes in a lot for this sort of thing.' He struck the barbed wire beside the track sharply with the ashplant.

'What, wire?'

'Yes. He's always trying to bag bits of the downs. He's got about fifteen hundred acres about here, and I suppose he wants a bit more. He doesn't approve of me,' he added, with a grin.

They were close upon the two men now, who looked up as they approached. Mr. Paradine, a small, hard-faced man in plus-fours was watching a large, youngish labourer with a red face, who was busy with the hinges of a five-barred gate which spanned the track.

'Afternoon, Mr. Paradine,' called Mendel heartily.

'Afternoon!' said the small man, with a cold and unsmiling little nod. He did not raise his cap.

'Having a bit of trouble with the gate?' asked Mendel, conversationally, coming to a halt.

Mr. Paradine looked at him stonily, without reply. The red-faced young labourer pushed his cap back on his forehead and straightened his back.

'Ah, the young limbs[71] 'as bin at en again,' he said wrathfully.

'Young limbs?' said Mendel inquiringly.

''Ad all on 'em off their 'inges las' night,' said the red-faced one. '*An*' fifty yards of wire broke down. Young devils.'

Mr. Paradine frowned.

'Well, get on with your job,' he said brusquely, 'and don't stand gossiping. And I'll tell Smart to keep an eye on it. If I catch any of them at it they'll pay for it.'

He turned on his heel and, ignoring the others completely, walked quickly away down the track towards the village. The red-faced man touched his cap and bent again to his work. Mendel gazed after the retreating figure of Mr. Paradine with a broad and mischievous grin.

'Polished manners the Owner's got, hasn't he?' he said delightedly.

'God, that man's a tick!' said Ruth.

The workman glanced up with a slow smile, and his eyes turned to the rapidly diminishing figure, but he said nothing.

'What's exactly the trouble?' asked Mendel, turning to him and producing his cigarette-case. 'It's all right—he's out of sight now. I thought he'd go if I stopped and spoke to him.'

The workman straightened his back and rather diffidently took the proffered cigarette in large cracked fingers.

'Thank 'ee, sir.'

'Who's been taking the gates off?' asked Ruth eagerly. The red-faced man smiled.

'Well, miss, we don't rightly know, see. Mr. Paradine 'e'd give a bit to know that, 'e would.' He smiled again and looked at them with queer, cunning yokel eyes.

'But why have they?'

'Well, see, sir, the folks down Leaford they reckon as 'ow this is downland, see? Common land, like. And that this track 'ere's a right of way. An' Mr. Paradine 'e reck'ns it's 'is, see?'

'But why does he put gates and wire up? He doesn't keep cattle here, does he?'

The red-faced man smiled his slow smile.

'Well, 'e *is* doin' now, miss.' He scratched his head reflectively. ''Course,' he added solemnly, 'it ain't right to break it down and damage property, see.'

'I don't see why not if he's trying to enclose common land,' said Rufus.

The workman shook his head. 'Well, 'course, 'e reckons it's 'is,' he said. 'T'ain't as though anyone *wants* to come along 'ere, see?'

'When do they do it?' asked Mendel. 'At night?'

'Ah, that's right, sir. No one to see them up here there isn't.' He bent again to the damaged hinge. 'I reckon it's some of the young lads as do it.' He looked thoughtfully at his handiwork. 'I reckon I've mended this gate a matter of ten or a dozen times now,' he said reflectively.

Mendel turned away.

'Well, more power to their elbows,' he said, 'if they're trying to prevent the Owner from grabbing a bit more of their property.'

The red-faced man shook his head.

'Ah,' he said, 'but they didn't ought t'damage property, see, sir.' He adjusted his cap and slowly resumed his work. 'But Mr. Paradine 'e's goin' to put Smart on the watch for 'em now. Serve 'em right, the young devils. Good day, sir. Good day, miss.'

'I don't know who Mr. Smart is,' said Rufus as they walked on, 'but I hope he doesn't catch anything but a cold.'

Mendel smiled. 'I wouldn't worry,' he said. 'I know old Smart. He's the keeper. He won't work himself to death on that job.'

Rufus was frowning into the distance. 'It's an extraordinary thing,' he said, 'how easily the natural man becomes a natural servant. Look at that chap. It's *his* land Paradine is taking—*his* birthright. But all he can think of is that they oughtn't to destroy property.'

'They're queer people about here,' said Mendel thoughtfully. 'I never know quite what to make of them. But there's one thing—'

'Well?'

'They're very seldom as silly as they look. They *are* silly, of course—incredibly silly sometimes. But at others they trade on the silliness. You remember the story of the Wiltshire Moonrakers[72]— the men who bluffed the exciseman by telling him that they were raking in the water for the reflection of the moon because they thought it was a cheese?'

'Yes. It's a grand yarn.'

'Quite. Well, these people are the descendants of the moonrakers. Sometimes they really *are* raking for the moon. Sometimes not. And you never know.'

'The peculiar beauty of the downs,' said Mendel as they halted at the top of a rise, 'is that there is nothing whatever to see.'

Rufus smiled as he gazed out over the mighty expanse. 'I should have said there was a great deal.'

'Ah, yes. But a great deal of nothing. That's the point. You have here, for example, a view of about fourteen miles. But fourteen miles of what? A lot of rather dull grey sky, about three miles of grass, a few rather apologetic trees and then just distance. There isn't any "scenery". That's the great virtue. Otherwise we should probably be surrounded by charabancs,[73] picnic-parties and gramophones.'

'In February?'

'Probably. Take Stonehenge.[74] There you've got an "object of interest". See what happens. I've never been by Stonehenge yet when there hasn't been a charabanc parked in the road outside.'

'I have,' said Ruth. 'One moonlit night. There wasn't anyone. And *then* it looked every day of its age.'

Mendel picked up a flint and flung it idly down the slope.

'There's a legend,' he said, 'that no one can count the stones twice and get the same answer each time. But if you *can* and you count them seven times nine times and then stand in the middle, you will see a terrific apparition and drop dead.'

'Have you tried it?' asked Rufus with interest.

Mendel shook his head. 'I was going to once. But they make you pay to go in now. I don't mind taking a chance on dropping dead—after all, the apparition might be worth it. But I'm darned if I'm going to *pay* to be stricken dead. Besides,' he added moodily, 'you can't do that sort of thing in a crowd.'

'I'm going to run,' said Ruth suddenly.

She turned and went dashing down the long slope without another word. They watched in silence as the small black figure, arms and legs flying in the effort of keeping its balance, tore headlong down the grassy road.

'She'll break her neck,' said Rufus rather nervously, as she just succeeded in recovering from a long stagger. Mendel said nothing. He was gazing after the rapidly diminishing figure with a curious cold smile.

'It's extraordinary how ugly a woman looks when she runs,' he said at last, 'that queer, knock-kneed, carthorse effect.'

'I think she runs rather well,' said Rufus defensively. He was becoming uncomfortably aware that Mendel's outburst of the morning was not an isolated phenomenon, and the sneering tone annoyed him. Mendel smiled, without moving his eyes from the runner, now a small figure far below.

'You're intended to,' he said dryly.

Rufus flushed. 'What d'you mean?'

Mendel sighed. 'What d'you mean?' he repeated. 'It's a queer convention that, isn't it? The convention of asking a person what he means when you know perfectly well?' He looked at Rufus with a thoughtful frown. 'I wonder how it originated? I suppose the idea was to give the man a chance to back out and put some perfectly innocent construction on what he'd said. Like this. "You're a bloody liar!" "What d'you mean?" "Well, I don't mean you're *deliberately* lying, old man, but I don't think that's true…" See?'

Rufus hesitated. 'As it happens,' he said quietly, 'I really wanted to know what you meant. Did you mean that you think Ruth ran down there for—for *my* benefit? Because–'

Mendel looked at him with wide-open blue eyes.

'No!' he said solemnly. 'She ran down there because she *likes* running down places. Why else should she?' He gave a sudden loud roar of laughter. 'Come on!' he cried, 'I'll race you to her! Come on!' He set off racing down the path at a breakneck speed. Rufus, recovering from his surprise, set off after him. Far down the track he could see Ruth. She had stopped and was sitting waiting on the bank. Mendel, his arms waving like a windmill, was roaring with laughter and shouting as he ran.

'Come on, Rufus—give her ten! Let her rip!' Suddenly in his great roaring voice he began to sing:

'Patron, Patron, Patron das macht der Wind,
Patron…'[75]

He trod in a rut and staggered.

'Careful!' yelled Rufus breathlessly, as with a mighty effort he drew level.

'Patron das macht der Wind!'

Chapter X

Copywriter Compromised

'I shouldn't do that, blossom,' said Mendel warningly.

'Why not?' asked Ruth, pausing, queen in hand, and gazing at the board with puckered brow.

'Because if you do I shall mate you in—let me see—yes, in three moves.'

'Rot!' said Ruth, without conviction. She replaced the piece and studied the position carefully, chin on one small brown hand. 'You can't do anything of the sort,' she added, defiantly moving her queen.

Mendel heaved a resigned sigh.

'Well, no one can say you weren't warned.' He moved a rook. 'Check!'

'Well, that's all right. I just do this.'

'Quite,' said Mendel, 'but then I do *this*.'

'Oh!' said Ruth, aghast. Mendel sat back in his chair and shook his head at her sorrowfully.

'A lack of brains,' he said, 'allied to an inability to accept well-meant advice. That's *your* trouble.'

'Wait a minute,' said Ruth, settling down, chin in hand. 'There must be *some* way out of it…'

Rufus laid down *Urn Burial*[76] and rose to his feet.

'It's darned hot in here,' he said, taking a mighty breath.

'Be quiet,' said Ruth, 'I am in desperate case.'[77]

'Ah, well,' said Mendel comfortingly, 'you'll soon be out of your misery.'

Rufus strolled over to the window and looked out. It was a bright moonlit night—so bright that one could see the grass track, glimmeringly pale across the face of the hill. The shadow of the big barn fell, silent and incredibly dark, on the farmyard. He turned.

'I think I shall go out for a bit and get a breath of air. It's rather a gorgeous night.'

Ruth nodded without looking up. Mendel, lounging back in his chair, lit a cigarette.

'All right. Don't get lost, though.'

A cloud was passing over the moon as he climbed the hill. Fascinated, he watched the quick-moving shadows sliding over the grass, streaming smokily away and leaving the calm clear flood of dead moonlight. He took the path that they had taken that morning as a precaution. He knew the neighbouring slopes well enough by now, but after his experience in the snow he did not trust his sense of direction.

It was not solely a desire for air that had brought Rufus out. Gazing upwards at the clear, glittering void above him, he admitted to himself that he was faintly but quite unmistakably worried. For the first week after his fortuitous arrival at Three Trees his chief sensation had been one of relief—relief at his escape from the hateful rush and noise of London, and the even more hateful disappointments of Leaford. Mendel and Ruth—their kindness and their casual, matter-of-fact acceptance of his presence—he had accepted in the same unheeding glow of thankfulness in which a man accepts the improbabilities of a pleasant dream. But in the last few days there had been a change. There had been time to think—to consider—to observe rationally. This, as Mendel had frankly said, was clearly not Eden. Nor was it the simple logical existence which, in his first daze of pleasure, he had been inclined to think it. In fact the more he considered the more clear he became that even at Three Trees there were problems which were not entirely concerned with eating, sleeping, or even running down hills...

He reached the top of the first rise and gazed thoughtfully back at the farmhouse, lying dimly amongst the thick black shadows. A faint glimmer of light showed between the curtains. Presumably they were still playing chess...

'Problem one,' he murmured, 'is them.' He turned and strolled slowly on along the track. What was it? This odd thing that had flashed out so unmistakably lately? What was the basis of Mendel's alternate moods of tenderness and resentment? Because resentment it clearly was. Rufus remembered with surprise that he had never heard Mendel criticise Ruth except in terms of women as a whole. Women—women—he hated them—resented them—lashed them with contempt—sometimes. And then again-

'And problem two is how I come into it...'

It was only in the last forty-eight hours, Rufus reflected, that he had 'come into it' at all. He had envied Mendel his mistress, it was true. But that was inevitable. He had looked at the dark, close-cropped head and the slim, firm figure and thought... well, all the obvious things. But until yesterday they had always seemed so completely one—so completely uninterested in anyone but each other. Now it was different. He remembered a dozen jesting things which Mendel had said—things which he had scarcely noticed at the time—which now took on a new significance. It almost seemed now as though the big man expected something—as though he were looking on fatalistically at some comedy which was being played before his eyes. Jealous? Suspicious? It was absurd. Rufus shook his head. He had never done more than silently desire her. And she—she had been almost disconcertingly unmoved by him. Neither arch nor defensive. Just cheerily and pleasantly indifferent...

He stopped suddenly as he heard a faint movement in front of him. The moon had passed behind a heavy bank of cloud, but as he peered along the track he fancied he saw a couple of forms flit into the darkness. He stood for a moment, but the silence was gigantic and complete, and with a shrug he walked on, fancying that his senses were playing him tricks. It was not until his foot struck against something lying on the ground that his mind rushed back to the scene of that afternoon, and the workman at the gate. He bent and felt beneath his feet. The gate had been torn from its hinges and lay with all its bars broken across the track. He chuckled, and as he did so, a hand touched his arm. He swung round with a wild chill of fright running down his spine.

'What is then, mister, what is it?' said a low voice.

Rufus peered into the darkness. Dimly he could see several shadowy figures. For a moment he fancied he was in the hands of Mr. Paradine's guards. Then the significance of the broken gate and the silent group became clear.

'Hullo!' he said, trying hard to make his voice as cheerful and friendly as possible, 'what are you chaps up to? Pulling down the gates?'

There was a moment's pause. 'Never you mind, mister,' another voice said dangerously, 'you mind your business and we'll mind ours, see?'

'Oh, all right,' Rufus said with a laugh, 'I'll go for a walk another way.'

'That's right,' said the second voice, 'there's plenty of room round about, ain't there?'

'Lots,' said Rufus. A great internal laughter was shaking him as he heard the voice. 'Pull the lot down and good luck to you. They've no right to be here anyhow.'

There was no answer. The figures stood in suspicious silence.

'The only thing is,' added Rufus with a chuckle, 'mind you don't get caught. Mr. Paradine's putting Smart on your track.'

There was a moment's pause.

'Ah,' came from one figure at last, 'we know all about 'im, don't us?'

'Ah,' said another voice, 'we do. Now, mister—it's a good night for a walk.'

Rufus turned. 'All right,' he said, 'good night and good luck.'

There was no reply. Then, as he walked away, the moon slid out from behind her cloud for a fleeting second, and he saw clearly the thing he wished to see, before they could turn quickly away. Rufus laughed.

'Good night, old man,' he called softly, 'and to-morrow you'll mend it for the eleventh time, I suppose.'

But the red-faced man had vanished with his friends into the darkness.

Ruth was alone when he returned. The chess-board still stood on the table, but Mendel had disappeared. Ruth was sitting in front of the fire, crouching in that characteristic attitude on the stool, her chin pillowed in her hand, and the red glow from the big log fire flickering on her face.

'Hullo, blossom! Where's Pip?'

She turned the small, fire-flushed face towards him with a smile of welcome.

'Out in the barn. Working.' She pulled the stool a little to one side to make room for him. 'Have a nice walk?'

'Grand!' said Rufus with a reminiscent chuckle. He seized one of the big old easy chairs and lugged it up to the fire. 'You know the bloke we saw mending the gate to-day?'

'Yes?'

'Well, he's out there now with some of his pals, breaking it down again.'

To his surprise she nodded calmly.

'Don't you think it's really rather a gorgeous situation? Being so concerned about comrade Paradine's property, and talking about the "young devils" from the village and then–'

'I'm not surprised,' said Ruth with a little smile. 'In fact I guessed that was it.'

'You guessed? But how?'

She shrugged her shoulders. 'He was too cautious with us and too humble with Paradine and too indignant altogether. I know they all hate Paradine. And when a Downsman hates a person he usually does that—draws back into his shell and is very humble and very silly.'

'Well, he took *me* in all right.'

'Yes. And I suppose he takes Paradine in. But neither of you know about places like this.' She looked at him with a smile. 'D'you realise that that man will be related to half Leaford? *He'd* know who was doing it, even if he weren't actually in it himself. He may have to work for Paradine—there isn't much else for people to do here. He owns the place. But he'll hate Paradine all the same. This is *their* place—his and his relatives, as you said to-day. And they'll think of Paradine as a thief—a new-comer—a gent from London. They'll take his money and touch their hats and be very humble. But they'll laugh at him behind his back and swindle him right and left. Paradine thinks they're fools and they let him. It suits their book—makes it easier to get back at him.'

Rufus nodded. There was a long silence. Ruth's eyes were back on the fire. He covertly studied her as she sat—the black boyish head and the slim neck—the firm outward curve of her small breasts, sharply outlined by the tight scarlet jersey—the slim shining legs which she gently stroked with one small brown hand.

His mind went back to the day they had gone tobogganing—to the soft weight pressing against him. Mendel had suggested that she should undress with them in front of the fire, but she had refused… Rufus swallowed hard and deliberately and carefully loosened his tightly clenched fist.

'Pip will find it pretty cold out there to-night,' he said in matter-of-fact tones. His voice sounded curiously loud in the silence.

'Oh, I don't know,' Ruth smiled at the fire. 'Sometimes he works out there for hours in the winter. It used to be much worse before he got the stove.'

'Does he go out there and leave you alone?'

She looked at him with a smile. 'Yes, Rufus dear. Quite, *quite* alone,' she said with mock pathos, 'and a very good thing too for all concerned.'

'You like being alone?' he said, foolishly.

She smiled again, the queer, almost mysterious smile.

'That depends entirely on the alternative.'

'I mean,' Rufus lied rather clumsily, 'I wondered whether my being here… spoiled it. Having me about and so on…'

She turned and gazed at him with the big dark eyes.

'That's always been a worry of yours, hasn't it?'

'Well, naturally, I mean–'

She shook her head. 'Then it's a very silly one.'

'Then… then do you like me?' Rufus blushed slightly at the inanity of the remark.

Ruth looked at him in silence for a moment. Then she nodded slightly and her eyes went moodily back to the fire.

'Yes, Rufus, my dear, I like you very much. I think you're nice,' she said rather wearily.

Rufus frowned. 'Nice!...' he said in rather hurt tones.

'Well, pleasant then. Pleasant to have tame about the place.' She paused in her idle stroking of the shining leg and examined the stocking closely. 'Damn—I've got a ladder.' She sighed. 'I suppose it's my own fault for wearing silk stockings in a place like this. But I can never quite face the prospect of nice, sensible wool.'

Rufus said nothing. He was aware of a curious, maddening electric tingle in his limbs which curled his fingers and toes into almost painful tension. Ruth had pulled her skirts a few inches above her knees, and was examining the ladder with resigned woe. Rufus swallowed hard.

'If you don't stop doing that,' he said in a low voice, 'I shall probably stop being either tame or nice.'

She looked up in surprise, the skirt hem still in her hand. 'Doing what?' she inquired.

Then, following his eyes, 'Oh, I see. Immodestly displaying my knees?' She smiled a rather crooked little smile. 'Come, come! Surely you've got past that stage, Rufus my dear? I mean to say—'

'As it happens, I haven't. Not at the moment, anyhow.'

She looked at him for a moment. The dark eyes were infinitely serious and he could have sworn to that queer flash of dread he had seen in them sometimes before. But her lips still smiled.

'But, Rufus—I must deal with this ladder…'

'Well, do it some other time, then,' he said harshly.

She hesitated, an impish grin playing over the wide-lipped mouth. Rufus leaned forward in his chair.

'See here,' he said quietly, 'are you looking for trouble?'

'No, ladders,' she said faintly.

'Well, then let me tell you that if—'

He paused as he met the dark, shining, challenging, frightened eyes. Then, suddenly he stretched out a hand.

'Come here!' he said coldly.

She hesitated, and then, rising slowly to her feet, came and stood before him. Her wide-open eyes never left his face. Her hands, tightly clenched, hung limply at her sides. He put out an arm and, encircling her waist, pulled her down, unresisting, on to his knees.

'What are you trying to do to me?' he said in a low voice.

Ruth made no reply. She sat upright on his knees, still staring into his face. Gently he laid his hand on the silken knee, and stroked the warm, soft firmness. Beyond the silkiness of the stocking there was a warmer, smoother satin, warm and alive and incredibly pleasant beneath his fingers. A shudder ran through her, her eyes flickered and closed. He shifted his position gently and drew the black head down upon his shoulder. It lay there, strangely heavy and inert. Rufus peered at the pale, lifeless face, and then, gently and experimentally, kissed the full red lips. They flickered for a moment into a smile. She opened her eyes and smiled up at him strangely. He was surprised and pleased, and kissed her again as gently as before. She slipped one scarlet woollen arm comfortably round his neck and wriggled her head into a more comfortable position.

'Nice Rufus,' she said softly, 'nice to have tame about the place.'

'You know, you're a bad girl,' he said, reprovingly. 'A thoroughly bad girl.'

'I'm sorry,' she said meekly, gazing up at him with the peculiar gamin[78] smile.

'No, you're not,' said Rufus. 'You're a deliberate and calculated hussy. And that business about the ladder was one of the most cold-blooded bits of depravity I've ever seen.'

'But there *is* a ladder,' she protested.

'So I observed.' He grinned down at her delightedly, pleased to find the curious, awkward tenseness dissolving into this familiar, vulgar, silly sex game. He gently pulled up the skirt and examined the silken knees. 'Yes, here it is. And it goes—'

'No, it doesn't,' said Ruth with a wriggle. 'That's me.'

'As a matter of interest,' said Rufus, exploring, 'do you *wear* underclothes? Because—'

She laid a gently restraining hand on his.

'Yes, but they happen to be rather brief. No, Rufus, no further except on business.'

'But I am on business.'

'No, you're not. Besides, I have moral scruples. One must draw the line somewhere and I draw it three inches above the top of my stockings.'

'All right, then, you're going to kiss me.'

She heaved a resigned sigh and, closing her eyes, held up her face with pursed lips.

'Oh, no!' said Rufus firmly, 'I didn't say I was going to kiss *you*. I said you were going to kiss me. Properly.'

She hesitated for a moment and the dark eyes opened. Then she suddenly drew his face down to hers, and he felt the brush of her tongue between his parted lips. The tingle of his limbs became a painful burning, and for a moment the playful coarseness and the tense awkwardness vanished together in a wild spasm of muscular contraction. The grip of his arms tightened as though he would crush the slim body.

'God, my love,' he whispered hoarsely. He was pleased, disappointed, happy, downcast, lusting and afraid.

Half an hour later, Ruth sat up, passed a tentative hand over her hair and said, 'I wonder how Pip's getting on?'

Rufus, who for some time had completely forgotten Mendel's existence, experienced a sharp pang of uneasiness, which might have been remorse, or self-reproach, but which felt much more like small-boy guilt.

He looked at Ruth inquiringly, feeling badly in need of a cue. The provocative way in which she had challenged him to make love to her and the mixture of tenseness and playfulness in her submission, had left him floundering badly. Was this sort of thing, he wondered, quite in order? Was it merely a part of the freedom of the odd household? Or was it a secret unfaithfulness, to be kept from an unsuspecting Mendel?

Ruth had risen from his lap and was staring out into the brilliant moonlight.

'If he doesn't come in soon,' she said, 'he'll be frozen stiff.' Her tone was conversational and unhelpful.

Rufus rose to his feet and, fumbling in his pocket, found and lit a cigarette. He was annoyed to find that his hands were shaking. He threw the spent match into the fire and, turning, was on the point of blurting out, 'I say, Ruth—do you think Pip will mind?' It suddenly occurred to him, however, that the question was an impossible one in his present state of ignorance. If Mendel *would* mind, it would imply that this was a mere flippant flirtation, which might hurt her feelings. If, on the other hand, Mendel would not, then she might be horrified at the mere suggestion of deceiving him. Rufus frowned and shook his head. The situation was decidedly obscure. But clearly his best course was to act as though he understood perfectly, and to take his cue from Ruth. At the moment the only thing for it was tactful silence.

Ruth turned away from the window and glanced at the clock.

'Come on!' she said. 'Let's go and dig him out.'

It was cold outside, but Mendel was still hard at work. They heard the steady rasp of a saw as they approached the barn, and through the window they could see him, cutting up a large plank by the light of a smoky oil lamp. Ruth pushed open the half-doors, and the familiar fragrance of the oil stove greeted them. Mendel looked up as they entered.

'Hullo,' he said.

'Haven't you nearly finished?' asked Ruth. 'It's almost eleven.'

Mendel glanced from one to the other and down again at his plank. 'I wish to God I'd got a circular saw,' he said inconsequently, 'this is like sawing concrete.' He straightened his back and, laying down the saw, lit a cigarette. Despite the cold, he had discarded his jacket and his rolled sleeves displayed the massive strength of his forearms and biceps. He brushed a trace of sweat from his forehead and ran a hand through the mop of yellow hair.

'Have a nice walk, Rufus?'

'Yes. I came on the chappie we saw mending the gate to-day. He was breaking it down again.'

Mendel roared with laughter.

'Great! With Smart the keeper helping him, I suppose?'

'I don't know. There were some others.'

'Did you give them a hand?'

'They wouldn't give me a chance. They just told me to go for a walk somewhere else.'

Mendel shook his head. 'You should have helped with the good work. Tell you what—let's have an expedition on our own one night with a pair of wire cutters and an axe. I'd love to have a go at that little swine Paradine.'

'They seem to be dealing with him quite well by themselves.'

Mendel rolled down his sleeves and, picking up his torn and disreputable tweed jacket, threw it carelessly over his arm. He turned out the lamp and led the way into the moonlit farmyard.

'Well, my love,' he slipped his arm through Ruth's, 'and have *you* had a nice evening?'

Rufus fancied that there was faint mockery in his tone.

'Most enjoyable, thank you,' said Ruth solemnly.

'Knitting by the fireside, eh?'

'Knitting by the fireside. Turning a very pretty heel, in fact.'

Mendel laughed and slipped an arm round her waist. Rufus, following them into the house, frowned in annoyance. This was all very well, but it did not answer the vital question. These queer, sarcastic, significant questions were one of Mendel's favourite ways of talking to Ruth. They might mean anything or nothing. Rufus found her hand in the darkness of the passage and squeezed it hard. She squeezed in reply, and retained it in hers for a moment. But maddeningly, casually, she released it before they passed into the lighted room, making the gesture neither significantly private nor equally significantly public. He looked at her questioningly and she smiled. But it was just the usual gamin grin and might have meant anything.

Mendel pulled up his favourite chair and sank into it with a sigh of relief.

'God, my back aches from the sawing!' he said. He hooked the stool towards him and placed his feet upon it. 'Quite soon I'm going to write a book on physical sensations. And in it backache will have a prominent place.'

'It's a queer pain,' said Rufus, politely, but rather vaguely, sitting down on the opposite side of the fire.

'Pain? But it isn't a pain at all. It's an ache. Aches and pains are entirely different. Pains are nearly always fundamentally unpleasant. But aches are usually rather pleasant. Like this.'

'How about earache and toothache and headache? Would you call them pleasant?'

'No. But they aren't real aches. They're pains.'

'Define,' said Rufus, wearily, glancing towards the door. Ruth had vanished into the kitchen.

'A true ache,' said Mendel firmly, 'is a thing which is annoying but funny. The sort of sensation which makes you groan and giggle at the same time. Backache. The feeling you get when you knock your elbow or your Achilles tendon. The feeling you get when something hits you hard on the thigh. Have you ever had that? It's excruciating. Excruciatingly funny. Rather like a mild edition of a sexual orgasm. Hullo, sweet,' he added, as Ruth appeared, 'what doing?'

'Making tea,' said Ruth. 'Tea at eleven o'clock at night is debauchery, but I thought we'd debauch.'

'Good,' said Mendel.

She walked slowly across the room and pulled casually at his thick hair. 'I thought you'd like it.' She kicked away the stool and perched herself on his knee. Rufus drew a quick breath. It was quite a normal thing for her to do, but at the moment it seemed significant.

'Here, no…' Mendel sat up, protesting. 'Get off, you lump. I'm tired.' He pushed her unceremoniously from her perch. 'I won't be sat on. I want to sit down and be quiet after all that sweating about.' He pointed to Rufus with a grin. 'Go and sit on him if you want to sit on anybody. He's young and active and he hasn't been working.'

Rufus looked at Ruth sharply. She was regarding Mendel with offended dignity.

'Very well,' she said with mock hauteur, 'if you don't want me there's plenty as do.' She extended a small piece of pink tongue and turned to Rufus. 'Aren't there, Rufus, my pet?' she said amorously. 'You'll have me, won't you?'

'Sure!' said Rufus, putting an arm round her as she coolly sat down on his knees. 'Come to Daddy.'

Ruth turned to Mendel.

'There you are! You're not the only lap on the beach. An attractive girl need never look far for a home.'

Mendel lay back in his chair and grinned his queer cynical grin.

'*What* a pretty pair,' he said mockingly.

Rufus smiled rather uncomfortably. Really, it was all very confusing. Mendel closed his eyes and continued to differentiate between aches and pains at some length.

At twelve, Mendel abandoned his thesis, finished his cold tea and fell silent for a while, staring at them unwinkingly with cold, thoughtful eyes. Ruth, who had never even simulated interest in his theory, was apparently asleep, her head pillowed comfortably on Rufus's shoulder. Rufus cautiously shifted her weight from one thigh to the other, and pinched experimentally at his numbed flesh. After half an hour even Ruth seemed extraordinarily heavy. He almost wished she would move. With Mendel present there was no possibility of exploiting the intimate position, and really she might just as well sit in a chair.

Mendel noticed the slight movement and grinned rather maliciously. 'Getting a bit heavy?' he inquired.

'My leg's gone to sleep,' said Rufus.

'They always get heavy after a bit,' said Mendel. 'It's very nice to have them at first, but after a while the weight begins to paralyse your limbs.'

Rufus did not reply, but gave another cautious wriggle. Ruth sat up suddenly.

'Sorry,' she said sleepily. 'Am I too heavy?'

'It's all right,' said Rufus.

She rose to her feet and stretched herself like a sleepy cat. 'I'm going to bed now anyhow.'

Mendel smiled. 'I thought you were going to spend the night on Rufus,' he said softly.

Rufus looked sharply from one to the other. Ruth was looking coldly at Mendel.

'I am going to spend the night in bed,' she said heavily. 'It's a habit of mine.'

'All right,' said Mendel, with a mocking little bow. 'We'll join you later.'

She hesitated for a moment as though about to speak. Then, changing her mind, she turned to the door. 'Good night,' she said non-committally, to the room at large. The door closed gently behind her.

Mendel leaned back in his chair and lit a fresh cigarette. 'The gentlemen are now left to their port,' he said quietly. Rufus smiled rather nervously. His instincts told him that something of a show-down was imminent.

'And how goes the pursuit of the simple life?' said Mendel with a faint smile. 'Still enjoying it?'

'Immensely,' said Rufus politely.

'That's right.' Mendel was rather too detached and cordial. 'Eden's proving satisfactory, eh?'

'Yes.'

'I rather wonder at that,' said the big man thoughtfully.

'Why?'

Mendel shrugged his shoulders. 'Because as I told you before, I don't believe you've got any very clear idea of what you want. You know a lot of the things you don't want, but you seem a bit woolly about what you do. Frankly,' he added, 'I should have expected you to be getting bored and restless by now.'

'Why?' asked Rufus again.

'Because at the moment,' said Mendel slowly, 'you aren't doing anything. Mental or physical.'

'But you yourself were very emphatic that one shouldn't rush round doing things.'

Mendel waved a hand. 'Oh, quite. If you're the type that *can* do nothing. But I shouldn't have said you were.'

'I'm fundamentally lazy,' said Rufus with a faint smile. Mendel shook his head.

'I doubt it. And even if you were it wouldn't affect my point.' He leaned back in his chair and looked at Rufus thoughtfully. 'You told me you left London because one half of you—the physical half—was moribund. Is it any more alive now?'

'In some ways,' said Rufus rather doubtfully.

'Oh, yes, I dare say. You now go for ten-mile walks where previously you travelled by Tube. But any bank clerk on holiday does that. When we run down hills you run down hills too, and think what jolly fun it all is. But you don't run down hills by yourself.' He flicked the ash from his cigarette with a gesture which was almost irritable. 'Don't you see what I mean? The one point in your being here is that you're free. Absolutely free to do what you like, within the limitations of the place and your own physical and mental limitations. You aren't just a guest who's more or less bound to do what we do. You can go and look for this physical existence you're so keen about in any way you like. But you don't. You come for walks with us. You run down hills with us, you play futile games with us, you eat with us. But you aren't an individual grabbing with both hands a chance to please yourself. You're just accepting *our* ideas about life now instead of somebody else's.'

Rufus flushed at the almost contemptuous tone.

'I'm sorry if I've been inflicting myself on you.'

Mendel gave a disgusted snort. 'Oh, for God's sake—' he said irritably. 'That's precisely the attitude I mean. That's just exactly what the bank clerk on holiday would say. *I* don't mind. I don't care in the least what you do. It's *you* I'm thinking about.' He leaned forward earnestly. 'Look here—a man who lives in towns and does an ordinary job of work is forced to accept the technique of life of the people he lives with. There's practically no scope for originality. He keeps the same hours—does the same work—eats the same food—amuses himself in the same way—as thousands of other people. He can't avoid it. The best he can do in the way of altering the technique of life is to try some piddling little precious unimportant change, like the man who had a pet lobster which he used to take for walks on a silver lead. Your Bohemian—your man who wants to cultivate a reputation for originality—simply lives like ten thousand other Bohemians instead of like forty million ordinary citizens. He can't really get away and be himself, because he can't get away from the stink and infection of other people of some sort.'

He threw his cigarette into the fire with unnecessary violence. Rufus remained sullenly silent.

'Well, you come here,' Mendel went on emphatically, 'and you have the chance to work things out for yourself. What happens?

Instead of getting on with it and not giving a damn about us, you simply drop in and accept what *we* do exactly as you accepted what other people did in London. The only difference is that there were eight or nine million[79] of them and there are only two of us.'

'But it happens that *I* like the things you do,' protested Rufus. 'This is just the sort of life I wanted. Only you happen to have thought of it first.'

'Rot!' Mendel swept away the protest unceremoniously. 'What you mean is that it's an improvement on your previous life. A nice ready-made holiday which saves you the trouble of thinking for yourself. You've got some woolly idea about leading a simpler more physical life, away from people and noise. You come here and find this place. It's in the country. Good. There are only two other people. Good. One goes for walks and runs down hills and toboggans and does a bit of amateur joinery. Good! The perfect physical life! Just what you've always been looking for. Ready made off the peg, and saves you all the trouble of getting your woolly ideas into any sort of shape.'

'Well, what the hell do you expect me to do?' demanded Rufus heatedly.

Mendel shrugged his shoulders.

'That's entirely up to you. *I* can't tell you. Nor can anyone else. Either you *know* what you want to do or else you're just an ordinary sheep which will accept anyone else's ideas. But you can't come here talking about a full physical life, go for an occasional walk, help me saw a bit of wood, and then say everything's perfect. It would be infinitely more to the point if you insisted on breaking the ice on the dew pond to bathe every day, only had a meal once in three days for the fun of feeling hungry, raped Ruth, hit me with a club if I protested, and set the place on fire to see what it felt like to be really hot.' He shook his head dolefully. 'Enterprise. That's what you lack. No ideas.'

'But fooling apart–' began Rufus with a smile.

'But I assure you I'm not fooling,' said Mendel earnestly. 'I'm perfectly serious.'

'But it's perfectly obvious that I can't…'

'*Can't?* Who's stopping you? That's the whole point. You can do dozens of interesting things if you like. That's the only reason for being here.'

'Well, then, why don't you?'

'Why don't I what?'

'Make exciting experiments?'

'I do. I have. Any I want to. This whole life *is* an experiment. An experiment of mine. But at the moment you will insist on sharing it instead of carrying out one of your own.'

There was a short silence.

'You wouldn't like it if I did,' said Rufus with a grin.

Mendel frowned. '*I* shouldn't like it?' he said irritably. 'But what the hell has that got to do with it? The only thing you've got to worry about is whether you'd like it.' He kicked angrily at the stool. 'I've told you already that I don't care in the least what you do, any more than I expect you to care what I do. If what you wanted and what I wanted happened to clash, I should fight tooth and nail to get what *I* wanted. But only by socking you in the jaw or something like that. Certainly not by appealing to your instincts as a gentleman or your public-school training. The trouble with you, Rufus, is that you want something new but not *too* new. You want it to be nice and familiar and easy to handle, so that you can apply exactly the same technique as you've applied all your life. You're the sort of man who thinks it would be grand to fight for your mate and hunt for your food. And you'd get a professional to teach you to hold your stone club with the overlapping grip, you'd want to fight Queensberry rules,[80] and you'd do your hunting in a scarlet coat.' He paused for breath.

'In fact,' said Rufus, 'you haven't much use for me at all.'

'None,' said Mendel with his sudden charming grin. 'You

seem to me completely pointless and rather deplorable. I shall now go to bed.'

They separated at the top of the stairs.

'Well, good night,' said Mendel with a smile, 'and I hope you have a really nice physical night.' The grin hardened slightly. 'From what I can see of the situation I should think it quite likely.'

He opened his door quietly and vanished without waiting for a reply. Slowly, shielding the flickering candle flame with his hand, Rufus walked along the narrow passage to his own room. A sudden thought struck him as he opened the door, and his heart gave a quick and painful thump. But the bed was chastely empty, and his pyjamas lay forlornly on the turned-down sheet.

Rufus undressed slowly and thoughtfully. One never knew with Mendel, of course, but unless he was bluffing even more childishly than usual he must realise that one wanted Ruth… 'Rape Ruth and hit me with a club if—' Judging from the earlier part of the evening, rape would hardly be called for… He climbed slowly into his pyjamas and shook his head bemusedly. But even there one was not really sure. Ruth had allowed herself to be kissed and fondled. But there had been that queer mixture of brazenness and fear. There was really no guarantee that at any moment the apparent abandon of both of them would not give place to an appalled respectability. After all, the most theoretically advanced of Bohemians had a nasty habit of becoming positively Victorian in a practical emergency. And the prospect of Mendel as a furious and outraged moralist was not inviting. He looked distressingly strong in the arms. Rufus shook his head again and climbed into bed. On the other hand, if one took Mendel at his word, it would apparently be quite in order to go along and demand the loan of Ruth for the night. Or she might just come. He sat up, struck by a sudden thought. Perhaps that was the meaning of the big man's final cryptic remark? Rufus considered for a moment and then, climbing out of bed, he gently unlatched the door and left it ajar. That, he reflected, at least showed an accommodating spirit. He returned to bed and, after a moment's hesitation, blew out the light and lay for some time listening intently. Once there was a slight creaking in the passage, and he could hear his heart thudding furiously as he strained eyes and ears. But nothing happened and quite soon he went to sleep.

Rufus was awakened the next morning by sunlight shining on his face. He wriggled sleepily for a while, but the sunlight was insistent, and at length he reluctantly opened his eyes and blinked up at the heavy oak beam which ran across the ceiling above his head. It was unusual to wake up of his own accord. Usually, Mendel or Ruth or both, fully dressed, and with every appearance of having been up for some hours, would arrive with hot water and loud sarcastic cries. He glanced out of the small, old-fashioned, leaded window. The sun had risen above the brow of the overshadowing hill and was shining brilliantly in a cloudless blue sky. The hillside looked fresh and green. He reflected that, if one had the energy, it would be nice to go out for an early morning walk. As he meditated, without much enthusiasm, on the possibility, he suddenly became aware that the sun did not usually strike his bedroom in the early morning. In fact– He fumbled under his pillow and produced his watch. The hands stood at nine-thirty. He sat up with a puzzled frown and held the watch to his ear. It was ticking faithfully. Listening intently he could hear no sound in the house. Everything was absolutely still. With a grunt he swung himself out of bed, slipping on the slippers and dressing-gown which he had borrowed from Mendel on a permanent basis. Clearly the household was oversleeping for once.

He padded softly along the passage to the top of the stairs and listened. There was still no sound below. He smiled grimly. It would be pleasant to rouse them violently and cuttingly in his turn. He paused at the bedroom door. All was silent. He tapped gently and entered.

'Hullo, Rufus,' said a voice. Ruth, wide awake, was lying in the large double bed, a book in her hand. There was no sign of Mendel. Rufus advanced into the room.

'Hullo. Where's Pip?'

'Out. He's gone for a walk. Said it was too nice to stay in bed.'

'So it is,' said Rufus without conviction. His eyes were on the sleek green satin pyjama jacket which covered the curve of her breasts.

'Do you know it's half-past nine?'

'Is it?' she said, stretching herself with lazy abandon, and gazing up at him with the shining dark eyes. 'What an awful thing!'

Rufus sat down on the edge of the bed and stared at her thoughtfully. 'Lazy!' he said reprovingly.

'But, Rufus, I was tired.'

He laid a hand on the figure beneath the bedclothes.

'Do you know what you ought to have done by now?'

'No,' she said peacefully. 'Tell me.'

'You ought to have sprung up with a glad cry, gone for a six-mile walk, fetched the milk, and cooked the breakfast, singing little snatches of song.'

'But I tell you I was tired,' she said pathetically.

'Tired!' said Rufus, 'bah!'

'Frightfully.' She looked at him accusingly. 'And anyhow you haven't shaved.'

'I was waiting for someone to bring me some water,' said Rufus plaintively.

'Poor Rufus.' She put out one bare arm and took his hand. 'But, love,' she added quickly, 'you're absolutely freezing.'

'No, I'm not; it's quite warm.'

'Rot. You'll catch pneumonia.' She threw back the clothes invitingly. 'Come into the office and get warm.'

He hesitated for a moment and looked at her steadily. She

smiled up at him, the curious urchin smile. The bedclothes flung back showed the slim, pyjama-trousered form, lying snugly on its side. Rufus stripped off the dressing-gown and kicked off the slippers and slid in beside her.

'That's better. Why, you're like ice.'

He put his arms round her and held her tightly.

'These are very pleasant pyjamas,' he said carefully.

'Nice, but old,' said Ruth.

They looked at one another for a moment and grinned. Honour was satisfied, and casualness had been paid its due. He ran his hands silently over the warm smooth figure. Then, gently and firmly, he unbuttoned the green jacket and slipped it off. Ruth assisted with a frank and accommodating wriggle. He placed a hand on the small, firm, warm breast.

'Nice,' he said quietly. He slipped his hands inside the elastic of the pyjama trousers and slipped them down over her feet.

'Take yours off too,' said Ruth.

He did so. She heaved a long sigh as their naked bodies pressed together and hugged him to her with all her strength.

Some time later, Rufus, returning from some unfathomable depth, heard her speaking softly and drowsily.

'Rufus, my love—'

'Yes, darling?'

'That was *very* awful, wasn't it?'

'Very,' said Rufus sleepily, 'at least it was for me. I hope it was for you…'

It was nearly half-past ten before they came down to breakfast. A used tea-cup, a loaf, and some butter showed that Mendel had fended for himself. They made themselves some tea and smoked, but neither wanted food.

Rufus was surprised to find how little change the last hour had made in the situation. When at last they had roused themselves, Ruth had at once retired into her shell of ordinary everyday friendliness. He knew now that it was not the detachment of *blasé* use. For she had made love with a peculiar tigerish intensity, mixed with a tenderness which made the idea of mere wanton unfaithfulness absurd. She had taken and given with all she had. But now, as she sat calmly sipping her tea, there was nothing to suggest this complete and ardent excitement.

'Pip must have gone a long way,' she said. 'He went out just before eight.'

'Yes,' said Rufus abstractedly. The question which had puzzled him for so long had reached the stage where an answer was imperative.

'Ruth,' he said suddenly, 'will he mind? About us?'

She looked at him and smiled. There was something a little hard and restrained in her face.

'Mind? Why no. He won't mind. Why should he? He didn't want me at that moment and he likes you.'

Rufus frowned. 'It's very queer,' he said thoughtfully. 'I can never quite make him out. Of course, being entirely logical I suppose one wouldn't mind. Not if one thinks like he does about things. But—'

'But what?' asked Ruth quietly.

'Well, I don't know. I suppose I'm old-fashioned. But it seems queer that he should love you as much as he does and yet—yet feel like that about it.'

'Does it?' said Ruth dully. 'I suppose so. Still, there it is.'

'Then it won't matter if we tell him?'

She looked at him in surprise.

'Tell him? What—that we've been to bed together? Why should we?'

'Then you'd rather just keep quiet about it?'

She rose suddenly and walked across to the window with a frown. 'You don't understand at all,' she said almost impatiently.

'Well, darn it!' said Rufus. 'Either we tell him or we keep it to ourselves. Clearly.'

Ruth blew a cloud of blue smoke from the window. It floated serenely out of the casement and vanished with a quick flicker in the gentle breeze.

'Can't you see,' she said gently, 'that it isn't a question of confessing our sins or keeping a secret? Can't you understand that Pip will neither like nor dislike it particularly? That he just won't be interested?'

'*Interested?*...'

'No. Of course he won't. It doesn't affect him directly, so he won't be interested. I tell you, he didn't want me at that moment. As a matter of fact, he doesn't want me much at all at present. You won't expect to rush up and tell him what you've had for breakfast, will you? And you won't think it necessary to keep what you've had for breakfast a deadly secret either. It just doesn't matter. He'll ask if he wants to know. As a matter of fact he asked me last night. Very casually.'

'What–?'

'If we'd slept together. I think he thought it was rather odd and amusing that we hadn't, but that was all–' She broke off and turned with a bitter little smile. 'So don't start worrying about Pip,' she said more cheerfully, 'because you can bet your life he'll never spend much time worrying about you.'

There was a long silence.

'I *don't* understand,' said Rufus helplessly. 'I don't understand either of you.'

She came across the room and kissed him lightly on the cheek.

'Poor Rufus! Never mind. You will one day when you grow up.' She slipped a hand through his arm. 'Come on and help me make the beds. I'm all behind this morning.'

An hour later Mendel returned. He was in high spirits and he carried a hare which he had been given by Smart the keeper.

'It's a darned shame to have killed it,' he said, stroking the long, black-tipped ears lovingly. 'But as he offered it to me I thought we may as well have it. The next best thing to a live hare is a jugged hare.' He threw the soft body on the table and, sitting down, lit a cigarette. 'What time did you slugs get up?' he inquired.

'About half-past ten,' said Rufus rather uncomfortably.

'Half-past ten on a morning like this! I suppose that's what you call a fuller physical life?' said Mendel, mischievously.

'It was,' replied Ruth calmly, picking up the hare and making for the kitchen.

'Was it, by God!' Mendel laughed. 'Well, look here,' he turned to Rufus. 'To-morrow, my lad, *you're* going to get up and come with me. I've found a tree.'

'A tree?' said Rufus, vaguely.

'Yes. A beauty.'

'What are we going to do? Climb it?'

'No. It's blown down. A beech. Beeches seldom blow down, but when they do they make grand logs—miles better than this damned elm stuff, which never burns properly.' He kicked contemptuously at the logs which stood on end before the fire. 'So to-morrow we're going to sally forth with saws, and cut it up and bring it in. See?'

'Sounds fun,' said Rufus.

'Yes. It's only about a couple of miles away and it'll be a nice job before breakfast.'

'You'll have to call me.'

Mendel grinned. 'I will.'

Chapter XI

Interlude – Trombone Tacet[81]

'Do you know,' said Rufus, thoughtfully, 'I only realised to-day that I haven't seen a paper for Lord knows how long?'

'Do you want to?' asked Mendel with a smile.

'No. I don't mean that. But it's odd to think that one doesn't miss papers here, whereas in London if you don't get your morning and evening paper you feel that you've definitely lost touch with things.'

'Quite,' said Mendel. 'You have, too. If you live in that world, you must have papers. And a wireless set. And a car. Because you're entirely dependent on other people, and if you depend on other people you must know what they're doing. Not long ago some peasants in Russia arrived at Moscow with presents of salt for the Czar. They didn't know there had been a revolution. Why should they? It didn't make any difference to them. It's the same here.' He picked up his jacket and put it on.

'Stopping?' asked Rufus in surprise.

'Yes. I'm tired of wood for the moment.' Mendel turned out the light and led the way into the farmyard. 'It's the same with one's sense of time,' he said, as they walked across to the house.

'When I first came here I always carried a watch. I couldn't get used to feeling that time literally didn't matter at all.'

'I can't yet,' said Rufus.

'No. You showed it then. You were surprised because I stopped working, because usually I go on longer than that. Longer in hours, I mean. But nowadays I realise that time is an absurd concept.'

'How d'you mean?'

'Well, people always tell you that sixty seconds make one minute and sixty minutes one hour, and that an hour is a measurable, invariable, mathematical thing which is somehow tied up with the sun and so on. But it isn't like that at all. One's common sense tells one so.'

He led the way into the big low room and, sitting down, lit a cigarette.

'How?' said Rufus. 'I don't quite follow.'

'Well, take the simplest possible case. Supposing I'm doing something which really absorbs me. I work for what my senses tell me is a very short time, and the fool clocks tell me that two hours have gone. Then again I am waiting for something and I wait what my senses tell me is an hour, and the clock says I have waited five minutes. Mathematically, the clock may be right. But it's ridiculous to order one's life by mathematics. Yet most people do.'

'Time was made for man and not man for time,'[82] said Rufus, smiling.

'More than that. Man *makes* time. It's a function of himself. For example, from my point of view I have worked for rather longer than usual this evening. Mathematically, you would say that I've worked for much less time. But the only person who can say is myself. Mathematical time multiplied by me equals real time. With me as the variable factor.'

'Very nice,' said Rufus, 'but scarcely practical for general application.'

'Of course not—that's why mathematical time was invented. So that all the sheep could baa together.'

Ruth came in from the kitchen.

'Hullo,' she said, 'finished?'

'Bored with wood,' said Mendel, briefly. He put out an arm and slipped it round her waist. 'What d'you say to going down to the pub? Rufus has never been and I feel a quite unusual yearning for my fellow men.'

Ruth nodded. 'All right.' She turned to Rufus. 'About once a month we go and contact civilisation in the Bell. It's rather a nice place.'

'I stayed in the Angel,' said Rufus, 'and that was a bloody joint.'

'Oh, yes, it is. But the Bell's quite fun sometimes.' She looked inquiringly at Mendel. 'How about food? Hungry?'

Mendel shook his head.

'Are you, Rufus?'

'Not very.'

'Good. Then we can go right away.'

Going down the steep hill towards the village, Mendel, his arm round Ruth's waist, burst into loud song.

'Should you do that *going?*' said Rufus, doubtfully. 'Surely one *goes* to the pub in silence.'

Mendel carolled on unheedingly. He was still singing as they reached the dimly-lit village street.

'That'll do,' said Ruth firmly, 'you'll get us all run in.'

Mendel paused in the middle of a stave. 'Perhaps you're right,' he said thoughtfully, 'but I do feel remarkably amused to-night.'

'By what?'

He threw back his head and roared with laughter.

'By you, my precious!' he said, tightening the encircling arm, so that they swerved unsteadily across the road, 'and by him. And more particularly by me.' He reached out and linked his free arm through Rufus's. 'We will now walk the Wobbly Wobbly Walk. By the left, go!'

There were a dozen or fifteen people in the small bar of the Bell, and the place was full of smoke and the clatter of broad, hard r'd conversation. Mendel was clearly known, for two men who were standing in the passage with mugs in their hands drew aside to let them pass and nodded civilly, and the landlord nodded from behind the bar and said 'Good evening, Mr.–' though, like a good landlord, he added no name.

Rather to Rufus's surprise, Mendel did not enter the bar, but passed on down the passage into the snug, a small room with a brightly burning fire, lit by a large hanging oil lamp, and furnished simply with two small marble tables and a few wooden arm-chairs. Mendel, who was leading, stopped abruptly in the doorway and then, with a cry of welcome, stepped forward and wrung by the hand a man who had risen from his place by the fire.

'Why, hullo, Mr. Kearns! Who'd have thought of seeing you?' He turned to Rufus. 'Rufus—let me introduce you to Mr. Fred Kearns. Mr. Kearns, this is Rufus. Rufus what, I've forgotten for the moment. He's staying up at Three Trees.'

Mr. Kearns shook Rufus by the hand.

'Pleased t'meet you, sir,' he said cordially.

He was a very small man indeed and, as he turned to greet Ruth, Rufus noticed that his body and legs were completely out of proportion. From the waist upwards, he was of normal build. But his legs were almost dwarf-like, and his shiny old blue serge trousers, at least six inches too long, hung in concertina folds over his boots. He wore a queer, old-fashioned flat white collar, with an old dove-grey tie threaded through a ring. His head was long, narrow, and covered with a few wisps of dirty grey hair, contrasting sharply with a thick, luxuriant moustache which, though grey at its edges, seemed by constant contact with the moisture of his lips to have gone rusty in the middle. His face was mild and somehow curiously peaceful, and as he beamed at them through his old-fashioned steel-rimmed glasses, his spaniel-like brown eyes took on a peculiarly kindly expression.

'Hullo, Mr. Kearns,' Ruth was shaking the little man heartily by the hand. 'Why, it's ages since we've seen you.'

'I'd quite given you up, miss,' the little man said in his gentle voice, as they seated themselves. 'Reckoned you'd gone and left us, I surely did.'

He resumed his seat, in which he sat bolt upright, with his little legs dangling an inch or two from the floor, like an ancient conjuror's dummy. 'Must be—ah—all of six months since I see you down here.'

'Well, we've *been* down,' said Ruth, 'but you weren't here. Twice we've been without seeing you.'

Mr. Kearns shook his head. 'Ah, well, y'see miss, I ain't bin *too* well. Nothing much really. But just not feeling meself. So I ain't been out, not any more than I must.' He jerked his head over his shoulder. 'You'll still be up at the farm?'

'That's right. Still there.' Mendel rose and struck the small brass bell. 'Have a drink? Pint?'

The little man gave a queer bob of assent. 'Thank you very much, sir.'

'Rufus, beer? How about you, sweet?'

'Ginger beer,' said Ruth. 'I will *not* drink alcohol to amuse anybody.'

'All right. There's no compulsion.' Mendel turned to the landlord. 'Three pints of beer and a ginger beer, please.'

He sat down again and lit a cigarette.

'Well, Mr. Kearns, and how's the band?'

The little man shook his queer long head with a gentle smile.

'Ooh, we goes on, sir, quiet like. I've known it better and I've known it worse.'

'Mr. Kearns is the bandmaster,' explained Ruth. 'How long is it now, Mr. Kearns, that you've been in it?'

Mr. Kearns smiled at Rufus through his thick glasses.

'Be sixty year come next Christmas, sir,' he said with gentle pride.

'Sixty years,' said Rufus in astonishment. 'But, good Lord, I shouldn't have thought you *were* sixty?'

The little man gave a quiet, pleased chuckle and looked whimsically at Mendel.

'Mr. Kearns is seventy-two,' said Mendel.

'Really?' said Rufus in genuine astonishment. 'Well, honestly I shouldn't have put you a day past sixty, if that.'

Mr. Kearns took a gulp at his beer and, setting down his mug, shook his head.

'Ah, I s'pose not, sir. But we wears well, all on us Kearnses. My father he died at ninety-two, and my mother she died last year, God rest her soul, at ninety-five.'

He removed the thick glasses and wiped them carefully with a big blue handkerchief. 'Yes, I'm seventy-two year old, shall be seventy-three come next Christmas. An' I first went out wi' the band on me thirteenth birthday, an' I've never missed a Christmas since, for sixty year.'

'What d'you play?' asked Rufus.

'You mean what instrument, sir? Cornet. Cornet I played as a boy and cornet I plays to this day.' He fumbled in his pocket and, producing a small black pipe, thrust his forefinger into the bowl, and struck a match. 'Mind you,' he added, pausing with the burning match half-way to his pipe. 'Mind you, I *have* played other instruments. Horn, euphonium, baritone. One time an' another, I reckon I've played most every instrument you'll find in a band. Brass band that is. No reed, sir.' He applied the match. 'But I always come back to the cornet in the end. Though I can't play like I used, y'see. Not with me teeth gone.'

Rufus shook his head. 'I should think that must be a record,' he said.

Mr. Kearns nodded.

'Aye,' he said tranquilly, 'I ain't ever heard of any that can beat sixty year. There's some old stagers in our band too. But none of them can't beat sixty year. Or come alongside it.'

He glanced up as two men entered the snug.

'Evenin', Tom. Evenin', Laurie.'

'Evenin', Fred.' The new-comers nodded civilly at Mendel. 'Evenin', sir. Evenin', miss.' They sat down quietly.

'You better, then, Fred?' One of them, a thick-set, red-faced man leaned across and murmured the question as though fearing to interrupt. Mr. Kearns finished his beer and, sucking the last drops from his moustache, nodded cheerfully.

'Oh, aye. I'm better than what I was. Sight better. 'Twas that cold spell, see, Tom, that's what 'twas.'

'Have another drink?' said Mendel. He rose and banged the bell and turned to the new-comers. 'Join us?'

'Thank you, sir.'

'That's right.' Mendel turned to the landlord. 'Same again and two pints as well.'

He resumed his seat. 'We've just been saying that Mr. Kearns here must hold the long-service record for bandsmen.'

The red-faced man shook his head and looked at Mr. Kearns admiringly. 'Ah, reckon he must just about.'

''Course bandsmen don't never die,' said his companion, a youth of about twenty in a brown suit, a cap, and a somewhat noisy pullover. 'No one ain't never seen a dead bandsman no more'n a dead donkey, 'ave they, Tom? It's the blowin', see?'

Mr. Kearns shook his head.

'I've seen plenty,' he said with a gentle smile.

'But *do* most bandsmen live a long time?' asked Rufus with interest.

Mr. Kearns raised his fresh tankard. 'Maybe they do,' he said. 'Ah, I s'pose they do. I've known some rare old uns meself.'

'I reckon it's the blowin',' said the youth again. 'Well, good 'ealth, sir. Good 'ealth, miss.'

'But I'll tell you what,' said Mr. Kearns, setting down his mug emphatically, 'long er short, they don't never stop *bein'* bandsmen once they start. Not no matter how old they get.'

'What about Fred 'Aines?' said the red-faced man slyly.

The youth roared with laughter. Mr. Kearns smiled gently.

'Ah, well, that were different. Fred 'Aines,' he explained, turning to Mendel, 'were a chap what vamoose with one of our euphoniums. Only bin in the band a month, 'e 'ad, and took it home, so say, to practise. Next mornin' Fred 'Aines was gone an' a nice silver euphonium—Hawkes euphonium[83]—were gone, too.'

'Well, that bears out what you say,' said Mendel with a grin. 'He wanted to go on playing wherever he was going.'

Mr. Kearns nodded with his gentle smile. 'Ah, p'raps you're right, sir. P'raps 'e did.'

There was a long pause. Mendel produced his cigarette-case and handed it round. The red-faced man had produced his pipe, but the youth, Rufus and Ruth accepted. There was a general striking of matches.

'It's a funny thing, is music,' said the bandmaster reflectively. 'The way it gets into a man, as you might say. Gets into his blood and never goes.' He shook his head thoughtfully. 'I've known many a man in my time—men maybe what didn't have much to make 'em happy like—what got more out of playin' with our band than out of anythin' else. Not educated men either. Just workin' chaps. An' they loved t'come and practise and play, maybe, out every now and again.'

'It's a wonderful gift,' said the red-faced man solemnly.

Mr. Kearns nodded. 'Ah. So it is, Tom. A wonderful gift is music.' He picked up his mug. 'D'you remember old Sid[84]—Sid Harland? He was a man what loved music, Sid was.'

'Ah,' said the red-faced man, 'I mind old Sid well. Used ter work fer Mr. Strange.'

'That's right.'

''Course, 'e died, didn't 'e?'

'Yes. He died. I was with 'im when 'e died.' The little old bandmaster turned to the youth. 'That's one o' the dead bandsmen I've seen, Laurie, me boy.'

'Caught a cold, didn't 'e?' said Tom.

'Ah,' said Mr. Kearns, 'it were his chest, see, Tom. 'Course 'e was never strong, Sid wasn't.'

He took a long pull at his beer and gazed reflectively into the fire with his mild brown eyes.

'It were a funny go altogether,' he said thoughtfully, 'about poor old Sid. One of the funniest goes in some ways as I ever heard tell of. 'Course, there wasn't anything funny in his dyin'. He hadn't never been strong. But it was the way of it, see?'

'What happened?' asked Mendel, flicking the ash from his cigarette.

Mr. Kearns turned his head slowly and looked at him.

'If I was to tell you, sir,' he said simply, 'you won't believe me. 'Cause it's a funny story, and if I didn't *know* maybe I wouldn't believe it meself, not the way of it, like.'

'Well, go on,' said Mendel with a smile, 'tell us, and we'll see if we can swallow it.'

Mr. Kearns hesitated and his gaze returned to the fire.

'Well, it was like this,' he said at last, settling back more comfortably in his chair, so that his short legs were pulled up quite three inches from the floor. 'Back over twenty years ago now— before the War—we had a chap come here as organist—chap by the name of Mr. Henry. Ah, a fine player he was, too.

Too good for here. You remember Mr. Henry, Tom?'

'Ah. Well,' said the red-faced man. ''E was a fine player.'

'Yes, he was. A real first-class player. He was only here two or three year and then he went away.' Mr. Kearns stuffed his finger into the bowl of his pipe and shook his head. Well, this Mr. Henry he was mad keen on music. Mad keen, he was. He got the choir together and he got them singing beautiful. An' not content with that he gets up a choir out of the village, see?' Mr. Kearns chuckled reminiscently. 'Rare lot of old bodies he got, first and last. Old gals what hadn't ever sung a note in their lives.'

'I know my missis was in it,' put in Tom.

'Ah. They was *all* in it. Well, after a bit Mr. Henry he said they'd do Handel's *Messiah*, see? 'Course, I'm not sayin' it isn't a lovely bit o' music, but o' course it was too hard for 'em—just village people like. Much too hard. Still, Mr. Henry he works away like a slave, same as he always did with anything. And then one day he comes along to me and says, "Mr. Kearns," he says (I can see him now—a youngish chap with black hair and spectacles and mighty big eyes), "Mr. Kearns," he says, "we're going to give a performance of the *Messiah* with the Choral Society, an' I'm going to have a band. Would some of your chaps come and play for me?" So I said, "Well, what do you want, Mr. Henry? D'you want us all?" "God, no," he says, just like that. "I want a couple of trumpeters and two tenor trombones an' a bass trombone," he says.

'"Well," I says, "I kin play the trumpet meself and so can Jack Slade." ('Course, y'see, it's practically the same as the cornet, really.) "An' there's Archie Simmons and Dave Ross for the tenor trombones and Sid Harland," I says, "fer the bass trombone." 'Cause at that time Sid played the bass trombone in the band, see? An' a very good player he was. "I don't care who it is," says Mr. Henry, "as long as they kin play. Will you ask them?" So I said yes, I would, an' the upshot was we went along the five of us to practise this *Messiah* music.' The bandmaster paused and, taking a mouthful of beer, shook his head with a chuckle. 'Well, we went along and then the fun began. Mr. Henry he'd got a rare scratch lot of us there, and there was some as *could* play and some as couldn't. 'Course, *we* was all right, see? There wasn't anythin' much to it, really—just like hymns most of it was. Not much harder, anyway. Only thing that put some o' the boys out was that some on it was in sharps keys, an' they wasn't used to that, all our music bein' written in flats, see.'

'But *is* all your music in flats?' said Rufus, 'and if so, why?'

'Well, y'see, sir, every instrument in a band's in a flats key, 'cept the bass trombone. So it's wrote in flats t'make it easier.' Mr. Kearns picked up his mug and dandled[85] it lovingly on his knee.

'Well, as I say, *we* got on fine, and after a bit so did most of the others. Not first-class, o' course—but quite a nice body o' tone— nice full band. But it so 'appened that poor old Sid he couldn't get used to havin' long rests. Not to havin' minutes together when he didn't play at all. And o' course there was plenty o' times when there wasn't no trombone in a sacred piece like that. It was the last chorus that always done him. Just singin' Amen it is all the time, and there was a matter o' seventy-two bars old Sid had to count, for a rest, see. Well, he could never count these seventy-two bars right. Never. An' o' course you get a man comin' in wrong with the bass trombone it sounds mighty queer. An' if ever he *did* count it right, Mr. Henry he'd stop the choir after about seventy bars and poor old Sid would have to start all over again.'

'Disappointing for 'im like,' said the red-faced man with a chuckle.

The bandmaster smiled. 'Ah, so it was. Poor old Sid!' He shook his head and refreshed himself with a pull of beer. 'So at last Mr. Henry gets a liddle lad to stand and count fer 'im, and after that it were all right. But in spite o' this poor old Sid were like a man in Heaven. Loved it, he did. He didn't say much. He were a tall, dark, quiet sort o' chap, what always looked as though a puff o' wind might blow him away. An' he never had much to say. But he come up to me after the first practice and he says, "'Cod, Fred, but ain't that some music, you?" That's all he said. But it were the *way* he said it. An' he used to come as regular as clockwork and sit in the corner by hisself, so as not to hit no one with his slide, see, an' play away lookin' fer all the world like a chap in Heaven.' The old man beamed round with his soft brown eyes and chuckled.

'His missis used to go on 'cause 'e would practise at home. Get one o' the youngsters to count fer 'im and play just his own parts like. But it were always the Amen chorus with the seventy-two bars that he liked best. That an' Hallelujah. Well, this went on an' the night come along an' we did the performance in the school, and very well it went considerin'. The paper it reckoned we'd done fine, and Mr. Henry he was very pleased and thanked us all very pleasant. An' I said, "Don't you mention it, Mr. Henry, we've enjoyed ourselves proper." An' so we had.' The bandmaster paused and applied a match to his pipe.

'Look here,' said Mendel, 'I thought you said we weren't going to believe you? Well—'

Mr. Kearns raised his hand.

'Half a minute, sir! I'm comin' to that bit now. Maybe I'm takin' a long time, but I wanted you to get it right, see, what had happened.' He leaned forward with his hands on his knees. 'But three months after that, poor old Sid he got ill. He wasn't never what you'd call a strong man, an' he was workin' up at Mr. Strange's and got hot, and then he cooled off like and it give him a chill, see. Well, I heard he was pretty bad, an' him bein' a bandsman, o' course I went round to see him. He were in bed and his missis had got Dr. Rose to him, an' I didn't like the looks o' him at all. In fact, I come away and said so. Grey he looked. You know—grey in the face, an' all hawkish. Well, it wasn't more'n a couple o' days after when I heard that poor old Sid was goin' fast. It was his chest, see.

So I jumped on me bike and went down to Brook Street where he lived, t'see if there was anythin' I could do. Well, o' course there wasn't nothin' you *could* do. His missis took me in an' I took one look at him an' I knoo it wouldn't be long. Still, his missis seemed t'like me to be there, so I sits down an' tries to talk to him, but he were too far gone to know me, see, or anybody else. Even his missis. He didn't seem to notice her even.' The old man paused for a long moment and shook his head thoughtfully.

'Well,' he went on at last, 'I sat there fer a bit sayin' what bit o' comfort I could to his missis, what were naturally very upset, and kept on asking Dr. Rose if there wasn't anything he could do. An' then suddenly I see Sid sort o' smile, like, an' start movin' his hands to and fro, to an' fro, like this. "What's he doin'?" Dr. Rose whispers to me, puzzled like. But *I* knoo what he were doin', after a minute. "He's playin' his trombone," I whispers back. An' sure enough he was. Moving his hand in and out, see, just as if he was moving his slide. Well, we sat there and watched, maybe fer five minutes, ol' Sid lyin' there and playin' away as happy as you please. An' then all of a sudden he sits up in bed and starts playin' harder than ever.

'I looks across at Dr. Rose. "Did he ought to do that?" I says, but he just shrugs his shoulders as if to say it didn't matter, like. An' then suddenly ole Sid jus' drops his hands down on the bedclothes an' looks up with a smile—ah, I've never seen such a smile on a mortal man before or since, sir—and he just says quite loud, "Seventy-two bars rest," he says, an' he lies down, sir, an' enters into them.'

The old bandmaster paused and in a long silence removed and carefully wiped his thick spectacles with the big blue handkerchief.

'There you are, sir,' he said soberly. 'An' I reckon that only goes to show what I said before. It's a queer thing is music, and the way it gets into a man, even if he is only a workin' chap. He'd never forgot it, see. His missis told me after that, he'd never finished talkin' about the *Messiah* music we did with Mr. Henry. An' that was his last thought, sir, an' he was tryin' to play it, an' he went on in his mind as you might say, till he got to "Amen" an' then he laid hisself down and entered into his rest as peaceful as any man I ever did see.'

'God, that's a story,' said Ruth almost under her breath. Her eyes were very bright. Mendel nodded slowly.

'It certainly is.'

The bandmaster replaced his spectacles. 'And that happened to me in this village over twenty year ago.'

There was a long silence.

'It's a wonderful thing is music,' said the red-faced man with a shake of the head. He finished his beer and looked round rather doubtfully. 'I don't know if you'd care to drink with me, sir… and… and… miss–?'

'No, look here,' said Rufus, rising quickly and smiting the bell. 'This round's on me.'

'The absurd thing, of course,' said Mendel, suddenly, as they walked silently up the hill, 'is that it should have been a bass trombone.'

'Why?' asked Rufus. There had been silence ever since they left the Bell.

'Well, think of it!—a bass trombone—one of the silliest, most unromantic, and clumsy instruments you can think of. Think just how awful it would have been if it had been a violin he played. The whole thing would have been a sort of appalling film plot. You know—the dying Paganini.[86] Everything else in the thing is sheer bad melodrama. The death-bed. The Amen chorus. The long rest. It's awful—*awful*. It makes you hot about the ears at the execrable taste of the Deity. But the bass trombone saves it. You cannot—*cannot* have a bass trombone in a melodrama. The thing's out of the question.'

'Personally,' said Rufus, 'I think it merely adds a peculiarly ghastly touch of comedy.'

Mendel threw up his head and gazed skywards.

'Comedy,' he said to the jewelled darkness. 'My God, you call that comedy?'

'I don't call it comedy at all. The whole thing is clearly tragedy with—'

'Or tragedy either!' Mendel threw out his hands in an appealing gesture. 'Christ, whoever thought of those bloody silly words in the first place? And why do people always want to label everything one or the other? "The Works of William Shakespeare. Volume One. Comedies. Volume Two. Tragedies." And, mark you, they put *Measure for Measure* and *The Merchant of Venice* among the comedies. As though *were* any "comedy" or any "tragedy" in that whole thorough-going sort of way!'

Rufus shrugged his shoulders.

'It's a convenient label.'

'A convenient label!' said Mendel with profound contempt. 'You might as well say that if I'm going from here to Glasgow it'll be all right to label my luggage Cardiff because it's a "convenient label". What the hell's the good of a label at all unless it's accurate?'

'But usually it is,' protested Rufus, 'quite accurate. There are undoubted comedies and undoubted tragedies.'

'Oh, yes, I dare say. In fiction. But that's because we demand it. We like to know where we are and to feel that everything's beautifully labelled and pigeon-holed. But there aren't in life. Life never goes on being persistently comic or persistently tragic in that nice well-rounded way, thank God. And perhaps that's why we find it a bit odd. It isn't what the books have prepared us for. It can't make up its mind, and it keeps mixing its style in a way which we feel is hardly good form.'

Mendel shook his head and stared thoughtfully ahead of him into the moonlit dimness.

'It's a funny thing, but we see it sometimes—this vital interdependence of comedy and tragedy. The great clowns have always seen it. Your Grock, your Chaplin[87]—they are always comic on the brink of disaster—always working on the old laugh-clown-laugh principle that makes us smile with a lump in our throats. I suppose we like it like that, because we're all so very fond of a good cry. But why not the other way? We like tragedy in our comedy? Why not comedy in our tragedy? We're all living the life. We all know that in real life Hamlet's rapier lands back from Polonius's cigarette-case—that Othello creeping towards Desdemona bangs his toe against the chamber-pot and wakes her. But we won't have it in fiction. It offends our taste. We're so keen to get away from a life full of bathos that we won't stand our nice cry being interrupted. It's so intolerably undignified. Only Shakespeare and some of the Russians have ever got away with it. And we cut it in Shakespeare and excuse the Russians on the ground that they're slightly mad.'

They walked on in silence.

'So you wouldn't call old Kearns's story comedy or tragedy?' said Rufus at last.

'Of course not. It's true. It's life, and life among very simple, unselfconscious people. And in life, as I say, everything is mixed up—difficult—uncomfortable—grotesque. But never in bad taste. Bad taste is a sham—a cheat—something trying to be what it isn't, like a Hollywood Duke. And life can't be an imitation of life. You might spoil that in the telling—old Kearns is a simple old boy, but even he nearly smade it into something it wasn't. But the thing itself remains genuine. Mixed—silly—bizarre, with the proper precarious feeling there all the time. So that you feel the truth—that one altered property, and the thing is something quite different. A banana skin, and tragedy is comedy. A badly written prescription and comedy's tragedy. A curtain held up one second too long and a drama's a melodrama. And in life the stage is littered with banana skins and illegible prescriptions, and the curtain is always held up too long.'

'Here comes the moon,' said Ruth, as they reached the crest of the hill.

Rufus did not sleep well that night. Normally, the country air, and long walks or carpentering, sent him to bed delightfully drowsy, in the happy certainty that he had only to get into his bed, blow out his candle, and lapse into the dreamy reverie which passes imperceptibly into sleep.

But to-night for some reason his brain refused to accept the usual signals for ceasing work. He lay for an hour staring out on to the pale moonlit hill, and then found to his disgust that, far from becoming more inclined for sleep, he felt if anything more wakeful than before. He lay for some time meditating the possibility of getting up and going for a walk in the moonlight. But somehow he could not face the prospect of getting up and dressing and stealing down in the darkened house. Moreover, his body did not share this appalling wakefulness. His legs ached slightly, and there was the unmistakable feeling of physical lassitude which reminded him that he had made vigorous physical love to Ruth only some fourteen hours ago. Rufus grunted and, rolling over on his back (a sure sign that for the moment he had abandoned the idea of sleep), resigned himself to one of his occasional bouts of concentrated and almost painful thought.

Two absurdly incongruous things were fighting for supremacy in his consciousness. On the one hand there were his own immediate problems. Ruth. What happened now. How much Mendel knew or cared. What part he was expected to play in the relations of the household. Was he soon to be accepted openly or tacitly, as her lover? Her occasional lover, or her only lover for the moment? And then, again, there was that grotesque business about the man who played the trombone. He was nothing to do with the case tra la, and there was absolutely nothing to be done about it. After all, *that* wasn't a problem. It had all been settled twenty years ago. But the fact remained that he kept butting in. Quite concretely and visually. One could *think* about Ruth quite nicely. But directly one started to visualise her—impossibly and enticingly innocent, throwing back the bedclothes and showing herself lying snugly in the green pyjama trousers, or naked with the small, firm breasts and the queer almost skinny brown arms and shoulders, looking… directly one did that there was the bass trombonist playing choruses from the *Messiah* and smiling like a man in Heaven. Only for some reason (a) He was a whole orchestra, or at least he made all the noises of one, and (b) He didn't blow. He just moved his slide and smiled like a man in Heaven, see above.

Rufus gave a violent wriggle and plunged his legs almost viciously to the bottom of the bed. Seriously, he reflected, seriously, here was a chance to think things out. If one *had* to lie as wide awake as this. He started again, without much conviction, with Ruth. Mendel and Ruth. But a moment later the bass trombonist… He decided coldly and logically to deal with and dispose of the bass trombonist. Taking, then, the bass trombonist first. Well, it was an odd yarn. Very odd. And, as told by old Kearns, very effective. Almost too effective to be pleasant in places. Ruth's eyes had been very bright and she had blinked rather more than usual. An odd, liquid brightness. Quite different from the hard, almost feverish brightness of her eyes when they challenged and she threw back the bedclothes and showed herself lying there, small, vulnerable, personal…

> 'By long and vehement suit I was seduced
> To make room for him in my husband's bed…'[88]

But she was not married to Mendel. He was married to someone else. And while they had committed adultery, he and Ruth only fornicated. Fornicated. His body gave a curious lecherous plunge at the thought. His muscles tensed and relaxed rhythmically. His hands clenched as he saw the little hard breasts and felt the terrific thrill of that frank, consenting little wriggle as she slipped from the green pyjamas. And then the bass trombonist came into his own again and played the whole of the Hallelujah chorus from beginning to end with full chorus and without interruption. His slide went rhythmically in and out, in and out… yes, of course, in and out, in and out!…

Despite his wakefulness, he had fallen into a doze. The faint rattle of the latch made him start upright in bed.

'Rufus!' she said very softly.

'Darling!' He stretched out his arms in the darkness. Mixed with his surprise and pleasure at her coming was an absurd and childish annoyance, which damned a woman who wouldn't let a man sleep. His hand brushed against something warm and silky. He put an arm round her thighs and drew her towards the bed.

'My darling love!' He pulled back the bedclothes and felt the small, night-chilled form slip in beside him. A small cold paw touched his bare neck.

'Fair do's,' his mind was saying mechanically. 'Fair do's. Even if you *are* sleepy…'

'You don't mind, Rufus?'

'My love!' He caught her in his arms and began to kiss her rapidly and violently. His hands slid quickly and eagerly over her. 'I love you,' he said, truthfully, and kissed her hard again. It would be all right. In a moment he would warm and not have to try any more. One always did if one kissed a woman and stroked her enough. And he loved her. It was only that he was sleepy. He pressed his body hard against hers.

'My sweet!'

Chapter XII

Sawing Through the Lady

Rufus awoke reluctantly from log-like unconsciousness to find that it was almost daylight, and that Mendel was leaning over him and shaking him gently by the shoulder. The recollection of the previous night came back to him with a rush, and for one insane sleepy moment he thought that this early attack was the result of jealousy. He half sat up in bed and blinked at Mendel drowsily.

'What's up?' he said vaguely.

'Don't make a row,' said Mendel in a half-whisper. 'There's no point in waking her.'

Rufus turned his head bemusedly, and realised that Ruth, still sleeping soundly, was lying beside him. Moreover, he realised, they were both quite remarkably naked. Rufus flushed slightly as he turned again to Mendel. The position seemed a little delicate. Mendel, however, seemed completely unmoved.

'Come on,' he said quietly, 'it's high time we started.'

'Started where?' said Rufus vaguely.

'You know. Our tree. I told you I'd call you. Out you get.' He turned away as Rufus, after a moment's hesitation, began to climb half-heartedly out of bed.

'I'll go down and get the stuff while you're dressing. Don't wake her if you can help it.' He went out, closing the door gently behind him.

Rufus slid cautiously and reluctantly out of bed and, padding over to the window, looked out rather gloomily. It was obviously still quite early, for the sun had not yet risen, and the early dawn light was cold and pale. A faint grey mist hung low on the hill. Rufus shivered and, turning, picked up his shirt discontentedly. It was bloody silly to go fooling around after logs at this time, when there was all day with nothing at all to do. He wished devoutly that he had never agreed to the fool plan. He reflected viciously that this was probably Mendel's idea of a joke—to come and drag him out of bed after… well, after a night like that. Clearly, a simple case of jealousy. Ruth had left Mendel and come to him, and now Mendel was getting his own back in this childish way…

He huddled, shivering into his clothes, and passed a hand over his rough chin with some disgust. His face felt sticky and dirty, but he had neither the time nor the energy to wash. He scratched disconsolately at his tousled hair and turned to the door. Ruth was still sleeping peacefully with her back to him. He looked at her for a moment and his face softened. Poor kid! He walked quietly round to the other side of the bed, and gently kissed the top of the black, close-cropped boyish head. There! To hell with Mendel, anyhow. He gave the poor little devil a hell of a time…

Mendel was waiting at the front door, impatiently smoking a cigarette. He carried a long cross-cut saw and a coil of rope.

'Come on,' he said brusquely, 'what a hell of a time you've been!'

'I damned nearly didn't come at all,' said Rufus, rebelliously. 'I think this is a silly bloody game.'

Mendel looked at him with a cold smile.

'You shouldn't do these things,' he said almost contemptuously. 'Then you wouldn't feel such a wreck in the morning.' He turned and led the way out of the farmyard without another word.

'I'll have one of those,' said Rufus grudgingly, putting out his hand for the rope. Mendel hitched the coil more firmly across his enormous shoulders.

'It's all right,' he said, 'it doesn't weigh anything.'

He turned to the right and went striding away up the steep slope, a powerful, ill-kempt, yellow-haired giant. Rufus said no more.

They walked in silence. The atmosphere was tense and unfriendly. Rufus could feel it in the tearing pace of Mendel's walk, which made him strain every muscle to avoid the indignity of being left behind. His legs were aching, and the keen bite of the morning air rather emphasised than cleared up the heavy thickness of his head. His heart was soon thumping rapidly with the exertion of striding up the steep hill and every thump produced a pulse of pain behind his eyes. He tried hard to breathe quietly, noting with fury that Mendel's lips were tightly closed, and that he showed not the slightest sign of distress.

'Where is this bloody tree?' he manged to get out as they breasted the top of the first rise.

'About a mile and a half,' said Mendel briefly, 'in that spinney beyond Lavell's Farm.'

Rufus nodded, but saved his breath. He was breathing in gasps and he was aware of black spots dancing before his eyes. He closed them and plugged blindly on. When he opened them again, it was to find Mendel looking sideways at him with the same cold smile.

'Walking too fast for you?' asked Mendel shortly.

Rufus shook his head.

'I like walking fast,' he said agonisedly.

Mendel nodded with a grim smile.

'Good. Whenever I'm out without Ruth I like to walk at a man's pace.'

Rufus took a deep gasping breath. 'Well, you're without her now,' he said huskily, 'so here's your chance.'

It got better after about half a mile. Whether Mendel relaxed his pace or not Rufus could not tell. But he had got his second wind, and they were walking now on the gentle slopes of the downs. His head was clearing every minute, and the awful fear that he would have to call a halt, or that he would simply be sick, was passing. Despite Mendel's silence he almost enjoyed the last mile of the walk. The sun was boiling up redly through the mist, and in spite of the queer hot crampedness of his leg muscles the sense of well-being of the morning was in him. He strode out more easily, and once when Mendel slackened slightly to give the coil of rope on his shoulders a hitch, he forged ahead for a few strides. Mendel sensed the change and smiled his grim smile.

'Beginning to feel more worth while?' he asked abruptly.

'Yes,' said Rufus guardedly.

He was still irritable, and not yet ready for amicable relations to be resumed. Mendel grunted.

'It always does,'[89] he said. 'That's the difference between night and morning. They're like a hot and cold bath. The hot bath's nice and easy to get into, but if you stay in it long it gets cold and you get out shivering and feeling as cheap as hell. The cold bath takes a bit of guts, but once you're in you feel all right and you get out feeling good.'

'Singing joyfully,' said Rufus, sarcastically, feeling in no mood for pretty simile.

Mendel smiled lazily. 'That's right,' he drawled. 'Singing joyfully.'

They walked on in silence to the spinney.

'Here we are,' said Mendel, throwing down the saw with a queer, flexible clatter, and unhitching the rope from his shoulders. Rufus pushed the smooth grey bark with his toe. The tree was a small beech which seemed to have been torn up by the roots. Its sleek grey trunk was about nine inches thick, forking after about seven feet into two big branches six inches in diameter. It lay prone amid its crushed branches, the earth still clinging forlornly to its long wide-spreading roots, which had pulled up the ground for some distance.

'What brought it down?' he asked curiously. 'They don't often fall. It can't have been the wind.'

'I don't know,' said Mendel. 'I wondered myself. It's on the edge, and its fallen outwards, so I don't see how the wind can have done it.'

He walked round and examined the roots. 'Several of the main roots have gone, but they don't seem to be diseased or anything.'

He peeled off his jacket and threw it carelessly on the dewy grass. 'Come on. Let's strip off some of the small stuff.'

He broke away a few small impeding branches and then, seizing a limb as thick as a man's wrist, gave a quick heave. There was a loud crack and the branch broke close to the trunk. Rufus followed his example, but the branch he tugged at resisted him stoutly and, rebounding, forced him back a few undignified steps. Rufus's lips set and, with a terrific wrench, he cracked the bough across.

'I don't think we'll take all this stuff,' said Mendel, tossing his branch aside. 'Let's just strip it off and take the main trunk and these two big chaps.' He patted the two smooth grey limbs, and broke off another small branch with one hand. Pausing for a moment, he looked at the fallen trunk with a regretful shake of the head.

'It's a beastly business breaking up a tree, and particularly a beech. But if the poor old thing can't stand up, we might as well burn it as let it lie here.'

After a while Mendel announced that the stripping process had gone far enough and proposed an attack on the main limbs. They picked up the big cross-cut saw and began the cutting up.

Rufus enjoyed it at first. The steady in and out movement was pleasant, and the weight of the saw alone seemed sufficient to send the big teeth deeper and deeper. He watched the scanty damp sawdust slide quickly down the grey bark to the ground, pouring out in a little stream as Mendel's strong thrust sent the blade out on his side. He speculated on the correct movement to employ. A body-thrust or a pure-arm movement? Normally it was the sort of question which he would have asked Mendel. But at the moment Rufus was carefully avoiding anything which might be construed as a friendly overture. Mendel was unconcerned and calm enough, but the contempt of his tone when they had set out still rankled.

The wood, however, was green and tough and, as the big blade sank more and more deeply into the limb, it became harder and harder to thrust it back towards Mendel with really satisfying briskness.

Rufus had followed Mendel's example and discarded his jacket and rolled up his sleeves. His right arm was beginning to ache, and his tense grip on the saw handle was straining his fingers. He looked curiously down at his bare arm. The biceps rose and fell rhythmically. He resented the aching muscle with a queer detached resentment. His arms were strong and well-developed. But he glanced across at Mendel's, with the huge biceps and triceps flexing and straightening heavily and commandingly, and resented the comparison. The ache was increasing with every thrust now. He wondered if Mendel's arm was aching too, and childishly hoped that it was. But the big man sawed steadily on, his brow puckered, and his eyes fixed unswervingly on the ever-deepening cut.

They were within an inch of the bottom of the limb. Unconsciously, Rufus strove to increase the rate of thrust in a wild aching end-spurt. But Mendel maintained the same steady rhythm to the end, and when the blade finally rasped through the lower bark, and the limb fell with a crackling of small branches to the ground, he quietly laid down the saw, which Rufus had thankfully released, and, picking up the heavy limb without sign of effort, threw it clear with a quick heave.

'Now the other limb,' he said without a pause.

The second limb was much worse. The ache in Rufus's muscles was cumulative and when he tried to keep his arm stiff and to thrust the blade through by the weight of his body he found that his back tired rapidly. His thrusts were no longer smooth and rhythmic, and once one of his desperate jabs caused the saw to jam in the cut and bend dangerously.

'Don't force it,' said Mendel calmly, 'just push it through quietly.'

Rufus looked up sharply. The cold blue eyes were fixed expressionlessly on the cut. Rufus swallowed hard and wearily forced his cramped and aching arm into the slow exasperating rhythm.

At last the cut was finished. As before, Mendel picked up the limb with exasperating ease and threw it aside. Surely, surely, thought Rufus, in an agony of apprehension, he'll stop for a moment now?

Mendel turned and picked up the saw.

'Now the trunk,' he said gently. 'I think we'll cut it into three.'

Rufus hesitated. He knew quite well that he could not manage another cut without a rest of some sort.

'Ready?' said Mendel inquiringly.

'Half a minute,' Rufus muttered. He turned aside with flushed face and, walking slowly over to his jacket, extracted a cigarette. His mouth was dry and parched and the smoke tasted acrid and unpleasant. But he gained a moment's respite as he slowly and deliberately lit it. Mendel stood silently and patiently waiting. Their glances met and, deep in the big man's eyes, Rufus thought he detected a spark of contemptuous amusement. A great childish anger flamed up in him, along with a wild desire to knock that faint smile from Mendel's face with his cramped hand. But he crushed it down and, passing a hand over his damp forehead, returned and picked up his end of the saw with seeming indifference.

'This is fun,' he said as lightly as he could. Mendel nodded without reply, as the blade scratched its first furrow across the sleek bark.

Half-way through the trunk Rufus knew he must stop. With the best will in the world he could force effective movement from his arms no longer. For some minutes he had merely allowed the blade to be carried to and fro by the power of Mendel's thrust and pull. Better, he decided, to call a halt quite calmly than to risk a comment. He straightened his back and loosened his grip on the handle.

'Do you mind if we stop for a moment?' he said calmly. 'This job makes my arm ache.'

It was an honourable and dignified acceptance of defeat.

'Why, of course!' Mendel stopped at once and stood up. 'I was forgetting.'

'Forgetting what?' asked Rufus dangerously.

'Why, forgetting you weren't used to this. It's purely a knack, and after a bit it doesn't need any strength at all.'

It was an innocent enough remark, but Rufus assumed that the smile which accompanied it was a smile of triumph.

'I'm glad of that,' he said, flushing angrily. 'At the moment I think it requires quite a lot.'

Mendel shook his head. 'All a part of a fuller physical life,' he said solemnly. 'You remember what I was saying about aches and pains? Well, it's quite true, isn't it? That tired ache in your arm is really a wryly funny feeling.' He looked at Rufus narrowly. 'It's odd,' he said thoughtfully, 'how little respect we have nowadays for the purely physical. With primitive man I suppose it was the only criterion of worth. Purely physical ability. But who cares, nowadays, if a man has muscles and eyes and ears and lungs?'

He pointed to the tree. 'We cut this up, quickly and skilfully. A job which calls for strength—skill—staying power. Who respects us for it? We might earn a bare living for it, but no one gives us authority—no one puts our picture in the papers—no one pays us ten thousand a year because of what our bodies can do. The only way in which physical ability is admired and rewarded is in silly specialised directions like hitting a ball with a racket or a club or a bat—things any narrow-chested weakling with a certain knack of eye and hand can do. Look at your sporting idols. Look at them as physical specimens. Those are *men*—those little fellows five feet high with hands like women. The physical cream of the race!' He flung out a hand with a bitter smile.

'So you'd like to go back to bulging muscles and stone clubs?' said Rufus, contemptuously.

'I?' Mendel shook his head. 'No. It's you I'm thinking about. You're the man who's returning to the physical existence. I'm only warning you of the disappointments of it.' He shot a quick glance at Rufus. 'Your bulging muscles won't get you anywhere much nowadays,' he added with a barely concealed sneer. They stared at one another in silence for a moment. This time the bitter antagonism in the blue eyes was unmistakable. Rufus threw away his cigarette and seized his end of the saw.

'Let's go on,' he said in a repressed voice.

Mendel laughed. 'Rested, eh? Right you are!' he cried in a queer harsh voice. 'But before we begin, I'll give you one word of consolation.' He paused, his hands on the saw, and gazed across the thick trunk with sparkling blue eyes. 'There's one bit of the world left which appreciates a man—a strong man—and that's women. They take strength from a man so they like him to have plenty.' He rasped the blade hard through the wood. 'Come on—use your muscles! They'll never get you anything else, but they'll get you something to keep you warm in bed, God send you joy of it!'

The saw rasped more quickly now. Far, far away, Rufus saw, in a glaring poster, the thick headline, 'Sawing Through a Woman'. In out, in out. Ruth lay there between them—between the tug and thrust of them, and they were sawing her in half. Mendel was no longer looking at the cut. He was staring across at Rufus with a queer, fixed grin. His face seemed to approach and recede with the rhythm of the saw, in a thick mist. One thrust more, one strong thrust of arm and body, and the saw would go through his body and out the other side. Rufus leaned forward with a grunt of effort. The misty face receded. But in another second he was thrust back and it was coming closer again—grinning, still grinning.

'Come on!' cried the mocking voice. 'Push, man, push. We're not half-way through yet!'

Rufus never knew how long they had been working when they stopped again. He awoke almost from unconsciousness to find that the maddening rhythm had ceased, and for one wild, crazy second he thought that Mendel in his turn had called a halt. But a moment later he saw that the thick trunk now lay in three neat sections, and that the big man was brushing back from his wet forehead a strand of yellow hair, and looking at the result of their labours with satisfaction.

'There,' he said, 'I think that'll do now.' His tone was normal and conversational. He did not look at Rufus, but turned aside and picked up the thick coil of rope.

Rufus sat down on the sawn trunk rather shakily. His legs felt weak, and he was sick and dizzy.

'How are we going to get it home?' he asked dully. All the strength had gone out of his body and he sullenly acquiesced in the assumption of casualness.

'Pull it,' said Mendel, calmly. 'That's what I brought this for.' He went on quietly uncoiling the rope.

'But we can't pull all that lot,' said Rufus involuntarily, 'it weighs God knows what.'

'Oh, it'll slide all right,' said Mendel, coolly. 'Once we get it moving.'

He separated the two towing ropes and turned to Rufus with a grin. 'Go on. You say what you think you can manage and I'll take the rest.'

Rufus looked at the thick grey limbs with sinking heart.

'We'd better divide it in half,' he said weakly. He knew the other man had won. It was a childish game. His brain was saying so. But defeat none the less was bitter.

'Can't very well do that,' said Mendel cheerfully, 'there are five bits.' He kicked aimlessly at the trunk. 'Tell you what, I'll take one of the limbs and these two bits of trunk, and you take the rest. That's about a fair split.'

Rufus looked at the tree. It was not a fair split. His portion was scarcely more than half the weight of Mendel's. He hesitated for a moment and then nodded wearily.

'All right,' he said, avoiding the sardonic blue eyes. He could play the mad competitive game no longer.

'Right,' said Mendel. 'Well, we'd better start lashing them up or Ruth'll be wondering where we are. If she's up yet.'

He rolled together the three great pieces of wood which were to be his portion and, running his rope round them, lashed them firmly together, with the saw resting on the top.

'You're never going to be able to pull that a mile and a half,' said Rufus in a low voice.

'No?' said Mendel, calmly. 'Why, then, you'll have to come back and lend me a hand. Let's see, anyhow.' He passed the tow rope over his head, and slipped his arms through it so that its sacking pad rested across his great chest. 'Now!' His great frame tensed as the rope pulled taut. He bent, straining forward, heaving at the dead weight with all the power of his great muscles. The logs shifted slightly, but that was all.

'I tell you it's impossible,' said Rufus with dull pleasure.

'It's only getting it started,' Mendel grunted. The veins on his forehead were standing out like thick wire. His face was darkly suffused with blood. He gave a final tremendous heave, and the load began to slide slowly forward. He took two or three straining steps, and then, as they gained speed, the logs began to slide more easily after him. In twenty yards they were sliding with a sort of sluggish ease like an immensely heavy sledge. Mendel dropped the rope from his chest. 'There you are. It's quite all right once you get them moving. Now, let's lash your lot.'

Rufus rose reluctantly to his feet and put on his jacket. They were on smooth, level ground. But between them and Three Trees, the ground undulated gently before shelving sharply away down to the farm. He looked at his burden. He might move it. He might even drag it painfully twenty yards, but a mile and a half?…

Mendel had already passed a rope under the logs and was lashing them tightly together. 'There you are,' he said. 'Get the rope round your chest, and try and get the thrust from your thighs and waist.' He paused with a hand on the load, as Rufus slipped into the rope harness. 'Get the sacking right or it'll cut your chest. I'll give you a shove off. Ready?'

He pushed hard as Rufus strained forwards. The load slid quite easily.

'That's fine!' called Mendel. 'Now, whatever you do, keep them moving!'

He ran across to his own load and, readjusting his rope, repeated the Herculean feat of starting his load from rest unaided.

Rufus struggled on. He was surprised to find that the logs, though heavy, were not the impossible load he had imagined. Once started, the smooth-barked limbs slid easily enough over the short grass. Apart from the pressure of the padded rope across his chest, there was little sensation of pulling a weight. It was rather as though one struggled forward through some very dense medium—like trying to run in water. The hippopotamus, he remembered foolishly, was said to be able to gallop along the bed of a stream. He glanced sideways. Mendel was walking parallel with him, bending forward against the strain of his heavier load, the muscles of his thick thighs and haunches rippling visibly beneath the scarecrow flannel trousers. Rufus looked down at the grass beneath him—the foolish absurdly detailed grass which normally was just a vague greenness, but which now, looked at closely like this, resembled earth seen from an aeroplane. How many blades of grass were there on the plain? Each step with this load was almost two feet, and it was about a mile and a half to Three Trees. That meant about two thousand five hundred yards or about—about four thousand steps… He began to count. One two three four five six seven eight nine ten… He glanced quickly back under his arm. The grey logs slid sluggishly after him, leaving a crushed and shining trail behind. They had come about fifty yards, which was one seventieth…

The down slopes did not compensate for the rises. It was a little easier to pull the load downhill than on the level. But on the up-slopes one bent almost double, with hands all but touching the grass, to keep the load moving at all. His eyes were fixed unseeingly now on the ground which passed slowly beneath and, despite the padding, the rope was cutting sharply across his chest.

'Keep it going!' he heard Mendel say breathlessly, 'or it'll be the devil to start here.'

He answered with a grunt which was almost a groan. And then suddenly a step was a fraction easier, and the next a little easier still and, raising his eyes, he saw that they had passed up the slope on to the level ground again.

It was the last slope which beat him—the last sharp incline before the precipitous slope down to the farm. His muscles were weak and quivering, and the rope was crushing his chest. He cast his eyes despairingly up the remaining forty yards and knew he could not do it; Mendel, bent almost double, was panting along some ten yards away. Rufus staggered on for a few more steps, the load jerking irregularly after him.

'It's no good,' he croaked hoarsely, 'I'll have to stop.' He saw Mendel's flushed face turn.

'No, don't. Hang on. It's only a few yards.'

Rufus gave a sudden drunken sideways stagger which drove the rope cruelly into his ribs.

'I—I can't.'

With a terrific effort Mendel swerved towards him. He saw the big man's hand come out and seize the taut rope.

'Let go, blast you!' he gasped furiously. But the load had lightened perceptibly and he staggered on.

'Come on, now, give her ten—' said Mendel breathlessly. He began to count like a cox,[90] timing the numbers to each two struggling steps. 'O-*one*, two-*o*, thre-*ee*—'

'All right,' said Rufus, hating, 'you've won.' He staggered over the crest and fell forward and was painfully sick on the grass.

With a final tremendous heave Mendel deposited his own load and, dropping his rope, stretched himself and took a deep breath. His chest was heaving hard. He looked down at Rufus with eyes that shone brightly in his flushed face.

'Rough luck,' he said, unconcernedly. 'You'll be all right in a minute. Just stay there and get your breath.'

He turned calmly and began to unlash the big grey logs. Rufus slowly raised himself on shaking arms. He was deadly pale, and still panting, but the sickness was passing.

'How're you going to get them down?' he said unsteadily.

'Roll them,' said Mendel, 'that's why I came a bit further round so as to miss the wire.' He turned and dragged a big section of trunk to the edge of the hill. 'Over you go.' He pushed it off. The big sleek grey cylinder rolled heavily forward. Then, gaining speed, it went careering down the steep hill, bounding and bumping over the rough surface, to roll thundering at last to rest beside the windbreak trees of the farm.

'Log rolling!' cried Mendel with a roar of laughter. 'Actual and literal, but not literary. Now for the rest.'

Chapter XIII

Fugue a 3 Voci[91]

February died hard, in a flurry of cold, beating wind and rain, which slashed bitterly across the sweep of the hills, and whistled through the creaking windbreak of the trees. But on the first of March, winter gave up the fight and lay quiet and exhausted. The sun came out warmly and the optimistic birds, always ready to proclaim the spring's triumph before the time, sang songs of rejoicing from every bush.

Ruth and Rufus paused at the top of the hill and gazed back silently at the sun-bathed stretches below them. The colours were still the dun and olive of winter. But on the plough there was a tinge of green, and in the dark brown of the spinney a hint of red that was new and hopeful.

'It's warm,' said Rufus, almost in surprise. 'Change the colours a bit and put some leaves on the trees and it might be May.'

'And in a week,' said Ruth cynically, 'it'll probably snow again.'

'In March?'

'Oh, yes. We had snow here once in the middle of March. The seasons are always later than you think really. It's hot in October and the leaves often don't turn till the middle of November. And then in February, when you think the back of winter's broken, you find it's only just begun.'

Rufus looked down at the sunlit roof of the farm, warm and browned with lichen. 'It must be glorious here in summer.'

Ruth's face clouded. 'Yes,' she said abruptly, turning away and continuing up the track.

They walked on in silence; one thing was uppermost and they could not escape it. Even a chance remark about the seasons— even that, brought it back, large and questioning in both their minds. Rufus glanced sideways at the pale, absorbed face.

'I should like to see this place in summer,' he said deliberately.

Ruth continued to gaze straight in front of her.

'Well, so you will, won't you?' The question was a very real question.

'I don't know,' said Rufus quietly. 'That's why I brought you out. To talk about that.'

She shrugged slightly.

'What is there to talk about? It's entirely up to you. You know that.'

'But is it?' said Rufus, quickly. 'Is it quite as easy as that?'

She turned and looked at him with eyes that were meant to be frank and unconcerned. 'Of course. You stay if you want to stay and go if you want to go. We've always told you–'

'I wasn't talking about "we",' said Rufus slowly, 'I was talking about you.'

'Leaving Pip out?'

'For the moment, yes.'

Ruth idly plucked a long stalk of coarse grass and began to pick it to pieces with great care.

'As far as I am concerned,' she said at last, in a low voice, 'I should like you to stay. You know that. It's—it's fun, your being here.'

'Not more than that?' said Rufus with a faint smile. She gave a sudden urchin-like grin.

'Why, yes. If you insist. Quite a lot more than that.'

He slipped an arm round her and, pulling her towards him, kissed her lightly on the lips.

'Nice to have you here!...' he repeated with a grin. 'Silly love!'

'Well,' said Ruth, smiling up at him mischievously, 'I was merely trying to be all cold and detached and so on. Because, seriously, I should hate you to stay here—well—just because of me.'

'But if I *wanted* to—you'd be pleased?'

She nodded. 'Of course, ass. And so would Pip.'

The smile faded from Rufus's face. 'That,' he said slowly, after a moment's pause, 'is the question.'

Ruth looked at him almost anxiously. 'What? Pip?'

'Yes. I'm not at all sure that he *would* like me to stay. In fact—'

'What?'

'In fact, I think he'd probably be damned glad to see the back of me.'

Ruth shook her head. Her eyes were back on the track before them. 'No,' she said thoughtfully, 'I think you're wrong. I think he likes it.'

'Then he's got some damned queer ways of showing it,' said Rufus, dryly.

She shook her head again, almost irritably.

'Oh, I don't mean that he likes it for twenty-four hours of a day. But altogether—in the sum, I mean—I think he'd hate you to go. I *know* he would, in fact.'

Rufus paused as they came to one of Mr. Paradine's gates— miraculously upright and undamaged for once. Climbing slowly up he sat on the top bar and gazed back at the farm.

'Why do you think that?' he said thoughtfully. 'I mean, have you got any—any reasons?'

Ruth perched herself beside him and swung the slim legs.

'Yes. As a matter of fact I have. Lots. Reasons that—that you don't know about.'

'Ah—' Rufus drew a long breath. He turned and took one small brown hand in his. 'Then, look here—will you tell me them? Because for a long time now I… I've felt that there was something funny about Pip. Something I didn't understand in his attitude about us. And I want to know.'

Ruth was gazing down at the ground.

'What don't you understand?' she asked in a low voice.

'Well, he's never seemed to be able to make up his mind whether he—he cared about us or not. It seems to vary from day to day. Sometimes he's quite all right and just rags us. And then a few hours later he seems frightfully—well, frightfully jealous. Almost murderous. Usually that's when you're not there. But what's he like with you about it? *Is* he jealous?'

Ruth hesitated. 'Yes. In a way. If you can call it jealousy.'

'Well, then, why on earth did he let you? I mean to say, he almost suggested himself that we should—sleep together. And he knows quite well that I should never have done it if he'd ever shown a sign… or if he'd just been neutral about it, for that matter. He positively encouraged us.'

'I think you're thinking of Pip in rather public-school terms,' said Ruth with a bitter little smile.

'No, I'm not. I can't get him right on *any* system, that's all.' He paused inquiringly, but Ruth was silent. 'I mean to say,' Rufus went on, shifting his position on the unsympathetic bar, 'it's perfectly obvious that he's very fond of you. Normally, therefore, you'd expect him to want to keep you to himself, and to be damned jealous if he couldn't.'

Ruth opened her mouth sharply and then closed it again without speaking.

'Well,' Rufus went on, 'instead of that he more or less throws us at one another's heads. Because he quite definitely *did*, sweet.'

'Oh, yes. He did,' said Ruth quietly.

'Well, up to a point I can even understand that. I don't think it's a thing I should ever do myself but, if you really feel as he says he does about things like that, I suppose there was no reason why we shouldn't sleep together if we wanted to a lot.'

'Exactly. No reason at all.'

'But what I *can't* get,' said Rufus irritably, 'is his attitude now. Is it that he thought he wouldn't mind and now finds he does, or what? And if so why the hell doesn't he say something about it, or kick me out or something? That's the only thing I can think of—that he *thought* he was very advanced and broadminded and so on and now he's finding he isn't. That's why I was wondering if I ought to go. And now,' he shook his head helplessly, 'and now *you* say he doesn't want me to.' Rufus swung his leg over the gate and sat astride the bar. 'Well, where the hell am I?'

Ruth slid down from the gate and, placing her elbow on the bar, pillowed her chin in her hands.

'Well, I can tell you where you are,' she said slowly. She looked up at Rufus with bitterly amused black eyes. 'You're about as wide of the mark about the whole thing as you can possibly be.'

'Wide of the mark?'

'Yes. About Pip. About me. About everything. You've got it all wrong, right from the start. At least, I think so. Even *I* can't be sure.'

'Well, then, for goodness' sake tell me,' said Rufus, irritably, 'because the present situation feeds me up. I'm tired of not knowing where I stand.'

Ruth hesitated for a moment.

'Go on,' said Rufus, shortly.

'You won't like it if I do,' she said with a shake of the black head. 'And, anyhow, I'm not at all sure that I can.'

'Never mind about that. Have a go.'

She passed a hand rather wearily over her eyes.

'Well,' she said slowly and reluctantly, 'if you're going to understand Pip you've got to think of him in—in terms of his background. You know he was married—*is* married, in fact?'

Rufus nodded.

'Yes. Well, as a matter of fact he was a barrister. Quite a good one, I believe. Anyhow, he was doing very well, and making a lot of money. Well, his wife was a bitch. I suppose I *should* say that. But she really was. She gave him a hell of a time and—and that was all she did give him. Anyhow, to cut a long story short, he got fed up, chucked up his practice and came down here. I'd known him for a long time, and we—we liked one another, so I came too. We hadn't any very definite ideas. At least, I hadn't. I was just in love with him. And all Pip wanted was to get away. From her. From work. From people. From the whole lot. And get back to a life where he could just do what he liked and be alive. Rather how you felt, I should imagine, only more so.'

'Well, you seem to have done it very successfully,' said Rufus. 'At least, I always thought so.'

'Yes. I dare say it looks like it to you. But as a matter of fact—' Ruth frowned down at the grass, 'as a matter of fact, we've only half succeeded. I suppose in a way it's my fault, but I've never been able to—to go all the way with Pip. I suppose I'm too disgustingly conventional. But, you see, partly because of the rotten time he's had, he's always been wildly keen on being—on being "natural". He wants everything to be natural and free and—and so on. And it so happens that what's natural to him isn't always natural to me.' She hesitated for a minute. 'And then you see I realised something. It's a bit difficult to explain, but as time went on I realised that— that I was only part of the scenery, really. That's why he'd brought me. And, you see, Rufus, I—I was very fond of him, so—'

'But look here, that's all rot!' said Rufus sharply. 'He's frightfully in love with you.'

Ruth shook her head. 'Oh, yes. He likes me all right—as a person. But he dislikes women fundamentally, and I happen to be one. So whether he likes me or not at any particular moment depends on just how fundamental he happens to be feeling. No. This is a thing I know about, Rufus. I'm here because a natural life involves having a woman. Just that. And what is more he resents it. He resents needing me. Like hell. The fact that he quite likes me doesn't alter that at all. In fact, it makes it worse sometimes.' She paused and picked a splinter from the wood of the gate. 'Which sometimes makes life a bit difficult as you've seen. Because I happen to be very fond of him.'

'I think you're talking rot,' said Rufus, without conviction.

Ruth shook her head. 'No. That's all quite true. You see, you've got to remember that Pip's absolutely selfish. Not selfish in the usual nasty petty little ways, but rather *grandly* selfish. He literally isn't interested in other people. Not even in me. I'm simply part of his surroundings; a thing that affects him at certain times in certain ways. If the house caught fire, Pip would be annoyed, not because it's a nice house in itself, but because not to have the house, which *he* likes, would be annoying. You see the difference? And if I died, he'd be annoyed because, since a woman is necessary to a natural life, he'd have to get someone else. You see? That's what I mean when I say he's sitting in the stalls all the time. He sits and notes how things react on him. Sometimes he's beastly to me, quite casually, just to see how it feels to be beastly. And then if I cry, which I usually do, like a fool—because I don't like it, Rufus—he comforts me to see how *that* feels.'

'The swab,'[92] said Rufus between set teeth.

Ruth shook her head. 'Oh, no, he isn't. It isn't like that at all. That's his attitude to everything.'

There was a long silence.

'Well, then how do *I* come into this?' asked Rufus at last. 'Am I part of the surroundings too?'

'Yes, but in a different way. You're sent straight from Heaven for him. You see, there are only a limited number of things that he can try with me. He can be beastly to me or nice to me. He can go about with me or stay by himself. He can make love to me or not, and so on. But after a time he gets to know how he feels about practically all of those possibilities, and it gets dull. He was very bored just before you came. Then you go blundering about on the Plain, and land at our very door. Don't you see what a chance that gives him? You're another man. It creates an entirely new set of circumstances. Put us together and how does he feel? What's it like to have someone else sleeping with your woman? How does it feel to be odd man out? How does one feel when jealous?... Don't you see?'

Rufus's face was very hard.

'Yes,' he said slowly, 'I see all right. Hence this competitive tomfoolery, I suppose.'

'Of course. Pip would say it's the natural thing when you get two men with only one woman between them. I expect he'd like to fight you for me.'

'That,' said Rufus viciously, 'would be quite all right with me.'

'And quite all right with him. Whatever happened. You can't get the better of Pip, you see, whatever you do. That's what makes him rather magnificent really. If you beat him, he'd just be coldly interested in what it felt like to be beaten.'

Rufus flushed as he remembered the beech tree. *And* in what it felt like to win? A sudden thought struck him and he turned to her sharply.

'Did you know all this before—before we began?'

Ruth hesitated. He put out a hand and turned the black head almost roughly towards him. The black eyes were hurt and afraid.

'Did you?'

She nodded slightly. 'Yes. Of course.'

'My God!' said Rufus in disgust.

'At least,' said Ruth with forced calmness, 'I knew that he did that sort of thing. As a matter of fact—' she hesitated, and her eyes were full of fear, 'as a matter of fact he suggested it.'

'Suggested what?' asked Rufus carefully.

'That I should get you to—to make love to me.'

Rufus looked at her for a moment with interest. Then he nodded slowly, and slid from the gate.

'I see,' he said quietly, 'well, in that case the question doesn't arise.' He threw away his cigarette. 'I think we'd better be getting back,' he said conversationally, 'it's getting cold.'

Ruth turned from the gate and laid a hand on his arm.

'Rufus–'

He looked at her coldly.

'I'm sorry. I told you you wouldn't like it.'

'So you did,' said Rufus sardonically, 'you were scrupulously fair.'

He started back along the track. Ruth walked mutely beside him. He did not look at her, but plugged silently along with his face expressionless. A tear suddenly splashed on the front of Ruth's coat. She brushed a hand hastily across her eyes. Rufus shot a glance at her covertly and flushed. Ruth crying, with the queer little face puckered and unhappy, and the long black lashes wet with tears, was a sight he could never bear with equanimity.

'It's no use crying,' he said savagely and uncomfortably.

Ruth produced a small handkerchief and blew her nose vigorously. 'One never cries when it *is* any use,' she said rather unexpectedly.

'As far as I can see,' Rufus said in irritated justification, 'that was just about the dirtiest thing you could have done to a man.' He was trying hard to prevent himself from taking her in his arms and saying that it was quite all right really. Not that it was. He was deeply hurt and bewildered. But at that moment his instinct was to change her tearful, unhappy face at any price.

'It wasn't like that at all,' she said wearily, 'if you only knew.' She dabbed vigorously at her eyes and thrust her handkerchief into her pocket. 'But there you are,' she added with a shrug, 'you don't know…'

'Don't know what?' asked Rufus sullenly.

'How it happened. It isn't what you think, at all!'

'Well, then, tell me,' he said almost brutally, stopping short and regarding her with sullen, resentful eyes. He did not hate her for what she had done. He only hated her for crying and unfairly making him feel guilty. Ruth hesitated.

'I don't know that it would help much if I did.'

Rufus shrugged.

'Please yourself,' he said coldly, 'but it's damn-all use to say I don't know and cry about it and then not tell me. Too like a cheap film with everybody having misunderstandings. I understood you to say that you made love to me to amuse Mendel. Because he egged you on. If that's so, it means that Mendel's played a dirty game and that you've helped him, doesn't it?'

Ruth shook her head.

'No. No, it isn't that, Rufus. You don't see. Pip wouldn't—he wouldn't play a dirty trick. Not in a—a personal way like that. It's just that he wanted to see something about himself and me–'

'I don't care *why* he did it. I don't care if he felt personal or impersonal about it. All I know is that he's been fooling me and that you've helped him. Haven't you?'

She looked at him for a moment with bright tear-filled dark eyes, and then glanced quickly away.

'In a way. But not how you think… Oh, I don't know–'

She dropped her face in her hands and her shoulders quivered. Rufus hesitated and then gently laid both hands on her shoulders.

'Darling,' he said, gently.

She did not look up.

'Darling—don't cry. Try and tell me what happened.' He slipped his arms round the small shaking form. 'It's all right, love. Don't cry. Just tell me what did happen.'

Quite suddenly her sobs ceased. She fumbled again for the handkerchief, and broke gently away from his arms.

'Sorry,' she said unsteadily. 'This is damned unfair. Crying at you about it. But all the same, I *will* tell you, because—because I wouldn't like you to think what you are thinking...' She slowly dried her eyes and started to walk on down the track. Rufus waited in silence. 'You see,' said Ruth at last, frowning into the distance with red-rimmed eyes, 'one of the things Pip had always complained about and been beastly about was the—the way I loved him. He—he said I hung on to him like a leech. I suppose he was right, but I couldn't help it. I loved him, though I knew he didn't love me in—in that sort of way. And I suppose I did pester him rather. At least, he always said I did... Well, he'd always said that what I wanted was a lover. Somebody else. Because then I should see that I didn't really want him alone—that someone else would do just as well.' She paused and glanced at Rufus rather nervously. 'So when you came he—he said we ought to be lovers. He said it would be good for both of us— that you wanted somebody and so did I. I didn't want to, really. I just wanted him. But he wouldn't have me much, and he kept on saying that I was too civilised and—and so on, and laughing at me, so at last I—well, I thought–' She swallowed hard. 'I'm awfully sorry, Rufus. But you see, I thought you wanted someone, and he kept saying I ought to and... and–' There was a long silence. Rufus was staring straight ahead of him with set lips. 'I know it doesn't make it much better really,' said Ruth helplessly, 'but I didn't want you to think I just did it to amuse him without thinking of you at all.'

Rufus smiled rather coldly.

'I see. Well, I suppose you realise that it's rather a shock to find that for weeks a woman's been letting you make love to her for—for purely experimental purposes?'

'But–!' Ruth turned to him in horror.

'It isn't pleasant,' he added bitterly, 'to find that you've been used as a—a sort of stud bull...'

'But, Rufus–!' She caught his hand in agony. 'You don't think that—you *can't!*...'

'Well, isn't that precisely what you've been saying? You thought you'd try an experiment and you did me the honour of selecting me to try it on.'

'But don't you see—!' She wrung his hand hard in supplication. 'Don't you see it—it was only like that at first. That—that first night and the next morning. But after that it was real. You know it was! Rufus, you don't think I've been doing it all this time?'

'You mean that Mendel was right?'

'How do you mean?'

'That as you couldn't have him I proved a satisfactory substitute?'

She stopped suddenly and looked at him. Rufus met her eyes coldly. Ruth slowly relinquished his hand.

'All right,' she said in a low voice. 'I suppose I deserve it. But I thought perhaps you'd see—'

She turned away. 'Never mind. Let's leave it at that. You were the subject of an experiment as you say, and I'm sorry. There's no more to be said.'

'Dramatic resignation,' said Rufus, brutally.

'Not at all,' she replied wearily, 'but it's no good trying to explain a thing to a person who understands and won't admit it.' She walked slowly on. 'Have you got a cigarette?'

'Surely.' Rufus produced his case, and lit her cigarette and his own. She blew a cloud of blue smoke into the air and looked at it with sombre eyes.

'I don't often generalise about men,' she said in a queer, impersonal voice, 'but there are some ways in which you're all very much alike, and I think that's the most general one.'

'What, dislike of being smade fools of?' said Rufus, acidly.

She shook her head. 'No. Never being content to write a thing off as finished. If anyone does a thing to you, you can never resist rubbing it in—if you happen to be in the right. Pip's just the same. If I do anything he doesn't like he doesn't just go for me and then stop. He prods. Sometimes he'll be nice in between. But he goes on prodding me about it for days. He can't stop once he finds he's on a sore spot and quite justified in hurting. I suppose it's the masculine feeling for justice—pious indignation and so on.' She turned and looked at him coolly and appraisingly. She was no longer afraid now of what he would do or say. Rufus realised uncomfortably that the strategic strength of his position was tottering.

'So you expect me to be ready to forgive you for making a fool of me directly you say you're sorry?' he said sarcastically.

She nodded. 'Of course. If you believe me. You know now exactly what happened. Of course you do. You're not an absolute fool. You know I did experiment with you—once. I've said I was sorry and you know it's true. But you must have your pound of flesh. You must pretend you think I've been doing it all the time.' She shook her head reflectively. 'It's queer how you like hurting, all of you.'

'It's rapidly becoming clear that the whole thing's my fault,' said Rufus with heavy irony.

'No. You're a deeply injured party, my dear. Don't you be done out of that. Stick to it. Have your money's worth. Make her squirm a bit. Make her cry a bit. And then, if she's worth it, relent. Slowly and with dignity.'

She stopped suddenly and turned on him. Her eyes blazed suddenly like blown fire. 'My God!' she cried, so suddenly that it startled him. 'The insolence of it! *I've* deceived you! *I've* taken your pure and holy love and experimented with it! But *you* haven't experimented with mine, have you? Yours was always pure and holy and idealistic, wasn't it? That first night, when you thought I was just a little tart, deceiving my lover, you were quite ready to do it. Pip had been decent to you—damned decent. But that didn't stop you from making love to me. I tell you I was playing this game straight days before you were. For days; while you were just amusing yourself and working off a few repressions on the nearest woman, which happened to be me. And then you have the nerve to go all wounded because I didn't fall in love with you at sight!...' She paused and stood there, gloriously angry, with heaving breasts and distended nostrils.

Desperately Rufus strove to frame a completely devastating reply. But she gave him no time.

'Don't worry!' she said. 'No one will ever suggest that it was your fault. It couldn't be. You're in on a good thing. You've had someone to sleep with and now you've got a grand reason for not sleeping with her any more. She's deceived you. What do you want better than that? Your conduct has been exemplary, and would be applauded in any Mess[93] in England. Leave it at that and don't spoil your lovely case by overworking it, that's all.'

Rufus stood for a moment, looking at the small proud figure. Then a slow grin spread over his face. Slowly and calmly he put out his hand and, pulling her, unwilling, towards him, methodically put his arms round her and kissed the face which she strove to avert.

'You little devil!' he said in fond surprise. 'You little hell-cat!'

'No!' she muttered, struggling vainly.

He continued to kiss her, gently and rhythmically.

'You talk to me like that, woman, and I'll put you across my knee and smack your bottom. Showing your nasty temper like that.'

She had stopped struggling now and lay limp in his arms. 'I slept with you,' went on Rufus, happily, 'because I wanted to. And I've gone on sleeping with you because I've gone on wanting to. I don't care in the slightest *why* you let me, as long as you did and liked it.' He raised a hand and turned the black head until his eyes were looking into hers. 'And as for Mendel, if he likes to look on, let him. And I hope he likes what he sees.' He bent his head and pressed his lips to hers. They quivered and opened. The grip of her arms tightened convulsively.

Ruth went to bed early that night. Despite their reconciliation, her relations with Rufus had scarcely returned to normal. As she had stood there, proud, angry and fearless, on the green track, the desire to take and kiss her—to comfort her—to say everything was as it had always been, had been irresistible. But after the spell of passionate kissing had passed, they had found themselves back on the uneasy debatable ground. Much which had puzzled Rufus was explained—her relationship with Mendel—the queer moodiness of the big man himself—the reason for her original brazenness. But a question still remained, uneasy and unanswered, which cast a shadow of awkwardness across their most casual conversation. She loved Mendel. That was certain. Despite his indifference— despite his egotism—despite his frequent unkindness. But she claimed that her relationship with Rufus was more than a mere cold-blooded experiment—she hinted that in it there had been a new happiness and a new sincerity. What was there in it for her in truth? That question still remained unanswered.

Rufus did not ask her. He had been on the point of doing so as they walked home from the talk in which he had learned so much and so little. But he realised, with a start of surprise, that had she put the same question to him, he could not have answered. Somehow the question of what he felt for Ruth had never arisen—never troubled him. She had been there. She had been willing. She had supplied a physical need. He had taken what was so fortuitously offered, like a small boy taking an orange at a school treat. But, like the small boy, the orange, the immediate objective, had been everything. And of his feelings towards the donor, he had scarcely thought at all.

He sat that night gazing into the big fire with a frown. Save for an occasional movement of the glowing logs, and the rustle as Mendel turned the leaves of his book, there was absolute silence.

Once, indeed, he looked up sharply, half afraid that in the stillness his very thoughts would be audible. But Mendel, leaning back in his chair, read calmly on, the blue eyes flickering from line to line, and the corners of the mouth drawn down in a slight smile of sardonic amusement. Rufus glanced at the cover of the book, and understood the smile. Mendel was reading Jeremy Taylor.[94]

Rufus turned again to the fire with wrinkled brows. Ruth. What did he feel for her? There were times when she was irresistible—when the feeling of the slim body in his arms was a sharp and hurting thing that– And she was never dull, never boring, never irritating, never jarring. It was not purely a physical attraction. Of that he could be certain. He knew he felt for her a hundred times—a thousand times—more of love than he had ever done for Marjorie, or for any woman before. But– He shook his head. Ruth was this life. And this life was queer—odd—in no way parallel to life as one had always known it. He tried to imagine her elsewhere. Ruth in evening clothes at a theatre. Ruth meeting strangers. Ruth even crossing a London street... He shook his head again in helpless irritation. Somehow it would not go. One could not see the two worlds mixed. Ruth was Three Trees—the downs—a scarlet jersey and a dark skirt—a bed—a naked body—Mendel. And amidst them all a lover—*the* lover. But one could not take them all away and see the lover alone. One could not substitute Piccadilly for the downs and a flat in Regent's Park for Three Trees, and stand back and estimate and assess the mixture. A phrase she had used to him that day flashed through his mind. 'A part of the scenery–' That was it. There, in the play they were all playing, she was cast for the lover, and one loved her with all the passion of a heartfelt part. But outside the theatre?... In another play?... He could not tell.

Mendel shifted his position slightly and looked up.

'J. Taylor,' he said conversationally, 'always seems to me the supreme example of the way Christianity improved on God.'

'Why?' asked Rufus, vaguely.

'Because he offers a perfectly good substitute for being a man: i.e., being a Christian. It's exactly as though he feels that God is an author who made rather a mess of his job and wants to suppress all the remaining first editions, and substitute a revised version. "God may have made you this way, but since then, he's seen the light and become more Christian." '

Rufus nodded unheedingly and returned to the fire. Mendel glanced at him keenly for a moment and then returned to his book with a slight smile.

And even if one could be sure of oneself, Rufus reflected, how about Ruth? She had said she was not playing and it was true. But what *was* she doing? Was there a degree between playing and… loving? Clearly it was not a case of 'off with the old love and on with the new'. She was insistent that she loved Mendel. And anyhow, no insistence was necessary. It stuck out a yard. Yet she had said she was not playing—that one was not just a substitute—a thing *faute de mieux*…[95] What was one, then? Could a person love two people at once? Belong to two people?... He frowned. Clearly, if she belonged to anyone it was Mendel. Of that there was no doubt. Belonged, perhaps, to Mendel, but did not love. Loved *him*, but did not belong…

'What did you quarrel about?' asked Mendel's voice with gentle interest.

Rufus looked up sharply. The big man had silently discarded Jeremy Taylor and was leaning back in his chair, looking at him narrowly.

'Ruth and I?' he said foolishly.

Mendel nodded silently.

Rufus flushed slightly. 'Why do you think we did?'

Mendel slowly lit a cigarette. 'Need I do a Holmesian exposition?'[96] he inquired with a little smile. 'All about red eyes and general gloom? What's up?'

'Why do you want to know?' asked Rufus shortly. Mendel raised his eyebrows.

'Merely general interest; besides, I might be able to help, or explain or something.'

Rufus looked at him coldly. 'I thought you weren't interested in your fellow men?'

'I'm not,' said Mendel with a lazy smile. 'But you and Ruth are scarcely my fellow men, are you? Besides,' he added with a grin, 'I hate to see these tiffs going on. Makes the house so depressing.'

'You prefer light comedy?' said Rufus bitterly.

'Infinitely.'

Rufus hesitated.

'Well, whatever we disagreed about it's settled now. So it will be quite all right for you,' he said sullenly. Mendel gazed reflectively at the end of his cigarette.

'Dear old Rufus,' he said softly. 'You're a cynical old cuss, aren't you?'

'No,' said Rufus, bluntly, 'but I'm rapidly becoming one.'

Mendel raised his eyebrows. 'Through me?'

'If you like to put it like that.'

'Why?'

There was a moment's pause.

'I don't see that it'll get us anywhere to go into that,' said Rufus quietly.

'But is that quite fair?' Mendel spread out his hands in mock appeal. 'I proffer help in your troubles, and you reject the offer with scorn. What have I done? After all, Rufus, though perhaps it's indelicate of me to mention it, I am like the good Lord. I have given you many things. Not the least of them—' He paused and glanced at Rufus, who was leaning tensely forward with eyes blazing.

'Well?' said Rufus swiftly.

Mendel smiled. 'Not the least of them a warm welcome to my house,' he said gently.

Rufus hesitated and then slowly leaned back in his chair. 'You see, whatever you do, you can't get the better of Pip…'

'I didn't realise that we were talking in terms of obligations,' he said slowly.

'We weren't,' said Mendel with his sudden charming smile. 'In fact, that was an absurd thing to say. It was only that I wondered why you had become so secretive, that's all.'

Rufus hesitated for a long moment.

Somehow at the sight of Mendel's charming friendly grin, all the dislike, suspicion and disgust which he had felt at what Ruth had told him seemed suddenly foolish and unjustified. When all was said and done, what *had* she told him? That Mendel was a queer fish. But he had known that before. That Mendel had proposed that they should be lovers. But even that might be part of the man's odd, crooked philosophy. It was unpleasant—uncomfortable—to feel that Mendel arranged things—experimented with one's life and looked on. But was it fair to judge Mendel by ordinary standards?… He did not claim to be an ordinary person.

'I don't want to butt in,' said Mendel gently, 'I only want to help if I can.'

Rufus nodded abstractedly and lit a cigarette to gain time. For the life of him he could not decide whether to lay his cards on the table—to tell Mendel that he knew. But as he flicked the match into the fire he suddenly saw that the thing was impossible. For after all—what did he know? That Mendel had cheated him? How had he? That he hadn't played straight? In what way hadn't he? It would not go into words…

He looked across at the big man and realised quite suddenly that he did not know him, and that now he never would. He might admire Mendel. He might even like him in a puzzled way. But he saw open between them a gulf which could never be filled again. Mendel was still smiling but, in the second that the match dropped into the glowing heart of the fire, Rufus made up his mind and gave Mendel up. And not even the smile could awake in him the confidence and trust that had been within an ace of returning. It was too difficult and he did not understand.

'Well, as a matter of fact,' he said evenly, 'I haven't told you because the thing we disagreed about was so silly and trivial that it would sound absurd to you. And anyhow it's quite all right now.'

He saw Mendel's eyes narrow a trifle, but the charming smile remained.

'Good. Well, then that's all about it. I'm glad.'

'You wouldn't like us to quarrel?' said Rufus slowly.

'Not unless you really want to,' said Mendel, still smiling. 'I'd like you to do just whatever will amuse you both the most.'

There was a moment's pause. Then Rufus rose abruptly to his feet.

'Bed,' he said wearily, 'that's where I'm going.'

Mendel grinned up lazily.

'Tired? So am I. But I think I'll do a bit more of Jeremy first. He's rather fun.'

'Good night,' said Rufus.

'Good night, Rufus. By the way,' Mendel added as he reached the door, 'have you any idea where our joint property is sleeping? *Chez* you or *chez* me?'

'I don't know,' said Rufus heavily.

Mendel grinned. 'Well, if you've been having a row I should think probably *chez* you. Anyhow, as the guard said to the passengers, you'll see when you get there. Good night.'

'Darling—'

'Yes, Rufus?'

'I want to ask you something. You needn't tell me if you don't want to…'

'What, love?'

'—do you love me?'

The warm body stirred slightly.

'No. Of course not. That's why I'm here.'

'No. But seriously, do you?'

Silence.

'You love him, don't you?'

'Yes,' slowly, 'I do.'

'Well, then—'

Another gentle movement.

'Rufus—' uneasily. 'It's awfully hard to explain. Do you want me to try?'

'Not if you'd rather not. But—'

'Well, then, can you understand this? I do love you—love you an awful lot. More than anybody else in the world. But it—it's quite different. That's all I can tell you really.' Pause. 'Will that do?'

A long silence.

'—yes. As long as you really do. Because I love you.'

'Rufus, my darling—if only you knew how much I do…'

Recurring decimal.

Chapter XIV

On Seeing Straight With a Black Eye

For a few days there was peace. Rufus saw little of Mendel. He disappeared early in the morning to his carpentry, or went for long walks on the hills alone. He was in his most solitary mood—the mood which seemed to demand, above everything else, that he should avoid contact with human beings. But on the few occasions when they were unavoidably brought together, he was always smiling and friendly, and there was no trace in his casual conversation of the previous tenseness and resentment.

Rufus accepted the change with a mental shrug of the shoulders. He had ceased now to try and keep pace with Mendel's rapidly shifting temperament. He lived exclusively in the present—the one thing which experience had taught him to rely on in the queer, gusty life at Three Trees. He was unfeignedly glad to be left alone with Ruth, and to Mendel he was rapidly becoming indifferent. He did not know to what this sudden relaxation of the tension might be the prelude. He did not even care. It was sufficient to be left in unhindered possession of Ruth, and to find Mendel agreeable and cheerful. He no longer felt uneasy or suspicious that things were not what they seemed. He *knew* they were not. And the assurance that fair weather could not last, made up, in a strange way, for his ignorance of what the change of weather might be.

He answered indifference with indifference quite as genuine, and enjoyed Mendel's long absences thoroughly.

With Ruth too, he lived only for the moment. By tacit consent, they had made no further effort to unravel the tangle of their feelings for one another. The future they never discussed. It was as though both, falling back exhausted from the high, blank, questioning wall before them, had turned with a queer resigned, but quite genuine happiness to the enjoyment of the sunshine on its known and familiar side. There was but one truth and one certainty—the present. And the present was long walks in wind, rain and sun, the slow death of winter, and reading and making love, and speculating on a thousand things which did not and could not concern them, but which had one supreme recommendation—they did not wring one with doubt and uneasiness, but could be slipped quietly and lovingly back into the library of thought without demanding action, or attitude, or resolve, or change.

Ruth made no comment on Mendel's solitariness. She accepted it in the same non-committal way in which she accepted all his moods. And in the meantime she turned unhesitatingly to Rufus.

At the end of a week, however, the clouds blew up again. At a midday meal Mendel was as smiling and cheerful as ever; but he did not get up and go with that clear air of relief which had marked the mood of the last few days. Instead he sat on, smoking a cigarette, and chatting gaily and inconsequently. Rufus was irresistibly reminded of his first few careful days at Three Trees—the days which had almost convinced him that in this man there was the art of existence. The recollection was a warning, and he watched, interested and philosophic, to see where the fire of light chaff and friendliness was leading. He had not long to wait. Mendel, leaning back in his chair, cigarette in hand, was complaining with mock bitterness at the inadequacy of the food at the previous night's meal.

'I don't mind its being uninteresting,' he was saying, 'I don't mind its being inadequate. But cold—congealed!...'

'Well, you should come in at a reasonable time,' said Ruth, defensively. We waited about half an hour for you as it was. It's your own fault for refusing to have regular meal-times like a Christian. If I ever *do* try and get you to come and eat, you're usually furious.'

Mendel sighed. 'There are,' he said plaintively, 'no fires before which my food could be stood? No oven in which it could be placed? No—'

'If I'd put it in the oven it would have been uneatable, anyhow.'

'All right. All right.' He held up a hand and winked at Rufus. 'Let it pass. Of course it was my fault. I was late. And time, of course, is always a matter of vital importance here, isn't it? I shall have to buy you a gong. Or perhaps a hooter. Like a factory.' He flicked the ash from his cigarette. 'Well, I tell you what. I'm not going to work to-night, so let's have a meal. A *real* meal. Eating for Eating's sake. It's an amusing thing to do sometimes.'

'Can't be done,' said Ruth promptly, 'not to-night. To-morrow if you like.'

Mendel shook his head.

'No, *not* to-morrow. To-night. I feel like gorging to-day and probably to-morrow I shan't.' He looked at her inquiringly. 'Why not to-night, sweet?'

'Because there isn't any food. At least not much. Besides, I shan't have time. We're going to the Devil's Leap and we shan't be back till about six.'

Mendel frowned. 'Well, that will leave plenty of time, won't it?'

'Yes, but don't you see, Pip, we don't want to go down to the village to-day. Otherwise we can't get over to the Leap and back at all. We were going straight away.'

Mendel raised his eyebrows. 'I see,' he said sarcastically, 'and how about me?'

'Well, as a matter of fact,' said Rufus, 'we thought you probably wouldn't want to come—that you'd be working. But–'

'But it would be much more fun if you would,' said Ruth quickly.

Mendel laughed rather unpleasantly.

'Oh, no,' he said. 'I wouldn't butt in and spoil the party for worlds. Three-sided picnics are a weariness of the flesh, anyhow.' He leaned forward and smiled his icy smile at Ruth. 'But I think it would be much nicer if you went there *to-morrow*. Then you could go down to the village and buy food for to-night.'

There was a moment's pause.

'You're very intent on your meals all of a sudden,' said Rufus suddenly. He had been looking forward to the walk.

Mendel turned to him with a smile.

'I am,' he said gently. 'Do you mind?'

Rufus met his eyes.

'When it makes you as bloody inconsiderate as this, I do,' he said hotly.

Mendel shook his head. 'I am deeply sorry about that,' he said tauntingly. 'Deeply sorry.'

Ruth was looking at Mendel with dark, steady eyes.

'All right,' she said quietly, 'just as you like. You shall have your precious meal to-night if you're so keen on it. What d'you want?'

Mendel smiled. 'Bacon and eggs,' he said coolly. 'Duck eggs, from Mr. Cooper.'

Rufus's fingers clenched instinctively. The provocation was so deliberate—so completely undisguised. Had he even coloured the ridiculous demand for a meal by asking for something difficult or complicated, it would have been less infuriating. But Cooper's farm was a good three miles away and, with his words, the deliberate interference with their plans became an open challenge. Rufus glanced at the girl. She was staring fixedly at Mendel.

'You shall have bacon and eggs,' she said slowly. 'From Mr. Cooper. And we'll go to the Devil's Leap to-morrow.'

'Excellent!' said Mendel calmly. 'I'm eternally grateful. You can't think what those eggs mean to me. Besides, doing something for me will be a change for you.'

She looked at him for a moment in silence, and then turning without a word, went to the door. Rufus laid a hand on her arm.

'Look here,' he said in a suppressed voice, 'I'll go. I shall be glad of the walk.'

Mendel flicked the ash from his cigarette.

'No, you won't,' he said gently. 'Ruth will go. By herself.'

'What the hell's it got to do with you?' said Rufus, turning furiously.

Mendel smiled lazily. 'Ruth will go,' he repeated. He looked at Rufus thoughtfully. 'It'll do her good,' he added deliberately, 'she's a lazy little bitch.'

He flicked his cigarette into the fire like lightning and half rose, as Rufus took a furious stride towards him.

'Rufus—!' Ruth caught his arm quickly. Rufus hesitated. Mendel smiled coldly and sank back into his chair. Rufus turned to Ruth. She was looking fixedly at Mendel.

'All right, Pip,' she said quietly, 'I'll go.'

'I know you will,' he replied curtly.

She pressed Rufus's arm slightly and went out. Rufus hesitated for a moment and then walked to the window. He stood there for a moment, his face very pale. There was icy sweat on his forehead. Mendel had lit another cigarette and was gazing into the fire with a thoughtful smile. Rufus saw Ruth emerge from the front door carrying a basket. She glanced back at the window and, seeing him, smiled and waved. He lifted a hand in reply and then, watching her well on to the track to the village, turned to Mendel. He knew quite well what he was going to do now. He had known even as her hand fell on his arm. There was nothing new in Mendel's unkindness to Ruth—nothing in his bullying that, in itself, demanded immediate and violent action. In the old days she had been his to treat as he pleased. But the last few days had changed all that. Mendel had left her and she had turned to Rufus; and to bully and insult her now was a direct challenge and unmistakably intended as such. Rufus knew that. He looked at Mendel and their eyes met. Mendel knew also. He still smiled. It was a happy, almost joyful smile, as though he welcomed a long expected gift.

'Well, Rufus?' he said gently.

Rufus looked at him dispassionately. Noted the spread of the great shoulders and the big pectoral muscles which rippled beneath the thin old shirt. They were interesting but not significant. 'I want to talk to you,' he said slowly, 'about several things.'

Mendel shook his head. 'No, you don't,' he said calmly, 'that's the last thing you want to do. But, still—go ahead if you really think so.'

Rufus glanced quickly out of the window at the green hillside. 'It's a nice afternoon,' he said.

'Agreed,' said Mendel solemnly, nodding.

'And a walk would do us both good,' said Rufus, reasonably.

'Agreed again. We might have gone and fetched the eggs, mightn't we?'

Rufus nodded. 'Yes. Well, as we didn't, how about going for a walk ourselves?'

Mendel sat up and looked at him thoughtfully.

'And talk on the walk, eh?'

'That's right,' said Rufus impassively.

Mendel stared at him for a moment in silence.

'A walk,' he said at last, 'is a thing I should really like. But—' a smile quivered at the corners of his mouth, '—you're quite sure *you* really want to go for one?'

He glanced up quizzically. Rufus's nails were digging into his hands. 'Quite sure,' he said calmly.

There was a moment's silence. Then Mendel rose quickly to his feet. 'Right!' he said briskly, 'I'm with you.' He yawned and stretched his great arms above his head. 'God, but this fire makes you sleepy!'

Rufus smiled a contemptuous little smile.

'Well, well—it enables you to be an impressively powerful figure when stretching,' he said coldly.

Mendel paused in the middle of his yawn and gazed at him in surprise. Then he suddenly roared with laughter and slapped Rufus on the shoulder. 'Oh, come, Rufus, old man—give me credit for a *little* more subtlety than that! Dash it!...'

They set off through the farmyard in silence.

'The arrangements for this walk are entirely in your hands,' said Mendel, lightly, as they reached the gate. 'Is there anywhere special you want to go?'

Rufus nodded. 'Up towards the spinney,' he said briefly.

'Right you are.' Mendel was accommodating.

They started to climb the hill side by side. Rufus's mind flew back to the last time they had done so. He smiled grimly at the recollection. To-day, there was no rope, no saw, no headache, no weariness. And somehow, surprisingly, the atmosphere was less tense, more simple, more understood...

Mendel's chuckle broke in upon his thoughts.

'D'you remember our beech tree?' he said with a grin, 'That was a rum go, Rufus.'

'You won,' said Rufus, briefly.

'No, that was the odd thing about it. I really lost rather badly. I had all the advantages. After all, you'd been having a rough night at sea with Ruth, and you were still half asleep when we started. But even so I never really cracked you.' He glanced sideways with a grin. 'After that I began to look at you with new interest.'

'You didn't expect much, then,' replied Rufus grimly.

'No. To be frank, I didn't. Not as much as that, anyhow. You're a husky[97] lad,' he added thoughtfully.

Rufus made no reply. The impersonal chatter about their queer private contest annoyed him. It seemed at the moment deplorably in bad taste. He hated Mendel to descend to polite small talk—to turn the edge of his enmity with friendly reminiscence. They were walking towards the end of a long battle and to discuss previous stages in this calm way was an ill-timed friendliness which he resented. He wanted only to walk in silence with Mendel to their walk's end, and then in silence to settle what would not go into words. So far they had understood one another. But now Mendel's talk was discordant and jarring.

Mendel apparently sensed his mood and fell silent. In contrast to their last visit to the spinney, they walked at an easy pace, breathing deeply and gently, as men will who know that breath and muscle must be saved and husbanded. Despite himself, Rufus could not fix his mind firmly on the business in hand, nor rivet his eyes on the still distant spinney. He looked around him and noted, with a kind of obstinate interest, the details of the changing season. The spinney itself was redder now with unopened buds, the grass was greener, and the air, which had been keen with the keenness of winter, was now only the fresh soft air of early spring. He strode on, feeling almost with surprise, the subtle play of his thigh muscles. There was something which brought comfort and confidence in the feeling of that awareness which was in him. He glanced sideways at Mendel and noted with detached admiration the powerful stride and backthrust shoulders. Interesting still, but still, with the spinney in full view, unsignificant. He suddenly felt, strangely, foolishly and exultantly happy. Two men walked silently across a stretch of bare down, with upflung heads and mouths tightly set. And they were good to look at. He stood some ten yards away and looked at them, and was very proud. They had no names, but they were alive in a living place, as men should be…

Mendel half paused when they were within half a mile of the spinney and regarded Rufus with a slow smile.

'When we started out, Rufus,' he said gently, 'you said you wanted to talk to me. There's no need if you don't really want to, but it might be interesting if you did.'

'I think you probably know all I wanted to say,' replied Rufus after a moment's hesitation.

'Probably. Some of it at least. But you might enjoy saying it, and I should certainly enjoy listening. And there might be something I didn't know.'

Rufus looked at him thoughtfully.

'There is a thing I'd like to ask you…'

'Yes?'

'How do you justify yourself—*to* yourself? Or do you? I know you don't attempt to justify anything you do to other people. But does that go for yourself too? Or do you work it all out so that you are really—really *right?* And if so, how?'

Mendel was smiling into the distance.

'That's a big question,' he said, with a little shake of the head, 'and I'm afraid it goes rather beyond the scope of our walk. But speaking offhand, I should say it's a mixture of the two. I never try to justify—even to myself. But sometimes I do, despite myself.'

'Convenient,' said Rufus shortly.

'Not altogether,' said Mendel calmly, 'not half so convenient as the way people like yourself work. You see, yours is a nice flexible system, really. You always seek justification for anything, and you get into such good practice that you always find it. Your average good husband and father, for example, would find half a dozen good justifications for being unkind to his wife.'

'And you?...'

'For me, the justification, if you like to call it that, is that I sometimes choose to be unjustifiable. Quite frankly and cheerfully.'

'The frankness and cheerfulness,' said Rufus, bitterly, 'is always in evidence.'

'I'm glad of that,' said Mendel seriously. 'I attach a good deal of importance to being quite truthful in my relations.'

'Truthful!' said Rufus, contemptuously. 'As you have been with me?'

Mendel turned the blue eyes full upon him.

'I have always been entirely truthful with you,' he said quietly. 'It isn't my fault if you have the sort of mentality which can't see the truth when it's given it.'

They were quite close to the spinney now. Before it lay the smooth patch of short lawn-like grass over which they had dragged their logs.

'There's nothing else?' asked Mendel.

'No.'

Mendel gave a sigh of relief.

'Frankly,' he said, 'I am rather relieved. I had an awful fear that with your queer crooked mind you would have got this all mixed up with quarrels and Ruth and so on.' He gave Rufus an ironic little bow. 'Once again, Rufus, I apologise for having underestimated you.'

Rufus looked at him in surprise.

'It is to do with Ruth,' he said grimly, 'and you know it.'

'Oh, indirectly, indirectly,' Mendel waved an airy hand, 'but not in a small personal sort of way. I should never have dreamed of coming away from that pleasant fire to quarrel with you about Ruth. Altogether too schoolboyish. No. The point is that we have been forced into competition by circumstances. Physical competition. And you've reached the stage where you feel that you can settle…'

'You can call it what you like,' said Rufus, shortly. 'I'm no longer interested in your theories.'

He stopped short. They were standing now on the smooth grass lawn before the spinney.

'I don't know if I can thrash you,' he said simply, 'but I'm going to try.'

Mendel smiled genially.

'I don't know either,' he said, 'but it will be pleasant to find out.'

Rufus slipped quickly from his jacket. Mendel, watching with a faint smile, followed his example.

'And if you succeed?' as they faced one another.

'Then I shall know that I'm right and that you're just a windbag and a bully.'

'But bullies can *always* fight,' said Mendel reasonably. 'Don't you believe that school story stuff…'

'Come on,' said Rufus, between set teeth. His heart was thumping heavily as he moved quickly forward. From far away the parting words rang in his ear. 'If you ever gets in a fight, Mr. Wade, you remember that the chap 'oo keeps 'is 'ead an' goes on 'ittin' with a straight arm wins…' He moved cautiously within distance. Mendel stood firm on his feet. His hands hung at his sides. The gentle, mocking smile was still on his lips. Rufus moved into distance and let go a quick left lead at the smiling mouth. He felt the knuckles brush the big man's chin. But Mendel had swayed away from the punch and it had barely touched him; and at that significant moment Rufus's lips tightened and he slipped quickly back from the expected counter. A novice might have blocked his blow or ducked. But that easy, beautifully-judged backward sway of the head…

Mendel had not countered. He stood still, loose, but wary,

on the defensive. Again, Rufus led quickly and followed up with a powerful right. This time Mendel did not move backwards. He slipped the lead with a flicker of the head and, even as Rufus's right fist smashed against his ribs, Mendel threw his great arms round his waist and, with a quick heave, sent the lighter man staggering back.

Mendel laughed aloud.

'Quicker!' he cried jeeringly, 'a lot quicker than that, Rufus!' And then, almost before Rufus had recovered his balance, the big man was on him. He struck out unseeingly and felt his left hand jar into Mendel's face. But a heavy blow crushed his lips and another, half guarded, glanced from his forearm and struck him dizzily on the temple. Mechanically he closed and for a few moments they strained silently together. His right arm came free and he struck vicious half-arm jabs at the big body pressed close to his own. Then he felt himself lifted clean off his feet and trees and sky whirled together to vanish in a sudden jarring red flash as the back of his head hit the ground.

Rufus rose dazedly to his feet. Mendel was standing with heaving chest a few yards away. His shirt was torn and blood was running from his nose, but the ironic smile was still on his parted lips and his eyes were shining brightly. Rufus brushed a hand across his puffy lips and noted with surprise that the back of his hand was covered in blood. His mind was icy clear now, as though the shock of his fall had broken away a dim window. Above everything, he thought, I must keep away. He's too heavy at close quarters… He advanced again, cautiously striving to avoid the bear-like grip of the huge arms. Twice he shot out the piston-like left, and the second time it landed squarely on the big man's cheek-bone. He grinned savagely as he saw Mendel's lips tighten, and took the heavy counter on his raised shoulder. Rufus feinted at the chin, got home a heavy smash as Mendel lifted his guard, and slipped the reply with ease. This was better. Mendel was not as good as he had thought, and he 'telegraphed' his punches most accommodatingly. If only he could keep away.

They circled each other cautiously. Mendel was no longer smiling. His lips were set and his eyes blazing. A lump was swelling rapidly beside his left eye, and he was breathing hard. He tried two short rushes, and once sent Rufus's head back sharply with a crack on the chin. But his blows were mainly wide swings, and Rufus had little difficulty in prodding him off with his invaluable left hand. Rufus found himself reflecting that that almost professional sway must have been a fluke… Twice more he slipped in and scored with quick snappy punches, which landed, though lightly. His confidence was rising with every moment now. Clearly he was a good deal faster than Mendel both in footwork and hitting, and the big man's superiority in reach was more than counterbalanced by Rufus's straighter hitting. Mendel seemed to realise it too, for he kept boring in, in an attempt to get to close quarters, where he could use his superior weight and vice-like arms. It was difficult to keep him away, and once, in slipping one of the heavy rushes, Rufus slipped and floundered for a moment helplessly. Mendel did not take advantage of the mistake, but hesitated with a crooked little smile, and Rufus, recovering, muttered 'Thanks!' and smiled in return, despite himself a little admiring.

Tiring at last of giving ground, he stood up finally to one of Mendel's rushes, and for a moment they stood toe to toe, hammering away with both hands, defence for the moment abandoned. But despite the whirl of blows, or perhaps because of it, neither could land an effective punch, and finally, as Mendel once more sought to come to grips, Rufus slipped away and, holding off his man with his left hand, returned to the long range which had paid him so well.

For a moment they circled one another cautiously. To his surprise, Rufus saw that Mendel was panting heavily and obviously distressed. He himself was breathing hard, and his mouth felt dry and rough. But clearly the effort of making his clumsy attacks was wearying Mendel more rapidly than his own more scientific methods. Rufus decided that the thing to do was to keep the big man on the move—to tantalise him—let him tire himself in cumbersome rushes until he became an easy target...

He saw Mendel relax and drove in like lightning to snatch the moment of indifferent balance. But his punch glanced off the side of the big man's head, and in a second they were once again wrestling furiously. He heard something like a chuckle from Mendel and strove desperately to break away from the bear-like hug which crushed his ribs. But Mendel's arms were like steel, and Rufus could feel his back weakening beneath the taller man's down-pressing weight. In desperation, he gave way suddenly and deliberately. They swayed for a moment and then, overbalancing, went to the ground with a jarring crash. Rufus gave a tremendous writhe as his shoulders hit the ground, and rolled the great weight from above him. He caught a glimpse of Mendel's distorted face as they rolled over and mechanically lashed out at it with his right fist. The blow landed on Mendel's jaw, but there was little force in it. He felt the great body beneath him give a furious and convulsive heave as if to roll them over once more, and braced his knee against the ground to maintain himself uppermost. Mendel's knees came up sharply and he fell forward over the big man's head. But he clung desperately to Mendel's chest with his knees, as a man grips a horse, and dropped back with his full weight on the recumbent form. And then suddenly he was kneeling with his knees on the great arms and his weight on the heaving chest, and Mendel was lying with closed eyes, the blood running freely from his face on to his torn shirt, and his breath coming in painful pants. Slowly and dazedly Rufus relaxed his instinctive grip on the big muscular throat. Somehow this sudden collapse bewildered him. A few seconds before he had been doggedly hoping that if he could keep the fight at long range all might be well—that he could tire Mendel out. But he had never visualised this sudden end…

'Well?' he said breathlessly, 'had enough?'

Mendel lay with closed eyes breathing heavily. Rufus hesitated, fearing a sudden spring. 'D'you hear what I say?' he demanded. 'Have you had enough?'

Mendel opened his eyes. They were heavy with fatigue. He nodded silently. Rufus scrambled to his feet and, brushing his hand across his painfully-cut lips, looked down at the huge prostrate form with contempt.

'Christ!' he said in disgust. 'And I thought you'd got guts!'

Mendel struggled slowly into a sitting position and passed his hand wearily across his blood-smeared face.

'You're a husky lad,' he murmured shakily.

'Husky be damned!' said Rufus roughly. 'You haven't got the guts of a louse!'

Mendel fumbled in his pocket and produced a handkerchief with which he dabbed gently at his nose.

'All right,' he said in a low voice, 'you needn't rub it in.'

He rose to his feet. Rufus started. There was something in the easy strength of the movement which sent a chill down his back. He himself had climbed slowly on to shaky legs…

'Wait a minute,' he said sharply. Mendel turned and looked at him.

'Well?'

'What the hell are you trying on?' said Rufus slowly.

'What d'you mean?'

Rufus took a quick pace forward.

'Why did you stop, damn you? You're all right. How you got up— You couldn't have done that if—'

There was a moment's pause.

'I'd had enough,' said Mendel sullenly.

'Why, you bloody funk, you—' He caught the sudden deep-down gleam in Mendel's eye and stopped. They stood in silence for a long moment. 'Why did you stop?' said Rufus in a low voice. 'You aren't licked.' He stared at Mendel for a moment. The blue eyes in the battered face were bright. 'In fact, you could have licked me,' he added dully.

'Did you want me to?' said Mendel quietly.

'I wanted you to fight,' said Rufus savagely. A vast sense of impotence and foolishness was swelling up in him.

'I did.'

'No, you didn't. You didn't try. You– ' The recollection of the first moments of their encounter flashed through his mind. 'You can box, can't you?' he said in a low voice.

Mendel hesitated.

'Yes, I can box,' he said at last.

'Then why the hell didn't you? Why did you fool about like that, damn you? I– ' Rufus stopped short. 'Oh, Christ, I don't see what you're up to,' he said wearily. His legs suddenly felt weak and the blood from his cut lips made him feel sick. His sweat-soaked shirt clung to him coldly.

Mendel was looking at him reflectively.

'Well, if you must know, I thought perhaps it– ' he hesitated.

'Well?'

'I thought perhaps it mattered more to you than me. That's all.'

Rufus looked at him with dull eyes. The big, beautifully-muscled form in the torn, blood-stained white shirt and ancient flannel trousers stood out sharply against the sombre background of the spinney. The disorderly mop of yellow hair stirred in the gentle air. He was a big man. A sickening sense of defeat swept over Rufus. He had fought hard, but the other man was bigger and carried too many guns. Bigger... bigger... bigger...

'What the hell did you do it for?' he said wearily. 'I didn't want you to do that.'

'Don't be silly,' said Mendel calmly. 'It was purely selfish.'

And there he goes, thought Rufus dully, spoiling it all by being just a bit too charming.

'You'd better put your jacket on,' said Mendel gently, 'or you'll catch pneumonia.'

Rufus turned slowly and picked up his jacket. Now home and Ruth…

He turned sharply—suddenly. Mendel was standing looking at him with that queer air of detached interest…

His mind flashed back to the scene at the gate. 'You can't get the better of Pip, you see. If you beat him, he'd just be coldly interested in what it felt like to be beaten…' Something seemed to crack in his brain, with a blinding flash of light. He dropped the jacket.

'Christ!' he shouted suddenly. 'I see! God, you–you–'

'What's the matter?' asked Mendel calmly.

Rufus sprang towards him. There was a strange and joyful smile on his face.

'You're a liar!' he shouted, 'that wasn't it! God, for a moment I thought you… you were big, like I used to think. But you're not. You're small and mean and petty!'

'What are you talking about?' said Mendel quietly.

'You say you did it for my sake. But that *wasn't* it! It was just your old game, wasn't it? Another little experiment at my expense…'

'You're off your head,' said Mendel shortly. His face was flushed.

'Am I?' shouted Rufus. 'We'll see.' He swung his arm with all his force and his open palm struck Mendel's face with a crack like a pistol shot. 'Now *fight*, you miserable–'

Mendel staggered back under the sudden blow, but quickly recovered.

'My God!' he muttered, 'be careful or you'll get hurt.'

'Hurt!' cried Rufus exultantly. 'That's what I want. Give up your shamming and cheating and fight!' He plugged forward and crashed his fist into Mendel's face. He saw the big man's lips go back, showing his white teeth, and then an avalanche struck him. He laughed as he guarded the sledge-hammer blows—laughed though he knew the end was near. He had a vision of Mendel's terrible face, and then, as he dropped his guard to catch a left-hand punch at the mark, realised too late that it was a feint. He saw the big right arm swing and, still laughing, heard a loud click and fell into the darkness.

Chapter XV

Waking Up and Dreaming

Rufus awoke slowly and foolishly, like a man awakening from the effects of an anaesthetic. At first there was nothing but an intense, numbing cold which made him turn slightly and strive to pull about him the cover which touched his chin. But the movement of his hand was sharply painful and, opening his eyes, he found himself staring into the sombre brownness of the spinney. He remembered and, sitting up, gazed foolishly round him. Something slipped from his chest, and he saw that the things which had covered him were his own jacket and Mendel's. The grass on which he lay was trampled and muddy, but he was quite alone in a gigantic silence.

He climbed stiffly and unsteadily to his feet and gazed out across the sweeping green slopes. They were serene and empty. Mendel had gone and left him lying. The jackets—how characteristic a gesture!... He smiled wryly.

Smiling was painful. He pressed a hand over his lips and found that they were swollen to twice their usual size. There was a crust of congealed blood on his chin, and he saw with surprise that the knuckles of his right hand were barked and still oozing blood.

Interested, he methodically took stock of his injuries. There was still a slight singing in his ears, like the faint hissing of a kettle. He tentatively opened his mouth, but the movement was painful. He gently touched the point of articulation at the side of his face. There was no dislocation. But just above, near his temple, there was a large, hard lump, which, for some reason, did not hurt at all. He prodded it with great satisfaction, and decided that, apart from his lips and a general feeling of weary soreness, the chief discomfort was his bruised and broken hands.

A slight breeze had arisen and it was cold. Rufus bent stiffly, discovering a bruised rib and, picking up his jacket, put it on. He bent again, with more respect for the rib, and threw Mendel's jacket across his arm. The least one could do—

Rufus sucked gently at his sore knuckles and considered. What now? The future, yes. That had settled itself. But the moment— Would Mendel have returned to the farm? He did not wish to see Mendel again. He was not afraid of Mendel. He was not even interested in him any more. But he did not like Mendel and there was nothing to say… He wondered vaguely if Ruth had returned from the village. If not, he might walk down and meet her. He could tell her what he had found, and there would be no reason to go back to the farm at all. Everything was very slow and clear somehow…

Rufus glanced down at the jacket across his arm and reflected that it was Mendel's and must be returned. He could not go to meet Ruth carrying Mendel's jacket. His glance travelled on, and he remembered that the clothes he was wearing were Mendel's. He frowned and shook his head. There was nothing for it but to go back to Three Trees and collect his own clothes. Perhaps Ruth would have returned. It did not matter. She had to be told. But all the same he would rather have told her alone. He disliked Mendel, but he did not hate him. And he did not want to tell Ruth in front of him.

Rufus walked back to Three Trees rather slowly. He was very tired and his legs were aching. Once it occurred to him that Mendel might have gone back and murdered Ruth and he walked faster. But his legs were aching, and he soon returned to his former pace. Besides, it was a silly idea. Why should he?

He was seized with a queer, newboy nervousness as he reached the top of the rise and saw Three Trees lying below him. How difficult was it going to be? He could not explain—it was all too clear to explain. Mendel would see that, of course, and even if he did not, it no longer mattered. But Ruth? He could only tell her that Mendel was a fraud—a sham—bogus. But would she understand that he had seen it—proved it? Would she be able, as he had done, to look into the blue eyes and see that it was all a lie, that Mendel was a lie himself—that there was nothing to love or admire or respect or like, and that all the pretty deceptive things were just stage properties?... He shook his head.

'She must see it,' he said aloud. 'She'll see it if she looks at him.' Perhaps it would be better if Mendel were there. He would tell her, and then say, 'Look at his eyes.' And she would look as he had done up by the spinney. And then she would see, as he had seen.

There was no one at the farm. The smoke was curling from the chimney, and he could see the flicker of the fire on the window. But he knew there was no one there while he was yet fifty yards from the house, for the silence was the silence of nobody, not the silence of life; and his senses were extraordinarily alert. He entered and called 'Ruth!', 'Mendel!' as loudly as his stiff jaw would permit; although he knew they were not there he was relieved when there was no sound, no reply.

He went into the big low room and, seeing his wrist-watch lying on the mantelpiece, picked it up and glanced at it idly and put it on. It was three o'clock. Ruth must be back soon, unless— A sudden thought struck him. Had Mendel returned and taken her? He went quickly into the kitchen. The big basket was still missing. She could not have returned. It was only an hour and a half ago and she had six miles to walk…

Rufus went slowly upstairs and along the passage to his room. His reflection in the mirror surprised and shocked him. He was very weary and his lips and knuckles throbbed painfully, but in the mirror his face looked a spectacular wreck. The entirely unpainful lump beside his temple was the size of the top of an egg and was rapidly turning a most engaging purple. His lips, covered with black congealed blood, were swollen grotesquely, and the blood from them had run down over his chin and formed a large mortal-looking blotch on the top of his shirt. Even his nose, which merely felt a little sore, seemed to have swollen considerably. 'Portrait of a Gentleman,' he muttered with a painful grin.

Slipping off his clothes, he padded naked over to the washstand and splashed out a basinful of ice-cold water. There were two large dark-red blotches on his lower ribs. It was as well, he reflected, that Ruth had not been in. Otherwise she might have been scared. The cold water stung his raw hands and lips sharply, and the water in the basin turned an unpleasant brownish colour, as he carefully wiped away the congealed blood and dirt, and dabbed gently at the cuts which were still welling blood. But the refreshing coldness silenced the last traces of the irritating singing in his ears, and when he had finished he felt entirely normal, save for the familiar sensation of refreshed weariness which always followed a wash after strenuous exertion.

After a prolonged search he found his own clothes, which he had not seen since his first few days at Three Trees. They bore no sign of his adventure in the snow. Clearly, Ruth had sponged and pressed them. There was something very satisfactory about putting on trousers with neat creases again. He carefully transferred his few possessions from the pockets of the borrowed clothes, and deposited the old shirt, trousers and jacket in Mendel's room. Returning, he took a last look round the room, as a man will look round the room of a hotel before vacating it; glanced reflectively at the bed; thought of Ruth; took a last look out of the window; and went quietly downstairs to await arrivals. The house was still deserted. He picked up a book at random and, sitting down, tried to read.

Half an hour later Ruth returned. He heard her step outside and sprang up, uncertain for a moment if it were she or Mendel. She came into the room rather wearily, carrying the big basket containing half a dozen large blue–green duck's eggs and a number of paper parcels. She stopped when she saw Rufus.

'Hullo!' he said rather awkwardly, waiting for the inevitable outcry of horror at his battered face. Rather to his disappointment it did not come. Ruth merely turned very pale and, setting down the basket, came slowly towards him.

'So you've been at it?...' she said, without surprise. Rufus merely nodded, feeling slightly foolish.

'I was afraid you would,' she said wearily, pulling off the little woollen cap and throwing it carelessly on the table. 'What bloody fools men are...' She looked round the room. 'Where's Pip?' she asked sharply.

'I haven't the faintest idea,' said Rufus, piqued and jealous at the urgency in her voice.

'Has he gone out?'

'No. He *is* out. He hasn't come back yet.'

She looked at him, puzzled. 'Look here,' she said with a rather painful smile, 'you haven't left him for dead somewhere, have you? Because—'

'Certainly not!' said Rufus indignantly. '*He* left *me* for dead. Up by the spinney… But God knows where he's gone now. I simply came home and he wasn't here.'

Ruth nodded. She was staring thoughtfully at his face.

'He won then? Or didn't anybody win?'

'Oh, yes, he won,' said Rufus happily, 'easily.'

'Of course he's miles too heavy for you,' said Ruth reflectively. 'How heavy are you?'

'About twelve six.'

'Well, he's quite fourteen. And he can box. He boxed for the Varsity.[98] I meant to tell you, but I thought it wouldn't help.'

'Yes. He is a bit heavy and he can box, and it wouldn't have helped,' said Rufus politely. He frowned in sudden irritation. 'But all this isn't getting us anywhere. I–'

'That's a nice suit,' said Ruth absently, putting out a hand and feeling the material of the lapel.

'Yes.'

'Why are you wearing it?' she said simply.

Rufus hesitated. 'Well, that's rather the point of what I was going to say. You see, I'm going.'

She frowned slightly. 'Going? But there's no point in going just because of this. There would have been much more point in going before.'

Rufus shook his head. 'Ah, but you don't understand. I've found out something. About him.'

'Oh?'

'Yes. So I'm going. There isn't any point in staying. You're coming too,' he added tentatively.

To his surprise she made no comment, but merely looked at him in silence for a moment. Then she walked over to the mantelpiece and, taking a cigarette from the box, lit it and stared thoughtfully out of the window. 'Why?' she said at last, turning to him with raised eyebrows.

Rufus frowned. He found her coolness very exasperating but,

even so, far less exasperating than his own. He had visualised this scene so clearly. Ruth frightened and agitated, himself commanding, imperious, and triumphant, beating down her feeble resistance and showing her so clearly why she could no longer stay with Mendel. And now she was icily calm and reasonable and he felt limp and extremely tired.

'Because you can't possibly stay with him any longer,' he said foolishly.

'But *why*, Rufus?'

'Because he's bogus,' said Rufus shortly.

She perched herself in a favourite attitude on the arm of one of the big chairs. 'Bogus?' she said slowly.

'Yes. Bogus. Absolutely bogus all through. There isn't a genuine thought or feeling or action in him. He's just a cheat and a sham.' Rufus shook his head. 'I never realised it until to-day. I always thought that somewhere underneath there was something big and unusual—something I hadn't got—that nobody else had got. And then to-day I found out that there was nothing there. I proved it.'

There was a long pause.

'How?' asked Ruth in a low voice.

'By what happened up by the spinney. Listen. After you'd gone I challenged him to fight. I thought I probably couldn't lick him, but I had to try, anyhow, after what he said to you. And I didn't care if I couldn't so long as I could hit him hard on the nose just once.'

Ruth smiled quietly. 'I suppose you don't realise that with him the word "bitch" is a term of endearment?'

'It may be sometimes,' replied Rufus grimly, 'but it wasn't *that* time. Anyhow, he was quite willing. I think he wanted it too. So we went up to the spinney and on the way he talked a lot of his usual rot about this all being impersonal and so on. Then we started and he foxed.'

'Foxed?'

'Yes. Pretended he couldn't box at all and that he was as slow as a cart-horse. Let me hit him and get all the best of it.'

Ruth's brow clouded. 'Yes,' she said briefly, 'that was certainly a bit low.'

'Wait a bit!' said Rufus more warmly. 'It was. But you haven't heard it all yet.' His eyes narrowed. 'After we'd been scrapping for just a minute or two—just caught each other a couple of clouts and wrestled about a bit—he pretended to collapse. Let me sit on his chest and said he'd had enough–' A bright flush mounted his face at the recollection. 'And like a bloody fool,' he added savagely, 'I let myself be take in. I… I thought he was just gutless, and told him so. And then–' He hesitated and took a deep breath. 'Then,' he went on in a lower voice, 'I suddenly spotted the way he got up. Not tired or anything, but obviously as fresh as paint if he liked. And then I saw what he'd been doing. I was furious and tackled him—told him I could see he wasn't licked and asked what the hell he thought he was doing. And–' Rufus stopped and moistened his sore and sticky lips.

'Well?' said Ruth quietly.

'He pretended for a bit that he didn't know what I meant,' said Rufus softly, 'and then when I stuck to him,' he added carefully, 'he said that he'd done it because he thought it meant more to me to win than it did to him.'

'Ah-h.' It was a long-drawn breath.

'Well, of course,' said Rufus gently, 'that knocked me all endways. A moment before I'd been thinking I'd licked him— that he was just a gutless lump and a bully. And then he said that and I suddenly saw that I'd lost—lost hopelessly. That he'd been like a big man humouring a kid. I just felt completely helpless. He stood there looking rather marvellous—and God, he can be a marvellous sight, that man—and I felt like a worm. I just wanted to give up and go away. I always used to feel, you know, that he was rather—rather grand somehow. Bigger than me, I mean. And this seemed to settle it once and for all. And then—' Rufus stopped and his cracked lips parted in a cold, painful smile. 'And then suddenly I thought of you and what you told me that day up by the gate, and it didn't ring true somehow. It was all—all a bit *too* neat and tidy. I turned round suddenly and looked at him standing there, and looked at his eyes, and he was *doing* it. Looking just like we said—standing back and seeing the effect. And then I saw it all in a flash. That it was all bogus and a lie. That he hadn't done it for me at all. That he'd always *meant* me to know he was foxing, because he knew that would break me. God, it was cunning, cunning! He'd given himself all the thrill of being beaten, and now he was having the thrill of being the big man, and seeing me realise it and—and feel small.' His voice had risen almost to a shout in his excitement. Ruth's sombre eyes were fixed on his face, but she did not move.

'So then,' said Rufus exultantly, 'I told him. Told him I'd found him out at last. He tried to pretend he didn't understand, so I slapped his face as hard as I could and *made* him fight. He saw it was no good, so he came at me like a tiger. I managed to catch him as he came in, right in the mouth, and then he got me with his right and knocked me out.' He shook his head slowly and thoughtfully. 'When I woke up he'd gone. He'd covered me with his own jacket as well as my own. The habit of being a big man dies hard.' Rufus paused and looked at her expectantly, but she said nothing, continuing to gaze at him strangely with an expression which he could not interpret. 'That's what I found out,' he concluded rather lamely.

She bowed her dark head in silence.

Rufus looked at her almost anxiously. 'Darling, you do see, don't you? You do see that—that he really *is* like that? That I'm not just imagining it?' He shook his head. 'I wish you'd been there,' he said almost to himself. 'You would—'

'There was no need,' said Ruth, breaking her long silence at last. 'I can see what happened. It's clear enough.'

A wave of relief swept over him. 'Then you see that I must go?'

She nodded. 'Yes. You must go. You're quite right. There's nothing left to stay for.'

'And that you must come with me?'

She hesitated for a long moment. Rufus took a step towards her and, putting his hands on each side of her face, gently turned it upwards towards him so that the big dark eyes looked steadily into his own. 'Darling,' he said quietly, 'do you love me?'

'You know I do,' she said tonelessly.

'Then you must come.'

She looked at him for a moment in silence, and then, gently disengaging herself, stared thoughtfully out of the window.

'Don't you see?' said Rufus quietly, 'you can't stay here now—knowing that. It isn't just that he's unkind to you. If he'd been what we thought, that wouldn't have mattered. At least, you might not have thought it mattered. But you can't stay now. There's nothing here for you any more than there is for me. You've seen that he's just bogus—just a sham. You can live with a sham as long as you think it's real. But not when you *know*.'

He took a deep breath and looked round the room with a frown. 'Can't you feel it?' he said in a low voice. 'Can't you feel that there's something unhealthy about this place—something queer and inhuman? For God's sake, let's get out of it, love, and back to—to real life. It may be a bit humdrum, but at least most of it's real and genuine, even when it's beastly. And here nothing's real and genuine. However nice it is, there's an atmosphere about it, as though you know we're all acting all the time, and that in a little while–' He paused helplessly.

'You've changed your mind, haven't you?' said Ruth with a quiet smile.

He hesitated. 'You mean about this place?'

'Yes. You used to think that—that *this* was real and that the other was—'

Rufus nodded. 'Yes,' he said, 'I have. But you see I hadn't really seen this properly. If it had been what I thought at first, it was perfect. But now it's worse than—than noise and boredom and so on. Because it isn't *true*. It's all just a—a bad play.'

There was a long silence.

'Well?' he said at last.

Ruth was staring thoughtfully out of the window.

'You don't realise what you're asking me to do,' she said with a shake of the head.

'Oh, yes, I do. I know how you felt about him. Because, you see, until this happened, I'd always felt that he was—well, the sort of man a woman *would* love. There is something rather grand about him until—until you know. But when you *do* know—when you know that he's just a gigantic sham—then there isn't anything left...' He rose suddenly and walked over to her. 'Do you believe what I've told you?' he said gently, 'about him?'

Ruth hesitated and then nodded slightly.

'Yes. I believe you, Rufus. I know, you wouldn't say that just—'

'Then there's nothing more to say. You must come. Because otherwise, you see, you'll have to live a sham...'

She hesitated for a long moment, and once she looked at him strangely and made as though to speak. But her lips closed again as she met his eyes, and she looked away again in silence. Then she slowly bowed her head.

'All right,' she said almost in a whisper.

Rufus seized her hand. 'You'll come?' he said quickly. She turned and looked at him with the queer unfathomable expression.

'Yes,' she said almost wearily, 'I'll come, Rufus. I—I don't see what else there is to do.'

'Darling!' he put his arm round her and kissed her. Gently, for his lips were very sore. She suffered herself to be kissed, neither resisting nor clinging, but lying quite limply in his arms. He saw her hurt eyes and was suddenly very sorry for her. He released her gently.

'I'm sorry if—if it hurt to be told that, sweet,' he said gently, 'but I had to tell you.'

'Of course,' she said with a brave little smile. Rufus stood up and glanced at his watch.

'We'll go at once,' he said. 'What time is there a train to London? Leaford's got a station somewhere, hasn't it?'

'It shares one with Standing. What time is it?'

'Just after four.'

'There's a train at half-past six, I think, that gets a connection at Salisbury.'

'Fine!' said Rufus briskly. 'How much stuff have you got?'

Ruth smiled. 'Nothing that I want to take,' she said quietly.

'Well then, we shall travel light enough,' said Rufus with a grin. 'Because I've got one hat, one overcoat, and just about enough money for our fares. Oh, and one toothbrush.' He glanced again at his watch. 'How long will it take us to get to—to the station?'[99]

Ruth rose slowly to her feet. 'We ought to leave ourselves quite half an hour. More, if anything. The station's half a mile the other side of the village.'

'Half an hour,' repeated Rufus thoughtfully. He looked round the room with a frown. 'Look here,' he said briefly, 'there's nothing to stay for, and I'm longing to get out of the place. Let's go now, and have tea in the village or something.'

Ruth hesitated and then, walking over to the window, gazed unseeingly out into the farmyard.

'Rufus,' she said slowly, 'I'm going to be a nuisance.'

'How, love?'

She turned. 'I must see Pip before I go.'

Rufus frowned. 'Why?' he asked shortly.

'I—I don't know. But I must. I'm sorry.'

Rufus sucked thoughtfully at his knuckles. 'It's rather silly,' he said at last. 'It's not as though there's anything to say. Wouldn't it be a good deal easier for all concerned if we just cleared out?'

She shook her dark head. 'No. I can't do that. Somehow—oh, I don't know. I can't just go and leave him without even saying good-bye. You see we… we've known each other a long time, and I shouldn't like to–' She stopped short, looking at him appealingly.

'Well, of course,' said Rufus slowly, 'if you feel like that about it, sweet–'

'I'll tell you what,' said Ruth, 'you go, if you don't want to see him, and I'll join you at the station. Oh, I'll *come*,' she added, with the sudden gamin grin, seeing his face. 'I won't leave you deserted on the platform. I'm not that sort of girl.'

'Ass!' said Rufus happily.

'But that would mean that you didn't have to see him.'

Rufus shook his head impatiently.

'Oh, it's not that. I don't care. There's no earthly reason why I shouldn't see him. I only thought that there isn't anything to say or do, and that it would be much less uncomfortable for all of us if we just went.'

'Well, then, you go.'

'No,' he said firmly, 'if you want to stay, do. And I'll stay too. We'll go together.'

She hesitated and then, seeing that his mind was made up, nodded. 'All right, darling.' She kissed him lightly on the cheek, and then, smoothing a hand over the black hair, looked at Rufus inquiringly. 'Then we may as well have some tea while we wait?'

'Tea,' said Rufus, 'would be an excellent thing. I'm frightfully thirsty.'

'Good.' Ruth picked up her shopping basket and went towards the kitchen. 'Poor Pip!' she said more cheerfully than she had spoken before. 'Now he'll have to fry his own duck eggs. And we shan't get any. What a waste!'

'Too bad!' said Rufus with a grin. 'Don't let's go.'

She stopped as she reached the door and dived down into the basket.

'Oh, by the way—I got you a paper in the village. I thought after what you said you were pining for one.'

She threw the folded newspaper on the table and disappeared into the kitchen. Rufus picked it up and unfolded it slowly and thoughtfully. He was conscious of an immense relief that it was all settled, but he realised with surprise that he had never visualised what would happen if Ruth had refused to come with him. From the moment when he awoke beside the spinney it had all seemed clear and settled, and he had never doubted that she would see and understand. But now it was all done he realised that he had asked her to take his word for something rather vague and inexpressible—to desert a man with whom she had lived for a long time on the strength of his single conviction, and to give up her whole life at his simple request. He had never doubted the result. But he felt a thrill of pride and love that she should trust him even in this last difficult, complicated and important issue. He looked towards the kitchen with an affectionate smile. Good kid. She had stood by him. She had not let him down.

Rufus sat down and opened the paper. The habit of years is not broken in a month, and to Rufus a newspaper was still a medium in which, with a skilled technical eye, one saw and approved or criticised the work of the advertising world. He noted with a grin that Bledisloe's were still running their old interview stuff for Maple Oil Hair Preparation. Almost ever since he could remember the advertising columns of the national Press had carried their touching and entirely unsolicited testimonials to the value of Maple Oil for the Thinning Hair. It was Bledisloe's only big account. Surely, surely, they could have found something new by now?

He turned the page and came suddenly upon the unmistakable lay-out of a Ritson and Partners advertisement. His idea of humour for Creamo had not been accepted, and Ritson's were still taking a three-column spread to say that Creamo existed and that children loved it. Rufus shook his head with a disapproving frown. Awful! And made worse by the fact that whoever wrote the copy (probably his successor, he thought, with a queer shock of surprise) had evidently made a desperate effort to infuse life where no life was. The copy said nothing, but said it in an appallingly confidential we're-all-friends-together-mother-aren't-we? style. Rufus shook his head again. You couldn't do that sort of thing with Creamo, unless you'd really got something to say. And this bird hadn't. He was saying all the old things as though he'd just discovered them...

A sudden thought struck him. Had George Gaskell's got anybody yet? Because they had been keen to get him, and now a job would be necessary, one might do worse... He turned rapidly over in search of the advertisement for the celebrated brand of toothpaste which was Gaskell's main account. He found it at last and was relieved to see that there was nothing new in the idea lay-out or copy. No sign of any major change there. He made a mental resolution to ring up Gaskell's as soon as he reached Town. A sudden idea struck him. 'Do you show your teeth when you smile?' Possible... Did many people? Rufus rose and walked to the mirror. But of course—his own lips were in too much mess to see. He sat down again. Ruth didn't. But Mendel did. 'Look at yourself in a mirror. Do your teeth show when you smile? White, strong, clean teeth? The sort of teeth which have been cleaned with—' He frowned. Clumsy. The thing would want working up. He abandoned the train of thought almost with an effort and returned to the paper. He looked rather vaguely through the news matter. Everything seemed much as usual. There was a grave situation in Bulgaria, but it was difficult to judge if this was a new one or the one which had been in full swing a month ago. Anyhow, the newspaper thought England should keep out of it and look to the Empire. The main item, which carried the big headings, concerned the trial of one Jacobs, which was now reaching its final stages. The evidence was given in full and from the occasional reference to the deceased and a body it was clearly a murder trial…

Ruth re-entered with tea on a tray. He laid down the paper.

'It's darned queer to see a paper again,' he said.

'Nice?' she asked with a smile.

'Yes, rather. Though nothing much seems to have happened.'

She set down the tray and, seating herself, began to pour out the tea. Rufus drank gratefully. There was a long silence as they munched bread and butter. Ruth was gazing into the fire with that queer, absorbed, sightless gaze he knew so well. Instinctively, Rufus put out a hand and began to stroke the boyish dark head. She rubbed her head against him like a pleased kitten, but her eyes never left the fire and she did not speak.

'You know, this is going to be awful fun,' he said almost shyly.

'Yes,' she nodded with an abstracted little smile.

'I've been thinking while you were out there. We can go back to the flat when we get to Town. It isn't very palatial, but it's quite nice. Then I shall go along and see Gaskell's. They offered me a job not long ago.'

She gave him a quick glance.

'A job?' she said slowly.

'Yes. Quite a good one.'

Ruth smiled at him strangely. 'You'd like to do that?'

Rufus raised his eyebrows. 'Oh, yes,' he said in some surprise. 'It would be all right. I might do far worse.'

Ruth nodded without comment.

'After all,' added Rufus, sensing her surprise and possible disapproval, 'I must do something, sweet. We've got to live and you know I haven't got any money.' He looked at her, anxious and a little hurt.

Ruth opened her mouth to speak, and then, changing her mind, nodded again in silence. 'Besides,' said Rufus, reasoning, 'jobs aren't very easy to come by. And I should get far more from Gaskell's, who want me, than I should from any other agency if I just went round looking for a job.'

'Agency?' said Ruth, with a flicker of a smile. 'You mean advertising agencies?'

'Yes.'

'But why advertising agencies?' she asked thoughtfully.

Rufus frowned slightly. 'Well, my sweet, it's the job I *know*. I should be darned little use at anything else, you see.' He was finding the conversation puzzling and rather irritating. 'You can't walk in and get a job worth having in something where you've got no experience and—and background.' He paused and wrinkled his brow. 'I *might* get a job with a firm or a—a Press job. But they wouldn't be as good as I can probably get with Gaskell's.'

'How good will that be?' she said slowly.

'I don't know exactly. They wanted me to go there as account executive[100] a little while ago. If that's still open I should think about a thousand a year.'

'A thousand a year?' she said in surprise. She looked up at him with the mischievous grin. 'More than you'd ever get as a farm labourer, Rufus.'

Rufus flushed. 'That's hardly fair, sweet,' he said quietly, 'the circumstances will be entirely different now.'

'Will they?' she said, seriously.

'Yes, of course. Why I... why I *wanted* that sort of thing in the first place was because there was something missing. And if I've got you there won't be.'

'You mean to say it was all as simple as that?'

'Yes. I'm sure of it now. That was all that was wrong. There wasn't any *point* in it all. And now there will be if I've got you.'

She nodded with the same strange, rather wistful smile. There was a long silence. Then she turned to him quickly.

'Rufus,' she said in carefully matter-of-fact tones, 'this isn't a question a nice girl asks her young man, but I must get it clear. Do you—do you want to get married or shall we just live in sin?... It doesn't matter, of course,' she added hurriedly, 'but I just wanted to know what you—'

Rufus looked at her in surprise.

'Don't be an ass!' he said with a grin. 'Of course we're going to be married.'

'All respectable?'

'All respectable. Directly we get back to Town. Why shouldn't we?'

'Oh, there's no reason why we *shouldn't*,' said Ruth quietly, 'as long as you really want to. But there's no need if you don't. That's all I wanted to be sure you knew.'

Rufus looked for a moment at the serious little face, and then, putting out an arm, drew her head against his knees and gently kissed the full red lips.

'Idiot!' he said fondly. 'God, I wish my lips weren't so sore.'

'But seriously—'

'I am serious. I love you and my intentions are strictly honourable. There. Will that do?'

'No,' said Ruth unexpectedly, 'it won't.'

'Why not?'

'I don't want your intentions to be honourable. I don't want you to have any "intentions" like that. I just want you to be in love with me, and to do just what you like, not what you think you ought to do.'

Rufus drew back and gazed at her in wide-eyed astonishment. Then he broke into a roar of laughter, which was brought to an abrupt end by a smothered 'Blast!' and an agonised clutch at his stiff jaw. 'Well, my *hat!*' he said happily. 'You're giving me credit for a rum sort of conscience. Why should I marry you if I didn't want to? I've never bothered about it down here.'

'Down here may be different,' said Ruth slowly.

'Why? I don't see that sleeping with you in Wiltshire is any different from sleeping with you in London. I don't *want* it to be different. I just want to marry you, that's all.'

She turned to him suddenly with a strange mixture of fear and entreaty in the dark eyes. 'Don't let it!' she said indistinctly. Rufus tightened the clasp of his encircling arm.

'Don't let what, my love?'

'Don't let it be different, Rufus. I don't want it to be different. I want it to go on being just the same…'

He drew her head down on his shoulder.

'Of course it'll be the same, silly. If you want to know, that's why I want to get married—so that it will always be the same.' He glanced down at her severely. 'You needn't think you're going to get anything out of it,' he said firmly. 'I'm not going to respect you or cherish you or anything like that. The idea is simply that we shall get married all respectable like, and people will say, "Oh, *look* at that nice Mr. Wade. *There's* a model husband and father if you like." And all the time you'll really be just my mistress and have a hell of a time. See?'

Ruth's eyes were closed. She smiled without opening them. 'That's right,' she said, snuggling her head more comfortably on his shoulder, 'that'll be nice.'

Rufus's hand tightened over her small firm breast. Regardless of his lips, he kissed her hard.

They had been sitting in the silence of close intimacy for a quarter of an hour when Ruth opened her eyes and, sitting up, passed a hand mechanically over her hair, and walked to the window. The early dusk was falling rapidly, and the room was already quite dark save for the flickering glow from the fire.

'What's the time?' she asked suddenly.

Rufus consulted his watch. 'Quarter to five.' He rose, and joined her at the window, a hand on her shoulder.

'I wish Mendel would come back,' he said impatiently. 'I wonder where the hell he is?'

Ruth's face was troubled. 'I suppose nothing's happened to him?...' She turned anxiously. 'Rufus—he *was* all right when you saw him last?...'

Rufus felt again the childish pang of jealousy.

'Apart from a bit there and a bit here,' he said viciously, 'he was a damned sight *too* all right to please me. Well enough to hit me a thundering crack on the jaw, anyway.'

'But he's got no jacket and he must have been hot. And it's getting colder now.'

'Well, he should have taken his damned jacket,' said Rufus, almost sullenly. '*I* didn't want it, and he might have known he couldn't work any more charm and nobleness on me.'

Ruth turned again and gazed out into the twilight. The rim of the hill stood out smooth and unbroken, a darker mass against the darkening sky.

'But I can't think where he can be. Unless he went down to the village to meet me. And even then he'd realise that he'd missed me and be back by now...'

'I suppose he's coming back?' said Rufus, struck by a sudden idea. Ruth turned and faced him quickly. The dark eyes were wide open and anxious.

'Why? What—?'

'I was just thinking,' Rufus explained with deliberate casualness, 'that it would be damned funny if he'd stolen a march on us and gone wandering off to Timbuctoo himself.' He looked coldly at her startled face. 'It would be a very characteristic act of heroic self-sacrifice,' he added maliciously, 'to wander away in your shirt-sleeves and leave the lovers together. Think what a kick Mendel'd get out of that!'

'He wouldn't do that,' said Ruth thoughtfully, apparently oblivious of his sarcasm. 'After all, it isn't so easy for him. *We've* got nothing here. But all his stuff is here. He—'

'I should say he was quite capable of it,' said Rufus with childish malice. 'After all, what's a house and furniture beside the chance of a real mental hot bath like he'd get out of this?'

Privately, he agreed with Ruth. He guessed—indeed, almost knew—that Mendel could not and would not have left Three Trees in the casual way that he suggested. But though he realised that he was being childish and unkind, he hated to see Ruth's smouldering anxiety, and could not resist fanning it gently.

Fortunately, she did not even seem to hear him. She merely nodded abstractedly and gazed out again at the darkening hill.

'Well,' said Rufus curtly, more annoyed than ever at the failure of his prodding to evoke a response, 'as far as I can see we can give him about another three-quarters of an hour at the outside. And if he hasn't come by then we shall have to go without kissing him on both cheeks. You can leave him a note or something.'

He turned away from the window and, taking off the thin glass chimney, lit the big hanging lamp. Ruth, unable to see into the darkness now the room was lightened, turned reluctantly away from the window and, collecting the used cups, placed them on the tray and bore them off to the kitchen. Rufus carefully turned up the wick as the glass warmed and cleared and, picking up his paper, sat down again by the fire. He smiled grimly to himself as he heard the faint swish of water and the chink of china from the kitchen. Ruth, unwilling to abandon ship leaving the dirty cups, was carefully washing up. It was a gesture, he reflected, which Mendel ought to appreciate, as completely in his own tradition. He turned to the murder trial and began to read the verbatim account of the evidence rather abstractedly. For his own part, he was hoping with great intensity that Mendel would *not* return before they left. He could appreciate Ruth's feelings in not wanting to leave without some form of good-bye, but he had felt from the first that the interview might be awkward, not for himself, but for her. He was not fool enough to deny, even to himself, that Ruth had been very fond of Mendel—had gone on in fact in the illogical dog-like feminine way being fond of him, long after any logical reason for affection had disappeared. But his dislike of the prospect of this farewell interview was not entirely due to jealousy. It was based rather on the impossibility of forecasting what Mendel would do in any given situation. With a normal man, about to be deserted by his mistress for someone else, one could fairly bet on anger, maudlin sentiment or unskilful heroics, none of which would be more than contemptible. But it was too much to hope that Mendel would neglect such a golden opportunity to be unconventional. He would be unlikely to choose anger, and if he decided for sentiment, heroics, or anything else, he would probably do it well enough to hurt Ruth considerably, and in a way one could not resent...

Decidedly, Rufus reflected, it would be better if Mendel did not come, even if it meant trifling and short-lived sentiment d'incomplétude[101] for Ruth. He glanced at his watch again. Ten minutes of the three-quarters of an hour had gone. In another half-hour it would be fair to suggest that Ruth should write Mendel a note, and that they should go.

He went back to the murder trial and read the evidence again with care. He decided that things looked black for Mr. Jacobs. His counsel was putting up a magnificent show against heavy odds, but the dead woman had undoubtedly been poisoned; the prisoner alone had access to her food and he had been positively identified by the chemist as the man who had bought the stuff two months before—

He looked up as Ruth came slowly in from the kitchen. Her

face was drawn and troubled, and Rufus wished devoutly that he could put time forward half an hour.

'Hullo!' he said, speaking as casually as he could. 'Did I hear you washing up?'

Ruth nodded and, going again to the window, pressed her face close to the glass and looked out into the darkness. Rufus looked at her with an uneasy frown.

'Darling,' he said tentatively, 'there's been such a lovely murder. No blood, but lots of arsenic and so on...'

She turned suddenly and faced him.

'Rufus,' she said almost defiantly, 'I'm going to look for him.'

Rufus smiled rather uneasily.

'Don't be silly, pet.'

'I am. I *must* see him. And I'm getting worried.'

'But what is there to worry about?' he said irritably.

'I can't think why he hasn't come back. Something may have happened to him. He may–'

Rufus rose to his feet and took her by the hand.

'But, darling, he may be *anywhere*. Where would you start to look? It's no use just wandering about on the downs in the dark.'

She shook her head obstinately.

'I must,' she said quietly, and turned towards the door.

'But supposing he gets back here while you're looking? Then *you'll* be lost. Far better just wait here and see if he turns up.' Rufus glanced at his watch. 'We can give him another half-hour. After all, if he isn't near enough to be back by then, you can bet he's gone wandering off somewhere and you certainly won't find him in the dark.'

Ruth did not reply but, gently disengaging her hand, walked over and picked up her hat and coat.

'Will you wait here?' she asked gently.

Rufus hesitated. 'You really *want* to go?' he said. A glance at her face told him the answer. He put his arms round her and kissed her. 'All right, sweet,' he said, 'we'll go. It's a damned silly thing to do and we shall probably miss him, but there—'

They slipped into their outdoor clothes and went to the door. 'Will the lamp be all right?' asked Rufus.

She nodded vaguely, but he could have sworn she did not hear or understand the question.

Chapter XVI

Loyalties

It was quite dark now. There was no moon and the sky was overcast and starless.

'Have you any idea where we're going to look?' asked Rufus as they stepped into the farmyard. 'I suppose he isn't out in the barn by any chance?'

'We should have heard him,' said the quiet voice from the darkness beside him.

'I suppose so. Still, we may as well make sure.' He walked over to the barn. It was silent and in darkness. He pulled open the squeaking half-door and paused on the threshold. The big low room was uncannily silent and black as the pit.

'Mendel!' he said quietly. There was no reply. The queer, frightened feeling of hide-and-seek-in-the-dark came to him—the fear that out of the blackness something would rise up in sudden violent movement. Or worse, that his hands would suddenly touch something warm, alive, and secret. He turned quickly away and went back to where Ruth's small figure stood outlined against the lighted window of the house.

'Not there, anyhow,' he said briefly.

She nodded and, turning, led the way quickly out of the gate.

'Where next?' inquired Rufus. 'I suppose he might have gone down to the village. How about the pub?' His eyes were growing accustomed to the gloom and he could see the shadowy outline of her face beside him.

'No,' she said quietly, 'he won't have gone there.' She turned sharply away from the track to the village and led the way up the southern slope of the hill.

'Why this way?' said Rufus. 'He left me up by the spinney.'

Ruth walked rapidly on without reply.

'Are you going somewhere definite? It's no good just wandering about.' Still she did not reply, but walked on up the hill for another twenty yards in silence. Then Rufus heard the quick long intake of her breath.

'I've got an idea,' she said slowly. 'I think I may know where—where he may be...'

'Where?' asked Rufus in surprise. 'I didn't know there was anything over here except just Plain?'

'There isn't,' she said briefly.

'Then where are we making for?'

Ruth hesitated. 'You've never been there,' she said evasively, 'besides, he may not be there at all.'

'But why do you think he's there? Why should he be?'

'I don't think he's there,' said Ruth maddeningly, 'I only think he may be. If he is, you'll see for yourself. If not... if not we'll have to look somewhere else.'

Rufus shrugged his shoulders and plodded on in silence. He pulled back his cuff and glanced at the glowing luminous face of his watch. It was twenty minutes past five.

'We shan't have to be frightfully long,' he said warningly. 'Particularly as we're coming away from the village.'

There was no reply. The sharp rim of the hill was close above them now, standing out in solid black mass against the heavy sky.

Rufus swerved sharply to avoid a thick dark patch of shrub—just such a bush of wild rose as they had demolished, at some incredibly distant time, in the toboggan. Ruth stumbled over a heavy tuft of grass and, putting out a hand, he slipped it through her arm to steady her.

They reached the top of the rise and, still arm in arm, set off unhesitatingly across the gentle grassy slopes. Rufus glanced back over his shoulder. Far below, the solitary lighted window of Three Trees gleamed clear and yellow in the darkness. The encircling windbreak of trees was a faint black shadow beside it, and the dark mass of the big barn could be felt rather than seen. But the rest was a black pit. Rufus turned again and strode on into the dark. Once he squeezed the arm linked in his own. There was a gentle immediate answering pressure. And then he felt her muscles tensed as she pressed his arm against her side with a sudden, surprising, almost frantic strength. But she did not turn her head, nor pause in her rapid confident walk, and Rufus found it impossible to question her again.

The pace at which they walked had warmed him, but a wind had sprung up and blew coldly from the east, making his face tingle and starting a painful throbbing in his sore and swollen lips. Rufus turned up his collar and, sinking his chin deeply in it, sent his body walking on into the night, while his mind retired thankfully into a warm and cheerfully lighted inner self, as it had done when he wandered in the snowstorm. He thought of Mendel, and remembered that wherever he was he had no jacket. Only a thin torn shirt stood between the big swelling chest and these icy fingers. He smiled secretly and grimly to himself as he reflected how completely Three Trees was playing its part to the end. He had come to it, lost and exhausted, in a snowstorm. And now, even in the last hour before he put it behind him for ever, he was walking blindly and confidingly across the hills, on a bleak and windy night, towards some mysterious destination and in search of a grotesque figure which no longer existed.

A sudden foolish conviction came on him that he still walked alone in the snow—that Mendel and Ruth and Three Trees were one with the mysterious ballroom of his nightmare, and that in a moment he would awake to find the darkness around him, the snowflakes stinging his face, and his tired feet still plodding mechanically forward through the soft, sluggish, impeding carpet. So strong was the feeling that he mechanically brushed his hand over the front of his coat, half expecting to feel the icy crust clinging to the cloth. But his coat was dry and soft, and his arm pressed upon another slim and warm, which did not melt beneath his touch. Ruth still walked quickly on in the same tense silence, and beneath their feet was no glimmering carpet, but the rough springiness of uneven grass.

'Where are we?' he said, less because he wanted to know than to break the charm of the dreamy, delusory silence.

Ruth shrugged her shoulders.

'We aren't anywhere,' she replied, in a low voice, 'you were quite right. There's nothing out this way for about ten miles.'

'Are we going far?'

'Not if he's there,' she said gently; 'there'll be no need.'

Rufus felt a spasm of profound irritation.

'I wish to God you'd stop being a sort of Oracle of Delphi,'[102] he said sharply, 'and tell me what all this is about.'

A sound came from her that might have been a sigh.

'All right,' she said resignedly. 'What d'you want to know?'

'Well, for one thing, where are we going?'

'I tell you,' she said irritably, 'we aren't going anywhere. It's just an ordinary bit of the Plain where you've never been, so it's no use my trying to describe it to you.'

'What, out in the open?'

'Yes. Of course.'

'But what makes you think he'll be there?'

'Because I think it's the most likely place to find him in the circumstances.'

'But why the hell should he come wandering about out here, unless he's off his head? Anyhow, what d'you think he's doing?'

Ruth hesitated. 'I don't know,' she said at last, 'I don't expect he's doing—anything.'

'Has he ever done this stunt of going off before?'

He heard a quick exhalation that was almost a laugh.

'Before? Of course he has. But usually I—I haven't had to go and find him.'

Rufus glanced quickly at his watch.

'Well, if he *isn't* where you think, we shall just have to leave it and go, if we're going to catch that train. We can't wander about here all night.'

To his surprise, she stopped dead, and he saw the faint glimmer of her pale face as she turned towards him in the darkness.

'What's up?' he said in surprise.

Ruth stood silent for a moment. Then she nodded.

'All right,' she said slowly in a strange voice which he did not understand. 'I'll make a bargain with you. If—if he *isn't* where I think, I—I won't look any more. We'll just go straight away and catch our train at Leaford. I won't even write a note.'

'Right ho,' said Rufus, pleased, 'that's fine. After all, if you don't see him you can always write to him when we get to Town.' He took her arm again as they walked on.

'How far is it now?'

'About a mile.'

Rufus nodded. 'Good. We can just about manage that in time. It's nearly twenty to six now.'

For a few minutes more they walked rapidly on, over the monotonous slopes of rough grassland. But then the ground began to slope sharply upwards, and Rufus could see above them in the darkness the mass of a high rampart of hill not unlike the great cuplike banking which surrounded Three Trees. Ruth was pressing forward faster and faster, her breath coming in quick excited pants. He no longer held her arm. To climb such a hill together at that speed was an encumbrance. His heart was thumping hard and his mind went back to the morning when he and Mendel had strained pantingly up the hill towards the beech spinney.

He raised his head and looked up at the crest, and noticed with surprise a curious redness in the sky above the summit, like the reflection of a fire. He was about to remark on it when a sudden smothered inarticulate cry came from beside him.

Rufus turned quickly. The girl had stopped dead. She had seen the curious glow, and stood gazing up at it with uplifted, shadowy white face. Then, before he could move or speak, she sprang suddenly forward, and went dashing up the hill in a sudden run, staggering and slipping on the rough damp grass, her breath coming in great sobbing gasps. Too breathless to speak, Rufus followed as fast as he could. Once his foot slipped back and he fell on his hands and knees. But Ruth staggered on unheeding and, reaching the summit at last, stood gazing down before her with heaving chest. Rufus stumbled up beside her and, stopping dead at her side, gazed silently at the scene below.

They stood, it seemed, on the rim of a great natural bowl. In the centre was an amphitheatre of flat short grass, forming an almost perfect circle about one hundred feet in diameter, smooth and well-kept as a lawn. Around the central space the high grass banks rose vertically to a height of almost a hundred feet. On the side where they stood the crest was sheer and open. But on the opposite side, for practically half a circle, a single line of beech trees stood on the rim of the crater, precisely spaced at distances of six or seven yards. Their branches, winter-bare, were lifted like fantastic arms over the circular bowl, which they seemed at once to menace and protect. All this Rufus saw unconsciously, in the strange flickering red light. But his eyes were riveted to the centre of the grassy space. A great cone-shaped fire of wood was blazing and crackling furiously. The sound of the crackling and shifting logs, borne on the wind, came clearly up the hillside to them. Before the fire a figure sat crouching, head sunk, arms encircling and clasping knees. The face and the torn white shirt glowed orange–red as they caught the flicker of the dancing flames. The figure seemed small and puny beside the towering walls of the crater. But the thickly muscled bare arms and the mop of yellow hair were unmistakable.

Instinctively, Rufus made to advance down the sheer slope. But at the first movement a hand seized his arm and pulled him back with urgent strength. He turned quickly. Ruth was not looking at him. She was staring down fixedly into the bowl with wide-open shining eyes. The flickering red glow was reflected in her pale face, turning it to a strange unearthly orange. She neither looked at him nor spoke. But he felt her convulsive grip on his arm tighten and, following her eyes, saw the crouching figure begin to move. He gave a little gasp of relief. For one moment its terrible stillness had sent him cold with the thought that Mendel was dead.

The figure raised its head slowly and gazed into the fire. The light flickered for a moment on the face half turned to them, and Rufus could clearly see the swollen sullen dark bruises on cheek and mouth. The brow was furrowed as though with a terrible weariness and despair, and as they watched they saw him pass a hand slowly and painfully across his eyes. Rufus turned to the silent girl.

'What is it?' he half whispered, hoarsely and almost accusingly. 'What's he doing here?'

Her eyes never left the crouching figure. She slowly shook her head. 'I don't know,' she said wearily.

'But why has he come here? What's the matter with him?'

'The matter with him?' Her voice broke a little. Rufus turned quickly. Her eyes were full of tears. 'Why—only that he's alone, Rufus. That—that's all.'

A sudden sob shook her and he saw a tear run down her face. But she neither put a hand to her eyes nor moved in any way. He tried to put out a hand—to comfort her—but somehow he could not.

Mendel had dropped his head again now. His face was hidden in his hands, which rested against his knees. Something made Rufus turn and look, away from the fire, into the vast empty blackness around them, and seeing it, and the small, wearily crouching figure, he felt suddenly a thrill of fear and awe. It was as though the figure of Mendel personified loneliness, crouching beaten and exhausted before its fire, alone in the great mocking waste. He turned and seized the girl by the hand.

'Come on!' he cried hoarsely and urgently. 'Come away. We can't stand and watch–' His words died away in a mutter. She turned now and looked at him for the first time.

'Away?' she said dully. He felt a chill run through him and dropped her hand at the single word.

'We can't stay here,' he muttered foolishly, 'we must go.'

She looked at him in silence for a moment, and then, without speaking, nodded significantly towards the fire.

'I know!' With a mighty effort he threw off the eerie spell which seemed to bind him and, turning, seized her fiercely by the shoulders. 'I know. But you said you would. You said you'd come. You're mine. You don't belong to him any more.' He felt the thin shoulders shaking in his grip. 'You must come,' he repeated savagely. 'Now. And leave him here. Or else you never will. If you go back now you'll never get away. He'll have you—*tight*—tighter than he had before. I shall be gone and you'll be dead. And you love me. You know you love me. It isn't as though this is real. He's acting again—*acting*—that's all—just as he always does. It isn't real. He isn't really– You've got to come. I'll love you if you come now.' He was shaking her in almost crazy anxiety, not knowing what he said. For a moment she seemed to hesitate, and for a triumphant moment she seemed about to yield. He clasped her to him in a wild foolish desire to topple her resolution over by sheer physical strength. She gave limply in his arms and suffered him to kiss her passionately. But she made no response, and as he paused and gazed at her, she gently disengaged herself and turned once more to the figure which sat beside the great fire. Something died in Rufus then, and he knew that he had lost. His arms fell to his sides and he suddenly felt very tired.

'Are you coming?' he said in a low voice, knowing the answer.

'No, Rufus,' she said quietly, her voice shaking a little.

He nodded mutely. 'Did you ever mean to come?' he said, not knowing why he asked.

'No.' She hesitated and then turned to him. Her lashes were wet. 'I'm sorry,' she said in a low voice. 'I—I don't know. I did mean to when I said I would. But all the time I—I knew.' She dropped her face in her hands and began to sob quietly. 'O God,' she muttered brokenly, 'and I do love you…'

The words neither surprised nor thrilled him. Something which he had never been able to understand before was now quite clear and simple. He put out his arms and drew her to him. He did not want to take her away now, nor to claim her. He only wanted to comfort her.

'Poor Ruth!' he said gently.

She looked up at him in supplication.

'But I do, Rufus—I do love you! You know I do?'

'Of course,' he said serenely, 'it's quite all right. Don't worry, love. I see.'

'I'd come if I could. If I could leave him. But… but–'

'It's all right,' he said soothingly. He was afraid—desperately afraid—that in her anxiety and wretchedness she would insist on explaining what needed no explanation. And that, strangely, would be intolerable. But she had fallen silent again. He held her tightly for a moment, and gazed down into the arena. The figure on the far side of the fire was very still and small.

'I must go,' he said slowly.

'Yes.' She gently released herself. Her sobs had ceased. 'Go now, Rufus. And try and—and forget about it.' She was staring at him with wide-open eyes, tear-filled still, but quite calm.

'And you?' said Rufus involuntarily.

'I shall go back, too,' she said gently, 'where I came from to meet you.'[103]

'I haven't spoiled it?' he said in a low voice.

'Spoiled it? No. How could you?'

'By telling you about him?'

She looked at him for a moment in surprise. Then she shook her head with a queer little smile. 'You still don't see,' she said gently. She turned and looked thoughtfully down at the fire. 'Do you really think you were telling me something I didn't know?' she said softly. 'Don't you see that I've known all the time that he's like that? That he's always playing—never quite genuine—never quite honest with himself or me?'

Rufus took a step forward.

'You *knew* that?'

She laughed quietly. 'Of course, my silly Rufus. That's why I must stay. He can't play by himself and if I went he might find out. And that would hurt him.' Her face was very gentle as she gazed down at the distant figure. 'He mustn't be hurt any more,' she said, and her voice seemed to Rufus to come from a vast distance. 'He's been hurt too much already and it mustn't ever happen again. I couldn't leave him alone, Rufus, with the fire dying down and the wind getting colder. But you—it's nothing to do with you. Go back—where you came from. That's your life really. It always has been. Go back where things are solid and noisy and—and beastly sometimes. You've never been really happy here—not really. You never would be. You're too young and too nice and too interested. It was just bad luck your meeting Pip and me—and this. You thought we were alive when you came. But we're not. We're dead. Dead and—and buried long ago. And we can't do anything, but go on playing—playing and pretending we're alive. Trying to make up a life of our own out of the bits we like, and funking the other bits, because they've beaten us. But they haven't beaten you, Rufus—the noise and the sweat and the people. You can go back and beat them and have it all—the real thing and know you've won. We've only got a few little easy things. Because we gave up—'

Her voice trailed away into silence.

'Good-bye,' she said quite suddenly and simply.

She put her arms round his neck and kissed him gently on the swollen lips. Rufus kissed her dazedly and mechanically. She released herself and, taking him by the arm, turned him round gently.

'Good-bye, Rufus,' she said again, 'you must go now.'

She turned away without another word and, walking forward, began to descend the steep wall of the crater. Rufus stood for a moment gazing stupidly after her. Then, raising his eyes with an effort, he looked for the last time round the great bowl. The fire was dying rapidly now, and he could only see the dim outline of the figure which crouched silently below the menacing trees. And then he suddenly realised that he must not see her go to Mendel and, turning, went blundering dazedly away down the steep slope towards the village. A curious sense of urgency was on him. There was time in it somewhere, and he instinctively glanced at his watch. It was nearly six o'clock.[104] He remembered.

Notes

1   *I have desired to go...* This is the full text of the poem 'Heaven-Haven' by the English poet and priest Gerard Manley Hopkins (1844–1889).

2   *S. J.* The abbreviation stands for 'Society of Jesus' and indicates that Hopkins was a member of the religious order of the Catholic Church also known as the Jesuits.

3   *And Life is Colour and Warmth and Light...* This is part of the poem 'Into Battle' by Julian Henry Francis Grenfell (1888–1915), a poet and soldier who distinguished himself during World War One before dying of wounds sustained during the Battle of Ypres.

4   *D.S.O.* Instituted in 1886, the Distinguished Service Order, or DSO, is a decoration awarded to members of the British armed forces in recognition of distinguished service during wartime.

5   *three-halfpence.* For the modern-day value of this sum (and others mentioned in the text) see the table on p. 293.

6   *the Goldsmith's and Silversmith's Company.* Founded in 1880 by William Gibson and John Lawrence Langman, the Goldsmiths & Silversmiths company was a well-known manufacturer of jewellery with retail premises in Regent Street, London. It was amalgamated with Garrard & Co in 1952.

7   *Honor Oak Cemetery.* Two large cemeteries, now known collectively as Camberwell cemeteries, are located in Honor Oak in south-east London. The first internment at Camberwell New Cemetery, which is what Rufus refers to as Honor Oak Cemetery, occurred in 1927, as Camberwell Old Cemetery had reached capacity.

8   *Boots Library.* More accurately known as Boots Book-Lovers' Library, Boots Library was a lending library run by the chemist chain Boots that operated

between 1898 and 1966. In 1935 it refused to stock *Simple Life* because it considered that Balchin had been too outspoken in his handling of the sexual scenes.

9   *Trafalgar Square Station.* In 1935, the arrangement of stations on the Bakerloo Line was slightly different to that which exists today. As suggested by Rufus's journey, Piccadilly Circus was followed by stops at Trafalgar Square and Charing Cross. When the Jubilee Line was built in the 1970s, Trafalgar Square and Charing Cross were renamed Charing Cross and Embankment, respectively.

10   *'general post'.* A general swapping of positions or locations.

11   *comptometer.* An early form of mechanical calculator.

12   *Bateman or Fougasse.* Bateman and Fougasse were two leading British artists and cartoonists of the 1930s. Henry Mayo Bateman (1887–1970) is probably best known for his 'The Man Who…' cartoons of the 1920s, which mostly depicted people committing terrible social faux pas. Fougasse, the pen name of Cyril Kenneth Bird (1887–1965), was renowned for his work for *Punch* magazine, as well as his Second World War propaganda posters, such as 'Careless Talk Cost Lives'.

13   *coupons.* In the 1930s, packets of cigarettes often contained coupons that could be exchanged either for more cigarettes or, in the case of the fictional Blenkin brand referred to here, a more desirable form of gift.

14   *You've got a liver…* Having a liver, or being liverish, means to be bad-tempered or unhappy.

15   *A tram went booming and clanging past them.* When *Simple Life* was first published in 1935, London's electric trams were just beginning to be replaced by trolleybuses but they were a ubiquitous feature of the capital's public transport network at that time. There were tram tracks on the Victoria Embankment, the road along which Rufus and Ted Lewis are walking when a tram passes them.

16   *Town.* London.

17   *The famous slogan […] blazed nightly above Piccadilly.* Since 1908, illuminated advertising hoardings have been a feature of the buildings that surround Piccadilly Circus in the heart of London although, in 2022, only one building (that between Shaftesbury Avenue and Glasshouse Street) now carries them.

18   *magnesia.* Better known as 'milk of magnesia', magnesia (magnesium hydroxide) is an inorganic chemical compound that is used in suspension as an antacid and laxative.

19   *forty-nine million people.* A slight overestimate on the part of Mr. Corder as the population of the UK was 46.1 million in 1931 and 48.2 million in 1941.

20   *attaining his majority.* To attain one's majority means to become an adult, as recognized by the law. In 1935, when *Simple Life* was first published, the age of majority in England was twenty-one. In 1970, it was lowered to eighteen,

and has remained so ever since.

21 *do a show.* To go to the theatre.

22 *sweeping a crossing.* Crossing sweepers were people (often young boys) who offered to sweep dirty urban streets in exchange for a small sum of money so that rich people could cross the road without getting dirt on their expensive clothes. They were particularly common in Victorian London and were embedded in the popular culture of the time as exemplified by paintings such as 'The Crossing Sweeper' by William Powell Frith (1858) and the character of Jo in Charles Dickens's *Bleak House* (1853). Especially in his early writing, Balchin frequently alluded to the job of a crossing sweeper as being the epitome of an undesirable occupation.

23 *steerage.* The part of a ship that provided the worst class of accommodation for passengers in possession of the cheapest tickets.

24 *Barker's.* Barkers of Kensington was a large, well-known department store in Kensington High Street. Founded in 1870, it closed in 2006.

25 *V.A.D.s.* The Voluntary Aid Detachment (VAD) was a volunteer civilian unit that provided nursing care for military personnel in the UK and other countries of the British Empire. Founded in 1909, it was particularly active during the First and Second World Wars.

26 *Mr. Baldwin.* Stanley Baldwin (1867–1947) was a British Conservative politician who served as prime minister on three occasions between the two great wars of the twentieth century. His final stint as premier began on 7 June 1935, almost exactly a month after *Simple Life* was published.

27 *Verbena.* An herbaceous plant with bright flowers. The oil derived from it has a citrusy smell and is used in perfumes.

28 *Scott and Black.* Charles William Anderson Scott (1903–1946) and Tom Campbell Black (1899–1936) were English aviators. Their exploits would have been fresh in Balchin's mind when he was writing *Simple Life* because they won the prestigious MacRobertson air race from London to Melbourne in October 1934, becoming world famous in the process.

29 *They might navigate by wireless beam.* From the early 1900s onwards it was possible for aeroplanes to navigate using wireless (i.e. radio) signals.

30 *'Oh freedom is a noble thing…'* These lines are taken from *The Brus* (*The Bruce*), a long narrative poem about the life of the Scottish king Robert the Bruce written by John Barbour (ca. 1320–1395), a Scottish clergyman and poet.

31 *Quiller Couch.* Sir Arthur Thomas Quiller-Couch (1863–1944) was a novelist as well as a notable literary critic. He was King Edward VII Professor of English Literature at Cambridge University when Balchin was studying there in the late 1920s.

32 *The League of Nations.* Established in 1920, the League of Nations was the first worldwide intergovernmental organization intended to maintain world

peace. In 1946, it was disbanded and succeeded by the United Nations. In his final year at Dauntsey's School (1926–7), Balchin belonged to the Junior Branch of the League of Nations.

33 *Emigration is the sincerest form of flattery.* Rufus is deliberately misquoting the proverb 'Imitation is the sincerest form of flattery.'

34 *this morning.* This is evidence of either drunken confusion on the part of Rufus or carelessness on the part of Balchin because we were told earlier (p. 33) that it was four o'clock in the afternoon when Rufus was summoned to attend his climactic meeting with Mr. Winstrowe and Mr. Corder.

35 *fisherman's gesture.* A fisherman traditionally spreads his arms out, at right-angles to his torso, to their fullest extent to indicate the size of a fish that he has caught (or that got away).

36 *'He either fears his fate too much…'* This is a slight misquotation (it should read 'That puts it not unto the touch') of the poem 'My Dear and Only Love' by the Scottish nobleman, soldier and poet James Graham (1612–1650), First Marquess of Montrose.

37 *'God bless the king…'* Rufus recites a slightly amended version of an ambiguously loyal toast (known variously as 'Which is Which' and 'Verse Intended to Allay the Violence of Party-Spirit') containing both pro- and anti-Jacobite sentiments written by the English poet John Byrom (1692–1763). The accepted version of Byrom's epigram is as follows:

> God bless the King! (I mean our faith's defender)
> God bless! (No harm in blessing) the Pretender.
> But who Pretender is, and who is King,
> God bless us all! That's quite another thing!

38 *Last time I went to St. Ives…* St Ives is a seaside town in the far south-west of England. 'As I was going to St Ives' is an English nursery rhyme in the form of a riddle:

> As I was going to St Ives,
> I met a man with seven wives,
> Each wife had seven sacks,
> Each sack had seven cats,
> Each cat had seven kits:
> Kits, cats, sacks, and wives,
> How many were there going to St Ives?

39 *Bulford Camp.* Located about two miles north-east of the town of Amesbury, Bulford Camp is a military camp on Salisbury Plain in Wiltshire. Opened in 1897, it still functions as a British Army base today.

40 *ambrosial.* The adjective derived from the word 'ambrosia', which means 'the food of the gods' in Greek and Roman mythology but which, in this context, means something very pleasing to the tastebuds.

41   *union-flannel.* A fabric composed of a blend of yarns, typically cotton mixed with either linen, wool or silk.

42   *headland.* The unploughed edge of a field.

43   *mould-board.* A mouldboard is the part of a plough that turns the earth over.

44   *'He leans to it…'* These lines are taken from the 1887 poem 'Harry Ploughman' by Gerard Manley Hopkins.

45   *Saul Kane had concluded the Everlasting Mercy…* 'The Everlasting Mercy' is a poem by the English poet John Masefield (1878–1967), the second longest-serving Poet Laureate. It tells the story of the drunken, violent womaniser Saul Kane, who turns to Christianity after a life of sin. At the end of the poem, Kane tries his hand at ploughing.

46   *throw them on the parish.* Leave them to rely on charitable aid organized by the church.

47   *the band.* Balchin once said that, at around the time when he left school in 1927, he ran a dance band for a while. He may therefore have drawn on his own experiences when writing about the band that perform at the Select Dance in Leaford.

48   *Pancho's Club in Villiers Street.* Villiers Street in central London runs alongside Charing Cross railway station, connecting the Strand to the Embankment. I have failed to find any record of a Pancho's Club existing there in the 1930s. It may therefore have been an invention of Balchin's.

49   *dickey.* A false shirt front.

50   *A fifteen-mile walk.* There is some evidence that Balchin wrote *Simple Life* quickly and perhaps did not pay sufficiently close attention to some of the factual aspects of the novel. Principally, he seems to get confused about times, distances and reasonable walking speeds. We are told that, after bidding farewell to the removal men, Rufus walks from 10 am until almost 1 pm. As most fit walkers struggle to maintain a speed of 4 mph for any length of time, it seems unlikely that Balchin's sedentary, city-dwelling hero could average in excess of 5 mph for close to three hours over unfamiliar terrain.

51   *Jermyn Street whore.* Jermyn Street is situated in the St James's area of central London. I have been unable to find any evidence of it being a favoured haunt of prostitutes in the 1930s but it is close to Piccadilly Circus, which certainly was.

52   *'Ensculptured, embossed…'* Either Rufus or Balchin is misremembering the last three lines of the poem 'To a Snowflake' by the English poet Francis Thompson (1859–1907), which actually read as follows:

> 'Insculped and embossed,
> With His hammer of wind,
> And His graver of frost.'

In this context, a graver is an engraving tool.

53   *He had walked for an hour and a half…* It is unclear which stretch of walking is being referred to here. In the next chapter, Rufus tells Mendel that he had begun walking at about 1 pm; he took 'the centre track' of three possible paths at some time before 2.30 pm; and he turned back at 3.30 pm precisely. None of the periods between those start times and 4.15 pm are equal to an hour and a half. This is further evidence of some carelessness on Balchin's part with regard to the times and distances referred to in *Simple Life*.

54   *'A traveller by the faithful hound…'* This is part of the poem 'Excelsior' by the American poet Henry Wadsworth Longfellow (1807–1882).

55   *'In dulci jubilo…'* Latin for 'In sweet rejoicing', 'In dulci jubilo' is a traditional Christmas carol.

56   *plus-fours.* Loose-fitting knickerbocker-style trousers that fall to just below the knee and were used by golfers in the 1930s. The name originates from the fact that the overhang at the knees required an extra four inches of material.

57   *a partially finished carving.* Balchin was an enthusiastic and skilled wood-carver himself.

58   *According to her lights.* An expression used quite frequently in Balchin's novels, it means 'in agreement with her personal values and beliefs'.

59   *sportsmen.* Balchin means that the removal men were good sports; he is not alluding to any athletic ability that they may or may not have possessed.

60   *lotus eat.* To indulge in luxury and pleasure.

61   *What was it Oscar Wilde said?* Ruth is alluding to one of the most celebrated aperçus to have issued from the pen of the Irish poet, playwright and novelist Oscar Fingal O'Flahertie Wills Wilde (1856–1900). The line in question is taken from Wilde's 1892 play *Lady Windermere's Fan*: 'I can resist everything except temptation.'

62   *a grand game played in the farmyard.* The game that Mendel and Ruth have devised sounds a little bit like real tennis.

63   *Salvationists.* Members of the Christian evangelical organization known as the Salvation Army.

64   *Lyons's restaurant.* Presumably Mendel is referring to the famous Corner Houses run by J. Lyons & Co in the West End of London, each of which contained several restaurants.

65   *the parable of the talents.* The Parable of Talents occurs, in slightly different forms, in two of the Gospels of the New Testament: *Matthew 25: 14–30* and *Luke 19: 11–27*. A rich man leaves his house to go travelling, and puts his property in the care of three of his servants. Each servant is given a number of 'talents' (a form of currency) according to his ability. When he returns from his travels, the master rewards his servants in proportion to how well they have invested the money they were given. The servant who had buried his solitary talent in the ground, as opposed to investing it wisely, is

reprimanded and dismissed.

66   *lilies of the field.* This expression (or a version of it) is found in the Gospels of both Matthew and Luke. For example, *Matthew 6: 28* has this to say:

> 'And why are you anxious about clothing? Consider the lilies of the field, how they grow: they neither toil nor spin.'

Here, the word 'spin' means to spin thread to make cloth for clothing. The meaning of this passage is that we should go about our daily work without worrying, and leave God to look after our worldly needs. P. G. Wodehouse used the expression 'lilies of the field' to refer to the idle rich who do not have to work for a living.

67   *afraid.* The title of Balchin's 1947 play-cum-novel *Lord, I Was Afraid* is a contracted form of the wording to be found in *Matthew 25* and the work itself was inspired by the Parable of Talents.

68   *the Ritz.* Opened in 1906, the Ritz hotel in London's Piccadilly has long been synonymous with luxury and fine dining.

69   *Maeterlinck's saying.* Maurice Maeterlinck (1862–1949) was a Belgian poet and playwright. He was awarded the Nobel Prize for Literature in 1911.

70   *ashplant.* A sapling cut from an ash tree and used as a walking stick.

71   *young limbs.* Young people.

72   *the Wiltshire Moonrakers.* There are many versions of this legend but the smuggling activities it describes may have been enacted in Devizes, which is only a few miles away from where Balchin grew up and he would probably have been aware of the legend from an early age. A moonraker is also a colloquial term for a native of Wiltshire.

73   *charabancs.* A charabanc was an early type of bus.

74   *Stonehenge.* The tourism 'problem' at Stonehenge has worsened considerably since the 1930s.

75   *Patron, Patron, Patron das Macht der Wind.* 'Patron, das macht der Wind!' is an aria from the cantata 'Geschwinde, Geschwinde, ihr wirbelnden Winde' ('The Contest between Phoebus and Pan'; BWV 201) by the German composer Johann Sebastian Bach (1685–1750).

76   *Urn Burial. Urn Burial* (or *Hydriotaphia*) is a discourse by the English author and physician Sir Thomas Browne (1605–1682) inspired by the discovery of some Anglo-Saxon pots in Norfolk.

77   *I am in desperate case.* If Ruth is quoting here then it is unclear exactly who or what she is quoting. Two possible options are Shakespeare ('And haste is needful in this desperate case.' – *Henry VI, Part 3*, Act IV, Scene 1) and the Roman historian Livy ('In difficult and desperate cases, the boldest counsels are the safest.' – *History of Rome*, Book XXV, Section 38).

78   *gamin.* It seems most likely that Balchin meant to write 'gamine' (meaning a girl who is boyishly attractive) as opposed to 'gamin' (meaning a street urchin).

79   *eight or nine million.* The population of Greater London (i.e. Inner and Outer London combined) was 8.1 million in 1931 and 8.6 million in 1939.

80   *Queensberry rules.* The standard rules of boxing, the preparation of which was supervised by the Ninth Marquess of Queensberry.

81   *Tacet.* A musical term denoting that an instrument is silent.

82   *Time was made for man and not man for time.* Rufus seems to be adapting the Gospel of Mark (*Mark 2:27*): 'The Sabbath was made for man, not man for the Sabbath'.

83   *Hawkes euphonium.* Hawkes & Son was a company founded in 1865 by William Henry Hawkes. It originally sold sheet music but later diversified into the manufacture of musical instruments. In 1930 Hawkes & Son merged with Boosey & Company to form Boosey & Hawkes. The company is still in existence today as a publisher of classical music.

84   *D'you remember old Sid...* The rather inconsequential tale that follows is reminiscent of some of the weaker stories in Balchin's short-story compendium *Last Recollections of My Uncle Charles* (1954).

85   *dandled.* The word is generally used to describe the action of bouncing a baby up and down. Mr. Kearns is evidently performing a similar sort of action on his knee with his beer mug.

86   *the dying Paganini.* Niccolò Paganini (1782–1840) was an Italian composer and, as a violinist, the most celebrated virtuoso of his era. He died from internal bleeding before a priest could be summoned.

87   *Your Grock, your Chaplin.* Grock (real name Charles Adrien Wettach; 1880–1959) was a Swiss clown reputed to have once been the world's highest paid entertainer. Sir Charles Spencer 'Charlie' Chaplin (1889–1977) was an English comic actor famed for his tramp persona.

88   *'By long and vehement suit I was seduced...'* This explanation of the begetting of Philip the Bastard in Shakespeare's play *King John* (Act I Scene 1) is spoken by his mother, Lady Faulconbridge.

89   *It always does.* This is an unsatisfactory continuation of the exchange initiated by Mendel a few lines earlier. Possibly, this part of the text was revised by Balchin—he may have taken something out—and he neglected to amend the resulting non-sequitur.

90   *He began to count like a cox...* In addition to steering a rowing boat, one of the duties of a cox is to call for increased effort from his or her crew members over a set period of time, and the duration of that effort may be indicated by counting in the same way as Mendel does here.

91   *Fugue a 3 Voci.* Italian for 'Fugue for 3 Voices', although note that the Italian for fugue is fuga. A fugue is a form of contrapuntal musical composition in which a melody is introduced by one voice and then successively taken up by the others, two in this case. J. S. Bach, Balchin's favourite classical composer,

wrote a number of fugues for three voices.

92   *swab.* An archaic term for a contemptible person.

93   *Mess.* A room in which members of the armed forces eat and socialize.

94   *Jeremy Taylor.* An English cleric, Taylor (1613–1667) achieved fame as an author during the Protectorate of Oliver Cromwell. His works include *The Rule and Exercises of Holy Living* (1650), which functions as a manual of Christian practice.

95   *faute de mieux.* A French expression meaning 'for want of a better alternative'.

96   *a Holmesian exposition.* Sherlock Holmes, the world-famous detective created by the English writer Sir Arthur Ignatius Conan Doyle (1859–1930), was renowned for deducing what was troubling his clients on the basis of his interpretation of non-verbal cues such as their mood, body language and physical appearance. In 1962, Balchin said 'I don't read detective stories [...] except Sherlock Holmes.'

97   *husky.* Big and strong.

98   *Varsity.* A university, but especially Oxford or Cambridge.

99   *How long will it take us to get to—to the station?* Previously (p. 105) we were told that Three Trees is situated 'about two miles away' from Leaford. As the railway station that Leaford shares with Standing is situated half a mile the other side of the village, Rufus and Ruth will have to walk very briskly (at an average speed of 5 mph) if they are to reach the station within half an hour.

100 *account executive.* An employee in an advertising agency who has responsibility for dealing with the firm's clients. A more senior position than a copywriter.

101 *sentiment d'incomplétude.* A feeling of inadequacy or of being unfulfilled. This psychological concept was first proposed by the French psychotherapist Pierre Janet (1859–1947), whose work subsequently influenced that of both Sigmund Freud (1856–1939) and Carl Jung (1875–1961).

102 *Oracle of Delphi.* Pythia, High Priestess of the Temple of Apollo at Delphi in Greece, was known as the Oracle of Delphi. As such, she acted as a medium, dispensing advice or prophecy to those who appealed to the gods for help.

103 *I shall go back [...] where I came from to meet you.* This is a curious and bewildering statement by Ruth and I confess that I am unable to explain it. If she means that she will meet Rufus in London, which is where she came from originally, then such an assertion is contradicted by the fact that, just a few lines further on, she clearly renounces Rufus and dedicates herself wholeheartedly to Mendel. Balchin rewrote the ending of *Simple Life* in February 1935, just a few months before publication. Perhaps he forgot to attend to this sentence because it makes little sense as written.

104 *It was nearly six o'clock.* See previous notes on this subject. At 5.20 pm, Rufus and Ruth set out from Three Trees and begin walking in the opposite direction to the village and the railway station. At 5.40 pm, by which time

it is fair to assume that they will have covered at least a mile, they still have about another mile to go to reach the place where Ruth thinks she might find Mendel. When they get there, they have walked at least two miles since leaving Three Trees. Therefore, if Rufus is still trying to catch the six-thirty train to London then he has more than four and a half miles to walk in just over half an hour, which is clearly impossible without running.

Table of Relative Values

This table is provided to enable the reader to gauge the modern-day value of sums of money mentioned in *Simple Life*. The conversion of 1935 monetary values to their 2020* equivalents has been performed based on the increase in the retail price index over the intervening period. An explanation of the rationale behind this methodology can be found at this very useful website: www.measuringworth.com

Page number	Sum of money mentioned in *Simple Life*	Relative value in 2020*
9	Three-halfpence	£0.44
10	£20	£1420
11	£700	£49,700
16	£4000	£284,000
17	£100,000	£7.1 million
22	£50,000	£3.6 million
26	Eighteen pence	£5.32
26	Five bob	£17.70
32	£1000	£71,000
34	£200,000	£14.2 million
38	Half a crown	£8.87
41	£170	£12,100
47	£600	£42,600
48	£2	£142
60	£10	£710

Table of Relative Values

Page number	Sum of money mentioned in *Simple Life*	Relative value in 2020*
61	£1	£71
61	£5	£355
81	One shilling	£3.55
84	Twenty shillings	£71
84	Twenty-five shillings	£88.75
95	Ten shillings	£35.50
95	Fifteen shillings	£53.25
95	Thirty-two shillings	£113.60
96	£300	£21,300
96	£400	£28,400
111	One pound four and eightpence	£87.50
123	£200	£14,200
201	£10,000	£710,000

* The most recent year for which data are available.

Nigel Balchin: A Condensed Biography

Nigel Balchin

Titles of novels printed in bold font identify those scheduled for republication as part of the Nigel Balchin Collection.

Nigel Balchin was, inter alia, a playwright, an author of non-fiction books, a Hollywood scriptwriter, a television dramatist, an advertising and marketing expert, an industrial psychologist and an authority on Oriental rugs and carpets. More pertinently in the current context, he was also one of the foremost popular novelists of the middle decades of the twentieth century. Balchin's fiction has long been revered by his peers: during his lifetime, his novels were praised by eminent fellow writers such as Anthony Burgess, John Betjeman, L. P. Hartley and Elizabeth Bowen; since his death, Balchin's admirers have included Clive James, Philippa Gregory, Julian Fellowes and Ruth Rendell.

For the purposes of this biographical sketch, I wish to focus primarily on the fourteen novels that Balchin wrote, and to show how the material for those novels was partly extracted from his own life experiences.

Balchin was born in Potterne, Wiltshire in 1908. His father was a small shopkeeper and his mother was the daughter of a railway guard. On his father's side of the family, Balchin was descended from a line of well-to-do gentleman farmers who tilled the soil in the Godalming area but, by the time of Balchin's birth, the money had largely gone and his father was forced to work long hours in order to support his wife and children. Balchin's third novel, *Lightbody on Liberty* (1936), is concerned with the fortunes of a small shopkeeper and aspects of the story were influenced by the experiences of William Balchin, Nigel's father.

Towards the end of the First World War, Balchin's parents moved from Potterne to another part of Wiltshire so that their youngest son could begin his secondary schooling at the Dauntsey Agricultural School, a minor public school in the village of West Lavington. In his teenage years, Balchin enjoyed a conventionally happy rural childhood on the edge of Salisbury Plain. When not occupied by his schooling, he played a full part in the social life of his village by indulging in amateur dramatics, singing in church concerts, attending village fetes and playing sport (as a schoolboy, he was adept at rugby, soccer, hockey, fives and cricket). He also undertook many long walks on the sparsely inhabited expanses of the Wiltshire Downs. This love of the countryside that he had found on his doorstep as a child informed Balchin's second novel, 1935's **Simple Life**.

In 1927, aided by a scholarship, Balchin took up an offer to read Natural Sciences at Cambridge. His college was Peterhouse and one of his fellow Petreans was the future film star James Mason, who remained a close friend for the rest of Balchin's life.

By the end of Balchin's second year at Peterhouse his interest in Natural Sciences was wearing thin. This was predominantly because the Ministry of Agriculture, who were funding Balchin's education, wanted him to specialize in the study of agriculture, with a view to obtaining a job as an agriculturist once he had graduated. Having no intention of following such a career, Balchin challenged the Ministry's diktat, got his own way and was able to study psychology instead of agriculture in his final term at university. This was a momentous decision, and one that would direct the course of Balchin's working life for at least the next fifteen years.

With the assistance of a charismatic psychology professor called Frederic Bartlett, Balchin secured a position with the National Institute of Industrial Psychology when he left Cambridge in 1930. The NIIP was a pioneering organization that attempted to use psychological techniques to solve practical problems encountered in British industry. As an industrial investigator, Balchin's job consisted of visiting factories and other places of work, where he sought to improve working conditions for the staff, primarily by making them more comfortable and removing handicaps that hindered them in their work. This portion of Balchin's life strongly influenced his debut novel *No Sky*, which was published in 1934 and described the work and home lives of a time-and-motion man in an engineering factory.

The highpoint of Balchin's five-year stay with the NIIP came when he was intimately involved in a large market research project that culminated in the launch of Black Magic chocolates in January 1933. But as Balchin's star rose, he became an asset that the NIIP could no longer afford to hold onto. Early in 1935,

Balchin left the NIIP to join Rowntree's, the manufacturers of Black Magic. He remained with them until the outbreak of World War Two, specializing in the consumer testing of different brands of confectionery.

Balchin's work for the NIIP enabled him to launch a parallel career as a writer. During the 1930s, he wrote a large number of articles for scientific journals and also for magazines such as *Punch*. Two collections of Balchin's *Punch* articles were spun off from the magazine and published in the form of his first two non-fiction books. These volumes—*How to Run a Bassoon Factory* (1934) and *Business for Pleasure* (1935)—saw Balchin in playful mood, satirizing the work he had accomplished for the NIIP.

Balchin married Elisabeth Walshe, a graduate of Newnham College, Cambridge, in 1934. They had met during Balchin's final year at university. Over the course of the following ten years the marriage produced three daughters, one of whom grew up to become the renowned child psychologist Penelope Leach.

Balchin began World War Two as a linkman between Rowntree's and the Ministry of Food before, in 1940, he transferred to the Ministry itself, where he took charge of the allocation of raw materials such as sugar and cocoa to food manufacturers. Balchin's horror at both the suffocating bureaucracy that impeded efficiency at the Ministry and the venal self-interest of some of the businessmen he had to deal with found the perfect outlet with the publication, in 1942, of *Darkness Falls from the Air*. Artistically speaking, this was Balchin's first really successful novel, and it would have sold much better had the prospect of substantial sales not been scuppered by the paper shortages extant at the time.

In the summer of 1941, Balchin left the Ministry of Food and enrolled in the army. He experienced a meteoric rise through the ranks of the military: appointed a captain in August 1941, he had risen as far as brigadier by May 1945. As well as advising on the practicality of new pieces of weaponry, Balchin also overhauled the army's personnel selection procedure, at the same time introducing the service to the concept of rudimentary computerisation in the form of Hollerith punched cards, which he had first used in connection with the Black Magic market research project.

Balchin's military career provided him with many of his best ideas for *The Small Back Room*, his 1943 smash-hit novel. Later successfully filmed by Powell and Pressburger, *The Small Back Room* was the story of a research scientist grappling with power struggles at work by day and his own personal problems—alcoholism and a fragile relationship with his girlfriend—by night. It made Balchin's name as a novelist.

Buoyed by the success of *The Small Back Room*, Balchin chose to become a full-time writer upon his release from military duties at the end of 1945. Published just a few months before his demobilization, **Mine Own Executioner**, Balchin's first post-war novel, was about a psycho-therapist who tries to help a Spitfire pilot who has made several attempts to murder his wife in the wake of brutal treatment at the hands of the Japanese. Its realism enhanced by information Balchin had gleaned from psychiatrists he had worked with during the war, **Mine Own Executioner** sold in vast quantities and was lavishly praised by the critics. It was also made into a respectable film, for which Balchin himself wrote the screenplay.

Accused by book reviewers of adhering to a formula when writing novels—the juxtaposition of work and domestic problems in the lives of middle-class professional men, set against the backdrop of the Second World War—Balchin decisively broke away from that formula as the end of the 1940s approached. First, in 1947, came *Lord, I Was Afraid*, a series of fantastical (and often satirical) dramatic scenarios presented in the form of a play. Despite being admired by Anthony Burgess and J. G. Ballard, the book sank without trace. It was followed a year later by *The Borgia*

Testament, an account of the life of the Renaissance tyrant Cesare Borgia written from his own perspective and in a very modern idiom. It is the only Balchin novel not to have been based at least to some extent on events from the writer's own life.

To the relief of his regular readers, Balchin then retreated to more familiar territory in 1949 with ***A Sort of Traitors***, a novel about two scientists tempted to commit treason in order to get some important research about the suppression of epidemics into the public domain. Predictably, Balchin's sales figures rebounded after the dips suffered by his two previous pieces of fiction.

Balchin's marriage to Elisabeth Walshe, despite surviving for almost twenty years, was never an especially stable one. At the beginning of World War Two it was damaged when Elisabeth had a brief fling with Christian Darnton, a composer of avant-garde classical music. Balchin's reaction was to savagely lampoon Darnton via the medium of Stephen, a self-pitying poet, in *Darkness Falls from the Air*. Then, in the late 1940s, Elisabeth began an affair with the painter and sculptor Michael Ayrton. Balchin permitted the liaison to drag on for several years, hoping that Elisabeth would eventually see sense and return to him, before bowing to the inevitable at the end of 1950, when he initiated divorce proceedings. Once more, Balchin used the creation of fiction as a pressure valve to release the frustration that had built up inside him as a result of Elisabeth's unfaithfulness. In *A Way Through the Wood*, published in 1951, he poked fun at Ayrton in the form of Bill Bule, an irresponsible aristocrat who steals the wife of the book's Balchin-like narrator. Raw and searingly honest, *A Way Through the Wood* is Balchin's most heartfelt novel.

In 1949, Balchin embarked on a new relationship with Yovanka Tomich, a Yugoslav émigré twenty-two years his junior who was initially employed to type his manuscripts. Energized by this upturn in the fortunes of his romantic affairs, Balchin's writing acquired a new vigour and this led to the creation of two of his finest novels. 1953's ***Sundry Creditors*** anatomized the workings of a Midlands engineering company with skill and precision and, like *No Sky* before it, was informed by the author's previous career as an industrial psychologist. But it also achieved contemporary relevance because it contained portraits—some affectionate, others much less so—of members of the Rowntree's top brass whom Balchin had dealt with over the previous few years, when he had served as a consultant on advertising and marketing matters.

The Fall of the Sparrow (1955) was completely different to its predecessor and saw Balchin once more boldly striding out into new territory. The book consisted of the life story, over a span of about thirty years, of Jason Pellew, a likeable but aimless drifter who suffers all manner of mishaps as a result of his unstable personality. To write this haunting and very believable novel, Balchin called upon his memories of Dauntsey's, Cambridge and his wartime research work for the army. During this very fertile period for Balchin's fiction, he also released a short-story compendium entitled *Last Recollections of My Uncle Charles* (1954).

During the second half of the 1950s, Balchin's working life was dominated by film scriptwriting. He won the 1957 BAFTA award for Best British Screenplay for the wartime espionage movie *The Man Who Never Was*, which led to a lucrative offer from Hollywood. Balchin toiled away in Tinseltown for three years in the employ of Twentieth Century Fox but he found the work uncreative and soul-destroying, and pined for Yovanka and the couple's young son Charles. The films he scripted in Hollywood were largely forgettable. The best-known movie he worked on was the infamous Richard Burton/Elizabeth Taylor remake of *Cleopatra* but his script had been mothballed long before filming began.

When his Fox contract expired in 1959, Balchin returned to Europe but, for tax reasons, he chose to live outside the country of his birth. After a brief spell in Paris, he settled in Italy. Here, he continued to write film scripts, but with no more success than previously. For a writer who relied primarily on his ability to convert events from his own life into sellable fiction, the film industry does not seem to have provided him with much inspiration: only the opening chapter of ***In the Absence of Mrs Petersen*** (1966) is concerned with the mechanics of movie making. But that novel focused more on Balchin's volatile on–off relationship with Yovanka (he had married his former secretary in 1953) and one of its main plot threads was inspired by stories about her Yugoslav relatives that she had told him.

Balchin returned to England in 1962, and settled there permanently. Written during his time in Italy, ***Seen Dimly Before Dawn*** was published the same year. Like ***The Fall of the Sparrow***, the new novel saw Balchin once more in nostalgic mood, as he summoned memories of his childhood to write an addictively readable story about a precocious fifteen-year-old schoolboy who falls in love, over the course of a summer holiday, with his uncle's tantalizing mistress. Balchin located the action in the Kent countryside, a part of the world he knew well as he had lived near Canterbury for several years immediately after the Second World War.

As the 1960s wore on, Balchin became increasingly troubled by alcoholism although, in truth, he had been a heavy drinker ever since his first marriage had begun to fall apart. His drinking badly affected the quality of his writing in the last few years of his life.

After ***In the Absence of Mrs Petersen***, an above-par thriller, albeit one that failed to emulate past glories, there was to be just one more Balchin novel. *Kings of Infinite Space*, a science-fiction story about a deep-space mission, was published in the autumn of 1967, when interest in the space race was approaching its zenith. Balchin had spent the summer of 1966 in America, meeting astronauts and visiting NASA locations. Although *Kings of Infinite Space* is true to life, and possesses some historical interest for those of an astronautical bent, it must be rated a failure at the ordinary narrative level and it supplied a disappointing full stop to Balchin's intermittently illustrious career as a novelist.

The final few years of Balchin's life saw a series of moves to successively smaller residential premises as he and Yovanka downsized in an attempt to preserve what little money was still dribbling into the novelist's coffers. Ideas for good novels continued to elude Balchin and the BBC rejected a number of projects he pitched to them. With a hint of desperation, he accepted a lucrative offer from the US-based Famous Writers School to work on a British version of a correspondence course in creative writing. He fell ill on returning from a meeting with the FWS in America and died three days later, on 17 May 1970. He was sixty-one. Balchin left behind a widow and five children from his two marriages. He was laid to rest in Hampstead Cemetery in north-west London. Glowing obituaries appeared in newspapers on both sides of the Atlantic.

Derek Collett

August 2021

Nigel Balchin Bibliography

Novels

No Sky (Hamish Hamilton, 1934)
Simple Life (Hamish Hamilton, 1935)
Lightbody on Liberty (Collins, 1936)
Darkness Falls from the Air (Collins, 1942)
The Small Back Room (Collins, 1943)
Mine Own Executioner (Collins, 1945)
The Borgia Testament (Collins, 1948)
A Sort of Traitors (Collins, 1949)
A Way Through the Wood (Collins, 1951)
Sundry Creditors (Collins, 1953)
The Fall of the Sparrow (Collins, 1955)
Seen Dimly Before Dawn (Collins, 1962)
In the Absence of Mrs Petersen (Collins, 1966)
Kings of Infinite Space (Collins, 1967)

Non-fiction books

How to Run a Bassoon Factory; or Business Explained (as Mark Spade; Hamish Hamilton, 1934)

Business for Pleasure (as Mark Spade; Hamish Hamilton, 1935)

Fun and Games: How to Win at Almost Anything (as Mark Spade; Hamish Hamilton, 1936)

Income and Outcome. A Study of Personal Finance (Hamish Hamilton, 1936)

The Anatomy of Villainy (Collins, 1950)

How to Run a Bassoon Factory; or Business Explained and *Business for Pleasure* (as Mark Spade, combined volume with an introduction by Balchin; Hamish Hamilton, 1950)

Other books

Lord, I Was Afraid (play; Collins, 1947)

Last Recollections of My Uncle Charles (short stories; Collins, 1954)

About the Nigel Balchin Collection

The novels reissued as the Nigel Balchin Collection have been specially chosen to comprise a comprehensive and representative sample of the finest and most interesting novels written by Balchin. At least one novel has been selected from each of the four decades during which he was active as a novelist. When complete, the Nigel Balchin Collection will constitute the widest selection of Balchin's fiction to be simultaneously in print since the 1960s.

Every novel has been freshly typeset and then carefully proofread against the first hardback edition to ensure fidelity to Balchin's original text. Each edition also includes a biographical essay about Balchin, an introduction to the novel in question and helpful explanatory notes compiled by Balchin's biographer, Derek Collett.

The following entries in the Nigel Balchin Collection have been published to date:

Number 1: *Seen Dimly Before Dawn* (November 2021)
Number 2: *Simple Life* (April 2022)

For the very latest information about the Nigel Balchin Collection, including likely publication dates for forthcoming volumes, visit the Nigel Balchin Website: www.nigelmarlinbalchin.co.uk

Enjoyed reading this novel? Like to know more about the man who wrote it? Then why not consider purchasing *His Own Executioner: The Life of Nigel Balchin*? The only biography of the author of *Simple Life*, this book tells the story of Balchin's life in a clear, engaging and authoritative fashion. Visit the Nigel Balchin Website at www.nigelmarlinbalchin.co.uk for details of how to buy this acclaimed biography.

Praise for *His Own Executioner: The Life of Nigel Balchin*:

'First-rate biography' – *The Literary Review*

'Collett paints a convincing picture' – D. J. Taylor, *The Times Literary Supplement*

'A riveting and revealing biography' – Cathi Unsworth, author of *That Old Black Magic*

Coming Soon in the Nigel Balchin Collection

Sundry Creditors: Welcome to Lang's engineering works, with its colourful cast of characters. There's old Gustavus Lang, the MD, a kindly, paternal type who believes in treating his workers like human beings. Walter, his half-brother, is cut from a very different cloth: a ruthless bully, he views business as a game, the object being to accrue as much power and money as possible. Jack Partridge, a young shop-floor worker, has a grudge against the bosses and regards Rosamund, Walter's beautiful daughter, as 'fair game'. Meanwhile, on the assembly line, Hilda Pinner wastes her working hours fantasizing about Lawrence Spellman, a dashing war hero and one of the directors of Lang's.

See how these very different people interact (amusingly, entertainingly, even scandalously at times) in this mesmeric novel, a real hidden gem among the works of Nigel Balchin.

9 781914 076213